ALSO BY ACE ATKINS

THE
FORSAKEN
ACE ATKINS

corsair

CORSAIR

First published in the United States of America in 2014 by G. P. Putnam's Sons,
an imprint of the Penguin Group

First published in Great Britain in 2015 by Corsair

1 3 5 7 9 10 8 6 4 2

A CIP catalogue record for this book
is available from the British Library.

ISBN: 978-1-4721-1428-0 (paperback)

ISBN: 978-1-4721-1429-7 (ebook)

Printed and bound in Great Britain by
CPI Group (UK) Ltd., Croydon, CR0 4YY

Corsair
An imprint of
Little, Brown Book Group
Carmelite House
50 Victoria Embankment
London EC4Y 0DZ

An Hachette UK Company
www.hachette.co.uk

www.littlebrown.co.uk

For Dutch Leonard and Tom Laughlin

Most men are more afraid of being thought cowards than of anything else, and a lot more afraid of being thought physical cowards than moral ones.

—Walter Van Tilburg Clark, *The Ox-Bow Incident*

If somebody's trailing you, make a circle, come back onto your own tracks, and ambush the folks that aim to ambush you.

—Rogers' Rangers Standing Order No. 17

THE FORSAKEN

1

July 4, 1977

After Diane Tull caught her boyfriend in the back of his cherry-red Trans Am making out with some slut from Eupora, she told Lori she didn't give a damn about the fireworks. Jimmy had run up after her, right in front of everyone and God, grabbed her elbow, and said she didn't see what she thought she saw. And Diane stopped walking, put her hands to the tops of her flared Lee's, wearing a thin yellow halter and clogs, big hoop earrings, and Dr Pepper–flavored lipstick. She wanted Jimmy to see what he was missing just because a six-pack of Coors had clouded his brain and he'd jumped at the cheapest tail he could find on the Jericho Square.

"I'm sorry," he said. "I swear. She just crawled on top of me."

"Here, would you hold something for me?" Diane said.

Jimmy smiled and nodded. Diane shot him her middle finger, turned on a heel, and walked through the Square toward the big gazebo, all lit up for the celebration, a band playing a half-decent version of "Freebird." There were a lot of old men and young men hanging out in folding chairs and folding tables, big metal barbecue pits blowing smoke off chicken and ribs, talking about

Saigon and the Battle of the Bulge. The town aldermen had called it a cele-bration of Tibbehah County's "Contribution to Freedom." Damn, Diane just wanted the hell out of there to go smoke a cigarette and settle in and watch Johnny Carson before her father, a Pentecostal minister, told her to turn off that Hollywood filth.

He was never much fun. He didn't even laugh when Johnny had on those animals who would crap on his desk.

"Let's get a ride," Lori said. Damn, she'd never forget that, Lori not want-ing to walk the two miles home. Diane remembered being mad at Jimmy in that seventeen-year-old heartbreak way, but also feeling the freedom of the summer and a night like the Fourth of July when Jericho actually felt like a place she wanted to be, with the music and good-smelling food and cold water-melon. All the boys with their big shiny trucks and muscle cars circling the Square like sharks, revving their motors, tooting their horns, and trying to get Diane and Lori inside like some kind of trophies for the boy parade.

"We could see the fireworks," Lori said. "After that, lots of people would give us rides."

Lori was three years younger and lots less developed, still sort of gawky, with her plastic glasses and braces, hair feathered back, wearing a tight Fleet-wood Mac T-shirt, ass-hugging bell-bottoms, and clogs identical to Diane's. Diane and Lori had lived next door to each other since they'd been born, and Diane for a long time felt like the mother before she became the big sister. She was glad that Lori saw that shit with Jimmy. She wanted Lori to know a girl didn't get treated like toilet paper, no matter if Jimmy was a senior and that his dad owned the big lumber mill and had bought him that red Pontiac for his birthday. You didn't take a goddamn tramp thrown in your face.

"I never liked that bastard anyway."

"The way he's always brushing his hair, thinking he's pretty," Lori said. "Talks down to me like I'm a kid. Like when he comes over on Sunday before your parents get home and he tells me to get lost. Who talks to someone like that?"

"He's a real jackass."

"Maybe this would make us feel better," Lori said, stopping in front of the closed storefront of Snooky Williams' Insurance, opening her purse and showing Diane a little baggie with a couple joints in it. "I stole them from my mom. She won't say anything because she doesn't think I know about her liking to smoke."

"Lori?"

"Yeah," she said, as they walked side by side around the shops, the Tibbehah Monitor, the old laundromat, Kaye's Western Wear, and the old Rexall Drugs.

"You're my hero," she said.

Around the Square, the old movie marquee showed The Exorcist II still. They wouldn't be getting that Star Wars movie for another two years. They turned away from the big celebration and followed Cotton Road to the west, out of town and into the country, and the little houses off County Road 234 where they lived. They made the walk a lot of days, sometimes coming into the Rexall for milk shakes or ice cream, mainly to meet up when there wasn't much to do, before Diane had taken that afternoon job at the Dairy Queen off Highway 45. Something else that her dad didn't like, again saying she'd come into highway trash. Diane thinking he must have a whole system of how to divide trashy people by geography.

The music was still loud coming from the Square a quarter mile away as they walked through people's yards and little gullies and on the soft gravel shoulder of the road. Headlights popped up only every few minutes, and they'd walk into shadows and away from the road when a car would be coming up on them from town. When they got to the creek bridge, just a little concrete span, they walked down the bank, a hell of a lot easier when they took off their clogs and didn't slide. There was a big flat rock where they could jump over the shallow sandy creek. They used to come here a lot as kids and play and watch the old men fish. Lori's stepfather and Diane's dad had been friends for a while but had a falling-out when Lori's parents had left the church and become Methodists.

Lori pulled out a joint and lit it with a matchbook from the Rebel Truck Stop. She sucked on it a few moments, coughed out most of the smoke, and smiled as she passed it.

"Listen," Diane said, straining to hear the music off the Square. "What's that song?"

" 'My Name Is Lisa.' "

"Yes," Diane said, taking a long pull. "Yes. Jessi Colter. God damn, I love Jess Colter."

"Anyone ever tell you that you favor her?"

"Jess Colter?" Diane said. "Um, no. You can't be high yet."

"You're dark like her," Lori said. "And the way you do your hair, all black and feathered. Makes you look like an Indian."

"I am part Indian," Diane said. "On my momma's side. Her daddy was full Cherokee."

"You never told me that."

"My daddy says it's an embarrassment to have Indian blood," Diane said. "He said those people were godless and did nothing but worship trees and rocks."

Lori passed back the joint. There was a very large moon that night and a lot of stars, the rock where they sat still warm from the hot summer days. They both heard cracks off in the distance and both turned to the sky above Jericho thinking that the fireworks had started.

"Shit," Diane said. "Just some rednecks shooting off pistols. Every Christmas and Fourth of July they got to make a lot of noise and raise hell. They'll be shooting all night long."

"You think we can see the fireworks from here?"

"Sure," Diane said. "Why not?" Diane reached into her purse and pulled out a pint of Aristocrat Vodka and took a swig.

"Are we both going to hell?" Lori asked. She said it with a great deal of seriousness, spending way too much time as a kid at Diane's daddy's church.

"All I really know, Lori, is that I don't want to be like my dad or even my

mother," Diane said. "What they do is not living. It's preparing to die. My dad won't be satisfied until he's fitted into his coffin, waiting to take the journey to heaven to square-dance and drink apple juice."

Lori laughed so hard, she spit out a little vodka. Diane smoked the joint, the idea of Jimmy making her laugh, too. The hair, all that goddamn blond hair, and that little joke of a mustache. He thought he looked like Burt Reynolds but really looked like he'd forgotten to wipe his face.

After a while under the moon, and finding warmth on that hot rock, they finished the joint and a lot of the vodka and walked back up the hill to the road. They slid into their clogs and laughed and walked over the bridge, a big expanse of cattle land stretching out to the north of them, cows grouped under shade trees as if they couldn't tell when the sun had gone down, and a gathering of trailers and little houses every quarter mile or so. Their road wasn't too far, a turn at Varner's Quick Mart and about a half mile beyond that into the hills. Diane would have to run straight to the bathroom to get off the smoke smell and brush her teeth, she could guarantee the pastor would be checking on her before he turned in from his nightly Bible readings at the kitchen table. And if he started in on her again, the animated yelling and screaming, her mother would be just assured to be back in their bedroom covered up and hiding, waiting to be bright-faced and beaming in the morning as if the words hadn't been said.

They were about a quarter mile past the bridge, laughing and talking, planning some kind of revenge for Jimmy, learning of two boys that Lori thought she could get once her braces came off, and deciding that if it came down to Jan-Michael Vincent and Parker Stevenson, that Parker seemed to be much smarter and better-looking. They both liked how he handled himself on the Battle of the Network Stars.

"Who's that?"

Diane turned and looked over her shoulder, walking kind of sloppy on the gravel, not caring to move back off the highway. "Who cares?"

"They're slowing down."

"Shit," Diane said. "Probably Jimmy wanting to explain how it was really that tramp's fault for jumping into his backseat and starting to make out."

The car had slowed to a crawl, but when she looked back again, she didn't see those telltale cat eyes of the Trans Am. This was a bigger car, black, probably a Chevy, with big headlights that switched onto bright and blinded them a bit, the engine in neutral and growling.

"Fucking asshole!" Diane yelled.

"Yeah," Lori said. "Fucking asshole!"

The engine growled again, leaving the high beams on, following them slow and steady. The creep really getting on Diane's nerves. She waved for the car to move on, and when that didn't work, raised her right hand high and shot the bird. The driver revved the engine and blasted up ahead of them and then just as fast hit the brakes hard. The car idled in the hot summer air up in the high gentle curve of the country road, the exhaust chugging, taillights glowing red.

"You shouldn't have done that."

"Someone is just messing with us," Diane said. "I'm not scared."

"Me either," Lori said. "Fuck you, man!"

They laughed and kept walking, waiting for the car to speed off, but instead it just sat there maybe forty yards away, and then the driver shot the car into reverse, heading back for them. The girls jumped off the shoulder and found themselves caught between the road and a long barbed wire fence. Diane felt the fence poking and catching her top and biting into her side. "Goddamn son of a bitch."

The car was a Chevy, a black Monte Carlo, and it waited at the roadside, both of the girls stuck down between the gulley and the road. Diane grabbed Lori's hand and told her to be quiet and just walk, and they followed the road as the Monte Carlo drove slow alongside of them. Revving the motor every few seconds, Diane now scared, scared as hell, because she didn't know this car or the driver and knew they were still a good ways from Varner's, where they could call someone, or scream near some trailers, and not be hanging out here in the night. She couldn't even imagine what her daddy would say if she told him.

The passenger window rolled down. She could not see the driver but caught part of his face when he fired up a cigarette and said, "You little dolls want a ride?" In half shadow, he was black and wore a beard, she could see, a jean jacket collar popped around his neck, something wrong with his skin, as if some of it had been burned at one time. The lighter went out and the girls kept walking. She held Lori's hand tighter. The younger girl was trembling and staring at the ground. That proud, sexy strut from the Square was gone; now it was fast and shameful and following that barbed wire path, her muttering that she should never ever have taken those joints, that they shouldn't have been drinking and messing about.

"Hush," Diane said. "Just hush."

The Monte Carlo revved. The man followed them slow but didn't say another word. Diane thought maybe they could run, but running might make it worse, show the man they were scared, although he probably already knew it and liked it.

When an old truck passed them on the road, one headlight busted out, and heading to town, the girls ran up to the side of the road and waved and yelled, but the truck just kept on puttering by them, leaving them full out exposed in the headlights of the Monte Carlo and caught in the high beams. As the old truck disappeared over the hill, there was still the sound of the big party, a mile away, playing some Tanya Tucker. "Delta Dawn."

Diane held on to Lori's hand tighter.

The driver's door opened and the shadow of the man appeared behind the lights. Diane tried to shield her eyes and yelled for the man to get the hell away from both of them. Lori was crying. And that made Diane madder than anything. "What the fuck do you want?"

The man had a gun and was upon them faster than Diane would have thought possible, snatching up a good hunk of her hair and forcing her back to his car. She screamed as loud as she could. Lori could have run. She could have run. Diane yelled so much she felt her lungs might explode.

The car door slammed behind them just as the fireworks started above, coloring their windshield in wild patterns, and the man sped off to the west. The soft crying of Lori in the backseat.

Lori was only fourteen.

2

I've always wondered, Quinn," W. R. "Sonny" Stevens, attorney-at-law, said. "Did you ever see your daddy work, doing those stunts, up close and in person?"

"Caddy and I went out to Hollywood a couple times when we were really young, back in the eighties," Quinn Colson said. "By then he was on *Dukes of Hazzard*, *A-Team*, and *MacGyver*. He let us hang out on set and see him race cars and flip them. It scared the hell out of my sister. But I kind of liked it. I once saw my dad run around for nearly a minute while completely on fire."

Stevens leaned back into his chair, his office filled with historic photos of Jericho, Mississippi's last hundred years, from its days as prosperous lumber mill and railroad town to the day last year when a tornado shredded nearly all of it. One of them was a picture of Jason Colson jumping ten Ford Pintos on his motorcycle back in '77. The office seemed to have remained untouched since then, windows painted shut and stale air locked up tight, dust motes in the sunlight, the room smelling of tobacco, whiskey, and old legal books.

"Maybe the reason you joined the Army?" Stevens said, smiling a bit, motioning with his chin.

Quinn was dressed for duty, that being the joke of it for some: spit-polished cowboy boots, crisp jeans, and a khaki shirt worn with an em-broidered star of the county sheriff. He wore a Beretta 9mm on his hip, the same gun that had followed him into thirteen tours of Iraq and Trash-canistan when he was with the Regiment, 3rd Batt. He was tall and thin, his hair cut a half-inch thick on top and next to nothing on the side. High and tight.

"You liked all that danger and excitement like your dad?"

"I liked the Army for other reasons," Quinn said. "I think my dad just liked hanging out with movie stars, drinking beer, and getting laid. Not much to the Jason Colson thought process."

Stevens smiled and swallowed, looking as if he really didn't know what to say. Which would be a first for Stevens, known for being the best lawyer in Tibbehah County when he was sober. And the second-best when he was drunk.

He was a compact man, somewhere in his late sixties, with thinning white hair, bright blue eyes, and cheeks flushed red from the booze. Quinn had never seen him when he was not wearing a coat and a tie. Today it was a navy sport coat with gold buttons, a white dress shirt with red tie, and khakis. Stevens stared in a knowing, grandfatherly way, hands clasped on top of the desk, waiting to dispense with the bullshit and get on to the case.

"OK," Quinn said. "How's it look?"

"Honestly?" Stevens said. "Pretty fucked-up."

"You really think they'll take our case to the grand jury?" Quinn said. "I answered every question the DA had honestly and accurately. Never believed they'd run with it. I thought I'd left tribunals and red tape when I left the service."

Sonny Stevens got up and stretched, right hand in his trouser pocket jingling some loose change, and walked to a bank of windows above Doris's Flower Shop & Specialties. The office had a wide, second-story porch and a nice view of the town square, most of it under construction right now as a good half was ripped apart by that tornado. There were concrete trucks and contractors parked inside what had been a city park and veterans' memorial. Now it was a staging area for the workers who were trying to rebuild what was lost. "I just wish you'd called me earlier," Stevens said. "The DA has had a real time turning a pretty simple, straightforward story into one of intrigue and corruption. I might could've stopped this shit from the start. But now? Politically, it's gone too far."

"What's to study on?" Quinn said. "Deputy Virgil and I met those men to get my sister and my nephew back. A sniper up in the hills killed two men, and when we looked to get out, Leonard Chappell and his flunky tried to kill me."

"And you shot them?" Stevens said, staring out the window.

"I shot Leonard. Lillie shot the other officer."

"Can you step back a little, Quinn?" Stevens said. "Tell it to me again, as straight and simple as possible. The cleanest and easiest version is the one a jury will believe. Start with Jamey Dixon. How'd you end up driving out to that airfield with him?"

"That convict Esau Davis kidnapped my sister and nephew, Jason," Quinn said. "Jason was four. Davis had sunk an armored car in a bass pond before he was incarcerated. He blamed Dixon for beating him to the car and taking the money."

"Did he?"

"Yes, sir," Quinn said. "Those two convicts had bragged to Dixon about all that money they stole and hid. You know Dixon was a chaplain at Parchman? He came out of there a full ordained minister."

"And started that church out in the county," Stevens said. "The one in the barn. The River?"

"Dixon used their confessions and told Johnny Stagg about that armored car, who used some of that money for Dixon's pardon and took the rest for his trouble."

"But that part can't be proved," Stevens said. "Just stay with the basics. Two escaped convicts kidnapped your sister, who was Jamey Dixon's girl-friend, and her young son."

"Yes, sir."

"And those convicts demanded their money back?"

"One convict," Quinn said. "The other one got killed while on the run."

"So that one convict, Esau Davis, wanted to exchange cash for your sister and nephew? You were scared as hell they might be harmed."

"Yes, sir," Quinn said. "Lillie found a vantage point in the hills by that old landing strip. She was to provide cover if Davis started shooting. You know Dixon only had twenty grand on him? And that wasn't from the bank job. That was from donations after the tornado."

"And how did Chief Chappell and his officer figure into this?"

"They were waiting for all of us to show," Quinn said. "They knew about the exchange and came for the money and to protect Stagg's inter-ests. They also had a sniper in the hills on the opposite side of Lillie who took out Dixon and Davis. When the shooting started, that's when Chap-pell and his man turned on me."

"Me and you both know Leonard Chappell was a joke as police chief and the head stooge for Johnny Stagg," Stevens said. "But one lawman killing another lawman makes for bad press and lots of political pressure on the DA."

"Leonard had no reason to be there but to steal that cash."

"Of course," Stevens said. "But the story the DA will tell is that they came to save the goddamn day and that you and Lillie killed them both to cover y'all's ass. That way all that money was yours without witnesses."

"Bullshit," Quinn said. "They had another man up in the hills. He killed the two men there to make the money exchange. No one seems to be wondering who killed those convicts, Dixon and Davis."

"They're going to say it was Lillie Virgil."

"Guns didn't match," Quinn said. "State tests prove it."

"They'll say she brought another gun."

"That's insane."

"You bet," Stevens said. "But you better prepare for that part of their story."

Stevens swallowed and moved from the window. He reached for a cut-glass decanter at a small bar near his desk and motioned to Quinn. Quinn declined. It was two in the afternoon. Stevens poured some bourbon into a coffee mug and swished it around a bit. He was deep in thought, looking across his old office, with all those barrister bookshelves and faded certificates, *Citizen of the Year* and *Outstanding Ole Miss Alumnus*, as he sipped.

"They can twist the story as they please," Stevens said. "We got two dead lawmen, two dead convicts, and a shitload of cash, flying wild and free, after this all went down. They claim nearly ten thousand is still unaccounted for."

"You know how many people went out into the hills after this happened?" Quinn said. "Families went there on weekends with butterfly nets and duffel bags. That money was found but never turned in."

"However this goes, it'll destroy your name," Stevens said. "They'll destroy Lillie's, too. They'll ask questions about y'all's relationship, relationships she might have with other, um, individuals. You got an election in April."

"You saying I should make a deal?"

"No, sir," Stevens said, sipping a bit more from the mug. His light blue eyes and red cheeks brightened a bit, him inhaling deeply as things were getting settled. "There's no deal to make. Not yet. Just preparing you for the shitstorm as we go into an election year. I don't think that fact is lost on anyone, particularly not Johnny Stagg."

"Mr. Stevens, how about we not discuss Johnny Stagg right now," Quinn said. "I just ate lunch."

"Whiskey makes it a little easier," he said. "Soothes the stomach. Stagg's been running the supervisors for a long while. I've gotten used to the fact people like him walk among us."

"Lillie saved my ass," Quinn said. "I shot Leonard Chappell because he was about to kill me. But Jamey Dixon and Esau were killed by someone else."

"Could've been any one of Stagg's goons."

"This individual wasn't a goon," Quinn said. "This person was a pro, a hell of a precise shot at a distance."

"You see anything at all?"

"Hard to look around when you hit the ground and crawl under a pickup truck."

"Imagine so," Stevens said. "And Lillie?"

"No, sir," Quinn said. "But you need to ask her."

"How could you be sure Leonard wanted you dead?"

"He was aiming a pistol straight at my head," Quinn said. "This was an ambush."

Stevens turned and leaned back against the windowsill and stared out at the rebuilding of downtown Jericho. Among the piles of brick, busted wood, and torn-away roofs, all that remained standing on that side of downtown after the storm was the old rusted water tower by the Big Black River. Now they were even repainting the tower from a rusted silver to a bright blue. New sidewalks. New roads. The Piggly Wiggly had reopened, with the Dollar Store not long to follow. There was word that Jericho might even be getting a Walmart.

"Did you hear Stagg is going to cut the ribbon when they reopen the Square?" Stevens asked.

"I did."

"To read about it in the papers, he is the sole person responsible for the rebirth of this town with the grants and handshakes he's made in Jackson."

"I guess anyone can be a hero."

"We'll get this matter straight, Quinn," Stevens said, "don't you worry.

Just keep doing your job. Lots of folks appre
place since coming home from the service."

"And what can I do while we wait to hear from

"Not much," Stevens said. "But if they indicate fo
beyond just an inquiry, you better have my ass on spee

In Memphis, Johnny Stagg slid into a booth at the Denny's on Union, across from the Peabody Hotel and down the street from AutoZone Park. He accepted the menu but shut it quick, telling the waitress a cup of coffee and ice water would be just fine, smacking his lips as he watched her backside sway in the tight uniform. His new man, Ringold, took a seat up at the bar near the kitchen, giving Stagg a little space for when Houston arrived. Houston had called the meeting, saying it was about time, as Stagg always had someone else talking business, making the exchanges, and figuring out just what in Memphis was black and what was white. Stagg had relayed one message since Bobby Campo was put in prison: All of Memphis was nothing but green.

Stagg toasted Ringold with his coffee mug. Ringold nodded back. Man probably didn't weigh a hundred eighty pounds or stand much higher than five foot ten. He was plain and bland as Wonder Bread, with a shaved head and stubbled black beard, his blue eyes almost translucent. While you wouldn't notice Ringold in a crowd, he probably had a hundred ways to kill a man with a salad fork.

Ringold had come to him that summer, not long after the storm, looking for work and laying out credentials that made him smile. He was three years out of uniform, a former Special Forces soldier, Blackwater operator, and all-around bad dude with a gun. Stagg had made some calls to some people Ringold had worked for and they couldn't say enough about how he handled himself. Stagg figured losing Leonard had been a damn blessing. He'd traded out a goddamn Oldsmobile for a Cadillac.

ucked a tooth, turned the Denny's fork, and grinned a good
, while when Houston and his four thugs walked into the restaurant.
Ringold stopped the thugs and motioned Houston to go take a seat in that
back booth facing across the alley to the Rendezvous rib joint. Houston
was black, short and muscular, wearing a flat-billed St. Louis Cardinals
ball cap and hexagonal rose-colored glasses.

Houston didn't look happy when he joined Stagg at the booth or when
he said, "No offense, Johnny, but we a package deal. My fucking boys
don't sit at no kids' table."

"C'mon, Mr. Houston," Stagg said, grinning. "You're the one that
wanted to meet. Come on. I'll buy you and your boys whatever you want.
Grand Slam breakfast? Santa Fe Skillet, Banana Caramel French Toast?"

"I wouldn't let my dog eat that shit," Houston said. "And he licks
his ass."

"How about coffee, then?"

"Don't drink coffee," Houston said. "I don't smoke. I don't do drugs."

"Ain't that something?" Stagg said. "What some folks might call
ironic."

"It's my fucking religion," Houston said. "I made it out. What I heard,
you made it out, too. Where you get your start? You don't look like you
came from no trust fund, coming out the cooch with a silver spoon."

Stagg just grinned at him, bony hands warming up on his coffee mug.
He wore the tattersall shirt he'd bought on the Oxford Square during
football season, with a red Ole Miss sweater-vest and pleated navy pants.
He wasn't ashamed to say he'd spent nearly three hundred dollars on a
pair of handwoven moccasins to be worn with fancy socks. Stagg recalled
when his momma made him and his brother exchange underwear on different days of the week because she hated doing wash. Stagg brushed at
his chapped, reddened cheek, motioning away the waitress with the nice
backside for a few moments while they discussed all the options Denny's,
America's Favorite Diner, offered them.

"My people from Marshall County," Houston said. "You heard of R. L. Burnside, the blues player? He was my great-uncle. Man could rip the shit out of a guitar. Women in France would rip their bras off and hand them over just to hear him play."

"Sure."

"You don't know him?"

Stagg sucked on his tooth, rotating the warm mug in his hand. "I don't listen to nigger music, Mr. Houston."

Houston grinned wide, showing some gold teeth. Stagg knew the man would like him to cut through the shit, get right to the point, that this wasn't about them becoming buddies and pals, but just how they would keep the goddamn Mexicans out of the city and keep a good thing going. There really wasn't much to consider. Stagg moved it. Houston sold it. Now Houston wanted more of a cut and that wasn't exactly surprising to Stagg. What was surprising is that Houston would want to be seen anywhere near Stagg, as you could bet sure as shit that the DEA or FBI or ATF or who the hell ever would be bugging their Banana Caramel French Toast this morning, wanting Stagg to follow his old pal and mentor Bobby Campo to the Cornhole Suite at the federal pen.

"You got kids?" Houston said.

"I got one."

"Boy or girl?"

"Boy," Stagg said. "Don't see that it matters."

"I got twelve kids," Houston said. "I got two of them with a Mexican woman I met when hiding out from Johnny Law down in Mexico. You ever been with a Mexican woman? Whew. Damn straight, with all that sweet brown skin and black hair. I'd live down there if those motherfuckers hadn't decided they wanted to have me killed."

"Those Mex sonsabitches mean business," Stagg said. "We had some of those boys in Tibbehah a year or so ago. They found out this local boy was trying to screw them out of a gun deal. Lord have mercy, they rode into

Jericho like they was Pancho Villa wanting to fill him full of a million holes."

"They kill him?" Houston asked.

Stagg shook his head. "Gave himself up to the Feds. I'm still waiting to read about him getting shanked by ole Speedy Gonzales in the shower."

Houston nodded. "Man, you a trip."

Stagg studied him, tilting his head a bit. "Son, are you wearing two watches?"

"Yep," Houston said. "One is platinum and one is gold. East Coast and Central."

"May I ask why?"

"'Cause I'm expanding."

Stagg laughed. Even through all that black shuck-and-jive bullshit that never made any sense to him, Stagg liked the boy. He liked that he'd called the meet, liked that he was going to ask for a larger cut, and liked that he'd crawled up from a world of shit to control his future. Stagg had been born to a manure salesman out of Carthage. Houston had come from a goddamn inner ring of hell in the Dixie Homes housing project.

"Sure you don't want breakfast?" Stagg said. "It's on me."

"OK," Houston said. "Maybe some of that French toast shit."

"With the fruit or without?"

"All the way."

"Figured that's what we got."

"Or maybe I want some of that goddamn Moon Over My Hammy," Houston said. "But that don't mean I'm gonna eat the whole thing. You can have your half and a few extra bites. I ain't asking to go equal on this shit. Just give me a little of that ole Hammy and maybe some hash browns and shit and a sip of Coke."

"I know," Stagg said, holding up his hand, "ain't nobody that goddamn stupid. I wouldn't be here if I wasn't in agreement."

Houston snapped shut his menu. The waitress arrived and he told her that he just wanted pancakes and hash browns and to bring a bottle of ketchup.

"A whole bottle?"

"You know, Mr. Stagg, you ain't at all like Bobby Campo."

Stagg nodded. "Appreciate that, sir."

"I never sat down at the table with Bobby Campo."

"He made a lot of mistakes," Stagg said. "He was reckless. A fuckup."

Houston readjusted his rose-colored shades and grinned. Two of his teeth were gold with diamonds inlaid. He smiled some more, adjusting each watch on each wrist. "Who you got up there by the door?" Houston said. "He don't look old enough to shave."

Stagg sipped some coffee. Put down the mug, warmed his hands as the heat curled up to his face. "Oh, just a new friend."

"Funny how you being all cool with the meet and greet and all that shit."

"Me and you got a good thing going," he said. "If someone were to try and break it up, I just want to make sure he knows he ain't invited."

"I think you and me gonna make a fine team," Houston said. "Don't let anyone fuck with my people."

"Good to hear that, Mr. Houston," Stagg said. "Much appreciated."

3

You could just marry Ophelia Bundren and move into her house in town," Lillie Virgil said, "or y'all could just move in together. Everyone in town knows y'all are screwing like rabbits anyway. People say you're the first warm thing that girl has held in her hand in a good long while."

Quinn hadn't been inside the sheriff's office two minutes when Lillie had walked into his office and started talking about his personal life. It usually took her at least four or five. Lillie was his chief deputy and was never really good at appropriate workplace conversation.

"I met with Stevens," Quinn said, tossing his ball cap on the desk and taking off his ranch coat. He hung the coat by the door and sat down behind his desk, propping up his cowboy boots. "He thinks the DA may go after murder charges on both of us."

"Hot damn."

"Seriously, Lillie?" Quinn said. "This might go to the grand jury when they're in session. They're going to say I killed Leonard Chappell in cold blood. And that you shot those three men yourself."

"Well, that would make me look pretty impressive," Lillie said. "But how exactly do they say I killed the two other men?"

"Stevens said you brought two rifles with you," Quinn said. "That's the reason the bullets don't match."

"Sure," Lillie said. "That's logical. Right as we start shooting, I put down my weapon and pick up a new one. How much money exactly did we make off this little deal we masterminded?"

"Two hundred grand, give or take a few pennies."

"Well, cut me in when you can," Lillie said, sitting at the other side of Quinn's desk. "I heard that new Walmart is definitely a go."

Mary Alice gave Lillie the stink eye as she came in and laid a hot mug of coffee on Quinn's desk. Mary Alice, who'd worked at the office for twenty years with Quinn's uncle when he was the sheriff, seemed to have a problem with Lillie's profanity and familiarity, all of a sudden. She looked a bit pious upon leaving the office.

"Stevens also thinks they might have a witness," Quinn said. "Two rifles. Premeditation, to get that cash. You can find shitbirds to say anything for the right price."

"Bring on some two-bit con saying he was squirrel-hunting in the hills," Lillie said. "Love to hear what he says. Watch ole Sonny tear his ass up on the stand. He's one hell of a lawyer when he's not drinking. By the way, how'd he seem today?"

Quinn tilted his head. "Sober," he said. "At least, while we discussed the important stuff."

Lillie shook her head. She nodded, thinking about what he said and then grinned very wide. "But I'm right about Ophelia?" Lillie said. "You gonna move to town and let Jean and Caddy take over the farm? Hot meal. Hot bed. The coroner right there at your disposal."

"Lillie," Quinn said, motioning to the door. "I have work to do."

"She's all right, Quinn," Lillie said. "She really is. Just because the woman embalms folks doesn't make her an abnormal person. She's the same as us only she's dealing with the shit that no decent person would want to handle. I'd say she's a stand-up person and loves the hell out of you. You can see that right off."

Mary Alice walked to the door and peered in. "Sorry to interrupt y'all's discussion of important matters but looks like Miss Thomas on County Road 112 had a break-in last night, says someone took her Sanyo television set and some clothing of a personal nature."

Quinn winked at Mary Alice. Lillie scooted her butt off Quinn's desk. She was strong and athletic, with curly light brown hair in a ponytail and wide hips and legs. She had on jeans and a SHERIFF'S OFFICE jacket today, lace-up boots, and a Glock on her hip, although as the former star of the Ole Miss Rifle Team she preferred a Winchester. If Lillie had wanted to take out every person at that airstrip last spring, she could've done it without much thought or effort. That's what was going to make the DA's argument make sense to a lot of folks.

"Why'd someone want to steal Miss Thomas's panties?" Lillie said, walking to the door. "The woman weights nearly three hundred pounds."

"Maybe they needed a tarp."

"I'll go with that theory," Lillie said, walking from the office. "And think about what I said, Quinn. Life is all about simplification."

Diane Tull had come back to Jericho fifteen years ago after her second marriage ended in Scottsdale, Arizona, and she found she could raise her teenage boys better back home. So she'd returned, trying to take back at least some of the crap she'd said about Tibbehah County, gritted her teeth, and started back to work at the Jericho Farm & Ranch. Her mother had run the place after she'd gotten remarried, this time to a gentle farmer named Shed Castle, whose family had owned some kind of dry goods store in Jericho since the early 1900s. Mr. Castle had died two years ago, and Diane's mother used to come in with her to help out until her dementia meant she just put things on the wrong shelf. The Farm & Ranch was now Diane's place, selling fishhooks, bullets, seeds, and feed every day of the year except Sundays, Thanksgiving, and Christmas.

Diane took down the sign for holiday hours but didn't put up a new one, figuring most people should damn well know by now when she opened and closed.

She set to work separating a new order of Carhartt work pants to the right sizes on the shelves when Caddy Colson and her son, Jason, walked in the door. Jason, who was five, said hello, not really looking at her, and ran straight over to the glass case where she kept the pocket watches and knives. Since he'd been three, he'd had his eye on a huge bowie knife that he said his Uncle Quinn would love. The kid had a deep country accent, which always seemed a bit odd to Diane on account of the boy being black, or half black. Caddy had come home with him some time back after some trouble in Memphis.

"No guns, no knives," Caddy said. "Don't you even ask."

Diane said hello and set down the pants. Caddy handed her a handwritten lists of things she needed to resupply The River Ministry: four bags of manure, twelve of mulch, two large bags of dog food, and one of cat food. She also planned to plant several rows of mustard and collard greens.

"When did y'all get a cat?" Diane asked.

"Showed up after the storm," Caddy said. "Jason wanted to keep it. Quinn being Quinn, he couldn't say no. Said we needed the help at the old house with the mice."

"And how's that working for you?"

"Having my place torn to shit with no insurance and then having to move in with my momma and brother into a house that was built in 1895? Not exactly heaven."

Diane smiled and took the list behind the display counter. Jason was still enthralled with all the outdoor gear for fishing, hunting, and hiking. Quinn had told her the last time he was in that Jason may even be a better tracker at his age then Quinn had been. That was something. She'd heard Quinn Colson had been some kind of kid hero back in the day with his outdoor skills. Daniel Boone, Jr. There was a story about that, headlined *Country Boy Can Survive*, when he'd been lost in the woods as a kid.

Caddy was a couple years younger than her brother. Slender and fair, her blond hair recently cut boy-short. She wore a pair of Levi's and a snug western shirt with snap buttons. No makeup and no jewelry. Still, Caddy Colson was feminine and petite, with men all over town liking to watch her walk.

Diane rang up the bill and told old Carl to get the manure and the feed and put them in back of Ms. Colson's truck. Carl just grunted, as that seemed to be the limit of his vocabulary.

"I've been thinking . . ." Caddy said, writing out the check.

Diane held up her hand. She knew where this was headed.

"I want you to talk to Quinn," Caddy said. "Something made you tell me what happened, and maybe it was the storm, or time, or pressure, or whatever, but people need to know."

"Did I mention rubber boots are on sale this month?"

"I'm serious, Diane," Caddy said, leaning in and whispering. "I know what it's like. I know what it's like to have evil in your life. If you don't address what's inside, it will eat away at you until you die."

"My insides are fine," Diane said. "I eat right, stay away from processed foods. Drink in moderation. By the way, I'm playing a set at the Southern Star with J.T. and a few other fellas. This band called Outlaw."

"I thought it was Tull and Friends?"

"That didn't sound as good," Diane said. "Reminded me of a cruise ship revue or had people thinking Jethro Tull, which we're not about."

"You're looking too good for the Farm & Ranch," Caddy said.

Diane stepped back and did a little twirl. Even at fifty she'd kept herself in shape, giving up the cigarettes and the crap food, going for walks and hikes, healthy living she'd learned out west. The same place she'd developed an appreciation for good boots, turquoise, and silver. She'd become more in touch with her Cherokee side, finding out they weren't just into worshipping trees and rocks like her daddy had said, finding out there was a lot of wisdom from her ancestors that had been kept from her. Besides, the whole western thing worked good for the cover band. When she wore feathers and turquoise against her dark skin and black hair, people still told her she looked and sounded just like Jessi Colter. And she'd always shoot back, "If only I could find my Waylon."

Jason wandered up to the register, laying down some lures and a tub of catfish bait he'd found in back. Without a word, Caddy slid it across and paid, this time in cash. The little boy took the sack and wandered out to the concrete platform and watched as Carl loaded down an ancient F-250 that had been Quinn's before he'd gotten that big official sheriff's truck.

"I appreciate it, Caddy," Diane said. "I do. But more time won't matter. It's been thirty-seven years."

Caddy reached out and touched Diane's wrist and said, "I've been praying for you. I told you my story. Quinn has his own. We're all still here and tougher for it."

"That's the Tulls," Diane said. "On our headstones. We know how to endure."

"Better to live," Caddy said, smiling as if reading Diane's thoughts and walking out the front door, the bell above jingling shut. "Quinn's waiting to hear from you."

4

When Jason Colson returned to Jericho, the mayor offered him the key to the city. But there was a catch, as there would be with someone as slick as Ben Bartlett. He asked if Jason might put on some kind of demonstration, you know, to bring people down from Memphis and see all Tibbehah had to offer. So Jason, never being one to shy away from a dare, asked if he might line up ten Ford Pintos and build a ramp at each end to his specifications. He'd bring along his custom-built Harley XR-750, nearly identical to the one Evel Knievel rode, only instead of an American flag, this one had the Stars and Bars on the gas tanks. Bartlett only asked where and when.

They'd decided to do it on May 16th of 1977 in the center of the Tibbehah County stadium, the town welcoming back its favorite son after Jason had been gone about seven years working out in Hollywood. Most recently he'd joined up with a crazy man from Arkansas named Hal Needham, who'd brought him into a little film called Smokey and the Bandit that looked to perhaps be the biggest picture of the year. In the South at least. It bombed with the Yankees up in New York.

That Saturday morning, Jason wore a Schott Perfecto with his name embroidered on the back, jeans with kneepads, and riding boots. The jump, while tough, wasn't as hard as some of the work he'd done with cars on

Smokey *or on* Gator *or on* Billy Jack Goes to Washington. *This was all about speed and timing and nerves. He had the nerves and had worked out the speed on a calculator. All the old stuntmen found it funny as hell he carried a calculator in his pocket. But he never did trust the changing wind or his math skills to protect his ass on a jump.*

For the past six months, he'd been dating the actress Adrienne Barbeau, living it up in Laurel Canyon. But as much as Adrienne had to offer, she'd seemed to lose interest, and there also was this redhead back home. He'd been thinking of her ever since he'd come home the last time. That was the real reason he'd been coming back and the real reason he was going to fly over the cars that morning, pop some wheelies for the kids, and sign some autographs.

It was a hell of thing to come back and show you weren't afraid of jack shit.

"You ready, Jason?" asked old Ben Bartlett. "I thought I might give the announcement and maybe you do a few tricks around the stadium. Just try not to burn up the end zone. We just had that resodded."

"And you give me the key after the jump?"

Bartlett grinned like a goddamn politician. "If you make the jump."

Who the hell says shit like "If"? Nobody said "If" to Jason Colson. Jason spit, looked up to the stands, and saw the redhead he'd been thinking about sitting there with the fat town sheriff who'd he'd just learned was her god-damn brother. A lot older brother who looked at Jason like he didn't stand a chance.

"What's that key open?" Jason said.

Bartlett may have been an opportunist, but he wasn't stupid. Jason looked up at that redhead, Jean Beckett, who he'd known a good long while but never since she'd become a filled-out, curvy woman. He pointed to her and gave her the thumbs-up.

Damn, that look on her face made it all worth it as he pulled on his helmet, adjusted his elbow pads and kneepads, and gunned the engine. He did two fast laps around the stadium, popping wheelies like a barnyard rooster, and then zipped down to the line he'd calculated for the run. He'd have to hit his top speed, running full-ass-out, when he hit that ramp. But he had to be careful. Start too soon and he'd overshoot the landing. Start too late and he'd be tasting goddamn Pinto for lunch.

He hit the mark and stopped, gunning the engine and staring down the space between the Harley and the ramp. He throttled the engine, its big, guttural sound shaking him and the bike, and making him realize for a split second he'd be just flying through the damn air on a seat with wheels and nothing else but the hand of God under him.

Jason Colson was good with that, toeing into first gear and running that bike faster than a scalded cat. The last thing he heard before hitting that ramp was the crowd yelling with excitement and fear.

And then there was only the open air.

5

Not that it always worked out, but when Quinn was on day shift, he was usually off at 1800 hours and drinking coffee with Boom at the Southern Star by 1815. Not that Quinn didn't enjoy decent beer and good whiskey, it was just the town sheriff couldn't, or shouldn't, be seen drinking in public in uniform or some might critique his judgment. Coming to the bar was more a nice way to decompress and swap some stories before heading home at dinnertime. Boom, his oldest and best friend, who'd given up the whiskey for a while now, would listen to Quinn complain about the slowness of rebuilding of his mother's house and how privacy was something he hadn't had since that twister had torn apart Jericho.

"But there is all that family love, that togetherness and shit," Boom said.

"Yes, sir," Quinn said. "All that shit."

"Man, you just pissed 'cause you can't get laid," Boom said. "You mad 'cause you and Ophelia can't walk around buck-ass naked and take care of business."

"And what's the matter, if that's the case?"

"You do seem just a little frustrated."

"How's that coffee?" Quinn said.

"Terrible as always," Boom said. "Why do we come here anyway?"

"Because there's nowhere else for forty miles?"

Boom nodded and toasted him with his mug. All around them people swilled beer and whiskey, a jukebox in the corner playing Willie Nelson's "Blue Eyes Crying in the Rain."

"You hear about that Chinese restaurant coming in?" Boom said. "Some family down from Memphis. I think they're Vietnamese but thought Chinese food would sell better. One of those buffets."

"Hell, yeah," Quinn said. "In Jericho, that's some fancy grub."

Quinn had known Boom since they were kids. They'd fished, hunted, fought, and raised hell all the way through high school until graduation, when Quinn signed up with the Army and Boom a couple years later with the Mississippi National Guard. Boom was a big, hulking black man who'd come back from Iraq with only one arm and a headful of PTSD. His water tanker had been blasted to hell and back when it hit an IED, and it had taken Boom a while to achieve what folks called the new normal. But he'd found what that meant, learning to work with a prosthetic, and even getting work tuning up the sheriff's vehicles at the county barn, with screwdrivers as fingers.

The long-haired and long-bearded bartender, a fella named Chip, poured them both some more coffee. Except for the Skynyrd tee, he looked like an authentic mountain man.

"Damn, Quinn," Boom said. "Why don't y'all just move in together? Let your momma and Caddy have the farm, just find a place for you and Ophelia."

"You know who you sound like?"

"Don't tell me."

"Lillie Virgil."

"God damn it all to hell."

The Southern Star was a long shot, narrow brick bar right off the Jericho Square, not too old since legal bars were something new to Tibbehah County. The bar ran along the left side of the room, the walls decorated with stuffed ducks, deer heads, and SEC and NASCAR memorabilia. A framed rebel flag adorned the wall in back of the bar, behind all the whiskey bottles. But Quinn's favorite thing in the Southern Star was that crazy stuffed wildcat, hissing and reared back, ready to bite. It was indigenous to Tibbehah County and the high school mascot.

There was a stage at the far end of the bar where J.T., the local muffler man, was plugging in his bass to the motherboard, and a drummer Quinn didn't know was setting up his kit. He turned to the door and saw Diane Tull walking in, proud and strong, holding a battered guitar case, wearing black jeans and a low-cut black top, turquoise necklace, and feather earrings. She was a good deal older than Quinn but still a very attractive woman. Quinn nodded to her.

Her face flushed as she passed and set down her guitar on the stage. She seemed to pause and hang there for a few moments and then clomped back to Quinn in her pointed rose-inlay cowboy boots and came up nose to nose. "OK," she said.

"Ma'am?"

"Caddy said we could talk."

"She did."

"How about now?"

Quinn nodded. He introduced Boom.

"You think I don't know Boom Kimbrough? His daddy worked at the Farm & Ranch for twenty years before my stepdaddy died."

"Ole Mr. Castle," Boom said. "How's your momma and them?"

"Doing fine," Diane said. "Appreciate you asking. And your daddy?"

"Working security at the mall in Tupelo."

And then there was a little bit of silence, enough silence that Boom was confident to excuse himself and say hello to J.T., who was readying the stage. Diane sat up with Quinn and motioned to Chip for two fingers of Jack Daniel's and a Coors chaser.

"That's pretty outlaw."

"Helps with the nerves," Diane said. "Whenever I have to sing, doesn't matter if there are two people or two hundred, I get a little shaky inside. A couple drinks stokes some confidence. Makes my voice sound smoother."

Quinn smiled, took a sip of coffee, and then checked the time. He needed to be back to the farm by 1900 to meet up with Ophelia and have dinner with the family.

"I really don't know very much," Quinn said. "Caddy said it would have to come from you."

"I think," Diane said, pushing back her black hair with her fingers, one silver streak hanging loose. "I think. Hell, I don't know. I don't know where to begin. You ever think something is as important in the dark of the night and then you wake up and find yourself trying to get some meaning out of it?"

"I do."

"Really?"

"Yes, ma'am," Quinn said. "You bet."

"Please don't call me ma'am," Diane said, leaning into the bar. "Makes me feel old as hell."

"Miss Tull?"

"Shit . . ."

"Diane?"

"Better."

"And so Caddy says you and me need to talk."

"That all she said?"

"Yep."

Chip laid down the whiskey and the beer. Diane threw it back and chased it with the Coors. She took another sip and stayed there all silent as J.T. hit some runs on his bass, the unknown drummer banging his kit, testing things for the show. Diane Tull's guitar set still in the case, waiting for her to come up and lead them through that Outlaw Country set, talking about raising hell, drinking, heartache, and love with such an absolute truth that Quinn wished he could stay for a while.

"Me and you haven't spoken that much," Diane said.

Quinn nodded.

"But you know who I am?"

Quinn nodded, studied her face a bit, and waited.

"I don't mean me the crazy lady at the feed store but the me you know for what happened when I was a teenager?"

Quinn took a breath. He slowly nodded.

"I never wanted to bring that up again."

"I understand."

"But all of this, what happened to the town, and other things that have come to light, have made me want to talk about it," Diane said. "Now I don't give a shit what you do. I don't care if you file a report or investigate or whatever it is you do. I just want to tell the sheriff, someone different than those men I told—no offense because I know Hamp Beckett was your uncle—but just to make sure there's some kind of memory, facts, to what Lori and I went through that night. It should be remembered."

"Lori was the girl who was murdered?"

Diane nodded. She breathed, licked her lips, and swallowed.

"I don't want to talk about it now . . . or here," she said. "Can I come by the sheriff's office tomorrow? I can take you out and show you where it happened. You know it's your sister who wants me to do this."

"Caddy has her way."

"Caddy gives me a shit ton of strength," Diane said. "What she did, taking on things after that tornado, helping out so many, despite her personal grief. Caddy Colson is my hero."

"Mine, too," Quinn said. "She's got a tough streak. I'm proud of her."

"Come by tomorrow?"

"Yes, ma'am."

"Appreciate you, Sheriff," Diane said. "But if you call me ma'am again, I'll try and break your fingers."

Diane Tull marched up to the stage and within five minutes, as Boom and Quinn were leaving the Southern Star, she launched into an old favorite called "The Healing Hands of Time."

Johnny Stagg ran most of Tibbehah County from a sprawling truck stop off Highway 45, not far from Tupelo, called the Rebel. The Rebel had a restaurant, a western-wear shop, convenience store, and place for truckers to shower, get some rest, and continue on to Atlanta or Oklahoma City or parts unknown. Lots of truckers made it the stop of choice in north Mississippi not only because of the fine facilities and the famous chicken-fried steak, but because of a smaller establishment behind the Rebel, also owned by Johnny Stagg, a concrete-bunker strip club called the Booby Trap. Tonight Stagg had on eight of his finest young girls, ranging in age from eighteen to forty-two, working the pole in spinning colored light to rap music that Johnny didn't understand or care to understand. But Johnny would've played "God Bless America" if it made the girls get their asses off the couches and shake their tails two inches from those bone-tired truckers.

Stagg had dinner at the Rebel with Ringold, as was his nightly custom, and walked over to the Booby Trap, toothpick swiveling in mouth, where he kept his real office, not the one for the Rotarians or his constituents from the Tibbehah County Board of Supervisors. This office, away from the bar and the stage, and down a long hallway of ten-inch-thick concrete blocks and rebar, was where he kept a safe full of cash from running drugs and whores all over north Mississippi and Memphis.

"Yes, sir?" Stagg said, walking into the office, finding the man from

Jackson sitting and waiting. Ringold nodded and closed the door behind him.

"Heard you been in Memphis," the man said. "So I waited."

Stagg didn't answer.

"I don't know how you do it," said the man, looking strange out of his stiff blue uniform for the Mississippi Highway Patrol. "Them people are animals up there. How you trust them blacks, Johnny? Good God Almighty."

"I don't see how my business is any concern of yours," Stagg said, not caring one goddamn bit for the man just showing up unannounced and taking a seat in Johnny's office. Stagg would have the ass of whoever opened his door up for the man and led him back. The man should've sat out in the titty bar like any professional, enjoying the jiggle, while Johnny finished up his pecan pie à la mode.

The Trooper smiled, black eyes flicking over Johnny's face, waiting, just knowing that Johnny was curious as hell why he'd come.

"He's getting out in a few weeks," he said. "That's official from the parole board."

Stagg leaned forward over his desk. "You sure?"

"It's a goddamn done deal," the Trooper said. "Figured you'd want to know straight off. But if you don't give a shit, hell, I won't bother you again."

The Trooper stood.

Stagg made a motion with his hand for him to sit his ass back down. Stagg looked up to Ringold, who raised his eyebrows and leaned against the wall. Ringold smiling a bit because he knew the possibility of this piece of shit getting out of prison had been one of the reasons he'd been hired.

When Ringold removed his jacket, you could see the man's brightly colored tattoos running the length of both arms. Stagg believed the daggers and skulls represented kills he'd made in and out of the service.

"But Johnny," the Trooper said. "Just 'cause the man's getting out doesn't mean he's coming straight to Tibbehah County. That bastard is sixty-fucking-six years old. He probably just wants to go and live a quiet life somewhere. I think you're putting too much thought into the past, buddy."

Stagg swiveled his chair around, looking at Ringold and then back to the Trooper. He could feel himself perspiring up under the red Ole Miss sweater and his face heating up a good bit. He reached into his pant pocket and found the key to his desk, unlocked it, and pulled out two neat stacks of envelopes, all of them postmarked from the Brushy Mountain federal penitentiary in Tennessee. "For twenty years, that son of a bitch has been writing me letters, saying what he planned to do when he came back," Stagg said.

"Why didn't you tell me?" the Trooper said. "Shit, the parole board would've found that pretty damn interesting."

"Been a good idea if the bullshit he wrote wouldn't incriminate me, too," Stagg said. "This man is one of the most cunning, evil, hardheaded sonsabitches I've ever met. He's gonna join up with those shitbirds down on the Coast, they're gonna put his old weathered ass back on the throne. Then they're coming straight back for me. He's going to do it. You know why? Because he goddamn promised he would, gave me his word, and now it's his time."

"That man sets foot in this place and we can arrest his ass," the Trooper said. "You got so many friends in Jackson, Stagg. People who owe you favors are waiting in line. This guy makes any trouble, coming after you, and his ass is in jail or shot dead."

"Y'all don't get it," Stagg said, rubbing his temples, standing up, and spitting the mawed toothpick in the trash can. "He doesn't want to do me harm. He just wants to get back in the saddle and slide into the world he left."

"And what's that?" the Trooper said, grinning. Ringold shuffled a bit on the far wall, those spooky blue eyes blank and almost sleepy, but he heard every goddamn word. His jacket bulging with a Smith & Wesson automatic.

Stagg looked at him, the pulsing dance music in the bar shaking the thick concrete walls. "You're sitting right in it," Stagg said. "Chains LeDoux says he's coming to take over what's rightfully his."

6

Quinn took the highway north headed toward Fate, the fastest way from town up into the hills and his farm, his family, and his cattle dog, Hondo. The setting sun gave all the busted-up trees on the way that in-between red-and-black glow, almost making the destruction pretty. Ophelia and Caddy were still outside, talking on top of a big wooden picnic table, while Jason ran around the bare apple trees with Hondo. Caddy smoked a cigarette but quickly extinguished it as Quinn got out of his truck.

The old farmhouse was a two-story white box with a tin roof and wide porch facing the curve of a gravel drive. The big colored Christmas lights still up from the holidays shined bright and welcoming as Jason and Hondo raced toward him. He picked up Jason, which got harder to do every day as the boy grew, and walked up to where the women sat. Hondo's tongue lolled from the side of his mouth as Quinn patted his head.

"Trouble," Quinn said. "Real trouble, with y'all discussing matters."

"Why's it men always think women are talking about them?" Caddy said. "You know, there are a lot more interesting subjects."

"Like what?" Quinn said.

"Embalming," Ophelia said. "Miranda Lambert's new album, and maybe taking a trip Saturday to Tupelo. Jason wanted to go see his Great-uncle Van."

"Embalming?" Quinn said.

"Been a busy week," Ophelia said. "Should I expect more business tomorrow?"

"Nope," Quinn said, smiling. "Slow day in the county. Although I saw Darnel Bryant at the gas station and he was looking pretty rough. Not long now."

Ophelia had brown eyes and brown hair parted down the middle, cut in kind of a stylish shaggy way when not worn up in a bun. When she worked, she didn't wear makeup, jewelry, or let her hair down. Working with the dead meant hospital scrubs and rubber gloves and masks, and Quinn was always glad to see her out of uniform in blue jeans and lace-up boots, an emerald green V-neck sweater scooped enough to show the gold cross around her neck. She wore her heavy blue coat unbuttoned.

She smiled back at Quinn. Very white straight teeth, nice red lips, and an impressive body under all those winter clothes.

"Grandma's fixing meat loaf," Jason said. "You like meat loaf, Uncle Quinn?"

Quinn looked to his sister, and she nodded, shooting him a look. Quinn nodded, too, and told Jason he liked it just fine.

"Momma says it tastes like shit," Jason said.

Caddy swatted his little leg, lightly but firm. "Where on earth did you learn to talk like that?"

Jason shrugged, unfazed. Quinn kept quiet, knowing exactly where he heard it.

The back field had been turned over, waiting for the spring, lying dormant until after Good Friday and planting time. Jean and Caddy both had a pretty ambitious list for the farm this year. Lots of corn, tomatoes, peppers, and peas. They already had cattle, but his mother wondered if they might get a milk cow, too. Quinn wanted to know who was going to milk it every morning when his mother moved back to town once her house repairs were done.

"Who was at the Star?" Ophelia asked.

Quinn shook his head. "Boom," he said. "Ran into Diane Tull."

Caddy looked up, Jason crawling up into her lap, watching Hondo chase after a brave squirrel who'd come down from a pecan tree. "When can I shoot?" Jason said. "I could shoot that squirrel. *Pow*. I could knock him outta that tree."

"You ever heard Diane sing?" Ophelia said, wrapping her arms around her body. It was a warm night for January, but it was still January. Quinn sat down next to her and put an arm around her. "She's got a gift."

The trees were leafless and skeletal, skies turning a reddish copper with long wisps of clouds. "Yep," Quinn said. "There's something about her that reminds me a bit of June Carter Cash."

"Most people say Jessi Colter," Caddy said, piping up, pulling a cigarette out of the pack and giving Quinn a *Don't you dare lecture me, you cigar-smoking bastard* stare.

"Just because you smoke Cubans doesn't make 'em any less dangerous."

"Dominicans," Quinn said. "Cubans are illegal."

Jason waved away the smoke with his little hand and jumped off the picnic bench, pointing up into the tree. "There's two of 'em. Look, Uncle Quinn. *Pow. Pow. Pow.* I can get both."

"And Boom?" Ophelia asked. "He's doing OK?"

"Hadn't drank in a long while," Quinn said. "Says he's fine with that."

"I couldn't get by without him at The River," Caddy said. "He comes by every day after work. Helps out on Saturday and after church, too."

"You do the true Lord's work." Ophelia plucked the cigarette from Caddy's hand and took a puff. "Y'all feed the poor and the sick and give people a place to stay when they have nowhere to go. You don't need to be a man or go to Bible school for that."

She handed Caddy back her cigarette.

Little Jason now talked about hunting deer and wild turkey and maybe he could buy that bowie knife at the Farm & Ranch. "Like the one in the book you read," Jason said. "About the king and that knife in the rock?"

Jean stepped out onto the porch and called them to supper. Quinn caught just a glimpse of his mother in the fading light, blue jeans and an old gray sweatshirt. Dressing up was a rare thing for her, only church, weddings, and funerals. His father had been gone nearly twenty years, and despite some men coming and leaving, she preferred to keep to herself. She was a tallish redhead, a little heavier, a few more wrinkles in her face over the years, but men still turned and looked at Jean Colson. She yelled again and stepped back inside.

Jason didn't seem excited about supper but walked on ahead with Caddy, Hondo trying to scoot into the kitchen door but someone pushing him back. Hondo, a coat of gray and black patches, ran up to Quinn and nuzzled his leg, flashing the saddest eyes he'd ever seen.

"Hondo's been banished from supper," Quinn said. "Jason was feeding him under the table."

"You always let him clean your plates."

"Yeah, but Jason was giving him too much," Quinn said. "That dog is getting fat."

Ophelia rubbed Hondo's ears and told Quinn not to talk that way. Quinn didn't say anything, just leaned in and kissed her hard on that tight red mouth. Glad to be alone with her again.

"How'd the meeting with Mr. Stevens go?" she asked.

"He said me and Lillie got nothing to worry about."

"You believe that?"

"Hell no," Quinn said, standing. "But, c'mon, let's eat. I hear the meat loaf tastes like shit."

When Diane Tull got home at midnight, his bright green Plymouth Road Runner was parked out front, him waiting on her and wanting to talk again. She'd told him to please call first, that he couldn't just come on over when he was lonely or bored and wanted to break out the Jim Beam and cigarettes and discuss his troubles. She told him last time she wasn't goddamn Oprah Winfrey or Dr. Phil, she was just a working woman trying to have a little fun in the middle years and that bringing up the past wasn't part of the grand plan. But there he was again, slumped behind the wheel, probably drunk but trying to hide it with the breath mints and chewing gum, trying to walk straight, be focused, and have them talk about Lori. Again.

"I'm sorry," he said, starting off the conversation like that. Who does that? *I'm sorry*. Really?

"I'm not in the mood, Hank," she said. "Can we let it alone for the night?"

"I started on it again," he said. "My daughter came to me in a dream."

"She did to me, too," Diane said. "For a long time. But I finally got brave enough to ask her to leave. And you know what? She did. Lori hasn't come back since."

"May I come in?"

"It's late," she said. "I got work in the morning."

"You sure are all dolled up."

"I sang tonight," she said. "At the Southern Star. I told you about it last week. You said you might come and listen. I was looking for you. Might've been able to talk there."

"I'm real sorry," he said. "I've been a mess. I bet you sure were something. I saw you and that preacher sing last year, that one who had that church in a barn and got himself shot?"

"Jamey Dixon."

"Yeah, Dixon," Stillwell said. "Y'all sounded pitch-perfect on those old hymns."

Diane leaned into the doorway of her 1920s bungalow, complete with rose trellis and porch swing, and just looked at him. He had a haphazard way of dressing, new blue jeans, an old Marshall Tucker Band tee, and a mackinaw coat that stunk of cigarettes. He had longish red hair and a red beard, both showing some gray. "Come on in," she said. "Jesus Christ."

"I just wanted to see how things went," he said. "With the sheriff. Did he know about what happened? He had to have known about it. Had to bother him, thinking this was all left unsettled in the county."

"It happened three years before he was even born, Mr. Stillwell," she said. "Sit down in the kitchen and I'll get you something to drink. You hungry?"

"Water is fine."

"Sit down," she said. "I'll get you a Coors."

"OK." Stillwell licked his lips. "Appreciate it."

He took a seat at the small kitchen table, slumped at the shoulders, hands laced before him. A hanging silver lamp in the center of the room shining over him. She opened up the refrigerator and grabbed a couple bottles, popped the tops, and placed one in front of him.

"Can I ask you something?"

"Sure," he said, seeming embarrassed to take a drink. "You can ask me whatever you want. Me and you, we're almost family."

"We're not family," she said. "We just have a pretty ugly connection. That's worse than being kin."

"That we do."

"Why do you keep coming to me?" she said. "Why bring all this up inside me? You do realize I left this shithole town for twenty years because I was tired of heading to the store for bread and milk and getting eyes of fucking pity. You know how many times people started laying hands on me in the damn cereal aisle, wanting to pray, when all I wanted was a goddamn box of Frosted Flakes?"

Stillwell licked his lips more and then drank a few swallows of the Coors. "I don't rightly know," he said. "I think it had something to do with the storm."

"The storm?" she said. "How's that?"

He coughed and gave a loose, weak smile. She drank some beer while she waited for him to think on things, mull over what he wanted to say. A beer always helped her come down from the high of singing, this group of them getting it right, finding a nice feel for some Haggard, that old bottle letting everyone down, feeling no pain at closing time. And finishing things off, closing out the last set with a bluegrass version of "Mama Tried." She and J.T. harmonizing on the chorus, J.T. setting down his bass for a mandolin, making each note sound like the turning of pins in a kid's music box.

"I lost everything in that storm," he said. "I knew then there might be no more time to make sense of it. I got to make sense of it before I'm gone. You remember how we used to always light candles for Lori every year on the Fourth. And then people just stopped showing up."

He looked down at the table, took a breath, and he started to cry. After a while, he wiped his eyes and his face and drank some more beer.

"Hell," he said. "You don't have to do nothin', Diane. I guess I just feel it's time to shine a light on this."

"Why me?"

"'Cause you were the one who was there," he said. "But I ain't telling you to do nothing. Maybe I just wanted some company. Or maybe I just wanted folks to remember her."

Diane reached up to the edge of her hair, feeling for that long streak of gray in all that black. She played with the end and glanced down at the gray, thinking maybe this would be the week to finally start dyeing it, making it all even. She tipped the Coors bottle at Stillwell and said, "I've never forgotten."

"I think about the last time I seen her," he said. "She came to me to borrow ten dollars at the body shop and I wouldn't give it to her. I'd got all over her about the way she'd been dressing. Embarrassed her. You believe that? She'd gotten all made-up for the carnival with a lot of lipstick and stuff on her eyes and such. You know what I did? I told her to go wash that shit off her face, said that she looked like a streetwalker. How you think that sounds from her daddy? No wonder she didn't call me when y'all needed a ride. When I had to go see her body with Sheriff Beckett, it was raining and all that goddamn paint was washing off her, making her look something foolish. Why did I talk like that? Like I was some kind of goddamn preacher. What kind of right did I have to be such a goddamn asshole? I deserve every bit of what's come to me."

Diane had heard this story perhaps a thousand times, the father playing it over and over again in his mind, trying to figure a way he might have found a new outcome. Sometime later, he became such a crazy-ass drunk that he'd been kicked out of the Born Losers Motorcycle Club as a liability. That fact would become Hank Stillwell's epitaph, *Too Fucked-up to Ride* with a bunch of hellraisers. The man still sporting the skull-and-crossbones tattoos on his nothing biceps and sagging skin. *Pig Pen* written in jagged ink.

"God damn, it keeps on hurting, Diane," Stillwell said, finishing the beer. "You think that'll ever stop?"

"No, sir," she said. "Not till you quit loving your daughter."

She stood and walked with him to the door and watched as he made his way down her stone path and back to a vintage Plymouth with shiny chrome wheels. He had to crank the car three times, but once it started it growled like a big cat before he rode away.

Diane took a deep breath. Tomorrow she'd lay it all out. Even if it didn't make her feel better, maybe it would keep both Stillwell and Caddy Colson off her ass.

The bugs had started to gather on her front porch. She clicked off the night-light and went on to bed.

7

Jason's younger brother Van had warned him: "Don't go and fuck with Big Doug and all his bullshit. I don't care how long y'all been friends. Something done broke in his head in Vietnam."

"We're just going to go drink some beer," Jason said. "What can be wrong with that?"

"You know who he rides with?" Van said. "You know about him and the Born Losers? They seen you jump the other day and wanted you to come out to the clubhouse. It ain't no beer joint, it's their private club where they shoot drugs, shoot guns, and raise hell. Do what you want, but I wouldn't go out to Choctaw Lake for nothing."

"Appreciate the advice, Van," Jason said, sliding into his leather jacket and snatching up the keys to his Harley. This was the Fat Boy, not the trick bike he'd used at the show. The landing had been a little off and, damn, if he hadn't bent the frame. He'd get her straightened out and smooth out the gas tank where it got all nicked to hell when he laid her down. He hadn't wanted to ditch the bike, but he came off the ramp hot as hell and headed right into the cop cars that had been parked in the end zone.

He rode out along Dogtown Road on a fine early-summer night, feeling the warm wind, smelling that honeysuckle and damp earth, and being glad he *was back down South for a while. The Fat Boy was baby blue, with a hand-tooled leather seat made by the same man who'd made saddles for Elvis. It was comfortable to be on the bike, comfortable to be back home among friends. The evening light was faded, a purple light shining off the green hills headed out to the lake, nothing but winding ribbon and yellow lines.*

The clubhouse had once been an old fishing cabin, a cobbled-together collection of boards and rusted tin. Outside, fifteen, twenty Harleys parked at all angles in the dirt, all of them custom, with tall ape hand bars, and sissy bars on the backseats for the women who rode with them. When Jason killed the engine he could hear an old Janis Joplin song blaring from inside the shack. A man with red hair and beard, wearing leather pants but no shirt, eyed Jason as he walked past. The man was turning over steaks on an open grill and smoking a cigarette. The man looked to Jason, cigarette hanging from his mouth, and said, "Who the fuck are you?"

"I'm Jason-Fucking-Colson."

The dude stopped, held up the end of a long fork to Jason's chest, and said, "You the dude who jumped the bike over all them Pintos?"

"Yep."

"I saw that," the man said. "That was some crazy shit. A bit wobbly on that landing, but some crazy shit, brother.

"My name's Stillwell, but they call me Pig Pen." He removed the fork from Jason's chest and offered him a big pat on the back, his hands filthy with grease. "Big Doug is inside with his old lady. Go on in, there's cold beer in some trash buckets, help yourself. Damn."

The windows had been busted out a long time ago and covered in plastic sheeting that bucked up and rippled in the wind off Choctaw Lake. There was a doorway but no door, and once Jason got inside it took some adjusting to get used to the darkness. The walls were decorated in those velvety glow posters of women with big tits, panthers, and Hendrix and Zeppelin. There were some black lights spaced around the room, keeping everything in a soft purple light. as men in leather vests and women in tight T-shirts stared up at him, everyone getting real quiet, just like folks in old John Wayne movies, and all he could hear was Janis daring a man to take another piece of her heart.

Someone messed with the music, turning down what he saw was an old jukebox on a dirty concrete floor, and Jason looked at the group, man-to-man, and over at the women, with long stringy hair down to their butts. He nodded and walked toward the beer, the reason he'd come to the party, since it was harder to find a cold beer in Jericho than a decent job.

And there was Big Doug, arms outstretched, big hairy belly exposed through a wide-open leather vest. He had long black hair and a long black beard and looked like he should be riding the high seas with men with wooden legs and eye patches. He walked over to Jason, wrapped him in a bear hug, and lifted him off the ground. Big Doug got the name honest: he was six foot six and about three hundred pounds. A woman, wearing a headband over her long blond hair parted in the middle, walked over and gave Jason a cold can of Coors.

"I knew you'd come," Big Doug said. "That pussy brother of yours try and scare you?"

"Which one?"

"Van," Big Doug said. "I tried to talk to him at the Dixie gas station a few days ago and he about pissed down his leg."

"Were you alone?" Jason said, grinning.

"Just out for a ride."

"All of you?"

"Yep," Doug said. "We ride with the club. We live with the club. It's a brotherhood. Hey, listen, I want you to meet my woman, Sally. We call her Long Tall Sally because . . . you know."

"She's built for speed?"

"Hell yeah," Big Doug said. "Man, you hadn't changed a bit. You look the same as when we graduated. You said you'd get out and, damn, if you didn't do it. Working with Burt Reynolds. Holy shit. You're an A-list L.A. mother-fucker now."

Jason nodded, drank some beer. The jukebox went silent and he heard that click and whir of a new song coming on. Wicked Wilson Pickett. "Mama Told Me Not to Come." Somebody's idea of a joke.

Since leaving the set of the last picture, Jason had let his hair grow out some, getting long for him, down over his ears and covering his forehead and eyebrows. He'd even grown a beard, feeling like a wild man and all natural, until being around this bunch made him feel like a clean-cut square. Some pussy businessman from Atlanta.

"How long you here for?" Sally asked. She had roving eyes and wore a man's tank top hiked up high over her belly. From the looks of her belly, she drank as much beer as Big Doug.

"Few weeks," Jason said. "Want to help my dad get settled after my mom died. Spend some time with Van. And Jerry is driving his rig in from El Paso. Should be here soon."

"Jason-Goddamn-Colson," Big Doug said, a little high and a little drunk. "Man, you were never scared of shit. Me and him did FFA together and he was the only one who'd compete with the men at the State Fair. He'd ride goddamn bulls. You remember that? Riding those big-nutted motherfuckers till they sent you flying."

"Good times."

"Good times?" Big Doug said. "You are crazy, you son of a bitch."

Jason finished the beer and Sally wandered off to get him a new one. His eyes had adjusted in the dim room, with the purple light, the haze of dope smoke, and a makeshift bar with a velvet painting of a nude black woman above it. The big glow of the jukebox shone across a group of three men who hadn't gotten up, still staring at Jason as he stood in the center of the clubhouse.

"Hey, come on," Big Doug said, just as Sally handed him the Coors. "I want you to meet the man. Come on."

Jason walked with him over by the jukebox, the music so loud it was hard to hear a word that was being said. A muscular man with no shirt and a lot of tats reclined in a big leather chair. A young girl was in his lap, arm around his neck, holding a cigarette for him and then taking a drag herself. She checked out Jason as Big Doug leaned in and said something in his ear. The man had wild eyes and long greasy black hair and a long beard. There was a lot about the fella that reminded Jason of goddamn Charles Manson.

Jason nodded at him. The scary fella just stared, took another drag, and then looked to Doug, who was grinning big as shit. Doug leaned over to Jason and yelled in his ear. "Meet Chains LeDoux, club president."

Jason offered his hand. Chains looked at him as if he'd just picked up a turd. Jason looked up over to Big Doug and shrugged. "Doesn't look like I'm wanted."

"Don't worry, he's always like that," Big Doug said as they walked away, Chains's wild eyes never leaving Jason. "He just is skittish of new people. He's protective of all of us. Doesn't like change. Always worried someone is going to be a narc."

"Do I look like a narc?"

Big Doug smiled and patted Jason's back so hard, Jason lost his wind for a moment. "You sure do, brother," Big Doug said. "You sure do."

"Appreciate the beer."

"You ain't going yet," Big Doug said, grabbing his elbow. "We're just getting started. And you're invited to ride with us tomorrow. We're going up to Shiloh, pay tribute to the boys."

"That gonna be OK with Chains?"

"He'll learn to love you as much as I do," Big Doug said. "Just relax, man. Be cool, brother. You're among friends."

8

"Let's get one thing straight right from the start, Sheriff Colson," Diane Tull said, "if there is any blame that goes to this, go ahead and blame me. I was the one who wanted to walk home. I was the one who froze up when that man stopped us, when Lori and I should have run like hell."

"The only blame is on the man who did this," Quinn said. "You were two kids. The man had a gun and had you both trapped. He was a predator out there hunting for something just like y'all. If it hadn't been you, he would have attacked someone else."

Diane was quiet, seated in the passenger side of his big green Ford F-250, the heater blowing, hot coffee in the mug holders, driving on out to the road to Jericho where all this had happened thirty-seven years ago. She said she wanted to make a run out to the old Fisher property before the Farm & Ranch opened at nine. Quinn had rolled on duty at 0600, but he had been up since 0430, running the hills up and around his farm and doing a short routine of pull-ups, push-ups, and flutter kicks, before shaving, dressing, and meeting up.

Hondo rode in the backseat of the cab, wanting to come to work today, his head slid up between the two front seats, panting.

"Your uncle sure loved that dog," Diane said. "He bought top-shelf food and kept a jar of pig ears for him. Always kept him in flea collars and heartworm protection. He was a good man, Sheriff."

"How about I don't call you ma'am and you don't call me sheriff?"

"You don't like to talk about him," she said. "Your uncle. Do you?"

"Nope."

"Always thought what they said about him were a bunch of dirty lies," she said. "People can be hateful."

"You bet."

"I know you hear things they're saying about you now, too."

"I do."

"And that's some dirty, shitty lies."

Quinn didn't say a word.

"People said things about me after all this, too," Diane said. "People said me and Lori picked up that man at the carnival and had sex with him. Some people even thought I may have shot Lori myself 'cause I was jealous or didn't want her telling what we'd done."

"People have small and idle minds."

"And you can't even do your job without people making comments."

"Of course, bullshit does go with an elected position."

"And this," Diane said. "All this I'm about to show you is just for you to know. Your sister wanted us to talk, maybe stoke a cold case and get some kind of air cleared about what happened. Is there still an old report?"

"There is."

"And you've read it?"

"I have."

A hand-painted sign out on the country road read *Dirt For Sale*. Quinn followed the rolling ribbon of cracked blacktop, the morning coming up bright and hard in early January. The trailers and small houses, the little farms, and closed gates to hunting lodges passing by. Quinn slowed after a few minutes, Diane telling him to keep driving, it was a ways up, but it was hard to tell anymore since the Fisher house had burned to the ground back in 1992. She pointed a finger a half mile down the road and Quinn slowed and drove off onto the shoulder, the old cedar posts and barbed wire still there, some of the posts replaced with solid metal T-bars. Cattle wandered far in the open pasture, trees dotting the land, cow pies dotting the worn-down grassland.

A tree in the distance caught Quinn's eyes, skeletal and alone, blackened from fire and spiky-branched. The dead tree resembled a black pitchfork.

Quinn shut off the engine. Diane took in a deep breath. Something about that old tree captivated him, like it was from a half-remembered dream.

"The house was up on that hill?" he said.

She nodded.

"You want to walk up that way?"

She took another long, deep breath. She rubbed her fingers over her eyes. She breathed again. "Oh, hell," she said. "Come on."

They got out of the truck, Hondo following. They walked through a cattle gate and then out into the pasture, among the growing weeds, wandering cows, and piles of shit. An old bull sat up on the hill, watching them without menace, just slow and lazy but curious, wide-eyed and snorting a bit. The other cattle grazing and chewing as Quinn walked side by side with Diane until she stopped and said this is where the man had taken them that night, under the full moon and with a pistol on them, telling them they were going up to that old abandoned house and sit a spell.

"'Sit a spell'?" Quinn asked.

"That's what he said," Diane said. "But you could see what he wanted from his eyes and the way he was sweating."

"I'm sorry," Quinn said.

"I'd like to say you forget in time," Diane said. "That some of all this is fuzzy. But that would be a goddamn lie."

The city and county leaders decided to hold the announcement at the Jericho Square. It had taken some time to remove all the debris and contractor trucks from the park and get it all looking straight again. The city work crews had strewn white lights in the newly planted trees and across the gazebo that had remained untouched after the storm, as well as the monument to the fallen heroes of the World Wars, Korea, Vietnam, and the Global War on Terror. The heads of the automotive components company had flown into Memphis and would arrive within the hour. Tibbehah was going to be supplying parts to that new Toyota plant in Blue Springs, one of the country's biggest. And already Johnny Stagg had spoken to no less than four news crews from Tupelo and Jackson bright and early that morning about what folks were calling the Tibbehah Miracle. Not only did it look like this little backwater county would survive after being hit dead-ass-on by an F4 tornado, but, damn, if it didn't look like it was going to be stronger and better than ever. A new industrial park, grants to rebuild the old downtown in the historical style of the original, and new road and highway improvements.

"People know it takes a good man to grease those wheels in Jackson," Ringold said, saying it in that flat, solemn way he spoke. "You're a hero. Folks say it takes a businessman like Mr. Stagg to get things done."

"Is that what they're saying?" Stagg said, grinning. He popped a piece of peppermint candy in his mouth and chewed hard. "The gratitude does keep me going."

"Are you going to speak?"

"No, sir," Stagg said.

"Senator Vardaman?"

"It's more his kind of show," Stagg said. "I just handle the introductions around here. I'm what you call a facilitator."

"You're also the man who pledged a half-million dollars to rebuild Jericho before any of this happened," Ringold said. "If I were you, I'd at least say a few words and take a fucking bow."

"People know what I done," Stagg said. "That's enough."

"Tupelo paper this morning called it an overall story of redemption," Ringold said. "They referred to you as the former owner of a roadside strip club turned entrepreneur."

"Is that a fact?" Stagg said. "'Former'? Bless their hearts."

The chamber of commerce president, Wade Mize, waddled on over with five folks who looked to be dressed for Sunday service. He wore a blue suit and bright gold tie, fat jowls recently shaved and smelling of cologne. He introduced a minister from Southaven, a couple businessmen from Memphis, and a couple women from Oxford who were looking to start a restaurant and maybe a boutique. Stagg grinned and shook their hands, smiling to all their praise, especially when the minister told him that most often miracles sprout from unlikely places. Stagg winked at the man and continued walking with Ringold. "Uh-huh," Stagg said.

"Mize sure seemed happy to see you."

"Funny, the people who call me Mr. Stagg these days," Stagg said. "Wade Mize's mother is a stone-cold crazy woman who's made it her personal mission to drive me from this town. I could take all the newspaper columns she's written about the old Rebel being a den of iniquity and we could wallpaper the whole truck stop. And you know what? I hadn't heard a damn peep from her after the storm. She still won't speak to me, but at least she shut her dry old mouth."

Stagg and Ringold walked on up to the gazebo where Stagg would stand behind Vardaman and the boys from the automotive company. There'd be talk about the opening of the production line and a grant to finally complete the industrial park right off Highway 45 that would bring jobs, money, and growth to northeast Mississippi. People had flyers and big blown-up pictures of the architectural drawings and such.

There would be a short prayer for the nine dead souls and a bell rung from the Baptist church at noon. After, the way Stagg understood things, they'd all go on over to city hall for a plate lunch of barbecue and catfish catered by Pap's.

Stagg looked out on the town square, taking a lot of pride in how much had been done in such a short amount of time. The broken shit had been hauled away and already a new row of four storefronts was being built. Stagg had offered the owners of the old stores a solid price for the destroyed property, telling them the recovery might take years—if at all. And now he already had agreements from a bank from Tupelo, a steak restaurant, and a combo coffee shop and tanning parlor.

"You think a dozen girls is enough?" Ringold asked. "For tonight?"

"Depends on the girls."

"Best we got."

"Make sure you got a couple real young ones," Stagg said. "That's been requested direct by one of the guests. Young, black, and happy."

"Yes, sir."

"Gonna be a hell of a party out at the ole hunt lodge tonight," Stagg said. "You better believe it. Those sonsabitches couldn't wait to get back to ole Jericho."

Stagg started to step down from the gazebo, walk across the park, and say hello to the meat manager of the Piggly Wiggly when he heard a guttural growl that nearly made him swallow the rest of his candy. He stopped cold on the steps and held up a hand for Ringold to do the same. "You hear that? You fucking hear that?"

He looked into the distance to see a half-dozen motorcycles with big engines and big pipes rip and vibrate the town square. The men had broad backs and leather vests worn over denim jackets. They had long hair and beards and looked as if they'd just stepped off horses from another century.

Stagg wandered out on the walkway, trying to get a glimpse of the pack rounding the Square, see if he recognized any of the bastards who'd come to town to make a stand and go ahead and squat and shit on his big day.

"Mr. Stagg?" Ringold said. "You OK?"

"Y'all didn't make it to the house?" Quinn said.

"No, sir," Diane said. Diane and Quinn stood in the pasture a few hundred meters from where the old house had been. "This is where he grabbed Lori and started to mess with her, putting his hands all on her, reaching under her shirt and into her jeans. He kept the gun on me and told me to sit, wait till he was done. I told him we needed to get to the old house, you know, just to keep him moving, trying to figure out a way we could get loose before we got inside."

Quinn nodded. Hondo broke into a wide circle and started to bark a bit at the cows, getting one big fat heifer to trot forward, the dog nipping at her heels. The dog barked some more and nipped at some other cows. Quinn looked up to the big bull on the hill and then back to Diane. The morning so gray and cold, he could see her breath as she spoke.

That black pitchfork tree loomed in the distance.

"He pushed her down to the ground," Diane said. "Right here. He told us if we didn't stop crying, he'd kill us both. He said if I tried to help her, he'd shoot me where I stood. I sat down and waited. He got to one knee, then pressed himself on Lori, and I just blurted out all of a sudden, I'm not even sure I'd said it, but I must have. I told him to come on with me first. I told him I'd let him have me first, not cry about it. I told Lori to go on, leave us alone. He didn't say anything, but she wouldn't leave us. She didn't go ten feet, just standing there with arms across her chest, crying, watching as that son of a bitch ripped off my jeans and underwear with a pocketknife and did what he wanted to me. He smelled like pure garbage, grunting and calling me filthy names the whole time, gun in his right hand until he finished up. Yes, it hurt like hell. I bled down there for weeks."

"You gave a pretty good description to my uncle," Quinn said. "You said he had burn marks on his face. A lot of scarring."

"On the right side," she said. "And some white scarring across his head where the hair didn't grow back normal. He wasn't a big man, but he had a lot of weight and muscle about him. Real compact. I'd never seen him before. When he got going, he spoke in biblical passages about whores and harlots. He told me he hated me."

Quinn nodded. Hondo looped back to him, tongue lolling, waiting for orders on more roundups.

"When he finished, he buckled up his pants and told me to get my ass up and to stand next to my friend," Diane said, hands in the pockets of a Sherpa jean coat, gray strand of hair falling across her eyes. "I pulled up my things, which were ripped and trashed, and walked over to Lori, putting my arm around her. I remember doing that much, telling her that as soon as we could we just needed to start running. She nodded, shivering like she was cold, even though it was hot as hell that night. I held her hand as we walked, like when we were kids, and I would look back at the man, him trudging along with a grin on his face till we got near that old tree over there."

She stood and pointed to the charred relic of what had maybe been a big oak.

"All of a sudden, he told us to run," she said. "He said run, get gone, he was through with the whores, and we ran to that old house, even though the house might've been worse. I always wondered why we didn't run to the road, away from this place, but the house was shelter and closer and I guess we were thinking he'd leave us and go back to his car."

"How far did y'all get?"

"From here?"

Quinn nodded. Hondo had wandered over to Diane Tull and moved his head and shoulders up against her leg. She had her right hand draped at her side and was rubbing his ears. She did not seem to be sad or uncomfortable, simply stating a historical fact of that horrific night, laying it all out for the law as she'd promised Caddy Colson. Quinn stood and watched her as she looked across the pasture and thought, her finally saying, "Maybe thirty feet, and then he started shooting. I heard the shot and then Lori slumped and fell and there was blood on me because we were running so close. When I stopped to help her, I felt the tear in my back and the crack of the shot and then two more. He shot me twice in the back and then I fell. The moon was so bright then. I remember that. That bastard getting plenty of light to do his shit."

9

Stagg had gotten the key to the hunt lodge from one of Vardaman's people, the senator providing the space, with Stagg bringing the booze and the women to the party. He employed a sixteen-year-old black kid named Willie James Jones, who carried in the crates of whiskey, while Ringold drove the Rebel Truck Stop van with eight girls from the Booby Trap. Before they'd come out, he made it absolutely clear this was in no way related to their duties, but if they wanted a shitload of tips, they were welcome to come along. Only problem with the offer was turning down a dozen girls. He decided to choose a couple young black girls, a Vietnamese, a Mexican, and four white girls. One of the white girls had the best goddamn tatas he'd seen in his life—natural, too—that she could wrap around a man's head like a hat.

"Where you want this, sir?" asked Willie James.

"Back bar underneath them ducks," Stagg said. "You see the ducks?"

Willie James nodded and kept walking through the open lodge over to the big fireplace and long bar. The walls were decorated with all manner of dead animals, stuffed ducks and deer and bobcat, Mississippi creatures. But the senator was also fond of going on over to Africa, and a game preserve in Texas, where he'd killed a rhino, a lion, and some wild animals

Stagg couldn't name. All the animals looked as dumb and glass-eyed as the girls who wandered in with Ringold, mouths hanging open since this was a good bit nicer than any of the trailers they'd been raised in out in Ackerman or Pontotoc.

"Please refrain from drinking unless y'all are asked," Stagg said. "These are fine men. They don't care for sloppy women."

The women nodded, the girl with the big tatas popping purple bubble gum as she listened. The two black girls wore identical pink kimonos, while the rest wore terry cloth robes over their bikinis and lingerie, already dressed for work.

"How about some music?" asked one of the black girls. Her name was Jaquita or Janiqua or some kind of crazy name. "Ain't a party with no music. Shit . . ."

"Sure," Stagg said. "As long as it's either country or western."

The girls sighed and Stagg walked out of the room back to the big kitchen where Willie James had laid out the cheese-and-sausage trays from Piggly Wiggly with some plates of cold fried chicken brought down special from Gus's in Memphis. Like always, the men could come into the kitchen, grab a plate of chow, and wander on out to the big room by the big stone fireplace to mingle with the ladies. The ladies were being paid by the hour, but the men knew it was customary to leave a tip, although there was this flunky from Jackson who gave a girl only two bits after intercourse. Stagg would never forget the low class of that fella or his people.

"Mr. Stagg?"

Stagg turned to see a little white girl, whose name he couldn't quite recall, come into the kitchen and ask if they might talk. She eyed the buffet of food and licked her lips and Stagg told her it was fine, go ahead and grab something to eat. "There might not be time later," he said. "While you tend to the business."

She didn't hesitate, grabbing an Ole Miss paper plate, and started to gather chicken legs, cheese, and sausage. "I ain't eaten all day, Mr. Stagg. Thank you."

Stagg smiled at her and waved a hand over the feast.

She inhaled the food so fast that Stagg worried she might choke, waiting for her to take a breath. "You had something you wanted to ask?"

"Yes, sir," she said. "But I don't rightly know how to say it."

Willie James peered up at Stagg from the long counter, where he was slicing up fruits and vegetables with as much skill as any Jap chef he'd seen on television.

"It's OK," Stagg said. "You want to whisper it?"

"Well," said the girl. "Last time, one of those men, a fat man from Tupelo who owns all those car dealerships . . ."

"Yes, ma'am," Stagg said, knowing his name and knowing the girl did, too. His big, florid face plastered on every billboard from Jericho to Batesville. *No Money Down. Bad Credit? No Problem.*

"Well," the girl said. "He had some unusual requests last time. I'd rather not be his date."

"What kind of things?"

The girl, short and small-boned, with hair like a pixie doll, leaned in and whispered into Stagg's ear. She was very direct and specific about the acts.

"Good Lord Almighty," Stagg said. He shook his head. "Man must've been raised in a barn."

"And then he wanted me to finish it with a . . ." the girl said, then whispering some more.

"I get the idea," Stagg said, feeling his face burn. "Hot damn. Well, all I can say is, keep a wide berth around that fella. I wouldn't let him near my dog."

"Yes, sir."

Stagg nodded, not listening anymore, standing back and appraising the table's bounty, the silver and finery that belonged to the absent senator. He watched as Willie James pulled gallon jugs of Southern Comfort and Smirnoff Vodka from boxes and laid them all out in a pretty-straight line. A nut tray with a silver cracker was offered next to the crystal glasses and cocktail napkins.

The girl took a breath, robe hanging open loose and easy, exposing a pink bra-and-panty set. She wore blue Crocs on her little feet.

"I guess we all got to pay them pipers," the girl said. "My daddy said the only way we'd ever sit at a rich man's table is to set it for him."

Staggs's face colored, with more blood rushing to his weathered old cheeks. He reached for a peppermint in his pocket. "How about you wait with the other ladies, doll?" Stagg said. "The gentlemen will be here right quick."

"Sure do appreciate y'all coming here this afternoon," said the DA investigator from Oxford, a man named Dale Childress. "I thought this would be a good spot, New Albany being a good midpoint."

Quinn and Lillie sat across from him in conference room at a Hampton Inn off Highway 78. As it started to rain on the way over, Lillie had declared the entire journey a big fuck-you. She said Childress didn't drive to Tibbehah because he knew about Quinn hiring Stevens. Here he could sit down and chew the fat, be pleasant, and make sure they all knew this was routine. Childress opened up a file and smiled across the table at Lillie. He'd offered them some bad coffee and stale muffins.

"So are you going to shit or get off the pot?" Lillie said.

"Excuse me?" Childress asked. He was younger than Quinn had first thought on the phone, maybe five years older than Quinn and Lillie, with thinning brown hair and a short-clipped mustache. He wore a wrinkled polo shirt that read *Investigator* over the breast pocket and khaki pants nearly two inches too short.

"We been through this already with another investigator," Quinn said. "Twice."

"Me and him rotate on the counties," Childress said. "On account of there's only two investigators for eight districts. Y'all sure you wouldn't like some coffee or muffins?"

"What we'd like," Lillie said, "is knowing how much longer this is going to last. We're hearing that y'all plan to take this to the grand jury. If this inquiry is trying to put together a case, we need our lawyer here."

Childress held up a hand and said, "Whoa. No, ma'am. This is just a fact-checking visit, like I said on the phone. I didn't want to show up in Jericho to make it appear to your constituents that it was anything but. I respect all law enforcement. I consider myself part of that team, and any-time I conduct an inquiry into official affairs, I'm not trying to buck the system. What y'all went through with them convicts sounded like pure hell. But if the DA didn't cross the t's and dot the i's on what happened to Leonard Chappell, people might wonder. He was the chief of police."

"And so crooked, they had to screw him into the ground," Lillie said.

Quinn reached under the table and grabbed her knee.

"I've met with Mr. Chappell's family and friends," Childress said. "They're still in a state of shock over the allegations and his death."

Lillie snorted. Quinn took a deep breath.

"That man came to kill me and another man named Jamey Dixon," Quinn said. "If I hadn't shot first, I'd be dead. He has a long history of ethics abuse and was out of his jurisdiction."

"Yes, sir," Childress said, tapping his pen at the edge of his legal pad. "That part sure is clear to me. What we are trying to figure out is who killed all those other men and why. Why did you, Sheriff, drive a former convict, Jamey Dixon, out to the scene? What benefit was he?"

"He was the goddamn trade," Lillie said. "Didn't you read the reports before you had us drive all the way over here?"

"Yes, ma'am," Childress said. "I read the reports several times. But some things aren't making sense to me. For me to get this gone and for all of us to go back to our lives, we got to make those weird pieces fit. It's all like a puzzle."

Lillie laced her fingers, clenched her jaw and leaned into the table. "I'm aware how it works, Mr. Childress."

"OK," he said. "OK. Let's just start off with some basic info. Sheriff Colson, you are former military, serving in the Army for ten years?"

Lillie sighed. Quinn nodded.

"Might I ask what made you retire and return back to Jericho?"

"Oh, hell," Lillie said. "Here it comes. Quinn, you have Sonny's ass on speed dial?"

Quinn stared across at Childress. He did not blink and set his jaw.

"There were several men shot out at a place called Hell's Creek," Childress said. "That was before you became sheriff. Can you tell me what that was all about?"

Quinn stared across at Childress, the man grinning like the sun was shining and all was right in the state of Mississippi. Quinn took out his cell phone and scrolled through to find Stevens's number. "I'll be right back," Quinn said.

The men came to the hunt lodge, exhausted from a day touring the tornado sites. They'd shaken a lot of hands and given a lot of hugs. There were prayers said, words of appreciation given, and many tears shed. Stagg had heard them all. There was the woman who'd been sucked out of a bathtub and landed five miles away. There was the old man who'd lost his wife of thirty years, his home, and his old black Lab. There was a cute set of orphans who rode it out under a table and an ugly woman who claimed Jesus held her hand while she sat on the shitter. Stagg liked hearing the stories, it gave the town some character and helped sell the forward momentum that Tibbehah County needed. Like the sign on Highway 45 read *Gateway to Mississippi's Future.*

"Mr. Stagg?" said the black stripper named Jaquita or Janiqua. "I think I sprained my wrist."

"Well, darling, I don't think there's any workmen's comp for tossing a man's pecker."

"That ain't what did it," she said. "I ain't done that tonight. One of those fools wanted to arm-wrestle and I thought he was joking but he took it real seriously. He was drinking Scotch from the bottle and kept on calling me his Little Hot Chocolate."

"Go see Willie James in the kitchen," Stagg said. "Let him get you a bag of ice. How about an extra fifty for the trouble?"

She left where Stagg sat alone at a big poker table facing the open room of the hunt lodge, thick pine beams steepled overhead, six bedroom doors opening out on the second-floor balcony. Every few minutes you could hear a woman's cry or a man's loud grunts as he finished his business. The whole party had grown sparse as the men and girls had paired off and left the silver trays of half-eaten chicken and picked-over, hardened cheese. Stagg made himself a ham sandwich to go with a tall glass of Alka-Seltzer and waited for the boys he'd called to show up. He'd deal with that mess and then drive on back to the Rebel, wait for Ringold to drive the van full of girls back to the Booby Trap and pick up eight fresh ones. This shit was going to go on all night or until the Viagra ran out.

At eight o'clock exactly, his cell phone rang. The ID reading BLOCKED meant the man was waiting outside for him. He got up and followed the stairs to the second bedroom door, knocking softly and hearing shuffling inside. The old gray-headed Trooper answered the door, looking pretty mad until he saw it was Stagg, and then grunted, "Let me get my pants and my gun. Is he here?"

"Yes, sir," Stagg said. "Waiting outside."

Stagg glanced through the cracked door and saw his little pixie lying on the bed, buck-naked and passed-out asleep. The old Trooper jerked a thumb at the girl and said, "Shit, Johnny. You git 'em young, don't you? When I got her clothes off, I felt like you'd laid out some jailbait."

"Were you disappointed?"

The man slid into his pants, smiled, and shook his buzz-cut head. He reached for his badge and gun on a chest of drawers. Two ducks petrified in midflight hung over the bed. He let himself out and followed Stagg through the big room and through the kitchen and outside. It had started to rain sometime in the last few hours they'd been at the lodge. A light mist fell across the headlights of a black Crown Vic with the windshield wipers going.

Stagg and the old Trooper stood side by side, waiting for the man to get out. The engine was still running as he met them in the headlights and asked how the party was going.

"Come on in," Stagg said. "We can fix you up a plate of whatever you like."

"No, sir," said the man. "I got to get home to Oxford. My wife would chew my ass if I get in too late."

"How'd it go?" the Trooper said.

The man shrugged, wiping the rain off his short-clipped mustache. His receding hair plastered down on his head. "You got it?"

"Yes, sir," the Trooper said. "Fuck, it's why I'm here."

The Trooper wandered off to a green Dodge pickup truck, saying he would never take an official vehicle off-duty, and opened up a passenger door and reached inside.

"Appreciate you making the trip," Stagg said.

The man looked nervous and unfocused in the bright hot lights of his car. "I got to go."

"Hold on, hold on."

"Who's inside?" the man asked.

Stagg just placed a finger to his lips and smiled.

The Trooper walked back to the men, carrying a rifle in a camouflage cover. He held it out in both hands as if presenting an official gift and waited for the other man. The other man hesitated for a bit, then took a breath and reached for it.

"Y'all got a warrant to search that dyke's house?" the Trooper asked.

"Almost."

"But y'all will take inventory of all them guns she collects?" Stagg said.

"Yes, sir."

"Good deal," Stagg said, grinning. "Sure is good seeing you."

He shook the man's hand and walked back to the hunt lodge to finish the second half of his sandwich.

10

When Quinn walked into Mr. Jim's barbershop the next morning, Luther Varner looked up from his copy of the *Daily Journal* and pronounced that rain was expected that afternoon, Ole Miss had screwed the pooch in the second half, and this country was still in the shitter. Mr. Jim was cutting the hair of Jay Bartlett, the esteemed mayor of Jericho, who was only six years older than Quinn and whose father had been mayor before him. Mr. Jim, a portly old man who'd served in Patton's 3rd Army, glanced up from his work and wished Quinn a good morning. Bartlett didn't say anything, looking to Quinn and then staring straight ahead at the TV on top of the Coke machine, the men checking out *The Price Is Right*, a special on celebrating Bob Barker's ninetieth birthday.

"Barker must be doing something right," Mr. Jim said. "Still got his own hair. Got good color and sense about him."

"You know he works with all them animals?" Mr. Varner said, spewing smoke from the side of his mouth. "I heard he paid a million dollars to save an elephant."

"Y'all ever watch anything else?" Quinn asked.

"Sometimes we watch *Days of Our Lives*."

"Sometimes?" Quinn said. "Y'all been watching it every day since I was a kid."

Luther Varner was rail-thin in dark jeans and a black T-shirt, his long, bony forearm proudly displaying a *Semper Fi* and laughing skull tattoos. He ashed the cigarette into his hand and walked over to the trash can to empty it. On the way back he shot a look at Quinn, tilting his head to Bartlett, before sitting back down.

"How you doing, Jay?" Quinn asked.

"Good."

"How'd it go yesterday on the Square?"

"Fine," Bartlett said, eyes never leaving *The Price Is Right*. A screaming fat woman had just been given the chance to win a small economy car.

"Damn," Luther said. "Don't think she could get in that car. What you think, Jim?"

"Part of her could get in," Mr. Jim said. "But the rest of her gonna have to hang out the window."

Bartlett kept on staring at the television. Mr. Jim put down the scissors and picked up a set of clippers, taking the hair off Bartlett's neck. Bartlett touched the part in his hair and fingered it off to the side, not being able to stand a moment that his hair wasn't spot-on. Mr. Jim put down the clippers and removed the cutter's cape from Bartlett's chest, dusting the hairs off his shoulders and neck. "Ready to go."

Bartlett reached into the pockets of his khakis and paid Mr. Jim. "Appreciate it."

Quinn hadn't moved. He simply nodded to Bartlett as he walked out, Bartlett only slightly returning the nod, something off and nervous about the man, as he passed and the door shut behind him with a jingle.

"That boy is sorrier than shit," Luther said.

Mr. Jim motioned for Quinn to take a seat. He fit the cape around his neck, finding the number 2 spacer he always used for the top of Quinn's head.

"He's a politician," Mr. Jim said. "It's in his blood. Them people don't think like decent people."

"Guess I won't expect his support this spring," Quinn said.

"Hell with him," Mr. Jim said, turning on the clippers, running the spacer over Quinn's head. Luther Varner shook his head at the sorriness of the whole situation, as he lit up another long smoke and turned his head to see if that fat woman had picked out the right numbers for the car. Mr. Jim finished up with the spacer and adjusted the clippers for the back and side of Quinn's head. Before he started, he launched into a coughing fit, turning his head and putting his hand to his mouth. Quinn and Luther didn't mention it, as Mr. Jim didn't want to discuss his illness.

He returned to the spinning chair as if it had never happened.

"I wasn't asked to attend the ceremony on the Square yesterday," Quinn said.

"Maybe they forgot?" Mr. Jim said, looking a bit more pale, breathing ragged.

"Bullshit."

"The supervisors got down on me early," Quinn said. "But I have to say I'm surprised by Jay Bartlett. His father was a decent man."

"Oh, hell no he wasn't, Quinn," Luther said. "Bartletts always do for the Bartletts. Ain't none of them ever stood for what's right. They stand for what people want to hear."

Mr. Jim held the clippers in his hand but hadn't turned them on yet.

"You think that's what people want to hear?" Quinn said. "You think it's gone that far?"

Luther squinted his eyes in the smoke and shook his head. "I don't know," he said, his voice weathered and cracked like a good Marine. "I try and not listen to bullshit."

"And if any of 'em bring it in here," Mr. Jim said, "my hand gets a bit unsteady."

"No one would have the guts to talk shit here," Quinn said. "Not here or at the VFW. What this town likes more than anything is standing back in the shadows and pointing fingers and talking about things they don't know a damn thing about."

"Ain't that always the way?" Luther said. "When I got home in '72, nobody was on the Square with a marching band and the damn key to the city. People who ain't been in it, been in the shit flying around them, can't wrap their heads around it."

"The worst of it," Quinn said, "is them stringing this thing out. They know exactly what they're doing."

"You deserve better than this county," Luther said. "I hate to say it. Jericho is my home. But hell, man, you know it's true. I know why you come back, glad to be a part of it, but I hope you'll find your own place. Somewhere that people deserve a good man."

Mr. Jim turned on the clippers and worked to keep Quinn high and tight. The whole haircut took less than three minutes. Quinn got up, reaching for his wallet, and Mr. Jim said there was no charge.

"How come?"

"'Cause you'll go broke keeping that hair that short," he said. "You know now that you're out of the service, you can grow it any way you like?"

Quinn grinned at the old man who'd been a friend to his uncle and to his father and had given him his very first haircut. He shook his liver-spotted hand. "I appreciate what works," Quinn said.

"You don't say . . ." Mr. Jim said.

"Shit," Mr. Varner said. "I hadn't cut my hair different since '65."

"These days, you got more hair in your ears than on top."

"Don't bother me none," Mr. Varner said. "Just pleased every day to see that old sun come up and not be among the dirt people. I hadn't forgotten what that goddamn twister did to my truck."

Quinn nodded at Luther. He'd been with the old man, helping the poor down in Sugar Ditch, when it hit.

Quinn grabbed his hat and coat from the rack and made his way to the glass door.

"It's good to see you, Quinn," Mr. Jim said, cleaning off his clippers and dropping his comb into the Barbicide. "Let me know when you get the new election posters. I'll post them bigger than shit in the front window."

"Did you talk to him?" Hank Stillwell asked.

Stillwell had stopped by the Jericho Farm & Ranch that morning, sitting out on the loading dock while Diane arranged sacks of feed, topsoil, and mulch. Wouldn't be long until the spring planting would start and people would be buying their seeds and small plants. Winter was tough. People didn't buy much when it was cold.

"We rode out to the site," Diane said. "I told the sheriff everything that I recalled. He knows everything I know."

Stillwell nodded, breathing in deep and hard through his nose. "Thank God."

"Did you want something or did you just stop by to talk?"

"I could use a new union suit."

"Inside," Diane said. "Go down the third aisle, with the work pants. They're down there."

"You got honey?"

"From Tibbehah bees."

"I'll get that, too," he said. "Y'all got a bit of everything here, don't you?"

"Yes, sir."

"I appreciate what you did," Stillwell said. "I know it was painful. Reaching back into those memories, that time. But I feel we owe it to Lori. Don't you? Her having no end to her story. No sense of knowing. Don't you want to know? I can't die and leave this earth without knowing why and who. I feel like my insides are done eaten away."

"Go on in and see if we got that union suit," Diane said. "I'll meet you inside. I got to finish stacking all this shit."

"You're a tough woman, Diane Tull."

"I'll meet you inside, Hank."

The store was nearly out of Diamond dog food, the premium, not the stuff for the pups or the old dogs. They were overstocked with topsoil and nearly out of manure, although most people around here scoured the cow fields for their own manure. Not buying your manure being kind of a point of pride for most folks who worked their own land.

Diane finished stacking the sacks on wooden pallets and checking the inventory. She needed some more wheat-straw bales and could do with some more sacks of corn for deer, people loving to get those animals close and captive, square and dead in their sights. Diane wore an old Sherpa coat with Marlboro Lights in one pocket and all her keys in the other. All the keys she owned: to her home, to her farm, the Farm & Ranch, to the cattle and chicken houses, feeling like it weighed a ton.

Stillwell lay down a small bottle of honey and an XL union suit, bright red with buttons down the front and an opener for the backside. Diane added the purchases to the register. "You mix this stuff in your coffee and tea and you won't get allergies come spring," she said.

"What do you think he'll do?" he asked. "Sheriff Colson?"

"He said he'd look into things."

"That don't mean shit," he said. "How long people been saying that? God damn."

"Maybe," Diane said. "But it's more than we had. You said you'd talked to Sheriff Beckett five years ago and he told you the whole thing was done and gone. Quinn Colson is an altogether different man."

Stillwell's face looked drawn, maybe more drawn than when he was drunk and hollow and passed out on her porch swing or slumped down in the seat of his old car. She finished ringing him up, and after he handed back the change, she put his stuff in a sack and walked out with him to the loading dock. It was bright and cold. She could see her breath, and the cold air felt good on her face and down into her lungs. Everything kind of clean and new that morning.

"It ain't right," he said. "It ain't fucking right. We got to make sense of things. Me and you."

"You're talking thirty-seven years ago."

"You're telling me that someone don't know?" he said. "Someone saw something. Someone knows something. This county ain't that big. Cowards keep shit to themselves."

Diane put her hands in her coat pockets, feeling the keys deep on the right side. She gripped the heft of them and nodded to Stillwell, wanting the old man to just go the hell away. She'd done what she'd promised. What else did he want of her? She wished he'd just leave her the hell alone and let them both go back to living their own lives, down their own paths. She never invited him.

"Do you want to talk to Sheriff Colson?" Diane asked. "Maybe that would help you and him."

"No, ma'am."

"But what you told me," she said. "Those are things he should know."

"If there comes a time when that's important," he said, "I'll do what's needed."

Diane lit up a cigarette and blew smoke into the crisp wind. "Can I ask you something?"

The old man spit and turned to her, waiting on the loading dock. A pickup truck turned in from the gates and drove up toward the Co-op. She wondered if Hank Stillwell had a job, had a woman, had anything in his wretched old life other than thinking about what happened to his daughter. It had seemed to become his main occupation, beyond any kind of obsession a normal person might have.

"What do you want to know?"

"Is it the truth you're hoping to find?" Diane asked.

"Goddamn right."

"Or is it what came later that bothers you?" Diane asked.

Stillwell swallowed hard, spit again, and seemed to stand up straighter. His breath came out in clouds as his face turned a bright shade of red. "I don't study on that time much."

"You don't?" Diane said. "What happened doesn't bother you?"

"Decisions were made and things were done," Stillwell said. "People were upset. Things just got set in motion. I couldn't stop it. Nothing I said could stop it."

"It wasn't right."

"No, ma'am," he said. "It was one of the most horrific things I've ever seen. I never wanted that. Never." Stillwell held the brown paper bag tight in his arms, hanging there on the loading dock, as a black woman crawled out of the pickup and asked if they had any collard greens. Diane smiled and yelled back for her to come on in, before turning back and whispering to Hank.

"You know it will come out," she said. "You can't bring up one without the other."

"If it helps learn who did this to you and Lori?" the old man said. "Fine by me."

He hobbled down the loading dock step and walked over to an aging Harley. He threw a leg over the seat, kick-started the engine, and roared out of the gravel lot. Diane squashed her cigarette and went inside the loading dock to help the woman.

11

Before Jason had left for L.A. the first time, he'd seen this corny biker movie at the old Jericho Drive-In, promising Brutal Violence Turned On by Hot Chicks and Burning Rubber. Maybe that's all he really needed to know about the Born Losers MC, although there'd been a lot of talk since he rode with them about brotherhood, respect, and being the kind of men who would not and could not conform to society. Chains LeDoux had gotten pretty ripped at Shiloh the night before, standing on the silent battleground and telling them all they were the sons of Confederates, Vikings, and the goddamn Knights of the Round Table, punching clocks and paying taxes were for the weak, the emasculated, the deadbeats. He then smoked down a joint, passed it on to Big Doug, and started into a karate kata that ended with a kick to the moon and a rebel yell.

Now, they'd been riding all day, most of it through foothills of Tennessee, and then down through the streets of Memphis and finally catching up with 78, where all of them were hungover, hungry, and getting a little worn in the saddle. Chains wanted to stop off at a little barbecue joint in Olive Branch run by a fellow Marine—Chains had been in 'Nam. The ex-Marine sometimes rode with the club and always gave out big plates of ribs, beans, and coleslaw when they got to town.

Jason just wanted to get home, check in with that sweet Jean Beckett, already calling her from a pay phone in Adamsville, and spend some more time with his dad and brothers before he'd load his bikes onto his truck trailer and head west. There was a new film shooting in a few months, again with Needham and Reynolds. A picture that promised to make stuntmen the real heroes. Needham wanted to jump a rocket car over a river.

The thirteen bikers plus Jason parked out front and used the toilets, the owner coming out and hugging the boys. Big Doug introduced Jason as a bad-ass potential member, saying he'd never met a crazier son of a bitch in his life. A Born Loser, if there'd ever been one, Jason learning "Loser" really meant an outcast from society.

"Big Doug don't say that 'bout anybody," the man said. "You want slaw and beans with them ribs?"

"Sure."

"Beers in the Coca-Cola cooler in the kitchen," he said. "Help yourself."

"Being with the club got perks," Big Doug said, "don't it?"

Jason nodded and made his way to a big circular table in the center of the room, a couple waitresses in white-and-red ringer T-shirts already laying down plates and handing out cans of beer and glasses of sweet tea for the boys. One of the other riders, that fella named Hank but called Pig Pen, took a seat across from him, the other bikers becoming friendlier and more open on the ride. He had wispy long red hair and a scraggly beard. Dirt up under his fingernails.

Chains LeDoux still couldn't even acknowledge Jason's presence. Chains had found a tree stump to sit on in his chaps and leather vest and smoke a joint, looking out at the cars going back and forth on the highway.

"Your ass hurt as much as mine?" Jason asked.

"Probably more," Stillwell said. "You get a chopper and the ride is smoother, just lay back, let the bike just take you where it wants to go."

"We know each other," Jason said. "Before the other night, when you almost stabbed me with that fork? Don't we?"

"I think you used to date my youngest sister."

"Don't say . . ."

"You remember her?"

"What was her name?"

"Darlene."

"Darlene what?"

"You dated more than one Darlene?"

"Oh, yes, sir," Jason said, grinning, a plate of ribs sliding in front of him. A cold Coors laid down at his elbow by the pit owner. "I can think of six just in Jericho."

"Darlene Stillwell."

"Hell yes, I know Darlene Stillwell," Jason said. "Sang in the choir. Twirled a baton that was on fire. Nicest girl you'll ever meet."

"She got married," Stillwell said. "Got two boys. She's a teller at the bank. They say she got management potential."

The men ate hunched over the plates, manners tossed aside, teeth on bone, wiping sauce on their bare chests and Levi's. Some of the boys started to throw rib bones at one another's heads. Nobody seemed to mind until Chains walked in and swept up a waitress in his arms and squeezed her ass, asking if she wanted to go for a nice long ride. The woman slapped his face and Chains just laughed, drinking more beer, some spilling down his beard, as he strutted over to the window of the restaurant. All the laughing and the jackassing and the cussing and eating slipping off when they heard the rumble of more bikes coming from the highway, Chains stood still at the window, not grinning about the waitress anymore but watching the parking lot, pulling a .38 from the back of his leather pants, telling everyone to get off their asses. "God damn, here they come," he said. "Ain't that somethin'?"

"Who?" Jason said, standing up. Hank looking like he'd just swallowed a big stone. "Who's coming?"

"Goddamn Outlaws," Stillwell said. "They claim this part of Mississippi.

They warned the owner here that if he served us again, they'd burn the place to the fucking ground."

"Oh, shit."

"Can you fight?" Stillwell asked.

"Yep."

"Shoot?"

"You bet."

"All right, then, come on," Stillwell said, joining up with all the boys in their leather and denim and man stink and testosterone. A couple had guns tucked in the waistbands of their wide belts; no shirts over their big furry-ape chests, and long beards. Jason the only one of them without a patched jacket. Big Doug stood up front with Chains, holding a two-foot-long section of metal pipe in his right hand and palming it into his left.

There were twenty Outlaws, just as hairy and ugly and big. The only way to tell the difference was by their leather vests and the big red-eyed skull and crossbone pistons. Memphis was an Outlaws town, and the Born Losers weren't but about fifteen miles from it.

"You jokers want to ride on into here, flying your colors, like it ain't no thing," said a big gray-haired bastard. "May not be nothing to you, but it's a big goddamn thing to me."

Chains looked to the man standing opposite to him, spit on the ground, and grabbed himself between the legs. "Suck it, motherfucker."

"Is that it?" the man said. "That's what you got? 'Cause I'm tired of talking shit with you, LeDoux. Let's take it back to the goddamn cowboy days."

Big Doug stepped up between the men and pushed the Outlaw guy square in the chest, knocking him back a few feet, and then every single goddamn Outlaw looked for a Born Loser skull to crack. There just wasn't any time for Jason to explain he had never really formally joined a damn thing, had just decided to ride along as a gag, on a dare. But a fight is a fight, and there had always been something in Jason Colson that made him love fighting in a real and authentic way. He grabbed the first son of a bitch he saw and punched him hard in the mouth, feeling good to really connect to some teeth, none of this fake throwing shit anymore, knocking the dude on the ground and looking for more. There were grunts, blows, kicking, and yelling and swearing, and then some blood spilled on the pavement at the barbecue joint. Somewhere, a dog on a chain was going crazy, wanting to get into the mess, and the hot summer wind had changed, blowing woodsmoke down through the brawl, making eyes water and the whole wild scene seem like something out of a crazy dream. It was Brutal Violence Turned On by Hot Chicks and Burning Rubber, only there weren't any hot chicks besides the two big-bottomed waitresses in red short shorts and tight ringer tees, screaming at them to either stop or beat some more ass.

Some Outlaw bastard had a big handful of Jason's hair and was trying to run his ass straight into a long line of Born Losers' bikes, but Jason rolled away from him, sweeping his legs out and then getting on top of the ugly man, punching him right in the ugly face, busting the man's lip and nose and reaching for his long greasy hair to slam his head on the pavement.

Somebody reached for him, Jason realizing it was two more Outlaws, one of them with a long metal chain that he fitted around Jason's neck and pulled, dragging him away from the bleeding man. Somewhere, someone fired a pistol. Someone yelled.

Jason could not breathe, thinking, God damn, this is how it all ends. You jump out of a helicopter, free-fall from a skyscraper, and plan to jump a car over a river, only to get your ass taken out by some redneck mad you ate his barbecue.

Jason was on his knees, trying for air and not succeeding a bit with the chain on his throat, when he heard a thwack and plunk and the pressure was gone, Jason rolling to his back, choking in long swallows of air. Big Doug appeared over him with the pipe, dripping with blood, and offered him a big meaty paw to get back to his feet and get on with it.

There was another shot, another cracking pistol. The women screamed, *and the barbecue joint owner was in the middle of them all, blasting off his shotgun, but not a damn thing stopped until they all heard those sirens coming off Highway 78, the men backing away, the kicking and punching slowing down, until they were still, Outlaw and Born Loser alike crawling back on their choppers, giving one another the bird and tailing on out of the parking lot. Jason's heart was jumping so bad in his chest, after not feeling that kind of worry for a good long while, that he nearly missed the fella laid out cold in the parking lot, a halo of blood spreading around the body and head.*

One of the big-bottomed waitresses was screaming like hell, holding the Outlaw's head in her lap, waiting for the law and medical help, and for the chaos to ride on down the road.

It wasn't a mile away that the fists of the bikers raised in the sky, high off handlebars, bikes crisscrossing and bikers high-fiving, on the back highways to Jericho.

12

You notice anything strange about that report in your hand, Sheriff?" Lillie said.

"The paper feels strange," Quinn said, looking up from the stack of files on the desk. "Onionskin. Pretty damn thin."

"And the report itself?"

"Real thin."

Lillie nodded. She sat down with Quinn in the SO conference room, not much to the room but a long row of file cabinets, a couple grease boards, and the coffee machine. There were old plaques on the wall for honors given to his late uncle by the state and a brand-new calendar from the Jericho National Bank. It was one of those big old-fashioned ones of bird dogs hunting through the brush, men in quilted coats raising guns to flying quail. The whole thing old-time wishful thinking, as the quail had died off decades ago, either from an influx of the coyotes or the invention of the bush hog, taking out their natural habitat.

Lillie set down a sack from the Sonic. "Saw you working when I left," Lillie said. "I got you a cheeseburger and fries. Everything on it."

"Reason I made you my chief deputy."

"Not because I had the most law enforcement experience?"

"I figured we needed to boost your self-confidence," Quinn said, reaching into the sack and getting the burger and fries, "since that's in such short supply with you."

Quinn already had a big cup of black coffee going on the desk. He didn't bother keeping track of how many cups he drank in a day. If Mary Alice wouldn't complain, he'd have a La Gloria Cubana going, too. Which he did, on occasion, when a window and fan were handy.

"After I came back from Memphis, your uncle wanted to go on and purge these files," Lillie said. "He always said he wanted to have a bonfire party on your land and clear the decks."

"He say why?"

"Officially?" Lillie asked. "He said the cases were closed and we needed the space."

"Unofficially?"

"He was a servant of the people and said there were a great many things in his file cabinet that would embarrass some fine folks and good families."

"Bless their hearts."

"Funny how you and Sheriff Beckett were related," Lillie said, stealing a French fry from the carton. "You could give a rat's ass about what people think. Or fine families and such."

"I don't care what they think," Quinn said. "But I do like to know how they might vote."

"Something happen?"

He told her about being at Mr. Jim's barbershop and Jay Bartlett being such a horse's ass.

"Jay Bartlett is a horse's ass," Lillie said. "A sorry little prick. He hadn't said two words to me in the last five years. He's been listening to rumors about me, too. He thinks that maybe I'm helping spread immorality and liberal ideas throughout Tibbehah County."

"Isn't that how you get your kicks?" Quinn said.

"Wouldn't you love to know," Lillie said. She placed her big combat boots on the edge of the desk and leaned back a bit. She had on her slick green sheriff's office jacket, hair in a ponytail and threaded through a ball cap with the insignia of Tibbehah County on it. "Now," she said, letting the front legs down on the chair and shifting her eyes down her stack of papers, "what's wrong with what you got?"

"I got nothing," Quinn said.

"Meaning?"

"Meaning there is the incident report with an interview with Diane Tull and a half-dozen people who saw them at the carnival that night," he said. "There were a couple half-assed and illiterate reports to follow about talking to people who lived out on Jericho Road near the old Fisher property and heard shots but didn't see a goddamn thing."

"Right."

"And an autopsy report."

"And what else?"

"Nothing."

"No follow-up reports, nothing filed with the state, no interview with local informants? You know your uncle always had a set of CIs on the payroll?"

"OK," Quinn said. "So it was half-assed and poorly done. Nobody ever said this sheriff's department was progressive. My uncle once tried to keep law and order. But he never thought of himself as an investigator."

"Stuff was taken out," she said. "That's not all that happened. Even if it was half-assed, there'd be twice as much here, just as routine."

Lillie took off her cap and placed it on the table, got up, and set her SO coat on the rack. She sat back down with Quinn and ate another few fries, thinking on things, and then took his last bite of cheeseburger. She thought some more as she ate. "Funny thing is how little people have talked about all this. What exactly did Diane Tull tell you?"

"Pretty much what she told my uncle in 1977."

"And nothing more?"

"What else could she say?" Quinn said. "How about you spell it out to me, Lillie Virgil?"

"OK, Sheriff." Lillie nodded, mind made up, and walked over to a long row of dented and scratched file cabinets. Using a key from her pocket, she opened one in the center, two drawers down, and pulled out an old manila folder, shut and bound with an old piece of string. "Call me when you get done reading this."

She slid the file far across the table to Quinn and he immediately wiped his hands on a napkin and opened it up. Stapled reports, autopsy files, several black-and-white photos that brought to mind many images of the hills of Afghanistan and burned-out homes in Iraq. He could recall the horrid smell of charred bodies. "Jesus."

"You bet," Lillie said. "They found this goddamn crispy critter on Jericho Road about three days after Diane Tull was raped and Lori Stillwell was murdered. You think nobody in this office thought about a connection?"

"Who is it?"

"A man," Lillie said. "A black man. That's about all anyone knows about him. You can read about all there is in the report, but it looks like Sheriff Beckett didn't so much as lift the phone to find out who he was, why he was here, or what happened to him. Seems like your uncle pretty much knew this all was a done deal."

"Son of a bitch."

"Like I said, call me when you're done," Lillie said. "I think it's about time you had a come-to-Jesus with Diane Tull and find out exactly why she's getting this thing opened far and wide. And if someone tells me this is about God's will, I'll punch 'em in the mouth. God may be strange and mysterious, but this didn't come out of nowhere."

Stagg met Craig Houston out on his two-thousand-acre spread out in the county, a good portion of Tibbehah that he'd controlled for decades, including what used to be a World War II airfield and some old hangars and barracks. Before and since the storm, Stagg had his crew out paving back over the tarmac, propping up those old Quonset huts and adding a few more, building up some cinder-block bunkers and then laying out miles and miles of chain-link fencing to keep the nosy out of his business. Stagg had told everyone he was working on his own hunt lodge, the airfield just part of his land, bringing in drinking buddies from Memphis and Jackson. "You like it?" Johnny Stagg said.

"All this shit yours?" asked Houston. "The fucking land? This whole damn compound?"

Stagg grinned and nodded. He stood against his maroon Cadillac, chewing on a toothpick, taking in the possibilities of his own little valley. A cold wind whisking down through the valley and across their faces.

"God damn, man. You ain't no joke. From here, we do what the fuck we want."

You didn't have to tell Houston much about how it would all work, the smart kid in the bright blue satin warm-up stood next to his bright white Escalade just smiling. He talked about their partnership, now a friendship, and how an airfield would get those Burrito Eaters off his back. Those Burrito Eaters now calling the shots from below the border in a town some had never even visited.

"Don't need no trucks coming in from Texas," Houston said. "Don't need no shit from New Orleans. We call it. Deal direct."

"And you can make it happen?" Stagg said. "You lived with those people down there for how long? Learned their practices and their ways?"

"Four years," Houston said. "They call my black ass Speedy Gonzales. Understand honor, respect, and that you shoot a motherfucker who don't. Shit, I didn't graduate fifth grade and now speak Spanish without no accent. Don't believe me? How 'bout we go down to the Mex place in Jericho and listen to me talk some shit beyond the chimichangas."

"Good," Stagg said. "Good."

"Who else knows about what you got?"

Stagg shook his head. The bright January wind was a damn knife cutting through that valley, rows and rows of old oaks and second-growth pines, and across the tarmac to where he stood with the black kingpin of Memphis. They both had come by themselves, Stagg leaving Ringold back at the Rebel and Houston leaving his people down in Olive Branch, where he ran things from the back of an all-you-can-eat soul food joint and Chinese buffet.

"When we start?" Houston asked.

"No sense in waiting," Stagg said. "You say the word, Mr. Houston."

"They ain't gonna like this," Houston said. "There's a lot of business gonna just be left hanging out there. Ain't like canceling your subscription to fucking *Playboy*. People gonna want answers. And if they get them, they gonna come for me and for you, Mr. Stagg."

"Let 'em come," Stagg said. "Like I said, those cartel folks been down here before. They know Tibbehah County ain't open to free trade."

"You ain't like the other Dixie Mafia folks I knew."

"There ain't no Dixie Mafia, son," Stagg said.

"But you part of that crew?" Houston said. "All those motherfuckers from around Corinth and down in Biloxi. That's your world."

"Dixie Mafia is something the damn Feds made up to cornhole us," Stagg said. "All those men I used to know, most of 'em dead or in prison, didn't do business unless we wanted. We don't have no blood oaths and hierarchy and all that Hollywood shit."

"But the old crooks?" Houston said. "They wouldn't been caught dead with no black kid from Orange Mound. You know that?"

"The South ain't the same," Stagg said. "Get that shit straight. I ain't never thought I'd have to worry about crazy-ass Mexicans coming up from Guadalajara with a chain saw, wanting to tell me how to run my business in Tibbehah."

"They killed eight of my people last year," Houston said. "One of 'em was my half brother."

Stagg nodded.

"Don't need 'em," Houston said. "Once you cut off the money, they gone."

"You bet," Stagg said, swiveling the toothpick in his mouth. "People come before me never saw a challenge coming. You got to think about the future every day of your goddamn life in this business, son. If you don't, you gonna wake up with a gun in your mouth or a cock up your ass."

"Damn, old man," Houston said. "That's hard shit."

"The plain ole gospel truth."

Houston walked across the weeds to the end of the airstrip, the concrete poured as smooth and straight as a griddle. He looked to the rolling Mississippi hills that protected each side of them, the open doors to the empty buildings, and the red wind sock, blowing straight and hard, at the other end of the runway. The morning sun was bright and wide across the valley.

Houston offered Stagg his hand.

"We need to talk," Diane Tull said.

"OK," Caddy said.

"Not here," Diane said. "In private."

Diane had found Caddy Colson unloading canned goods and fresh vegetables from the back of her old blue Ford pickup. She was stocking the storerooms in a barn that doubled as a church, a place called The River, which served the poor and downtrodden of Greater Jericho and Tibbehah County. Caddy was being helped by Boom Kimbrough, a hell of a strong man even with one arm. He hoisted big boxes and unwieldy gallons of milk up in his one massive arm and supported it all with a prosthetic hook.

Caddy looked to Boom, Boom pretending he hadn't heard any of the conversation, but he walked away with a flat of canned baked beans. "Come on," Caddy said. "We can go on inside the sanctuary. All right?"

Diane nodded and followed through the big open barn doors, still strange as hell to her to call an old livestock barn, painted red with a sloping metal roof, a church. The outreach and ministry of the late Jamey Dixon. Diane knew how much Caddy had loved Dixon, worshipped and believed in him, and believed that her turnaround as a human being came through meeting him and forging her belief in a Christ who forgave prostitutes and tax collectors. And who was Diane to judge, Caddy did certainly seem like a changed person.

She was fresh-scrubbed in Levi's and shit-kicker boots, a long sweatshirt on under a blue barn coat, her boy-short hair ruffling in the wind as she walked Diane into the barn and closed the large doors behind them. The January wind whipped up good around them and whistled through the cracks of the church. Long homemade pews stretched out in three directions from a stage and pulpit, bales of hay and galvanized troughs making the point of no one getting over the humbleness of his surroundings.

"How far can I trust your brother?" Diane said.

"Depends on what it is."

"I've started up something again, Caddy," Diane said. "I wish to God I'd never done it. I want Quinn to just stop, leave it alone."

"Quinn's never been much good at leaving things alone."

"But if I ask him or you ask him, he'll do it," Diane said, "right? There's no need to open things up if the survivors want it closed. That should mean something to him."

"You want to sit down?"

"Not really."

"You look a nervous mess, Diane," Caddy said. "Sit."

They found a center pew, four spaces back from the stage, Diane wondering if indeed she did look like shit since she hadn't looked in a mirror since getting to work that morning. She hadn't dressed up or down and thought she was handling her conversation with Hank Stillwell pretty damn good, considering what he'd said. She now knew his obsession wasn't just about Lori but about himself and about things haunting him as a man. Diane wanted out.

"What happened?"

Diane told her about meeting with Quinn and driving out to Jericho Road, riding out to a spot that she hadn't visited in years, not ever wanting to see the place since coming up on it made her feel like she was coming up out of her skin. But she said she swallowed the fear, wanted to face things again, not let what happened control her and maybe put those events off her conscience and into the hands of the new sheriff, since the old one never seemed to listen.

"And what did he say?"

"He said he'd heard the stories and knew what happened to us," Diane said. "But he needed to look at the old reports and talk to some people. I don't want him talking to anybody. He starts talking to people and then things are going to come back on me. People are going to start to talk and point fingers, and, Caddy, I'm too old for that. This was too long ago. I can't have that happen. And I can't have anything else happen, either. People might get hurt."

Caddy sat cool in the pew next to Diane, shit-kicker boot crossed at the knee, leaning up against the pew ahead, resting her chin on her forearm. A big cross made out of cedar logs hung from the rafters, swinging lightly in the breeze that cut in from outside.

"Don't worry about Quinn," Caddy said. "He takes care of himself and doesn't scare easy. You're the one sweating and it's not even forty degrees outside."

"This shit is making me think on things I hadn't worried about for a long time," Diane said. "Things happened, some of it I recall, but other things feel like part of a dream. Things I heard whispered by my parents and some of the old people, who'd drop little comments on me, giving me a wink like I knew what they are talking about."

There was a pleasantness to the old barn, the rough-hewn slats of wood, the still-present smell of feed and hay, even as support beams budded with speakers and the stage had been outfitted for a country gospel band. White Christmas lights wrapped most of the rafters and support beams, and there was a stillness about the place, even though people were hammering and talking outside. Lots of people, working to keep the ministry going.

"You don't have to talk to me," Caddy said. "But you need to let this all out to two men."

"Jesus Christ and Quinn Colson?"

"Yes, ma'am," Caddy said. "Both can help you."

"I might need the one carries a gun on his hip."

"Tell Quinn," Caddy said. "It doesn't matter who out there wants you to keep things quiet. If it's still important, still going on, he needs to know. He'll look out for you. We'll all look out for you. You've been a part of us since the beginning."

Caddy reached out and squeezed Diane's hand. Diane hadn't noticed she was crying until she felt the wetness on her cheeks. She wiped it away with the back of her hand and snuffled a short laugh. "Something better not happen to me or you'll have to rework Sunday's service."

"I got you down for 'You'll Never Walk Alone' and 'There Will Be Peace in the Valley,'" Caddy said. "Momma is thrilled. Two of Elvis's favorites. To Jean, something's not really holy unless Elvis sung it."

"I'll do my best," Diane said.

Caddy gripped Diane's hand more and squeezed tighter. She looked her right in the eye and smiled, so much strength and confidence that reminded Diane of Jamey Dixon, him being the one who'd first brought Diane to The River and got her to sing onstage, said she had a gift and he needed her to be a part of the rebirth of this county.

"He sure loved you, Caddy," Diane said, regretting saying it before the words were even out of her mouth. Caddy withdrew her hand, stood abruptly but kept the smile going, and told her again to speak to Quinn.

"And after that?"

"Lay it all down for Jesus, sister," Caddy said.

13

"You take me to the nicest places, Quinn," Ophelia Bundren said, looking cute and warm in a snug blue V-neck sweater dress and gray tights. "Are you trying to spoil me?"

"Blue plate special is chicken spaghetti and two sides," Quinn said. "Depends on what you want for the sides."

"To be honest, it's just nice being away from work," she said. "We had two funerals this morning and another one on Saturday. All of them people I know. All of them old. Do you know how hard it is to make old people look good when they die?"

"I imagine it's tough to make any dead person look good," Quinn said.

"You'd be surprised," Ophelia said. "Some people look better in the box than on the street."

"Is that a fact?"

"Take Miss Nelson, for instance," Ophelia said. "In life, she wore that crazy red wig and enough paint on her face for a circus clown. I chose a different wig and toned down her cheeks and eyes. Gave her a softer look. Her husband whispered to me after the service it was the best she'd looked since her wedding day."

"You are an artist, Miss Bundren."

"I'd like to think so," she said. "I just have a different canvas than most."

"You want the special?" Quinn said, looking up at the waitress, an older frizz-haired woman named Mary. Quinn was pretty sure Mary had been at the Fillin' Station diner since the day they opened. She'd been bringing food to Quinn since he was in a high chair.

Ophelia sighed and put down the menu that hadn't changed much, either, over the years. "Only live once," she said.

Quinn showed two fingers to the waitress and Mary walked off to the kitchen, Quinn and Ophelia framed in the front plate-glass window of what had been a Texaco service station. The owner had even found a couple of those glass-topped pumps from the thirties to place under the portico and hang some old-time gas signs in and around the restaurant. The room smelled like grease and cigarettes.

"You too tired to talk shop?" Quinn said.

"I thought this was a date?"

"If this was a date, I could do better," Quinn said, pushing the file of the unknown man of '77 toward her. "I might even take you to Vanelli's in Tupelo for some Athenian lasagna. This is an autopsy report from before we were born. It was done by old Doc Stevens and contains a lot of medical information I need deciphered. Also there are a few photos in there that should help. I wouldn't advise you look at them before lunch."

"Seriously," Ophelia said, "I see plenty of that before I even have breakfast. How bad can it be?"

Quinn didn't say a word. He'd learned when a woman announced she had a certain thing on her mind, he was not one to get in her way.

"Jesus God," Ophelia said, putting a hand to her mouth.

"Body was found out on Jericho Road not far from where a couple young girls were attacked," Quinn said. "The body was never ID'd. But it looks like they have some dental records, and maybe some DNA left somewhere."

"Damn," Ophelia said, reading. "This wasn't just murder, it was a punishment. What the hell happened?"

"I have some idea of what occurred but no idea of who he was," Quinn said. "I'm hoping you might be able to tell me what could be done about it now. He had no ID on him, reports say he was homeless, a hitchhiker who'd come to Jericho. He was living like an animal off the Natchez Trace, had some kind of lean-to he'd fashioned out of old scrap wood and tin."

"Why?" she asked. "Why would someone do this to another human?"

"I can tell you more later," Quinn said. "Just take the file and let me know what I need to request from Jackson. I guess we start with the dental records."

"Sure," Ophelia said. "And you said there might be some DNA?"

Quinn shrugged. "There's mention of bloody and burned clothes placed in evidence. Maybe a pair of boots. I can't find any trace of them right now; my uncle had sort of a scattered filing system. But Lillie and I are looking. Also checking with the court archives in Oxford."

"A black male, late twenties, measured at a little under six feet," Ophelia said. "That's it?"

Mary brought them two large sweet teas and blue plate specials. They'd forgotten to ask which sides, but the cook had just ladled on some green beans and fried eggplant. Not bad choices. They started to eat and didn't talk. Quinn and Ophelia had been together long enough, and during some tough times after the tornado, that they felt solid around each other, no need to say much. They were the only ones in the restaurant, the time getting close to two, way past when normal folks ate lunch.

Ophelia had dark brown eyes and long brown hair with sideswept bangs she'd often push from her eyes as a nervous habit. When she was curious, skeptical, or worried, her mouth would turn into a thick red knot, holding what she had to say until she had chosen her words right. Most folks in Jericho considered her shy, or mousy, but she was more standoffish, slow to reveal herself in the typical Bundren way.

"This may not be the time," Ophelia said, "but there's nothing wrong if you were to stay with me in town a few days. I don't give a good god damn what anyone says about me. And, hell, bring Hondo, too. You need some space of your own. And I'm closer to town."

"People seem to be talking about me enough."

"All bullshit."

"Of course."

"The ones that matter don't talk that way."

Quinn nodded. "I hope not," he said. "It's the ones who whisper that give you trouble."

"How about a toothbrush at my place?" Ophelia said. "We start with a toothbrush . . ."

"Roger that," Quinn said. "Always liked to travel light. Be prepared for whatever comes my way."

Quinn rode with Lillie up into the hills around Carthage late that afternoon to find a man named E. J. Royce, who'd worked as a deputy with his late Uncle Hamp. Royce was an odd duck, as anybody in Jericho was guaranteed to echo if asked. How else would you describe a man who'd turned his back on all his people and came to town only for the most basic supplies? He preferred the company of dogs—coon dogs, to be exact—five or six of them meeting Quinn's truck on the highway and following it on each side, baying and barking, until they got close to Royce's shack.

The shack was fashioned together with plywood, Visqueen, and spit. Royce telling anyone who'd listen, from his children to his church, "I don't ask for nothing I don't need. I tend to my business. I take care of my own damn self."

The dogs barked and bayed some more. Quinn and Lillie got out of the big F-250, walked to the front porch, and knocked on a little door that sat oddly low even for a short man like E. J. Royce.

The old man opened the little door with a broad grin, wearing Liberty overalls and a trucker cap from Tibbehah County Co-op, the main competition for Diane Tull's Jericho Farm & Ranch. "Well, shit," he said.

Royce always greeted Quinn that way.

"And you, too."

Royce smiled. He almost never could remember Lillie's name, always referring to her as that big-boned girl with grit.

"Good to see you, Mr. Royce," Quinn said. "You got some time?"

"Y'all ain't come to arrest me?"

"You do something wrong?" Lillie asked.

"Stick around a bit, darlin'," Royce said, grinning, scratching the white whiskers on his chin. "I just might. Damn, you're a tall drink of water."

He invited them into his shack, waving to an old sofa covered in stacked clothes and fixed in places with duct tape. A couple of the dogs followed them inside and Royce shooed them away, telling them they knew better and needed an ass-whippin', they didn't watch out. But the old man patted them on the heads as he led them out and closed the door. Boxes lined the walls, bundles of clothes that Quinn knew had been dropped off by the Baptist church that he never used. A television set on top of two older television sets played an episode of *Gunsmoke*.

Quinn nodded to the television. "Always liked Matt Dillon."

"Didn't know it was back on the air till the other day," Royce said. "Good to see something worth a shit on."

Lillie took a seat on the couch, nodding at Quinn to do the same. Lillie was always getting onto Quinn about his abrupt military manner interfering with real investigations. She often told him to act nice, be friendly, make the other person comfortable. But, then again, a couple weeks ago Lillie promised an abuser that she would kick in his goddamn teeth if she ever again saw a mark on his girlfriend.

"How y'all been?" Royce said. "Your sister brought me a plate of supper the other night. I told her she didn't need to be gone and doing that. You know, I don't ask for nothin' I don't need. I tend to my business. And I take care of own damn self."

"I think I may have heard that, sir," Quinn said.

Royce found an old kitchen chair toppled over under some clothes and brought it near the sofa. He smiled at Lillie and she smiled back. On television, Matt Dillon just killed three men and was walking down the center of the street in Dodge City. No one said jack shit.

"We need to talk to you about a murder that happened some time ago," Lillie said. "I think you're the last deputy around from the seventies."

"Hal Strange is still kicking," Royce said, "but he moved to Gulfport a few years ago."

"I heard he died," Lillie said.

"Nope," Royce said. "Just got a Christmas card from his wife said they'd taken in some culture travels up in Gatlinburg, seeing some shows and all. Dinner theater and dancing."

Lillie had brought in the file but didn't open it. She just took her time, Quinn always letting her take the lead in an investigation. "Do you recall when those two girls were attacked on the Fourth of July? This was in 1977."

Royce, who'd been smiling, now quit. He rubbed his hands over his old white whiskers, his flannel shirt as threadbare as possible without becoming translucent. "Sure," he said. "That's the stuff what'll stick hard. I don't know how y'all still work in law enforcement. Seems like them things happen more and more. But back then, that was something not regular. Things like that didn't happen in Jericho."

Quinn knew the local history but did not correct the old man.

"You ever catch the man who did it?" Lillie asked, the file placed between her knee and forearm that answered that very question.

"No, ma'am," he said, "we sure didn't. Sheriff Beckett took that shame to his grave. I don't think he ever gave up trying to find that man. The father of the dead girl. What's his name?"

"Stillwell?"

"Yes, Stillwell," Royce said. "Sure made a mess of that fella . . . sloppy, crazy-ass drunk."

Royce nodded with certainty, the mountains of clothes, garbage, and boxes of useless shit reminding Quinn of the state he'd once found his uncle's farm in. There were a lot of empty bottles of Old Grand-Dad lying about the shack, too, and coffee cans filled with cigarette butts.

Royce lit up a cigarette. Lillie joined him.

"So y'all had nothing?" Lillie said. "Not even some rumors or something to go on?"

"Sheriff Beckett must've paid out nearly a thousand dollars to informants," he said. "Doc Stevens offered a big reward. Judge Blanton got some highway patrol folks to come over and look into things, taking the man's description across the state. This shit looks bad for a town. Looks worse for law enforcement. It made the papers and the TV station in Tupelo. I remember for a few years they used to have a candlelight vigil on the Square. That lasted for a while and then I guess people just forgot about that Stillwell girl."

Lillie tilted her head and bit her lower lip, cigarette still in hand. She flicked her eyes at Quinn and sat back in the duct-taped sofa.

"There was a second murder about that time?" Quinn said.

"Don't recall that."

Quinn nodded. He did not smile at the old man.

"You wrote the report," Quinn said. "It was from July 6th of '77. Man had been shot several times, his skull fractured, neck broken, and then his body was dragged out into the county and burned, his attackers probably trying to get rid of any evidence."

The old man's eyes narrowed at Quinn. He smoked a bit more and then stubbed out the cigarette under his old boots right there in his living room. "Something like that comes to mind. Sure. What of it?"

"Didn't y'all think maybe these two events were connected?" Lillie asked.

"What do you mean?"

Lillie swallowed and took in a very long breath. Lillie Virgil had trouble with patience but could wrangle her emotions when needed. "Victim was a black male in his late twenties," Lillie said. "Perp in the rape was a black male in his late twenties."

Royce had a wide look of confusion on his face, sort of like a man you'd see lost in a big city, wandering around, trying to find something familiar.

"I just don't know, doll," he said. "I just don't know."

"It's Deputy Virgil," she said. "My name is Deputy Virgil."

"And this was a long time back," Royce said. "Wish I could be more help. Y'all want some pie? I got two old women who bring me more pie than a dozen men could eat. I think I got some chocolate and maybe some pecan? Y'all stick around. I think *Gunsmoke*'s gonna start again in a second."

Quinn looked to Lillie. She frowned but stayed put. Royce had already stood, stranding between the couch and a cleared path through the junk to the kitchen.

"The report on the second crime was incomplete," Lillie said. "And we can't seem to put our hands on the evidence you logged."

"Forty years ago?" Royce said. "Hell. Come on, let's eat some pie."

"Thirty-seven," Quinn said.

"Long time."

"Yep," Quinn said.

"What's it matter now?" Royce said.

"One of the victims has made an inquiry," Quinn said. "A cold case always matters to those who've inherited it."

"Kind of like shit rolling downhill?" Royce said.

Lillie nodded. She finished her cigarette, dropped it in a nearby Maxwell House can, and stood.

"Wish I could help y'all," Royce said, "but I been retired for twenty years. Sure wish your uncle was still with us. He'd know. Lots of things he didn't put in a report like they do now. He was a lawman, carried thoughts and ideas with him until he could follow through."

"Until he ran out of time," Quinn said.

"He was a fine Christian man," Royce said. "What people said about him being on the take was pure and complete bullshit."

"Appreciate your time, Mr. Royce."

"Did y'all try and ever talk to Stagg?" Royce said. "I know y'all's history, but he might know something that could help."

"The thought had occurred to me."

"I don't think a man can fart in this county without ole Johnny T. Stagg knowing about it."

Lillie walked out of the shack without a word, tugging on her sunglasses as they walked back to the Big Green Machine. "Hmm" was all Lillie said before Quinn cranked the engine.

"That wasn't much help," he said.

"Sometimes I forget how much I hate this fucking county," she said.

"You don't mean that."

Lillie was quiet, mirrored glasses reflecting the road ahead.

14

Quinn removed his Beretta M9 at the door, locked it away in his Army footlocker, and took a seat at a long kitchen table with his mother and Jason. Jean had made fried chicken that night, along with collard greens and cornbread. She brought Quinn a cold Bud, knowing he wanted one before he even asked, Jean Colson never being the kind of mother to turn her nose up at her children drinking beer. She was a woman who bought wine by the box.

As they ate, they listened to Elvis's *Moody Blue* album, a personal favorite of Jean's. She especially liked "If You Love Me, Let Me Know," a song she used to sing to Quinn and Caddy as babies and later to Jason.

"What happened to Boom?" Jean asked.

"He's at The River," Quinn said. "Caddy said he'd met a girl there."

"If it's the one I'm thinking about," Jean said, "he better watch out. She's a fast operator."

"He doesn't tell me much," Quinn said. "Not about that stuff."

"What stuff?"

"His personal life."

"Y'all have known each other your whole life," Jean said. "I find it hard to believe there are some subjects off-limits."

Quinn shrugged. Jason refused to eat any collard greens, but seemed good with the chicken and cornbread. He sat right next to Quinn, pushing his small shoulder up under Quinn's arm as he told him about some kids who'd been mean to him on the playground.

"How old are they?" Quinn asked.

"Old," Jason said. "I think they're in first grade."

"That old?" Quinn said, chewing off a bit of fried chicken breast, still hot as hell inside and good and spicy. His momma did something with the meat before she cooked with milk and Tabasco. "What'd they say?"

Jason shrugged. "They said I smelled."

"Why'd they say that?"

Jason shrugged. He looked embarrassed.

"What'd you do about it?"

"I said I'd kick them in the privates."

Quinn started to agree with his nephew, but Jean held up her hand and gave him the eye. "You know what today is?" she asked, changing the subject.

"Wednesday?"

"It's Elvis's birthday," she said. "You know he would have been seventy-nine?"

"You don't say," Quinn said. Jean going on again and again about Elvis Presley. Just part of the deal with having dinner with his mother.

"I bet next year they'll have a big thing at Graceland," she said. "But, for the life of me, I can't imagine Elvis at eighty. I think maybe it's best he died when he did and never had to get old. I saw him a year before he died. And, yes, he'd gained some weight. But that voice. That voice never left us."

"No kidding, Momma," Quinn said, having heard these stories since he'd been Jason's age.

Jean pretended she was about to throw a drumstick at Quinn's head. But she instead put it down and picked up her wineglass. Elvis had moved on into "Let Me Be There," with the Stamps providing background vocals, J. D. Sumner giving a lot of bottom of soul. His voice something almost supernatural.

"He did this song," Jean said. "I saw it. I heard it."

"You knew Elvis?" Jason said, eyes brightening.

"I saw Elvis Presley seventeen times in concert," Jean said. "He once touched my hand."

Quinn looked up from his chicken, wiped his mouth with a napkin. "And I'm betting he gave you a yellow scarf, too."

"You want a spanking, Quinn?" she said. "You're not too damn old."

Jason found the idea of Uncle Quinn getting a spanking to be the funniest thing he'd ever heard. He laughed and laughed.

"Well, I bet you didn't know this," Jean said. "I once went up to Graceland to meet him. This was only a few months before he died. When we got up there, he was upstairs in his bedroom and wouldn't come down. I heard his voice at the top of the steps, but when I turned to look, Elvis was gone. All of it very strange. Hard to remember."

"With Dad?" Quinn said.

"Your dad was friends with some of Elvis's bodyguards," Jean said. "When he found out I how much I loved Elvis, he took me to Memphis on his motorcycle. We stayed down in the Jungle Room and listened to music. We played pool downstairs until dawn. He had the kindest old black woman who cooked for him. She made your father and me some eggs and bacon. At Graceland. Can you imagine?"

"You're right," Quinn said. "You never told me that story."

Jean took a big sip of wine. She shrugged back at Quinn. "Part of it was a pleasant memory," she said, "if certain folks hadn't been a part of it."

Quinn nodded, brought his empty plate to the big farm sink, setting in the stopper and starting to fill it with water. He added in a box of suds and went ahead, starting with the glasses on the counter.

"Leave it."

"No, ma'am."

"Leave it."

"You made dinner."

Soon, Quinn was elbow-deep in the sink, and Jean was slow-dancing with Jason to "She Thinks I Still Care," getting ready to put him to bed. After he finished the dishes, Quinn grabbed a La Gloria Cubana and wandered down to the fire pit. He added some branches and dry leaves, and then some busted-up logs, to the ring of old stones. In the fall, he'd cut some trees for firewood and left some large logs on each side of the pit. It had been so cold, he hadn't had much company lately. Caddy was still at The River.

Halfway into his cigar, a truck pulled into the driveway by the house and he heard the telltale squeak of Boom's old door. He was a hulking shadow, making his way from the hill, where the farmhouse was perched, down to the stone pit, taking a seat on a log across from Quinn. The fire crackled between them, Quinn poking at it with a long stick.

"Watching a fire sober isn't as much fun as when you're drunk."

"I'm not drunk," Quinn said.

"You like to think on things," Boom said. "I used to drink to turn all that shit off."

The right arm of his coat had been neatly cut and pinned at the elbow. Lately, Boom didn't wear the prosthetic outside the garage.

"You got a smoke for me?" he asked.

Quinn reached into his ranch coat and found another cigar. He stood and passed it to Boom's left hand. Boom bit off the end and Quinn lit a stainless steel Zippo etched with an America flag.

Boom got the cigar going, blowing out the warm smoke into the cold air.

"I tried you at the office," Boom said, "but Mary Alice said you were out with Lillie."

"Went out to see E. J. Royce."

"That motherfucker is crazy."

"Yes, sir."

"Left you a message," Boom said. "Guess you didn't get it."

The logs had started to smoke and flames started to rise high off the dry oak as Quinn poked at the edges. The red oak smelled very good and sweet on a cold January night. The cigar smelled of rich, aged tobacco and a cedar wrapper.

"I was working on Kenny's engine today," Boom said. "You know he really does need a new vehicle? That Crown Vic has about had it. A true piece of shit, even with my touch."

"Working on it."

"Well, I had my head up under the hood, doing my thing, minding my own business."

Quinn smoked the cigar and watched the fire. The sky above him was big and black, speckled with a million stars. Everything bigger out in the Mississippi hills, wilder in the country.

"Well, I heard Chuck McDougal out in the lot talking to Mr. Dupuy," Boom said. "I had the bay door open and they didn't even know I was there or I could hear them."

"Dumbasses," Quinn said. "What'd they say?"

"They gonna smoke your ass at the supervisors' meeting," Boom said. "Dupuy guaranteed his support to ask you to step down until the DA has cleared you. McDougal is going to say this shooting is an embarrassment to our great county."

"Son of a bitch."

"Both of 'em," Boom said.

"Sometimes I wonder why I came back."

"Sometimes?" Boom said. "Shit, I wondered that from the first moment you stepped foot back in Jericho."

Boom clenched the cigar in his teeth and grinned. The wind fluttered his empty right sleeve. Quinn took another puff of his cigar and tossed it deep into the fire.

On the front porch of her old bungalow two blocks from the Jericho Square, Diane Tull kept a collection of wind chimes, now tinkling and twirling in the January wind. Diane was getting ready for bed after spending the last hour talking with her son Patrick, who'd just moved back to Phoenix and found work at a bookshop in Scottsdale. Her other son, David, didn't call as much. He lived in Nashville, waiting tables during the day and singing for tips outside Ernest Tubb Record Shop at night. Her second husband, their father, had been a frustrated singer/songwriter who thought of himself as the James Taylor of the Southwest, singing about Indians and sunsets. At first, he'd seemed charming to Diane. Later, she knew he was completely and utterly full of shit.

Diane was glad to be in her own home, one of the fortunate folks who'd gotten through the storm with a place to live. A big oak had crushed the roof over her living room, but she'd never had to move out, all the repairs going on under a blue tarp while she was at the Farm & Ranch. She'd even gotten a few improvements to her kitchen with the insurance money: new counters, new sink, and a brand-new dishwasher.

When did her life get so boring that she got excited about a damn dishwasher?

The wind chimes clicked and spun outside, cold wind whistling through windowsill cracks and under the doors, making a bad racket, enough to make people in town nervous, the way they were now, whenever a storm blew through. Diane took off her wet towel and changed into some gray sweatpants and a white tank top, finding a spot on her bed to read a new novel by James Carlos Blake until she fell asleep. She'd be back at work at seven a.m. to sell that feed and seed.

Diane heard the creak of the slats on her front porch and the clunk of boots.

Diane closed the book and stood, listening to the soft-thudding footsteps outside, and then turned off the bedside lamp to see a little better in the dark.

The front porch light had already been turned off and at first she thought it was Hank Stillwell again, drunk as a goat and not having any sense of decency about the time. But even in the darkness, she could tell it was a young man with long hair and a beard, walking from end to end on the front porch, reaching up and touching a glass wind chime, making the sound stop for a moment and then start again as he moved away. He leaned toward the window to her living room and peered in for a long moment.

Diane Tull kept a loaded J. C. Higgins 12-gauge under her bed and knew how to use it. She got to her knees, reached through the boxes to find it, and pulled it up on top of her thighs, squatting there and listening.

The man walked off the porch and down the steps. She stood and peered through lace curtains again, seeing nothing of him, wondering if maybe he'd been at the wrong house looking for the wrong person. Since the tornado, lots of folks didn't know one end of town from the other, all the wayfinders and landmarks ripped out in a few seconds.

She caught her breath and walked back to the kitchen, shotgun in right hand, for a cold drink of water. The wind blew violent as hell outside, Diane wishing she'd never collected so many of those damn chimes, people always bringing them to her now from vacation spots. There were wind chimes from New Orleans, Gulf Shores, and even a set from New York City, with little chimes hanging beneath the Empire State Building. Now all she needed was a goddamn cat to let the town know she'd gone crazy.

She laid the shotgun on the kitchen table and drank the cool water. The wind knocked hard outside, tree limbs brushing the window. And then there was a sharp buzz and flickering of light and her damn power was out.

"Son of a bitch."

She lit a candle, finished her water, and had turned back to the bedroom when she saw the bearded man looking through the back door window straight at her.

She dropped the glass, it shattering to the floor. Diane reached for the shotgun as she heard the rattling and twisting of the knob.

15

Quinn slipped out of bed with Ophelia at midnight, finding his creased Levi's and stiff khaki shirt folded across a chair. She stirred from the bed, ran a hand through her dark hair, and rose up to look at the clock. She was still naked, the covers only concealing her from the waist down.

"Stay," she said. "It's raining."

"I got to be up in five hours."

"What happened to your toothbrush?"

"I already brushed my teeth."

"Or razor?"

"You told me to hold off on the razor."

"God damn you, Quinn Colson."

Quinn pulled into his jeans and slipped on his shirt with the star stitched on the sleeve. He sat on the bed as he worked the buttons. The rain pinged the tin roof of Ophelia's house and wind shook the shutters. In the dim light, he could see his badge and gun on the nightstand. The television still flickered in the living room, where they'd watched about five minutes of *Man of the West* before making their way back to her bedroom and getting down to business. The routine of it all had been quite pleasant.

"You really pay fifty dollars for a pair of panties?" he asked.

"You think they're worth it?"

"Didn't keep 'em on that long."

Ophelia smiled at him, not trying to cover up her full breasts with their large dark nipples, and watched him. She lay sideways, elbow on mattress and head crooked in hand.

"Until a few months ago," Quinn said, "I never knew about that ruby in your belly."

"I've had that since high school," she said. "You wouldn't know because you were already gone."

"Maybe I would've come home more often."

"Maybe so."

"You probably had lots of women at Fort Benning."

"I knew a few girls in Columbus," Quinn said. "One girl in Phenix City wasn't too bad."

"What happened?"

"She took little pride in her underwear."

Ophelia rolled on her back and laughed, tucking a pillow up behind her head, stretching her arms high. "Come back."

"Five hours."

"I thought Rangers could work on little sleep, no food."

"That's true."

"Why don't you consider me a test?"

"Kind of like doing PT?" Quinn said.

"Exactly."

The wind was pretty damn violent and the rain sounded like pennies hitting the metal roof. He started to unbutton his shirt again when he heard his phone buzz by his gun. The screen flashed on, lighting up the room. Ophelia just shook her head and said, "Shit."

Quinn picked it up and got Kenny, who was on night patrol. "Sheriff, dispatch just got a call from Diane Tull. She's got a creeper around her house. I'm headed that way now, but I'm clear up to Fate."

"Roger that," Quinn said. "Meet you there."

Quinn stood and rebuttoned his shirt and scooped up his gun, badge, and pair of cowboy boots as he walked to the living room. Ophelia followed, slipping into the tight black T-shirt she'd had on earlier with those high-dollar lace panties. She kissed him at the door and he walked out into the rain.

He paused for a moment.

Six houses up, on top of a hill, was Anna Lee Stevens's big Victorian, the low green light shining from her screened-in porch, half the house ripped away and now rebuilt with unpainted wood and brand-new windows. But that side porch was the same. And that damn green light that shined every night all night.

Quinn looked away and sped off in the opposite direction. Glad not to have to study on that too long.

She saw the man and he saw her. And then he was gone. In the darkness and by candlelight, she lifted the phone off the hook and called 911, saying she had a creeper, a fucking pervert, wanting to see her naked. But as soon as Diane put down the phone, she was filled with such a goddamn almighty rage that some son of a bitch had invaded her space, her home, her yard, that she went out into the wind and the rain with the J. C. Higgins to make sure the bastard damn well knew.

She followed the short steps off the door from the kitchen and out into her backyard, turning to the right and left, shotgun tucked up under her right armpit, raised and ready to scatter some buckshot.

The wind chimes were going wild on the front porch, rain coming down hard now, falling sideways, making things tough to see in the night, as she took a wide berth around the side of her old house, looking from the tree line to the crepe myrtles and azaleas. Even thought it was deep winter, some of her daffodils had started to barely poke from the front lawn, now crushed under her bare feet as she moved onto the driveway, which seemed a lot longer than usual. She didn't see a thing along the street, all the other houses in darkness, as she made her way to the mailbox. She dropped the shotgun down for just a moment to use her forearm to wipe the rain from her eyes.

She knew all the cars and trucks on her little street. She worried for a half second about what she looked like, in pajama bottoms, a man's tank top, barefoot, and cradling a gun.

She was turning back to the house when she saw the man dart from the hedges on the other side of her house, running for the road, as she picked up the gun, leveled it at him, and yelled for him to "Stop, you stupid son of a bitch!"

Of course he didn't listen.

"I said, fucking stop, you fucking bastard."

She squeezed the trigger, the man running off from the blast from forty, fifty feet away. Diane felt like she was in a trance, moving past her black mailbox hand-painted with curving colorful flowers. She jacked another shell into the breech and leveled the shotgun again and fired again. And then again. The shotgun ramming hard into the crook of her shoulder.

The man was gone. Diane just stood there in the rain, on the road, trying to catch her breath. Lights flicked on in all the houses down the little street. Dogs barked.

From down the road, two little streets down, she heard a motorcycle kick to life, making a great noisy racket, kicking into gear, the engine growling as it turned into her street. Diane just saw that single taillight as the rider rushed past, too far away for another shot, and made it up and over the hill.

She walked back toward her house, waiting on the police, when she noticed what he'd done. The son of a bitch had slashed her tires, the rims lying flat and hard on the ground.

And the fella had also decided to spray-paint a few words on the driver's door and the truck bed.

In sloppy, loose letters, the message read *SHUT YORE GD MOUTH*.

God damn it, Diane thought, shotgun resting up on her shoulder. If she could've just gotten a little closer, she might have taken a nice hunk out of his ass.

Shut your GD mouth.

Now, that was fucking original.

"You're soaked," Quinn said.

"So I am," Diane Tull said.

Quinn kept his eyes front and center on her forehead; her man's tank top was wet to the point of being translucent.

"Let's head inside, ma'am."

"I thought we covered the ma'am thing," Diane said, giving a nervous laugh. Hair in a ponytail, black, with that one silver streak hanging down loose. "I can't take that shit tonight, Sheriff. You say that again and I'll punch you."

Diane was still holding a shotgun and she seemed agitated and quite nervous. The wind and rain had grown worse, blowing across the headlights of Quinn's still-running truck. His dispatch radio squawked inside the cab.

"Do you mind, Miss Tull?" Quinn said. He opened his right hand and Diane handed over her shotgun. An old J. C. Higgins, the house brand of Sears & Roebuck. His uncle and his dad had similar guns. He studied the gun, mostly in an effort to keep his eyes averted from her chest.

They walked back into her driveway and she showed him what he had done to her truck. Quinn shined a flashlight across the driver's door.

"Well," Quinn said, "he can't spell worth shit. Who spells *your* like that?"

"Some dumb shit."

"And your tires?" Quinn said, shaking his head. "That's just plain mean."

"Seeing that bastard's face in my kitchen window was enough to give me a start."

"I bet," Quinn said, following Diane out of the rain, around her old white bungalow, and up some steps and into her kitchen. She had a candle going, on account of the power being out, and she lit two more and found a little battery-powered lantern to set on the kitchen counter.

"You get a decent look?" he asked.

"Hell no," Diane said. "He was a white man with a scraggly beard and long hair. He had on jeans and a red flannel shirt. That could be half the fucking rednecks in north Mississippi. Fifty people on a Saturday at Walmart in Tupelo."

"How tall?"

"A little shorter than you."

"Less than six feet?"

"Just under."

"Build?"

"Skinny."

"Age?"

"I can't say for sure," Diane said. "Not old. Not young."

"Thirties?"

She nodded. "Sure," she said, "I figure."

"Eye color?"

She shook her head.

"Hair color?"

"Could've been lighter, but it seemed brown," she said. "He was wearing a ponytail and his hair was wet. Oh, hell."

Quinn nodded. The kitchen was very small and intimate, Diane Tull standing on one side of the counter in front of the stove, Quinn sitting on

117

the other side, writing into his notebook. He noted the time of her call, her address, her Social Security number, and the basics of what had happened before she had discovered the man had vandalized her truck.

"And he just ran?"

"I shot at him," she said. "Twice. Damn, I was too far away."

Quinn nodded. "What direction?"

"Toward the Square," she said. "He got two streets down and got on a motorcycle. I saw him ride away, up over the hill, to the Square."

"I know it was raining and dark, but did you see anything about the bike?"

"No," she said. "I heard it more than saw it. It had those special mufflers folks have, really loud, you could've heard the damn thing ten miles away."

"Any chance you got him with the shotgun?"

Diane's face looked drawn, hands trembling around a glass of water, as she shook her head. "I wish."

"I'm going to call dispatch with what we know," Quinn said. "Then I'm going to look around your house some more. We have a deputy headed this way. He'll sit on your house all night."

"That's not necessary," she said. "I don't think that bastard's coming back."

"Maybe not," Quinn said. "But I'd feel better with Kenny sitting on things."

"Kenny?" she said. "Really?"

"He's tougher than he seems."

"God, I hope so."

Diane put down the glass of water and wrapped her arms around herself. She shivered a bit and used a dishtowel to dry her face. She was more than twenty years older than Quinn but didn't look her age, still attractive, with her high cheekbones and black hair with its long streak of silver.

Diane Tull wore Levi's and work shirts, and had been a good friend to his mother and Caddy, helping Caddy, even though Caddy wouldn't admit it, after Jamey's death and on through the mess of the storm. Quinn couldn't even recall all the free stuff she'd donated to The River.

"Who else knows you and I spoke?" Quinn said. "Caddy and who else?"

"That's it," she said.

She looked away, thinking on something. Quinn tilted her head, watched her face, and stayed quiet.

"Well, there's another. But he'd never say a word. He's too sensitive about things."

"Who?"

"I'd rather not say," Diane said.

Quinn removed the spent shells from the shotgun. He asked if she had more and she nodded and said she had boxes and boxes in her bedroom.

"If he's the only other person," Quinn said, "stands to reason . . ."

Diane swallowed and nodded a bit. "Hank Stillwell."

"He upset you're bringing all this up?" Quinn said. "Has to be sensitive to him."

"No," Diane said, shaking her head, wiping the rain off her arms and across her chest and over her wet tank top, "not at all."

"How can you be sure?"

"He's the one who come to me and asked me to stoke it," Diane Tull said. "He said you're the only man who can find out who murdered his daughter."

"This may not be the time," Quinn said, "but there's something I've been meaning to ask you."

"The man who got burned up?"

Quinn nodded.

"It's been a hell of a night, Sheriff," she said. "I got to get those tires changed before I get to work in a few hours and then figure out how to get those cusswords off my truck. I'd rather not churn all that up right now."

"Yes, ma'am," Quinn said. "Kenny and I can help you with those tires. I'll call a friend."

"Appreciate that, Sheriff," she said. "You're a good man."

"Your vote in this spring's election would be much appreciated," Quinn said, tipping at his baseball cap.

16

"My brother isn't too fond of your friends," Jean Beckett said, sitting on the back of Jason's baby blue Shovelhead Harley, looking pretty as can be, running her mouth over a soft serve vanilla cone.

"They're not my friends," Jason said. "Big Doug is a friend. But the others are just some boys I met. They're good fellas, a little hot-tempered, but good fellas."

"My brother said y'all got into a rumble with another gang up in Olive Branch," she said. "One man got hurt real bad at some barbecue pit. He's still in the hospital in Memphis."

"Your brother is the sheriff," Jason said, licking a little bit off his chocolate cone. "I guess he hears things."

The yellow-and-red glow from the Dairy Queen shone down on the parking lot and out into the rolling Big Black River, not far off Highway 45, out on Cotton Road.

"He's just looking out for me," Jean said. "I think he's more concerned that you've left your roots and gone Hollywood."

"That much is true."

"You're all Hollywood?" Jean said.

"Through and through," Jason said. "How'd you like to come out west with me? I leave in a couple weeks and I'm driving through Texas, New Mexico, and Arizona. You've never seen any country like it. You ever been out of Jericho?"

"Hell yes," she said. "I've been to New York City."

"How many times?"

"Once," Jean said, looking away, smiling. "With my senior class. I've been to New Orleans a bunch. I've gone to Mardi Gras three times."

"How'd you like to ride on the back of my bike up the PCH?"

"Depends on what the hell's the PCH."

"Pacific Coast Highway," Jason said. "We follow the ocean all the way up to San Francisco. We'll camp out at Big Sur, eat crabs at Fisherman's Wharf, make love on the beach at Santa Cruz."

"I think you're getting a little ahead of yourself, Jason Colson."

Jason grinned. He wrapped his arm around Jean Beckett's narrow waist, feeling the warm tautness of her belly, lifting her red hair off the nape of her neck, and kissing her at the hairline while she finished up the soft serve.

The Dairy Queen was an odd little building, looking queer and out of place right at the edge of that dirty old river. It was just a cinder-block box with big neon sign above the open-air counter, where teenage girls served burgers, dogs, and milk shakes. They wore tight white shirts and kept their hair in ponytails and most nights played a rock 'n' roll station out of Memphis.

Jason kissed Jean's neck and she rubbed his beard.

"I'm not supposed to say this," Jean said, "but Hamp thinks your running around with those boys is going to get you into trouble. He thinks maybe it'd be best if you left town for a while. He calls the man who runs things, what's his name? Chains? He says he's a stone-cold sociopath."

"He's not my biggest fan," Jason said. "But I think he got his eggs a little scrambled in 'Nam. I just don't think he can stand for people to tell him what to do, doesn't care for the way most people live by laws and old-fashioned kind of phoniness."

"I'd watch my step," Jean said. "He sounds batshit crazy to me."

Jason finished his ice cream and tossed the rest of the cone toward a trash barrel. The speakers at the stand were playing Elton John, recalling for Jason some sweet times down in San Diego with a young actress he'd dated a couple years ago. Dune buggies and wet bathing suits and burning driftwood on the beach. Jason had felt he was on another planet than Jericho. He hoped he could do the same for Jean. This wasn't living.

"Before we go any further," Jason said, "I need you to understand something about me."

Jean leaned back into Jason, shoulders pressing into his chest, that red hair blowing in the hot wind off the river, driving him crazy.

"What's that?"

"I don't like people telling me what to do," Jason said. "Since I was a kid, I hated when someone said I was too scared or I couldn't do something. My brother Jerry got rich taking bets from kids in town about what his brother might try next. I could climb the tallest trees. Dove off that bridge over there when I was ten. Headfirst."

"That is crazy."

"That's just the way I am," Jason said. "It's the way I make my living. Every day I'm out there, someone in L.A. is playing chicken with my livelihood. The day I say no mas, my reputation is done. That's one of the many things I've learned from Mr. Needham."

"So you want me to know your profession is being crazy," Jean asked. "And riding with some real cutthroats while you're back home is just another way of proving yourself."

"Every day, Miss Jean."

She got off his slick Harley, Jason watching her walk over to toss the rest of her ice cream in the trash barrel. She had on cowboy boots, with cutoff jeans and a white peasant top that was next to nothing. Jason's heart just kind of caught for a moment as she turned, smiled, and walked toward him. Jason moving up on the seat, kicking the bike to start, and Jean Beckett crawling on back with him, wrapping her long arms around his waist. "Just where are we going, Jason Colson?" she whispered.

"Don't have any plans."

"Just promise me one thing," she said, her words hot and warm in his ear. Jason revved the motor. The little girls working the Dairy Queen squealed.

"Don't you ever lie to me," she said. "When that happens, there's no second chances."

17

Quinn liked to get up before dawn, feeling like he had a jump on the morning, some alone time for himself when he pulled on his PT gear and ran a fire road up behind his house. He'd fashioned an old section of pipe between a couple four-by-fours, where he could do pull-ups, and had a concrete pad he'd poured for push-ups and sit-ups. He liked to train in the elements, appreciated the cold and wet, and was happy to burn off a good sweat before showering, shaving, and putting on his uniform. That uniform almost always ironed, with starched jeans, a khaki or Army-green button-up shirt with a patch on the shoulder. He'd pin on his tin star and collect his M9 Beretta, about the only thing he took from his time in the Regiment. His cowboy boots were always shined and ready to go on top of his footlocker, and by the first cup of coffee, and sometimes a cigar, he was watching the sun rise over the big rolls of hay he kept for his cattle.

Jean was up next. And then Jason got up, bleary-eyed in Superman pajamas and a little pissed at the early hour. Jean made them both fried eggs with bacon and biscuits. Then Jason hurried back to his bedroom to get dressed for kindergarten while Jean packed his lunch. Caddy was already up and gone, serving food to homeless families at The River. This had been the way since they'd all moved in after the storm.

"You had a late night," Jean said.

"Diane Tull had some problems," Quinn said, telling her about the peeper and the damage to her truck.

"Why in the hell would someone do that to such a nice woman?" Jean said. "She's the only one around here who sells decent American-made clothes for kids. And boots. She helped Jason into a new pair of boots this fall. She's good with kids. Raised two boys of her own."

"Lillie has a theory," Quinn said.

"And what's that?"

"People can be mean as hell and dumber than shit."

"Miss Tull have any idea who might have slashed her tires?"

"No, ma'am," Quinn said, not wanting to get into opening back up the events of 1977 with Jean. Caddy may have told her, but Quinn wanted to keep much of it confidential. He crumbled the bacon on top of the eggs and dashed them with Crystal sauce.

When he finished off the last bit of biscuit, and washed out and filled up his Thermos with black coffee, Quinn walked out onto the front porch and out to the Big Green Machine to warm it up for Jason. On days he came in late, Lillie would cover for him. And when she needed to watch her daughter, a baby girl she rescued and adopted at six months old, Quinn covered for her.

The day was bright and bleak, sun not supposed to take them much above forty degrees. The trees were leafless and brittle in the wind. Quinn poured some coffee, steaming from the mug, and tuned his radio to the Drake & Zeke morning show out of Memphis. As he listened to the latest jokes about Memphis politicians and the decline of modern culture, Jean brought out Jason and helped get him in his safety seat. They were off, riding up the long dirty road from Quinn's house, through some logging land, and then turning toward Jericho and the elementary school.

"Uncle Quinn?"

"Yes, sir."

"You never said what to do about them bullies," he said.

"Your momma would want me to say to tell a teacher."

"What'd you say?"

"Did they hurt you?"

"No," Jason said. "They just said I stunk."

"How's that?"

"They said black people smell funny."

"You know their names?"

"No, sir," Jason said. "But they said the creamies smelled worse than the blacks. I guess I'm a creamy."

Quinn took a long breath, turning the wheel of the truck. "I'll tell your momma to talk to the teacher."

"But what do I do when no one's looking?"

Quinn nodded and drove, catching up with Highway 9 and heading due south. He'd turned down the radio as they spoke, Drake & Zeke taking a station break, playing one of Chris Knight's latest tracks about loneliness and heartache in the backwoods.

"When I was a little older than you, I had this kid always wanted to fight me," Quinn said. "Never knew why. But he rode the bus with me and would get up in my face. I figure he just didn't like my looks."

"Did you kill him?"

"No, sir," Quinn said. "I guess I was more scared of getting in trouble with the principal than the fighting. I used to get in a lot of trouble and there was talk of getting me suspended."

"What'd you do?"

Quinn looked in the rearview to where Jason was strapped tight in the safety seat. They rode over the busted back highways into town, passing Mr. Varner's Quick Mart, work crews crawling out of trucks and buying chicken biscuits and bottles of Mountain Dew to start their day. A refueling truck had parked at the Dixie gas station, filling the pumps.

"I told your grandmomma about it," Quinn said.

"Why didn't you tell your daddy?"

"Wasn't around," Quinn said. "Your grandmomma had to sort of be both to me. I figured when I told her, she'd say for me not to fight or else I'd rip my clothes. She was always getting onto me about tearing up my jeans when I climbed trees or went out to shoot squirrels with Mr. Boom. But she didn't. She just told me I'd know the right thing."

"What? What was it?"

"Well, one day that kid got off at my stop and that boy followed me down Ithaca Street to our house," Quinn said. "He kept on coming and knocked on my door, telling me it was ass-whippin' time."

"An ass-whippin'?"

"Yep," Quinn said. "Don't repeat that. Your grandmomma just handed me my hat and coat and said to go take care of that son of a bitch. She said don't ever let someone come into your territory."

"Some other kids laughed when they said I stunk."

"Don't let 'em say that," Quinn said. "You stand toe-to-toe and smile in their faces. When they're not looking, punch them in the gut."

"What if they hit me back?"

"Hit 'em harder," Quinn said. "You got a Colson head. It'll hurt even less if you give 'em back twice what they gave you. They count on you being scared, not on you coming full out."

Quinn lifted his eyes up at the rearview and winked at Jason. Jason grinned. He seemed very pleased with that answer.

"Uncle Quinn?" Jason said. "Momma says you got a mean streak."

"Your momma might be right," he said. "About some things."

Quinn turned onto Cotton Road and headed toward the Square and due east for the school, much of it still covered up in blue tarps and most of the classrooms out in emergency trailers. The playground had taken a beating but remained the same as when Quinn had played there. Teachers waited outside the front of the school, administrative still inside, to walk the drop-off kids to the classrooms or trailers.

After a woman helped Jason from his seat and sent him down the path to his class, Quinn noted a little bounce in the kid's step.

"You might try some brake cleaner on that," Lillie Virgil said, getting out of her Jeep, hand over eyes in the harsh morning sun.

Diane Tull had parked at the side of the Farm & Ranch, using a hose and soapy brush to work on that spray paint from last night. She had on an old barn coat over a flannel shirt and jeans and wore a pair of high rubber boots. She hoped she could get this shit off her truck before customers started coming in.

"I'd hoped it wouldn't set," Diane said.

"Can you scratch it off with a fingernail?"

Diane picked at some of the lettering. "Some of it. Some has set."

"Nail polish remover," Lillie said. "Some kids defaced some county vehicles a few years ago and Mary Alice just reached in her purse and showed how easy it works. That woman sure is proud of her fingernails. Like eagle claws. That was on tractors, but I don't think you'll mind damaging that coat a little bit."

"It's an old truck."

"Nice one," Lillie said. "'Sixty-five?"

"'Sixty-six," Diane said, putting the brush in the bucket. "The two-tone paint is original and the AM radio still works. My daddy bought it brand-new at a dealership in Columbus."

"Sorry about what happened," Lillie said. "Don't wash too much of it yet. I need to take some pictures."

"Sheriff Colson took some last night," Diane said.

"Need a few more, in the daylight," Lillie said. "I know he already pulled some prints off the door handle."

"It was locked," Diane said, warming her hands in her blue barn coat. "And Quinn thought the prints looked to be mine, thumbprint the size of a woman's."

Lillie walked back to her truck and pulled out a little point-and-shoot Nikon that she said belonged to the sheriff's office. She took eight or nine pictures from different perspectives and then slipped the camera in her side pocket. She hadn't worn a hat that day, her brown hair tied up and pinned in a bun. Lillie Virgil was tall and competent, intimidating to some people. People around town whispered that Lillie didn't care much for boys, but Diane didn't believe it. She thought people in Jericho couldn't handle seeing a woman so tough, she could outshoot, outcuss, and outfight most of the men.

"You got a few minutes?" Lillie said. "Got a few questions."

"Not much to say," Diane said. "Didn't see much and shot at just a blur of him."

Lillie closed one eye in the harsh light and smiled at Diane. Diane had the bucket in one hand and walked over to the spigot to turn off the hose. The flowing water was ice-cold that morning.

"Not about this."

"Oh," Diane said, standing there, last bits of water draining from the uncoiled hose. "I guess I expected Sheriff Colson."

"You rather talk to him?"

"No," Diane said. "Guess it doesn't matter. Just didn't feel like discussing it last night. I don't know how much to add, either. I guess it's no secret what happened. That old story has gotten to be pretty famous."

"Seems like it was a secret for a lot of folks."

Diane nodded, turned, and dumped out the dirty water from the bucket. She'd gotten some paint off the side of the truck, now the message reading *YORE GD*. Lillie said she was pretty sure that nail polish remover trick would work, but it would be a hell of shame to mess up that red-and-white paint job. The old truck being a real work of art. Diane stepped back, looked at her dead stepdaddy's truck, and agreed. Those rotten bastards for doing this.

"We've reopened the case," Lillie said. "Both of them."

Diane hung next to her truck, leaning against the tailgate, and nodded. She asked if Lillie wouldn't mind going inside, "My hands feel like they've frozen solid."

Lillie followed her up the ramp and into the big storage area where they kept the feed and fertilizer and overflow from inside the farm supply. Diane sat on a big stack of dog food and lit a cigarette, blowing smoke into the wind.

"You want one?"

"Trying like hell to quit," Lillie said.

A flyer for an upcoming rodeo at the Tibbehah Ag Center fluttered in the cold wind. The event promised the grand spectacles of monkeys riding dogs, and that proceeds would go to disaster relief. Lillie turned her head to read the flyer. "Don't think I've ever seen a monkey riding a dog," Lillie said. "Must be something."

"They don't really ride 'em," Diane said, "they're more tied to cattle dogs. The cattle dogs work the sheep and it looks like the goddamn monkeys are cowboys."

"They dress the monkeys as cowboys?"

"Oh yes, ma'am," Diane said, blowing out another stream of smoke. "Hats, chaps, six-shooters. The works."

"Signs and wonders."

Lillie just stood silent and watched Diane smoke the cigarette, no other vehicles in the gravel parking lot that morning. It was still early and the Farm & Ranch wasn't even officially open yet. She'd left the front cattle gate unlocked and slightly open for a feed delivery, now sort of wishing she'd locked up behind her as she most often did. She wasn't ready to get into all this again and wished liked hell she hadn't let Hank Stillwell stir up the muck from the bottom.

"So everyone pretty much knew this man was killed because of what happened to y'all?" Lillie said.

Diane nodded.

"I wasn't even eighteen."

"But you do know who did it?"

Diane shook her head. She tossed the cigarette and started a new one. Lillie brought out her notebook and left it hanging by her right leg, not even opening her pen.

"But you knew," she said. "Everyone knew?"

"I knew right away that a black man had been taken out and hung and then burned," Diane said. "I'll be real honest with you, Miss Virgil. You know how I felt?"

"Relieved."

"Yep."

"And now?"

Diane Tull's face twitched a bit, sitting there on those sacks, mind back into the summer of 1977. She gave a nervous laugh, hands shaking a bit, holding the cigarette, as she blew out some smoke and wiped her eyes. "What I feel about it now?" Diane said. "How about shame? Embarrassment? Guilt? You want me to keep going, keep coming up with words on the horror of what they did?"

"You're a hell of a person," Lillie said. "If a man did that to me and to my friend, I don't know if I'd care where he ended up."

Diane's face shifted into a bitter and knowing smile. "Shit," she said. "Y'all don't know?"

"What's that?"

"Wasn't him," Diane said, shaking her head, looking away, crying again, feeling embarrassed for it. "I saw the man who did this to us not six weeks later. I told Sheriff Beckett and he told me to keep quiet. I told my daddy and he told me the same thing. No one would listen. I guess this story seemed a lot neater if they'd hung the right man."

Lillie swallowed and took a deep breath, at first not seeming to know what to say or ask. "Then who'd they get?"

"First black man they could find," Diane said. "Looking for the first tree they could find. I never knew the man's name or his people. And I don't think anyone else did, either. Can you imagine the horror of those bastards coming for you?"

"Who?" Lillie said. "Who were they?"

18

"You know there's an easier solution to this, Mr. Stagg," Ringold said. "We need to consider some creative options on this issue."

Stagg grinned, liking the official manners and formal way Ringold spoke. But the man was off base about his plans, not understanding the way this county worked. "You mean just kill the bastard?"

"Pretty much what I had in mind," Ringold said.

Stagg glanced over at the black-and-white surveillance TVs stacked on the wall: restaurant register, truck stop register, wide shot of the Booby Trap stage, wide shot of the diesel pumps, and long shot of the parking lot behind the Rebel. They hadn't had an armed robbery in seven years, not since that teenager from Pontotoc had come over and held up a couple working girls with a hunting knife. Stagg hadn't had to do a damn thing other than disarm the boy, call the sheriff, the boy busted and bleeding and crying by the time he got there. The girls, all six of them, deciding to take matters into their own hands, inflicting a world of pain with their long nails and tiny fists.

"If you got a fucking copperhead in a jar, I wouldn't advise you let it loose," Stagg said. "You might have a plan for that son of a bitch, but them sidewinders are unpredictable, finding nooks and crannies and laying low till you don't see them. That's what this man is like, who he is. You think I hadn't thought about just shooting the son of a bitch dead? How 'bout every day for the last twenty years."

"He's a threat," Ringold said, arms crossed over his chest. "To your business and to all you've done around here."

"OK," Stagg said, picking up a toothpick, working a little meat from a back molar. "Let's say we blast this bastard's grits all over north Mississippi. Right? He's gone, but our troubles are still with us. No, sir. You being an Army man, top shelf, with all that Secret Squirrel ninja training and all, should know not to prepare for what you think might happen but what could happen."

"Yes, sir," Ringold said. "I follow."

"This man has a lot of friends," Stagg said. "He's the goddamn Will Rogers of shitbirds. They love him. Follow him to hell and back and beyond. They been waiting and planning for his release since his ass pranced into the doors of Brushy Mountain. If we take him out, they're still coming. That's what he'd want and what they'll do. We ain't dealing with rational people here. They don't have any belief system other than to fuck up the order of the world."

Ringold stood cocksure, with erect military posture that always reminded Johnny Stagg of that goddamn Quinn Colson. Ringold was the flip side of the coin: tough, good with a gun, but knew on which side his bread was buttered. He didn't think Colson had all of Ringold's tattoos, skulls and daggers and spears for the number of men he'd killed overseas. Colson was a Boy Scout, a non-realist, someone who needed to be taught the lessons of the world.

"But, tactically speaking . . ."

"Sure," Stagg said, "he gets out. Yes, sir, he's coming this way."

"And what happens next?"

"That's why I plan to keep that fucking snake in the jar," Stagg said. "We do that and all the plans and bullshit and threats are gone. He wants to lead a revolt, a movement. He wants to come back to Jericho not 'cause it's the best thing for his people. He wants to come back to Jericho to cornhole the shit out of me, the way I cornholed his ass more than twenty years back."

Ringold nodded. His bald head catching in the light, the stubbled beard on his face more than the fella had on his head. Stagg was pretty sure he'd never seen the man as much as crack a grin, which suited him just fine. Ringold was the pure and unfiltered killing machine he wanted, and if Chains LeDoux wanted to ride his Harley and nasty ass on into the Rebel like a fucking parade, that Ringold would be there to greet him at the door.

"So how's it work?" Ringold asked. "To keep him incarcerated?"

"I got things in motion," Stagg said. "This man has secrets. Fucked up a lot along the way. And I got a long memory of this town. Even if some of our citizens think their asses are lily-white."

Stagg swiveled a bit in his leather chair, the executive model in the catalog, pushing forward with the tips of his oxblood loafers. He nodded, again glancing over the surveillance screens, seeing a fat woman buying three Moon Pies and a Coke inside the Rebel, and one of the working girls not giving but a half-assed effort on the pole, looking dog tired or drunk. She'd need a talking-to. You work the pole, you work the pole. You didn't know how to sell it, go back to your momma and tin can trailer.

"This sack of shit ran drugs and guns out of Tibbehah since he got out of the service," Stagg said. "Talking back in the Vietnam days."

Ringold nodded. He was chewing gum, watching Johnny Stagg as he stood by the doorframe, listening, waiting for what needed to be done. He wondered if Ringold had a problem with killing another military man, some kind of ethical conflict, since the guy was a vet. Or maybe he'd just been mixing up Ringold and Colson in his head.

"I don't know what he did over in Southeast Asia," Stagg said. "Don't care. He ain't from here. He came down here sometime around 'seventy-four to raise hell down at Choctaw Lake. I think this was a stopover for them, heading down to the Coast, and they built some kind of fucking clubhouse out there. One of those shitbirds owned the land. He did it fair and legal. They shot guns and drank whiskey, smoked dope. That was what it was all about back then. People smoking dope, dropping acid, doing pills. Those fellas, the Born-Fucking-Losers, would mule all this shit from New Orleans and bring it up into north Mississippi and Memphis. Ain't nobody fucked with them. Ain't nobody around here seemed to care much. They were bad for business. I was an honest family man, trying to run a friendly little ole gas station here, and them scroungy fuckers would shoot up on their bikes, riding like they'd just come out of hell itself. People didn't like it. Didn't want to be around it."

"What about the law?"

"You know the law back then was Colson's uncle, a good ole boy but a weak man named Hamp Beckett. Hamp Beckett was lazy, greedy as hell. He wouldn't go looking for trouble unless the county was up in flames. These boys tended to keep to themselves down at Choctaw Lake and what they did in Memphis or Birmingham wasn't the concern of Sheriff Beckett. At least the way he told it."

"So how'd you go about it?" Ringold said, the boy rushing his story, Stagg preferring to illustrate the story, the situation, the setup, the players, before dropping the punch line.

Stagg leaned back in the executive-model chair and crossed his nice shoes at the corner of his desk. A big old Kenworth had just rolled on under Rebel's tin roof and was sucking down some diesel. It sure was something just to be able to sit back and watch people spend cash on gas, groceries, and pussy.

"Why you think it was me?" Stagg said, grinning. "Who did something?"

"'Cause I know you, Mr. Stagg."

"Hmm," Stagg said. "Well, I guess you can say I got frustrated being cut out of the action here in Tibbehah. As a young man, I done got myself involved in timber, land deals, and such. And when I opened up the Rebel, I got money not only for what was headed out of Jericho but what was headed through. To see all that money, all that opportunity, going to a bunch of nasty folks who didn't shave or shower just didn't sit well with me. And I tried to work with them. God knows, I tried to turn it into a good situation."

"Threats?"

"Let's just say I made some arrangements with some folks in Memphis," Stagg said, inhaling, sweetly recalling that time when he sprayed a can of Raid on that nest. "And they made sure their little clubhouse got shaken to pieces and them boys got scattered to the wind. It wasn't no easy thing and ended up with me being beholden to some folks in Memphis for nearly twenty fucking years. But that's done. LeDoux went to jail and now I get to rule the roost."

"I still say kill the bastard," Ringold said. "One shot. No trouble."

"I never figured the son of a bitch would be cut loose," Stagg said. "But we're gonna stop that cold. Nothing to worry about."

Ringold stood silent. Man was a goddamn rock.

"I understand what you have in mind, sir," Ringold said. "But you're also about to flush the sheriff down the toilet. You do that and his investigation stops. All this is shot to hell. I just don't understand how one benefits the other."

"Shit," Stagg said, laughing to himself. "You think I'm flushing Colson down the toilet? I'm about to get that cocky son of a bitch right where I want him. And where I need him."

"And where's that?"

"In the palm of my fucking hand," Stagg said. "Just like his ole dead uncle."

. . .

"Some boys at school were calling Jason a little creamy," Quinn said. "Where do kids hear crap like that?"

"You know as well as I do," Lillie said, "their shitty parents."

"Caddy's going to be pissed at my advice."

"Let me guess," Lillie said, both of them sitting in Quinn's office, running through last night's reports and her talk with Diane Tull. "You told Jason to whip their asses, right?"

"You want some more coffee?" Quinn said.

"Am I right?"

Quinn poured some more coffee from his Thermos into Lillie's cup, no good way of telling Mary Alice that her stuff was god-awful. "And Lillie Virgil would've said different?"

"I may be lots of things, Sheriff," Lillie said, "but I'm no hypocrite. Some kids start calling Rose a beaner or a wetback or that crap and I'll tell her to punch them right in the throat."

"Little girl's going to be a tough one."

"Smart, too," Lillie said. "Those big brown eyes see everything."

Quinn got up and propped open a window, taking a seat on top of his desk, and firing up a half-finished cigar. Lillie didn't seem to mind or notice, only occasionally noting her uniform had started to smell like a Havana whorehouse. Quinn had started the cigar after dropping off Jason and put it out when walking in past Mary Alice.

"And that's all you got out of Diane Tull?" Quinn said.

"All I got?" Lillie said. "I think that's a gracious plenty."

"She knows who lynched that man," Quinn said. "If she's got that kind of guilt and remorse, she's heard things. People can't keep a secret like that this long."

"She said a couple days after, her lying up in a hospital bed, some man came to her parents and told them it was all done," Lillie said. "That some men from town had taken care of the man who'd done it."

"Who came to her parents?"

"She didn't know," she said. "She said this was at the hospital and happened out in the hall, her only getting pieces of loose talk. First feeling good about it and happy the man was dead."

"And the men who did the lynching?"

"Diane said she didn't want to know," Lillie said. "Too much shame in it. That's some heavy burden on a teenage girl. Not only was she raped, shot, and had to witness the murder of her friend, she then believes she caused the death of an innocent man."

"You really believe she doesn't know more?" Quinn said.

"Nope," Lillie said. "She realized we knew about the lynching and it didn't take too much to connect what happened. She's got a lot of remorse and guilt about what happened. She said when she saw the shitbird who really raped and shot her a few weeks later and tried to tell her parents, no one would listen. She said all of Jericho was pleased and happy that justice was done."

"Seems like my uncle was, too."

"Surprise you?" Lillie said.

Quinn shook his head. Mary Alice knocked on the office door and peered in, waving her hand in front of her face and telling him to at least cut on the ceiling fan. "Y'all want some coffee?"

Quinn told her they were good. Mary Alice, all made-up, hair tall and coiffed, and wearing a friendly snowman sweater, shut the door.

"Where would you start?" Quinn said. "With both of them? The killer and the victim?"

Lillie cut on the fan as Mary Alice had requested and sat back down. She mulled it over for a few minutes. "I'd ask around Sugar Ditch," Lillie said. "Reach out into the black community with a description of both."

"Don't know much about the victim."

"Maybe we will soon," Lillie said. "As long as it wasn't burned and buried, it'll show up."

Quinn puffed on the cigar and ashed the tip in a COLSON FOR SHERIFF coffee mug. "What else we got going today?" Quinn said.

"Goddamn Chester got drunk again and busted the window at the florist shop," Lillie said. "He's into some kind of feud with Miss Doris over that alley where he takes a piss now and then. And we got some kind of family squabble out in Providence with Missy Hayes. She says her uncle tossed all her shit out of a house where she was staying. The uncle says she was a renter who didn't pay and that she'd been warned. Kin or not."

"Who's her uncle?"

"Levi Sims."

Quinn nodded, puffed on the cigar some more. "Between those two, I wouldn't know who to believe."

"That whole family is fucked in the head," Lillie said.

"Make sure to put that in the report," Quinn said.

"You bet."

"I'll talk to Boom," Quinn said. "Might be good if we ride together in Sugar Ditch, talk to some folks we know."

"Are you saying people in the Ditch are mistrustful of white folks?" Lillie said, taking the cigar from Quinn's mouth and taking a puff. "And you need Boom just to get them to loosen up and talk a bit?"

"Yes, ma'am."

"Damn," Lillie said. "You're turning into a pretty good investigator, Sheriff."

19

"Appreciate you stopping by, Sheriff," W. D. "Sonny" Stevens said. "But I'm afraid I got some right shitty news for you."

"Terrific," Quinn said.

They stood out on Stevens's balcony on the second floor of his law office. The repair work and construction around the Square now a common racket during the week. Twenty or so contractor trucks were parked in and around the Square, filling in the holes and gaps that the tornado left. Lots of hammering and saws, big chunks of Sheetrock lifted off trucks and fitted on the studs. Blue tarps fluttered from a few rooftops still waiting for repairs. New permits being pulled every day.

"DA wants you in Oxford Friday for a sit-down," Stevens said.

"OK."

"This is a step up from the informal, friendly stuff," Stevens said.

"Fine by me."

"Getting ugly."

"That's expected," Quinn said. "Let 'em get to it. If they want to ruin the election, now's the time."

"They also have a search warrant to check Lillie's house," he said. "I learned this from a trusted friend in Oxford. So tell her to act surprised when they show up."

"Don't worry," Quinn said. "Lillie will give them an earful."

"How'd it go last time?" Stevens said. "With that investigator in New Albany?"

"He was slicker than shit."

"Friendly?"

"Too friendly," Quinn said. "He didn't stop grinning the whole time. What could they possibly have, Mr. Stevens?"

"DA's trying to tie you both to all that money," Stevens said. "That's it, right? You and Lillie ambush those two convicts making an exchange and, when the Jericho police showed, y'all shot them, too. So, I'd guess the DA either found a witness or they're trying to show an uptick in your personal finances."

"Hell," Quinn said. "You know how much I make a year?"

"Shameful," Stevens said, shaking his head. "Just shameful."

Quinn leaned over the wooden banister and looked out at the Square. The old movie house built in the thirties, which for a short time became a church, was now coming back as a movie house. Some woman from Oxford had moved into town to start a coffee shop and tanning parlor, and there were two restaurants—a Greek and a Chinese restaurant—moving into spaces that had been vacant since Quinn had been a kid. What was a tragedy was now deemed an economic miracle.

"I never intended to go for second term anyway," Quinn said. "I came back to bury my uncle and then left the Regiment to finish some things. I've done my part."

"But you don't care for being forced out?"

"No, sir," Quinn said. "You know that scene in *Butch and Sundance* when Sundance can't stomach being called a cheater? He makes the man across from him ask him to stay at the poker table."

"Other fella was Sam Elliott," Stevens said. "Before he grew the mustache."

"That's pretty much how I feel."

"I don't like it, either," Stevens said. "And don't care for the way it smells."

"Like bullshit and diesel?"

"Got Johnny Stagg all over it."

"Yep."

"You need to inform Miss Virgil that she'll be served with a search warrant sometime later today," Stevens said. "We'll all head over to Oxford tomorrow and see what the DA is about to throw down. Maybe he has a deal on the table."

"No deals."

"You'd like to be asked to stay awhile."

They watched all the activity on the Square for a bit. Neither of them spoke until Quinn turned to the older man. "Mr. Stevens?"

"Yes, sir."

"This may be off topic," Quinn said, "but do you recall a couple young girls attacked in 1977? One girl was shot and killed. The other raped and left for dead."

"Diane Tull," he said. "And Hank Stillwell's daughter."

"Do you know what happened after?" Quinn said. "A man was snatched up and lynched."

Stevens swallowed. His fine gray hair blowing wild and scattering over his head. He leaned into a space by Quinn at the banister and spit down on the sidewalk below. Quinn could smell the bourbon on his breath, but he seemed clear-eyed and sharp. "That was one of the most disgusting acts I think ever happened in this town."

"So who were they?" Quinn said. "The ones who could pull it off and no one would question it?"

Stevens shook his head, reaching up and patting down his scattering hair. They both stood there, young man and old man, leaning over the railing and watching the rebuilding of the new and improved Jericho. The American flag flying next to the gazebo and an old cannon by the foot of the veterans' monument. More hammering and sawing and commotion carried on below, signaling movement, improvement, and change.

"That's been quite a while."

"Doesn't make things any better."

"I might know someone who can help y'all out," he said. "Let me ask around."

"Someone wants me to shut my goddamn mouth," Diane Tull said. "They wanted it so badly, they wrote it on the side of my pickup truck."

"That don't seem right," Hank Stillwell said. "Maybe someone's just joshin' you."

"And they slashed my tires and came up to my home, peeping in the windows," Diane said. "No, sir. They're not joshing me. They mean business, and, at this point, I'm a little confused by your motivation here. Do you want to find out who killed your daughter or just stir all this shit back up?"

Diane had called the old man to meet her on the Natchez Trace at noon. That way, she could get loose from the store without anyone asking a bunch of questions. And the more Hank Stillwell's muscle car was parked outside her house or at the feed store, the more people would start thinking they were having an affair. Just what she needed, folks think she was hopping in bed with a man twenty years her senior. Hank Stillwell. Jesus, she sure hoped not.

"I just want to help," Stillwell said. "I figured you'd want the same."

"Who's doing this pushing?" she said. "Who doesn't want this to come out?"

"That's a hell of a long list," Stillwell said. They stood under a covered viewing area where you could look out at Indian mounds rising up from the flat, grassy ground. This was the place, according to the official park map, where the Choctaws came to bury their dead with pieces of pottery, weapons, and tools. There were two different viewing points and a building with public restrooms.

"I don't really care who this embarrasses," she said. "Do you?"

"No, ma'am."

"But you rode with these people?" she said. "This could get you in trouble, too."

"I've been clean now for more than twenty years," Stillwell said. "I have a good many years of my life that I don't even recall. After Lori died, I just wanted to make myself numb to the world and with the help of some lucky pills I succeeded."

"But they're back?" Diane said, cars and trucks slowly driving past them on the Trace. "Aren't they? I've seen them coming back in town, buying things at the store, heading back out to that clubhouse y'all used to have. Are they the same folks?"

"Yes, ma'am," Stillwell said. "Some of them. Some are new. Others are dead."

"And the more this comes out," Diane said, "the more it shuts them down."

Stillwell's face was covered in reddish gray stubble, looking as if it had been a couple days since his last shave and maybe last bath. He wore a red-and-black checked coat, threadbare trousers, and an ancient pair of pointy-toed cowboy boots. "What they did was wrong. That man gets out of prison and he's going to turn this town inside out. He's been sitting there up at Brushy Mountain thinking on things, making plans for when he comes back. You and me don't step up, tell what we know, we're going to find this county in worse shape than after the storm."

"One man?" she said. "You really believe he can do all that?"

Stillwell nodded. "He's got a list of people he wants cleared out and I'm number one on that list."

"So you're trying to save your own skin?"

"I'm the dumb son of a bitch who put him in prison," Stillwell said. "I turned informant on the whole crew and testified in federal court. Chains LeDoux calls me his own personal Judas Iscariot."

"This isn't about Lori," Diane said. "This isn't about me."

"It's all the same, Miss Tull," he said. "We're just all caught up in it until we see it all through."

"I should go."

Stillwell touched her arm as she passed. He looked into her eyes, shivering as if the coat didn't offer him any warmth in the setting sun. "Please," he said. "All I need you to do is tell the sheriff that these people got the wrong man. Tell them that you saw the fella who did this to y'all after that man got hung."

"I already did, Hank," she said. "And now I'm done with whatever angle you're working. Please leave me the hell alone."

20

By the time Quinn got back to the farm, he'd already picked up two drug addicts who missed their court dates, talked a woman out of filing charges against her fifteen-year-old son for poking a fork in her butt, helped an old woman riddled with dementia get home from the Piggly Wiggly, and wrote an incident report for a crew down from Byhalia who'd had a thousand bucks' worth of tools stolen. He hadn't even made it up the front steps when Caddy met him at the door with one of those pissed-off Caddy looks, screen door slamming behind her. Her hands on her hips and staring down at her brother, not saying good to see you, welcome home, how was your day? But instead, "What the hell did you tell my son this morning?"

"Hey there, Caddy," Quinn said, not breaking stride, walking up the brick steps to the front porch and taking a seat in an old rocker.

"What did you tell him, Quinn?" Caddy said. "I had to pick him up early from school. He has bruises all up and down his body and his eye is nearly swollen shut."

"Did he win?" Quinn said.

"Damn you."

"He's a kid," Quinn said. "He's a boy. Besides, do you know what those little bastards said to him on the playground?"

"I don't give a crap," Caddy said. "He's five. I don't want him fighting. I don't want him to respond to those kind of taunts. You don't think I've laid awake at night thinking about what these little rednecks will make of some half-black kid? You think it's bad now? It's going to be a hundred times worse in high school. I think about him asking a girl on a date and, no matter if they're black or white, what they'll say. It breaks my heart."

"Sit down."

"I'd rather stand."

"Sit down, Caddy," Quinn said. "Let's talk. It's been a hell of a day and I did my best with Jason. I just gave him the same advice Momma gave me when that turd Carl Rose wanted to kick my ass."

"I remember that," Caddy said, sitting. "I recall everyone talking about it. You broke his nose."

"Yep," Quinn said. "And Carl Rose hadn't been worth a shit since."

"Well, Jason isn't you," she said. "And there were two boys doing this to him."

"He can't let people talk to him like that," Quinn said. "Saying he smells 'cause he's part black. Jason's going to have to learn to fight sooner or later."

"At five?" Caddy said. "Have you gone crazy? I'm not trying to raise a fine young soldier, I'm trying to raise a good boy with a good belief system. If I tried to fight every bastard that had done me wrong, I wouldn't have time to breathe."

"Well," Quinn said, leaning back in the rocker, "I'm sorry."

"Really?"

"Shit, yeah," Quinn said. "Wasn't my place. I don't have kids. I'm just trying to help out some."

Caddy was on the porch swing, some of the red-hot color gone from her face. She had on a man's button-down over a George Jones T-shirt. "OK," she said. "I appreciate you trying. I really do. But I don't want Jason to be a kindergarten hell-raiser. I want him to make better choices than we did. Smart ones."

"Isn't ass-kicking in the Bible?"

"Maybe you forgot to read the second half of that book," Caddy said, smiling a bit. The old swing kicked up and back slowly on chains from the curved beaded-board ceiling. Quinn had painted it a light blue, the color of the sky, as the old-timers had way back to keep the bad spirits away, finding some of the original paint when he'd scraped it clean.

"What's for supper?" Quinn said.

"Mom's got something going," she said. "I think she's frying up some of that deer you just got processed. The cubed steak with some sweet potatoes and green beans."

It was quiet and still between them in the falling shadows. Quinn could hear bird songs and the skittering of squirrels. Deep over the pasture, a hawk circled, making its final hunting rounds in the last light of day. "You doing OK, sis?"

"I'm fine," she said. "Why?"

"You hadn't stopped working in almost a year."

"I don't want to stop," she said, placing a hand on Quinn's knee. "I slow down and all I can do is think. I read somewhere that when you're going through hell, just mash the pedal to the metal and keep going."

"I think that was Jerry Reed."

They stayed on the porch, front door closed to Jean and Jason. Caddy said Jean had gotten some ice on Jason's eye, helped tend to his cuts and bruises. The older boys who'd done it were suspended and she said Jason took some kind of comfort in the justice of that. Quinn hadn't expected the boys to really take it out on him.

"How'd everything go with Diane Tull?" Caddy asked. "Every time I start feeling sorry for myself, I think about what that woman has gone through."

"You've been through plenty."

"But to be raped and shot, lying there and knowing your best friend was dead."

"Hard stuff," Quinn said. "I just hope I can help."

"Did Uncle Hamp ever do anything?"

"Nope."

"Not even questioned someone?"

Quinn took a deep breath and stood, stretching his arms and back. Being in the truck for most of the day was making him more stiff and sore. He needed to get back on the fire roads even earlier tomorrow. "We both know Uncle Hamp was pretty good at looking the other way when he thought justice was served," Quinn said. "What he did wasn't legally correct. But he surely thought it was right."

"He turned his head from something bad?"

"Diane Tull thinks so," Quinn said. "Some men around here killed the man they believed hurt her and she's having some trouble with that part of things. I don't think she ever wanted that part of it to come up. She believes the man they killed was innocent."

"Good Lord."

"Took him out to Jericho Road where it all happened and hung him from that old oak," Quinn said. "It's still there but dead, black and charred. I think it was hit by lightning. Our uncle just sat off on the sidelines and let the whole thing go. She came to him later when she spotted the real killer and our uncle ignored her."

"So who was the man?"

"Nobody ever knew," Quinn said. "He's buried in an unmarked grave."

"Jesus God."

"Yes, ma'am."

. . .

After supper, Quinn picked up Boom and drove south out of Jericho down to Sugar Ditch, an old black community of shacks and hovels. Most of the people there lived in the bottomland along a creek that flooded with every rain. The buildings weren't up to any sort of code—the county had no building code at all—and many of them didn't have indoor plumbing. Most people didn't own the houses, if you could call them that. They paid rent to the man who ran the district, a former pimp and car thief by the name of Dupuy. There weren't a lot of places you could complain, as Dupuy also represented the district as county supervisor and conveniently fought against any building code proposals as "government interfering with our rights as property owners." He drove a big white Jaguar, smoked Newports, and Quinn didn't think he'd ever seen the man without a cell phone screwed tight to his ear.

Boom suggested they start off at Club Disco 9000, a place where Boom used to hang out before he quit drinking. One night, he'd beaten the hell out of four men—after the loss of his arm—because of a slight to his honor.

"Don't have much reason to come here anymore," Boom said.

Quinn pulled his truck into the gravel lot by the old cinder-block juke house. It was Wednesday night and there were six or seven cars and trucks parked outside. The music was loud, but since the place was set way back from any houses or trailers, no one ever complained. Most of the time the music came from a jukebox, but on weekends there'd be a band who'd play blues or Chitlin' Circuit soul.

"They still pissed at you busting the place up?"

"I made good on it," Boom said. "I paid off what I broke."

As soon as they entered, the owner and chief bartender, an old black man named Spam, looked straight at Boom and then to Quinn and just started shaking his head. He leaned against the bar as they took a seat,

Spam just taking his own sweet time walking down the bar, towel over his shoulder, before saying, "Please don't start some shit tonight. I can't take it."

"I paid you for that table," Boom said.

"What about the chairs?"

"Money should've covered the chairs, too," Boom said.

"Hmm," Spam said. "Thought part of our deal was that you didn't come down here no more. People afraid when they see you, Boom. They don't know if you're gonna hug 'em or kick the shit out of 'em."

"That was a while back," Boom said. "This ain't about that."

"What's this about?"

"Sheriff got some questions for you," Boom said. "Appreciate if you help him out."

Spam looked to Quinn and raised his eyebrows. "You fucking with me, man? You bring Boom Kimbrough down here to give me that gotdamn fist bump and tell me you're cool. I know the damn sheriff. And you ain't exactly the Good Housekeeping Seal, Boom. Got damn."

"How long you been living in Tibbehah?" Quinn asked.

"Since I popped out of my momma," Spam said. "I left for Memphis. I came back. Man, you know."

"Were you here in 1977?" Quinn asked.

"What the fuck you saying I did?"

"Man's not saying you did shit," Boom said. "Calm the hell down, Spam. Just listen. He needs some help."

"Mmm," Spam said.

"You remember a man drove a black Olds," Quinn said. "Probably new. Had shiny wheels and black leather inside."

"You got to be shitting me."

"Fella was a black man but had some kind of scarring on his face," Quinn said. "Like he'd been burned."

"Like Boom?"

"Yeah," Quinn said, "like Boom. Only Boom hadn't been born yet."

Spam shook his head, both palms flat on the bar. The jukebox playing a song with a woman singing "You Got to Lick It to Stick It." Some of the folks in the bar laughing at the refrain, drinking some big quart Budweiser with a side of illegal moonshine that Spam made special. A few of them would glance over at Boom and then away, Quinn used to the stares about his buddy's arm but also knowing these people were probably scared of the old Boom, the one who first came out of Guard damaged and beaten and into just tearing shit up.

"Man, Sheriff," Spam said, "I don't know. You talk to Dupuy?"

"I'd rather not."

"Y'all ain't friends?" Spam asked.

"I don't think much of how he treats folks around here," Quinn said.

"Before him, it was his daddy, and before his daddy was a white man named Bertrand Sinclair. And he was the worst of them all, 'cause he didn't just give folks a shitty place to live. He made them work for it, pay for it, and end up dying for it."

Boom looked up from the bar. A man walked past Boom and offered his hand. Boom offered his left and the man wandered off.

"I got it," Spam said. "Fucked-up face. Cool car. Hadn't been around these parts for almost forty years. Ain't nothing to it."

"Can you ask around for me, Spam?" Quinn said. "I'd consider it a favor."

"Sure, man," Spam said, offering his hand. "I'm just fucking with you. You're all right, Sheriff Colson. You ain't your uncle. Nobody can say that the law don't care about the Ditch."

Quinn looked at the man and shook his hand. "I do need to ask you something else about that time."

"Hold on," Spam said, heading down to the other end of the bar and popping the tops of two quart bottles of Bud. He gave the men two jelly jars filled with a shot of shine on the side. Spam didn't have a business license, alcohol being illegal in Tibbehah County outside the city limits, and he was operating what would be known in the dusty statutes as a beer joint. "OK?"

"A black man was killed that same summer," Quinn said. "Some men got together and took him out and hung him from a tree on Dogtown Road. Nobody claimed the body, but I was thinking he might have been from the Ditch. Maybe his people too afraid to claim him?"

Spam reached into his shirt pocket and pulled out a pack of cigarettes. He thumped one free and screwed into his mouth, lighting up with a disposable Bic. "Shit, yeah," Spam said. "I do know something about that. Everybody remember that day. Jericho went back to being a goddamn sundown town. You know? White folks thought this man had killed that little girl. But that man didn't do nothing but get in their way."

"Who was he?" Quinn said.

Boom watched them from his seat beside Quinn. There was laughter and good conversation and a very large woman on the dance floor with a very skinny man. With cold drinks in hand, they looked to be having a pretty good time in the low, soft neon light. A slow soul song came on and they embraced each other, moving smooth and easy. The woman wore the uniform of a maid from the Choctaw casinos.

"Man was crazy," Spam said. "Just showed up that year with a bag. He stayed with some woman he know and then she kicked him out. He slept out in the woods for a long time. You know, out on the Trace. I don't think he had a real job, people just called him Echo. Call him Echo 'cause he ended up only repeating you. Not answering you back."

"Where was he from?"

"Don't know."

"Who was the woman?"

"Man," Spam said, "long time ago. All I remember is when they strung his ass up for those little girls, ain't nobody could believe it. Hardest part to think about was like you said, the dude who did that to those girls had a car and could talk, to threaten them. Echo didn't have jack shit. Wouldn't hurt no one. Just walked the highways with that bag on him, wandering around, looking for some day work."

"What kind of bag did he carry?"

"Army bag," Spam said. "Man had been in Vietnam and got out with his brains scrambled. Always carried that bag with him, wearing them Army boots."

"Man," Boom said.

Quinn's cell started to ring and he stepped out into the gravel lot to answer. It was Lillie.

"Well," she said. "Sonny Stevens does know his shit. Those fuckheads are here now, going through all my shit, my bedroom, my shed, and even into Rose's room. I don't like this, Quinn. I don't like what they're doing. I don't like what they're implying."

"What do you think they're looking for?"

"They're taking all my guns," she said. "They're going to try and nail me for Dixon and Esau Davis and make their bullshit stick."

"Where's Rose?"

"Right here on the porch," she said. "I'm waiting for them to be gone."

"I'm in the Ditch with Boom," Quinn said. "Hang on. Headed your way."

21

The Born Losers called it a church meeting, and although they talked about not believing in a damn thing, they took the church meeting pretty serious. There was an old card table placed under a swinging light and the core members would sit at that table: Chains as president, Big Doug as sergeant at arms, a skinny dude name Deke was the club treasurer. There was an enforcer named Gangrene who also worked at J.T.'s body shop in town, taking care of most of their bikes. Jason had heard he'd killed a couple men in a brawl outside Little Rock, but he seemed like a decent enough guy. Gangrene had taken the Harley to his shop to straighten out the frame and get the dents out of the gas tank. He was married, had two kids, and owned his own trailer.

Chains knocked on the table with a bottle of Jack Daniel's, it being the gavel, telling everyone who was milling about, playing darts, pinball, and pool, to shut the fuck up and open their ears.

Jason had been playing darts and he stopped. It was midday but dark and hot inside the clubhouse. It was nearly a hundred degrees outside and the fans inside weren't doing squat.

"I'm sorry to say that scumbag Outlaw didn't die," Chains said. "Now they want a truce. We stay out of Tennessee and they stay out of Mississippi. It's that clear."

The men nodded. Somewhere, a "Hell, yeah."

"They ain't scared of us," Chains said. "They're scared of fucking Johnny Law, who has a hard-on for their skag business and the whores they're running out of those trucker joints on Lamar and at the airport. They don't need the pressure and the shit. I say we deal."

"For now," Big Doug said.

"Yep," Chains said. "For now."

Deke, skinny-faced, with a long, flat nose that looked like a penis, and droopy, sad eyes, nodded. "Money's tight," he said. "We got two hundred bucks and some change left. Can't afford a war."

"Me and Gangrene making a run down to New Orleans," Chains said. "We'll be back in four days. Don't worry about money."

"But we're through with the Outlaws?" Big Doug said. "One of those motherfuckers kicked me in the balls. Hell, they tried to kill Jason."

"If they'd killed your pal, that ain't on us," Chains said. "He's not riding with our colors. He gets hurt and that's on you, brother man."

Big Doug leaned back into the folding chair and folded his big fat arms over his chest. He wore a black Molly Hatchet tee with the sleeves cut off. "Fuck me."

Jason met eyes with Chains LeDoux, noticing the way the man had just trimmed his black beard, his hair still down past his shoulders. He wore no shirt and skintight jeans with combat boots, a cigarette hanging out of his mouth. His eyes, those fucking gray eyes, just lingered on him. "You got a fucking problem, dude?"

Jason held the look, chalked up the pool cue, and said, "No problem."

A couple fat boys at the bar exchanged a look, the big-titted black woman with the Afro lying prone in the velvet painting looking down at them. A man in the background of the painting peeked out from behind a curtain as the woman beamed in the spotlight.

They all heard the cars at the same time, tires on gravel. One of the boys went for the door and yelled back inside that it was the fuzz.

"God damn, son of a bitch," Chains said.

Jason leaned over the table and broke apart the balls. Two solids went in. He stepped back and checked out the next shot as the club members walked to the door and filed outside. Jason took another shot, missed, looked up, and saw his partner, redheaded Hank Stillwell—Pig Pen—had left, too.

Jason shrugged and took a sip of beer, leaving the bottle at the edge of the table, and filed on outside.

Two patrol cars with Tibbehah County sheriff's insignias sat parked at crooked angles outside the clubhouse. A hot, dry wind blew off Choctaw Lake, the lake dry and low as hell, as the sheriff came forward from his vehicle and asked, "Which of you boys they call Chains?"

Chains stepped forward. "I'm Chains."

Big Doug stepped forward. "I'm Chains."

And Deke rubbed his long, rubbery nose, stepped forward, and opened his mouth. "I'm fucking Kirk Douglas."

"Y'all are true comedians," said Hamp Beckett, who Jason had met on one prior occasion. Beckett, a Korean War vet and the longtime sheriff, had not been impressed with his Hollywood stories.

Beckett looked over Chains and the boys to Jason, hanging by the clubhouse door, and now looked even less impressed. He just shook his head and spit some Skoal out on the ground.

"I seen the pictures, and you seen the pictures, where the lawman comes out to harass the bikers," Beckett said. "Me and you fellas playing a goddamn game like Wile E. Coyote and that fucking bird. But I don't care about your long hair or your scooters or whatever y'all do out here on the lake. This is your place, and as long as nobody gets hurt, it's not my trouble."

Big Doug took a step back. Little Deke twitched for a moment, turned his head, and then did the same. Chains stood alone, with his tight jeans and combat boots and loose cigarette in his fingers.

"I got a call yesterday from the police chief up in Olive Branch," Beckett said. "He knows y'all boys got into a rumble with some more scooter lovers up there. He ain't issuing any warrants because I don't think his jail is big enough to hold each and every one of you. But he wanted me to deliver a message. Go get your barbecue in Byhalia, stay out of his town. Is that too much to ask?"

Chains flicked the cigarette. He nodded with understanding and walked up to Sheriff Beckett, whispering in his ear, patting him on the back, and handing him the last couple hundred dollars in the club fund. The sheriff beamed and laughed, not saying a word, sticking the wad of cash into his uniform trousers and walking back to the patrol car.

"Y'all ride safe," he said, before backing out and kicking up a billowing cloud of the dry and dusty road.

22

Quinn and Lillie waited at the DA's office in Oxford the next morning with Sonny Stevens telling them everything was going to be just fine. "I don't think they found what they were looking for," Stevens said. "And now they want to slide something across the table? We'll listen to their bullshit, thank them for their time, and then walk over to Ajax and have a Bloody Mary. What do you say? Be a shame to waste the trip."

They sat together in the front conference room of an institutional-looking building off Monroe Avenue that had once been the local health department. The office still smelled like ammonia and old people. The floors were a dingy, worn linoleum under skittering fluorescent lights. Someone had tacked last year's Ole Miss football schedule on the wall. As always, the scrawled *L*s outnumbered the *W*s.

"I didn't care for the way I was treated yesterday," Lillie said. "Dale Childress and his partner came to my front door, shoving that warrant into my face. They acted like they were raiding a drug dealer's house, tracking mud on my kitchen floor, waking up Rose. They didn't have the sense or decency to put anything back."

"So noted," Stevens said. "This entire matter has been disruptive as hell to y'all's lives and that of the sheriff's office."

"I don't think they're making an offer," Quinn said. "I think they're about to show us their cards. Grand jury meets in a week. I don't like the timing."

"Don't get your dick in a twist," Stevens said, looking sharp today in a navy blue suit, white shirt, and red tie. He straightened his collar and cuffs. "Excuse me, Lillie. Sorry to be so crude. But let's wait and see. I just don't care to do all this sitting around. We've been in this goddamn place for almost thirty minutes and my ass is starting to hurt."

Not two seconds later, the door opened and in walked Childress, followed by a fat man in a blue suit with a florid face and enormous gold glasses. The fat man looked as if he'd just jogged twenty miles to make the meeting. He offered a sweaty hand all around: "Trey Wilbanks, Assistant District Attorney." Trey knocked over a coffee mug as he was shaking hands, but it was Quinn's and empty and only made a minor thud as it fell to the floor.

"I appreciate y'all driving over this morning," Wilbanks said.

"Didn't know we had a choice," Lillie said.

Stevens flicked his eyes at Lillie but quickly returned a calm, pleasant gaze back to the men, hands folded in front of him. Wilbanks flipped through some papers as if trying to recall exactly what this meeting was all about.

Childress hadn't offered to shake hands. He sat beside the fat ADA and slumped into his seat, not smiling or making eye contact with Quinn. All of Childress's good ole boy *Aw, shucks* act from their first meeting was gone.

"Deputy Virgil, do you own a fifty-cal sniper rifle made by the Barrett Firearms Company?" Wilbanks asked.

"No, sir," she said. "You looking to purchase one?"

Wilbanks wiped his sweating face with a napkin. He smiled and glanced to Childress before continuing, showing no emotion as he spoke. "Seems you had one in your garage under lock and key."

"That's a lie," Lillie said. "I know my guns."

Wilbanks grinned a bit more, sending a *What can I do?* look to Sonny Stevens, who had ceased smiling a few seconds before. Stevens's entire posture changed, listening to the questioning. The old man had his index finger covering his mouth, eyes flicking over the sweating young attorney as if trying to shush himself and not let go a tirade he was holding close.

"Our purpose of this meeting is to give y'all a chance to talk things over and perhaps offer another version of the events that gibes with this new evidence," Wilbanks said. "We found fifty-cal shells in the hills above that old airstrip in Tibbehah County and bullets in the bodies of the two dead men. The fifty-cal rifle we found at Deputy Virgil's home is now with a state lab with rush orders to get results. None of us want to make law enforcement look bad."

Quinn took a breath, steadying himself. He stared at Childress, waiting for that sorry son of a bitch to meet his eyes. But Childress didn't have the courage, keeping his eyes down, a good old dog.

"We're just trying to make some sense of the events," Wilbanks said.

"I shot one man," Lillie said. "I shot a corrupt officer trying to kill Sheriff Colson. I used my Winchester model 70 and turned that weapon over to the state. But y'all can go straight to hell if you believe that in the heat of the moment I put down a gun I've been shooting since I was a teenager and picked up a tactical fifty-cal to cover my tracks. That's the dumbest shit I've ever heard."

"What's strange to us," Childress said, finally speaking, looking up from the floor, "is that some of these puzzle pieces got some weird edges."

Quinn had to hold on to the armrests of his seat, dig the hell in, or else he felt he might launch over the conference table and grab the bastard by his wispy hair or mustache and bang his head on the table.

"That weapon never belonged to Deputy Virgil," Stevens said. "Are y'all gonna charge my clients today? Or did you just want to piss a little in their morning coffee?"

Wilbanks coughed into his hand and wiped his face, sweating even more, as the meeting continued. He looked over at Childress and licked his lips. "We'd hoped to get some kind of statement from Miss Virgil regarding these events. To clarify."

"Chief Deputy Virgil," Sonny Stevens said.

Wilbanks apologized and looked down at the legal pad on his desk. He tapped a pen on some penciled notes, waited a few long seconds, and looked across the table. "Do you mind if we change topics for a moment?" he asked. "We did have another reason for calling this meeting."

Stevens cut his eyes over at Quinn, smoothed down his tie, and circled a couple fingers for him to go ahead, tell them what he wanted.

"You've reopened a cold case from 1977?" Wilbanks asked.

Quinn nodded.

"How's that coming?" the fat man asked.

"I'm a little confused here," Quinn said. "What's that investigation have to do with the shooting last April?"

"Our office has taken a big interest in that case," Childress said, speaking up. "The district attorney wanted us to ask personally how y'all were making out."

"Well," Lillie said, "we'd be further along if we weren't being called out for bullshit questions. Or having to wait around while you boys creep my house. Do you know what a fucking mess you left my panties drawer?"

"Just doing our jobs," Childress said.

"Just like us," Quinn said. "Without question."

"Why's the old case so important?" Stevens asked. "With eight counties, it's not like y'all are sitting around with your thumbs up your asses."

"This one has caught the attention of the DA," Childress said. "It has a lot of personal significance for him."

"Did he know the victims?" Quinn asked.

"Victims?" Childress said. "I know of only one."

Quinn stared at Dale Childress and said, "Just which case are we talking about?"

"The lynching," Wilbanks said. "That black fella who they strung up in the tree, shot and burned."

"How'd you know about that?" Lillie asked.

"You're not looking into what happened?" Wilbanks said.

"We didn't say that," Quinn said. "But why would you want to know about something that happened nearly forty years ago? Our investigation is tied to a completely different case."

"The DA would be grateful for y'all making some headway down in Jericho," Wilbanks said. "The racial edge to this crime is something he'd like to see addressed. We know about the rape and murder that may have sparked this crime. But the law was ignored and this man's rights were violated."

"I don't know whether to punch y'all," Lillie said, "or stand up in salute."

"How about both," Quinn said.

Sonny Stevens raised his hand, trying to quiet his clients. "And why would your office entrust an important case to law enforcement officers they say they don't fully trust?"

"We have to follow up with the shooting," Childress said. "Just as sure as y'all will be following up with that lynching. Now that new witnesses have come forward."

"Y'all really keep tabs on Jericho," Lillie said. "Did you find that out before or after y'all went through my panties?"

Sonny Stevens held up a hand, telling everyone to settle the hell down. "Am I hearing some kind of quid pro quo situation on the table? Some folks charged in exchange for an end to this ridiculous investigation of my clients?"

Wilbanks swallowed, patted his sweating head, and looked to Quinn and Lillie and then back to Stevens. "No, sir. We're simply stating the DA and his entire office would be grateful if some headway could be made in a pretty ugly chapter here in north Mississippi. The two items are unrelated."

"Well, god damn," Stevens said, shaking his head.

"What's that, sir?" Wilbanks said.

"Politics do trump all," Stevens said, stood, and buttoned the top button of his suit coat. Quinn stood more slowly, Lillie following them both, walking out the door. No handshakes, no words said, until they were out of the stale, sour-smelling building and in a parking lot, facing the back of the Oxford town square.

"Sneaky motherfuckers," Stevens said. "They wouldn't admit it with their feet to the fire and their cojones in a vise. But they want y'all to come up with results and make this local turd into the next attorney general."

"I never owned a gun like that in my life," Lillie said. "They seeded it to make sure."

"Guess they thought y'all needed some extra incentive," Stevens said. "But what in the world would make y'all not follow through on an investigation you're already working on? And this case has been around almost forty years. Who the hell is in such a rush for something so goddamn old?"

Stagg heard them as he was finishing up a plate of fried catfish, coleslaw, and beans at the Rebel. The sound was something terrific, drowning out even the 18-wheelers rolling in off Highway 45. He watched from the red-padded back booth and saw a good thirty, forty of those shitbirds on two wheels zip between the gas pumps and the restaurants, finding a place to gather above the semi lot. Mr. Ringold excused himself to go out and get himself a better look. Stagg stood, dropped a couple bucks on the table as was his custom with the waitresses, and walked down the long row of stools at the dining counter, past the truckers hunched over their meat loaf and chicken-fried steak not giving one shit about the noise shaking the plate glass. Only a couple of his longtime waitresses gathered by the register, witnessing the entire Born Losers Motorcycle Club come back to town.

Stagg kept standing there with hands on hips, reaching over by the candy displays and finding a couple peppermints in a big white bucket, offered on the honor system to benefit a home for abused kids over in Grenada.

He walked out slow and easy, seeing the men getting off their bikes, taking in the bright and cold day. The sound of their growling pipes still ringing in his ears as he made his way to the pumps and over to the higher ground where they'd parked. *Hot damn.* Here we go.

One man separated himself from the others. He had a shaved head and wore a thick black leather jacket with leather pants with high leather boots. He had on dark sunglasses and his face was a mess of tattoos, ink on his chin and down his cheeks and over his throat. The closer he got, Stagg could make out that the ink on his chin was that of a devil's goatee and the one on his neck was one of those dreamcatchers that he sold in the Rebel for four dollars and ninety-nine cents. Genuine Choctaw but made in China.

"You Johnny Stagg?" the man said. His voice was gravelly and thick, accusing as an old woman's. Stagg figured the boy was in his late forties or early fifties, hard to tell without any hair and all those goddamn crazy tattoos.

Stagg just nodded.

"You sure don't look like much."

Stagg didn't say anything.

"I hear you run this shithole."

Stagg grinned, not being able to help himself, this boy was the genuine article of swagger and bullshit. He was pretty certain that even this boy's momma didn't love him.

"Y'all's food any good?" the man said. "We've been riding all morning from Meridian."

"Why don't you see for yourself?" Stagg said. "Try the lemon pie."

"And the titties out back?" the man said. "We talking local talent or Grade A? I don't want some toothless, pregnant skank grinding my pecker for a dollar."

"The bar doesn't open till four," Stagg said. "You might have noticed that on the billboards if you boys could read. You sure do have a mess of them with you."

"Johnny Stagg," the man said. "Damn, it's good to see you. I sure have heard a bunch of things."

"Is that right?" Stagg asked, not giving a damn but drawing things out, seeing Ringold making his way out through the dozens and dozens of parked trucks and finding some land up above the Rebel.

"I heard you were sneaky as hell," the man said. "Smart. Tricky. That if a man turned his back on you, you'd stick it hard and high inside him."

Ringold was just a shadow on the ridge over the tattooed freak's shoulder. Stagg just now caught the glimmer of a rifle scope from above. Money well spent.

"Might be true," Stagg said. "Might be true now."

"We didn't come for trouble," the man said. "We came to eat country chow and see some big ole titties. If they ain't dancing now, you better go wake them up and say you got company. Shake 'em hard and long."

"We don't open the Trap till four."

"The Booby Trap," the man said. "That's clever as hell. You think of that all by yourself, Mr. Stagg?"

"I sure did," Stagg said. "And it's made me a rich man."

"But you didn't get really rich until about twenty years ago," the man said. "I was there. I remember. You just don't remember me, do you?"

"What's your name, son?"

"Animal."

"Your momma name you that?"

"It's what you'll call me from now on," the man said. "And, sir, we'll be regulars here for a while. Just getting things ready."

"I've been expecting y'all," Stagg said. "As long as you tend to your manners, there won't be no trouble. Buy your gas, buy a plate lunch. Y'all can go in like normal folks to the Booby Trap when we open. But, son, just don't try and get tough with me. I got myself a real weak stomach and the indigestion."

"You know that hell is coming," Animal said. "Right?"

"I've gotten his letters from Brushy Mountain," Stagg said.

"This is our county now," he said. "Understood?"

"Is that so?" Stagg said. "Hmm."

"Goddamn right."

"OK," Stagg said. "But I sure would be careful about gloating too much on your big ole fucking hog. There's a high-velocity rifle aimed right at your head, boy. Have you ever seen what one of them things can do to a watermelon? When it explodes, it makes a hell of a goddamn mess."

The man, Animal, kind of laughed. But when he turned to look over his shoulder, his face turned a few more funny colors. He didn't say jack as he walked back to his men and their rows of shiny chrome Harleys.

Stagg flipped a peppermint into his mouth, crunching it with his back teeth.

23

Diane noticed the old truck following her not two seconds after leaving the Jericho Farm & Ranch. Not that a beat-up white Chevy was strange, but it was clear to her the driver had been waiting. He'd been parked on the gravel, westbound on Cotton Road, and after she drove east, he made a U-turn and kept on her truck real close. She'd promised that these bastards wouldn't spook her any. She'd decided just to pretend they weren't even there unless they got too close and she'd call the sheriff to get them off her ass. She headed on to the town square, following up and around, and then spit out the other side of Cotton Road, toward Highway 45, following it past where the old Hollywood Video had been and the Dollar Store, coming up into the lot of the Piggly Wiggly. The storm had torn the ever-living shit out of the Pig, the metal roof of the store sucked into the tornado and most of the goods either taken or given away.

But now, it looked like the same old Pig that had been there since the late sixties. Diane parked in the lot, saw the white Chevy roll past her, up and around the lot, and park back toward the Shell station.

Diane would not let the bastards scare her or change her routine. She wanted to pick up some beef cuts, potatoes, and vegetables for a stew. If someone wanted to make something of it, she had a fully loaded .38 Taurus in her handbag.

Despite all the repairs to the roof and the foundation, not much had changed inside the Pig. They had the same old registers, the same manager's box perched above the gumball machines, and a little café where they served fried chicken and biscuits. Diane started off in the produce, getting some red potatoes, carrots, onions, and some celery. She wished they had a good bakery in town, tired of all this crummy, tasteless white stuff they kept. She'd never made bread herself, but maybe she needed to learn.

Diane looked over her shoulder, not seeing anyone or anything, and kept on heading over to dairy. She loaded a jug of milk and butter into her cart. The speakers above her were as new as the ceiling, but the manager still played the same music, that soft elevator stuff of not-so-recent hits, an instrumental of Kenny and Dolly's "Islands in the Stream."

The butcher shop was along the far back wall and she searched through the plastic-wrapped packages for something cheap, but not too tough, that she could leave simmering in a Crock-Pot. A woman at her church once told her you could leave an old shoe in a Crock-Pot and make it soft. But that wasn't altogether true. The meat was the base for everything and you might as well spend a little extra.

"Y'all having steaks tonight?" said a man behind her.

She turned to see a short, odd, crummy little guy in thin Liberty overalls wearing a trucker hat. He was somewhere in his seventies and had a nose that looked like a rhubarb.

"I'm sorry," she said, "do I know you?"

"E. J. Royce," the man said, smiling.

"Mr. Royce," she said. "I apologize."

"That's all right," he said. "It's been a while. I switched over the Co-op on account of it being closer to my house."

"So I see," she said. Royce had on a Tibbehah County Co-op trucker's cap.

"How your boys?"

"Moved away."

"How old are they?"

Diane told him, and she placed the package of stew meat in her cart and started to turn away. "Good seeing you."

"And your momma?"

"Not well," she said. "She has Alzheimer's."

Royce edged his cart gently in front of Diane's, cutting her off, the old man smiling, face chapped and worn. His flannel shirt so thin, it didn't look like it could stand another washing. "Listen," he said, "Miss Tull."

Diane stared at the man. The music above them playing more instrumentals, "Always On My Mind" sounding as syrupy-sweet as possible. She backed away the cart but studied the old man's face and the eager look in his faded blue eyes. "Did you just follow me?"

"Me?" he said. "No, ma'am. I just came in here to get me some of them Hungry-Man dinners. I swear to you, you don't need to cook nothing. They make a hell of roast beef and potatoes. But their chicken and gravy is just like something your grandmomma might make."

"Do you drive an old beat-up Chevy truck?"

"Ma'am," Royce said, "I don't want to take much of your time. I just seen you in here and thought to myself, 'Yep, that's Diane Tull.' I was just talking about you the other day with some old buddies. You know, I used to be in law enforcement. I proudly retired after twenty-five years of commitment to this county."

"What do you want?"

Royce removed his hat, showing he didn't have hair except on the sides, and scratched his bald head. He didn't have anything in his cart. She moved back her cart another few inches, wanting to get away but at the same time curious about why Royce was following her. A bearded young man on a motorcycle. And now this old coot. Maybe she just attracted the crazy folks like those bugs to her porch light.

He slid the hat back on his head, leaned his forearms on the cart's basket, and looked in either direction. "I hear you gotten curious about some things might have happened after y'all had all that trouble."

Diane Tull looked at Royce right in his cataracted eyes. "What of it."

"Don't blame you," he said. "You may not recall, but me and Sheriff Beckett were the first ones who got to you, after you walked a spell out on Jericho Road. That trucker seen you all bloody and called it in on his CB."

"I remember."

Royce nodded, all serious. "God help y'all for what you girls went through."

"I just came here to make some stew," she said. "I don't need anyone laying their hands on me in the meat aisle. I don't think Jesus makes visits to the Piggly Wiggly."

"I just think you need to be more appreciative to those who took care of your troubles."

"Come again?"

"You don't need to embarrass the folks who looked out for you and Miss Stillwell when y'all needed them," he said. "You weren't in no shape to be put through a trial. Things got done that needed to be done."

"I can't believe it," Diane said. "I can't fucking believe it. You've followed me into town to tell me to shut my mouth about y'all hanging an innocent man."

"You don't know what you're saying," Royce said. "You were nearly dead when they found you, bled-out."

"I saw the man who did it," she said. "I saw him six weeks after y'all hung that poor man from the big oak."

Royce nodded, backing his cart away, showing a path for Diane to follow if she wished. He thumbed at his nose and said, "I think you're misremembering some things. I think you need to know what was done was in y'all's best interest."

"Says who?" Diane said. "I never asked for any of that."

A fat man on a scooter zipped down the aisle past them, cart loaded down with cookies, white bread, Little Debbie snack pies, and two liters of Diet Dr Pepper. "Good seeing you, ma'am," Royce said, raising his voice a little, nodding.

"You need to stay away from me."

"I'm just the messenger, ma'am," he said. "Some fine folks did the right thing. Don't go dragging names through the mud. Thank the Lord we had people in this county had the sand."

Royce rolled the cart away, heading down the cereal aisle to the tune of "Don't It Make My Brown Eyes Blue."

"You want a beer?" Lillie asked.

"Yep."

"Aren't you still on duty?" she said, walking into her kitchen.

Quinn loosed his tie and yanked it off his neck, tossing it onto a chair. "Kenny and Dave Cullison are on patrol," he said. "They'll call if they need us."

"You want a Coors or a Bud?"

"Long as it's cold," Quinn said.

He sat in a chair in Lillie's living room, her daughter Rose, now almost two, watching him with suspicion from a big overstuffed sofa. The little girl turned her head to *Dora the Explorer*, a personal favorite since the little girl found some kind of kinship with the character. They were both brown-skinned girls with brown hair and brown eyes who spoke Spanish. Lille had rescued her from a filthy trailer in north Mississippi in a human-trafficking case and later adopted her as an infant. It had been important to Lillie the girl learned her native language, along with some choice English expressions that were pure Lillie.

Lillie handed him a beer and sat down next to Rose. Lillie had a beer, too, and took a swig. It was nearly 1700. Quinn had to be at the county supervisors' meeting in an hour to present the monthly crime stats and the budget for the New Year. He would've been more excited about a visit to a proctologist.

"When I came home, after my mom got sick, I told myself I'd never stay," she said. "I had friends and a life in Memphis. This was a job and temporary. But then Sheriff Beckett died and you came home. And now there's Rose."

"Lots of ungrateful people."

"I should have had Sonny Stevens cataloging everything in my home," she said. "We should have tagged everything in the house so they couldn't pull that shit."

On TV, Dora had just befriended a magical talking llama. The llama was apparently also friends with a Spanish-speaking flute.

"They would've found another way," Quinn said. "They would've searched the SO's office and thrown it down there. They had the gun and would have made it work."

Lillie put her hands over Rose's ears. "So these goddamn shitbags," she said, "are working with and knew that sniper."

"Yep."

"That sniper not only shot back at me, he was trying to punch your lights out, too."

"Yes, ma'am," Quinn said. "He continued to shoot after I got Caddy and Jason in the truck. He was there to tie up loose ends."

"I hate this," Lillie said. "But they sure got us beat."

Lillie took her hands off Rose's ears. Rose was so intent on the cartoon that she'd barely noticed they'd been talking. The evil Swiper, a bandito fox, lurked in some bushes, waiting for Dora, the magical llama, the flute, and Dora's monkey.

"How'd you like to attend the county supervisors' meeting with me?"

"That's tonight?"

Quinn nodded. He drank some more beer. "Maybe if I keep on drinking for the next hour, I can show up drunk. And they can fire me."

"They're going to try and do that anyway."

"They're going to try and embarrass me tonight," Quinn said. "You, too."

"They may wait for the charges to come."

"No," Quinn said. "It's tonight. Boom heard a couple those sonsabitches conspiring at the County Barn. They have a quorum to ask me to step down until the investigation of us is completed."

"They can't do that."

"Nope," Quinn said. "But this is the official launch of the mudslinging."

Lillie tipped back her beer. Her home was a small cottage with beaded-board walls and clean, spare rooms. She had a lot of antiques from her mother, lots of old photos of people who'd lived in Jericho a long time before Quinn and Lillie. Men with big mustaches and boiled shirts and women in thick, ruffled, uncomfortable-looking clothes and tall lace-up boots. On a side table was a framed picture of Lillie and some woman Quinn had never met, dressed-up and seated in some nice restaurant.

"They're hoping you'll turn," Lillie said. "That's what the talk of manslaughter is about. They want to get me for killing Leonard's stooge, Burney, and probably try and make that convict my accessory."

"That's something," Quinn said.

"How so?"

"That they are so goddamn stupid, they think I'd sell you out," Quinn said. "I can't imagine what they're hoping to accomplish. What's their objective here? Just to get us both gone?"

"That seems like a done deal."

Lillie leaned back into the sofa and reached for a throw to cover Rose's small body and bare feet. The girl was bright-eyed and beautiful. As she grew, her Indian features became more pronounced. The large black eyes, the nose and high cheekbones. She'd been a miracle for Lillie, even with the tantrums and the night terrors and the screaming that came out of nowhere and grew more intense. Sometimes, Lillie said, she seemed completely detached, trapped inside her own head. They had seen specialists from Jackson to Memphis, everyone realizing whatever abuse and trauma the girl had experienced, even as an infant, wasn't done with her.

But now, in front of the television, cuddled with Lille and watching *Dora*, she was happy.

"I got to go," Quinn said, rising.

Lillie looked up at him, her eyes meeting his, and said, "Give 'em hell."

24

Johnny Stagg always hated having to conduct his business in public, once a month, center stage, in the Tibbehah County Building, spending hours talking about things already been decided. But this was the law, had been the law for a hundred years or more, and, as he looked out into the seats, he was surprised to see them filled. The Board of Supervisors meeting wasn't exactly a hot ticket in Jericho unless you planned on getting your road paved or wanted to complain about logging traffic. Most of the time, folks just asked for an improvement in public utilities, which didn't have a damn thing to do with them. But here they were, country-come-to-town, wanting to know just what was going to be done about their sheriff killing a fellow lawman in cold blood.

Stagg waited for things to begin, taking center seat on the dais, right next to that fat old Chuck McDougal, who represented District 3, and Mr. Dupuy, who represented District 4 down in Sugar Ditch. Sam Bishop, Jr., ran things within the city limits of Jericho and was the son of a Boy Scout troop leader. Bobby Pickens ran things out toward Drivers Flat, District 5, down into the bottomland that was white, all the way to the border with the Choctaw Nation. You couldn't rely on Bishop or Pickens. Pickens's mind could be swayed, but Bishop thought his opinion mattered two shits.

"Call to order," Stagg said. "Glad to see so many interested faces with us tonight. Mr. McDougal, would you please lead us all in the pledge and a short prayer?"

Dupuy was on his cell phone, talking to some woman he was courting. McDougal had been clipping his fingernails under the dais straight onto the floor. His daddy had been the biggest crook this county had ever seen and he'd have been the same if he'd had half a brain.

McDougal stood, pig-eyed and porky, and put his hand to the American pin on his chest. He gave a lot of effect to saying "under God," as that had always been his election platform. He told people in Tibbehah that the government wanted to take the Lord out of schools.

Stagg stood, hand on chest, spotting Quinn Colson in the center row. He was in uniform and sitting with the county coroner, a nice-looking piece of tail that the sheriff was fucking. He looked right at Stagg. Stagg nodded to him. Quinn's expression did not change.

"Lord, please grant our nation's leaders, in particular our president, some sense of wisdom and Christian values," McDougal said. "To represent this great God-fearing nation in the ways of our forefathers and not just immigrants."

Lord, if that boy was dumb as dirt, Stagg thought, he'd cover a few acres.

Stagg watched the Bundren girl lean into Quinn, whisper something, and Colson smile. He couldn't blame them. McDougal was a Grade A moron.

"Any comments or questions should be held until the end of the agenda," Stagg said. "We got lots to cover and a packed house. So y'all please bear with us tonight. We'll go as quickly and efficiently as always."

There were grading projects, cell phone towers, and a new subdivision plot needed approving. All of them decided on weeks ago, kickbacks already divvied up. There were improvements requested to the old bridge over the Big Black. The Fire Department needed two new vehicles because of those damaged in the storm, and there was a reimbursement needed for the town clerk for prep and copying of tax rolls.

"And we got some property to remove?" Stagg said. "From the sheriff's office. Sheriff Colson?"

Quinn approached the dais, ramrod straight, and read off a request to remove a Vertex handheld radio, whatever that was, and a 2007 Ford Crown Vic. Both would be headed to salvage.

"We're also having issues at the SO building," Colson said. "The roof repairs were patch jobs and have started to leak. We need to look to a permanent solution, along with the damage to two of our holding cells."

"Fine by me," Stagg said. "Does the board have any questions?"

Stagg leaned back, stifling a yawn. This was the part of the show that he enjoyed. Colson had his hands flat on the lectern, not showing any emotion in that buzz-cut head of his.

McDougal cleared his throat and leaned forward into his microphone. "Yes, sir," he said. "I got a few things to discuss that ain't on this matter but having to deal with sheriff's business."

Stagg covered a slight grin with his hand.

"I've spent a lot of time out in my district, as I always do, speaking with my constituents who are concerned about this ongoing legal matter with you and Chief Deputy Virgil," he said, coughing more into his hand. "Have you heard any new information when this inquiry will be done? I'd like to pass on some comfort to my people up in the hills."

Quinn did not shuffle or move. His eyes just shifted from Stagg to McDougal's puffy face and reddened cheeks.

"We've met with investigators from the DA's office," Quinn said. "We've answered all their questions."

McDougal smiled wide. He puckered his mouth and shifted his eyes over at Dupuy's midnight-black ass. Dupuy dressed tonight like he was on his way to a Sunday fish fry, with a five-button green silk suit with yellow hankie in the pocket. "Mmm-hmm," McDougal said. "I guess we're getting some conflicting information. I just spoke to the DA's office and they said you and Chief Deputy Virgil have been combative and unhelpful."

"That's a lie," Colson said.

"Excuse me?" McDougal said. "Excuse me?"

"I said that's a lie," Colson said. "We have been cooperative in what was a justified shooting. If someone says different, they're either uninformed or stupid."

Dupuy jerked forward in his chair, eyes wide, Stagg enjoying a fine bit of old-time theater. "Come again, Sheriff? Come again? You don't think y'all being investigated for killing Police Chief Chappell is important? You think this is some kind of joke? My people take it real serious. Mr. McDougal's folks, too. I imagine you should know your place around here, Mr. Colson."

As expected, Sam Bishop, Jr., and Bobby Pickens were silent. They were told to steer clear of things and that was exactly what they'd do if they wanted their projects to go through.

"Sheriff Colson?" Bobby Pickens said.

Stagg turned quick to look at that red-faced peckerhead. Pickens had his hands over his mouth, contemplating this dumb-shit move.

Colson stood there.

"Some on this board feel this investigation into the shooting last April is complicating your sheriff's duties," he said. "What do you say?"

"I can do my job the same," Quinn said. "I stand behind my actions."

"Yes, sir," Pickens said.

That goddamn son of a bitch.

"At what point would you step down?" McDougal asked. "If you was arrested?"

From the crowd in the pews, Stagg saw that old drunk Sonny Stevens rise and walk down the aisle to stand with Quinn. God damn, this was fun. The only disappointment was Stevens seemed to be walking in a straight line. And when he started to speak, he didn't slur his words. "This line of questioning is improper," Stevens said, "and could and might be slanderous. Sheriff Colson has not been accused of a crime."

McDougal leaned back into his padded leather seat and belched. Dupuy looked down at his cell phone, starting to text. Stagg nodded and nodded, knowing he was going to have to get through to the whole town, and county, what exactly was at stake. "We're concerned, Sheriff," Stagg said. "We are worried about how this affects our people and the county you serve. We're not saying it has to be permanent, but perhaps until the investigation is completed, you and Deputy Virgil should step down."

"And when will that be?" Quinn said.

"I guess nobody knows that."

"Seems to me," Quinn said, "you know a lot of things before they happen or before they can be found."

"Sir?"

"I got a busted radio and a patrol car that need to be junked," Quinn said. "There's been two burglaries in the county, nine drug arrests, eighteen speeding tickets, and fourteen cases of assault since we last met. That information has been printed and handed out, as always. Are we finished?"

There was a mood in the room, a shifting nervous energy that Stagg could sense and feel and hoped Colson could as well. Lots of whispering and glares among the business owners, the players, and the busybodies in Tibbehah life. No one seemed satisfied with Colson's answer. He was being put on notice and everyone knew it.

Old Sonny Stevens leaned into Quinn, whispered into his ear. The young man and the old man walked out together. His girlfriend remained alone in the center seat, giving Stagg an *Eat shit and die* look. Damn, she had a fine little red mouth.

It was early night, darkness at 1930, as Quinn stepped out into the parking lot and saw the Big Green Machine parked sideways and off toward the main road. He and Sonny had parted at the back door, Sonny wanting him to come to his office first thing and work on some strategies to keep the coyotes at bay. "Best thing is to stay focused on the job," Sonny had said. "That way, when the shitstorm is over, you can hold your head high and stroll through the cannon smoke."

Boom had done a fine job on the used F-250, Quinn making damn sure to furnish his own vehicle rather than take the tricked-out truck Stagg and the Board of Supervisors had offered when he first took office. This one had a big engine, dually pipes, a roll bar, KC lights, and no strings attached. The Army-green paint gleamed in the fluorescent light from a recent waxing. He hit the unlock button in his coat pocket, his breath coming out in cloud bursts, and got halfway there when he spotted Stagg's man standing close to his vehicle.

"Cold night, ain't it?" the man called Ringold said.

Quinn nodded, maintaining eye contact, and opened the door. Hondo was inside, sleeping in the back on a horse blanket. Hondo stirred, yawned, and got to his feet.

"Mr. Stagg would like you and him to meet," Ringold said.

"What'd you call that in there?"

"In private."

"If Stagg wants a meet," Quinn said, "tell him to call Mary Alice at the SO. I'm off duty." He reached into his shirt pocket and pulled out a fresh La Gloria Cubana. He punched the bottom, lit the end, and propped a boot on the truck's running board.

"It would be in y'all's best interests."

"How do you figure?" Quinn said, smoke filling the air.

"Mr. Stagg has a proposition."

"Should have said it tonight," Quinn said. "I don't make deals in back of a jerk shack."

"You're a hard one, Ranger," Ringold said. He grinned a little, wearing a snug-fit denim jacket, Carhartt khakis, and tan combat boots. He kept a chrome Sig Sauer on his belt, as was his right. There was no doubt the man had a permit, but he'd check anyway.

"Good night," Quinn said.

"Which battalion?"

"Third Batt," Quinn said. "Fort Benning."

Ringold nodded. "I knew some of you," he said. "You know Ricardo Perez?"

"I do," Quinn said, hanging there, door open. Hondo moved up to the driver's seat and stood there, poised, growling nice and low.

"I figured," he said. "I knew him at Fort Bragg."

Quinn nodded. Ringold waited a beat, like he wanted Quinn to ask him about Bragg and the Special Forces, but Quinn stayed silent, staring at him. Quinn had heard Ringold had been 82nd Airborne and then Special Forces, but him knowing Ricardo was the first proof of it. Ringold brought it up because he wanted Quinn to know who he was dealing with.

"Can I ask you something, Sheriff Colson?"

Quinn nodded.

"Ain't it hard to slow down?" Ringold said. "Some days, I feel like I'm just itching out of my skin for a little action."

"What you do now is your call."

"And what is it that I do?" Ringold said, a streetlight shining off his bald head. He rubbed the stubble on his beard and grinned.

"You walk behind Stagg," Quinn said.

"Sure," Ringold said. "But not too far, Sergeant."

Quinn shrugged. The man was compact and hard, short and muscled, still dressing as if he were on patrol in Kandahar. His eyes were very light, with a strange intensity that was either high intelligence or batshit crazy.

"So you're saying no to a meet?"

"That's what I said."

"Mr. Stagg is a man of compromise."

"We could sit here for the rest of the night and debate what Mr. Stagg is a man of," Quinn said. "But I've got better plans."

From the reflection in his truck's side mirror, Quinn saw Ophelia Bundren wandering out of the county building, speaking with Sam Bishop, Jr., and Betty Jo Mize of the *Tibbehah Monitor*. The old woman leaned into Ophelia, whispered in her ear, and Ophelia walked away with a smile. She joined Quinn at his truck and he opened the passenger door, helping her up into the seat of the tall truck.

Ringold nodded to Quinn as Quinn passed him at the front bumper, neither man moving out of the way, Ringold closing in on Quinn's personal space. Ringold just stood in Quinn's headlights, flat-footed and immobile, as he backed out and turned out of the lot and onto the road.

"Just what was that all about?" Ophelia said, staring.

"He wanted to give himself a proper introduction," Quinn said.

25

"Do you think we might have a normal night, Quinn?" Ophelia asked. "We both turn off our cell phones. I'll make us some supper and we can sit on the couch and watch some television. No interruptions. No professional talk. We just act like regular folks."

"I'll turn off the scanner," Quinn said. "But I better keep my cell on."

"I guess you're right," she said. "Son of a bitch. I better, too. I just figured I'd try."

Ophelia had on a pair of faded Levi's and a tight black shirt. She'd twisted her brown hair up into a bun at the top of her head and had kicked off her shoes. Her toenails a bubble gum pink.

"What's for supper?" Quinn said.

"Well," Ophelia said, "I'm not cooking that greasy old Southern food like your momma. How about some pasta and a healthy salad? I have a bottle of red wine somewhere around here. We can sit on the couch and watch *The Bachelor*, forget all about those shitbag supervisors, Johnny Stagg, and murders from long past."

"What the hell's *The Bachelor*?"

"It's a show where one guy gets to date twenty-five women over a few weeks," she said. "At the end of the show, the bachelor gets to decide which one he's going to marry."

"In a few weeks?"

"Yeah, but they go on a bunch of dates at beaches, travel to exotic countries, and listen to a lot of crappy bands the producers are trying to promote. If you get picked each week, he gives you a dethorned rose. The only trouble comes when the bachelor, or sometimes it's a bachelorette, starts to make out and grub with multiple folks. You'll see drunk crying, catfights, people screaming at each other and throwing shit."

"I want to see that, I'll just go back on patrol."

"What'd you rather see?"

"I heard *3:10 to Yuma* is on tonight," Quinn said. "The real one, with Glenn Ford, not that god-awful remake."

"Don't you watch anything else besides westerns?"

"When I was younger, I used to watch a lot of action movies from the seventies," Quinn said. "But then Caddy pointed out that all I was doing was looking for my dad, running all the stunt sequences in slow motion, trying to get a glimpse of my father. After Caddy brought it to my attention, I just stopped."

"What about war movies?"

Quinn shook his head. "Hell no."

"Suit yourself," Ophelia said. "But you'd really like *The Bachelor*. Half the time the women are wearing flimsy little clothes or bikinis. They had one girl a few weeks ago that walked around the house without a stitch of clothes on. Of course they had her privates all blacked out. But, can you imagine doing that on national TV?"

"Pasta?"

"And salad," Ophelia said. "And red wine."

"Just me and you?" Quinn said. "On the couch, pretending to be normal people with normal jobs?"

"And Hondo, too."

Hondo was already on the couch, making himself at home, resting after a long day of roaming the farm and chasing deer, cattle, and rabbits. Ophelia uncorked a bottle, Quinn not being one to drink much wine but not wanting to make a thing of it. She poured each of them a glass and then started to cut up the vegetables for the salad. Ophelia, as she should, showed excellent precision with the paring knife.

"I don't want to complicate plans," Quinn said, "but you did leave me a message about something you'd found?"

"I found something in that file you gave me," Ophelia said, chopping and slicing carrots with a lot of dexterity and speed. "May not mean anything given the time frame. We can talk about it later, if you like."

Quinn drank some wine. Wasn't bad. But he would've rather had a cold Bud or Coors anytime. "I'd like to know."

"There was some correspondence between your uncle and the FBI office in Jackson," she said. "In the letters, it appeared that he'd sent them the remains of the dead man's burned clothes and a pair of boots that were pretty much intact. It seems like old Dr. Stevens did take a dental record or at least tried to. The body was a mess and back then there wasn't any DNA testing or reason to take tissue samples."

"What happened to the body?"

"Potter's field," Ophelia said.

Quinn drank some wine and his face must've shown something, because she reached into the refrigerator and popped the top of a can of Coors.

"Gracias."

She poured the rest of his wine in her glass and then got out a pot to boil some water. Quinn stood there with her, all of it feeling nice and normal. Ophelia could fill out a T-shirt, and her bare feet were cute as hell. Something really comfortable about her little place, all the low light and the sparseness of the rooms, with paintings of old barns and pastures and wildlife. Quinn just hoped the damn cell wouldn't ring in the next few hours, which would be a minor miracle.

"I'll call the Feds tomorrow," Quinn said. "We didn't have a lot of luck with the DA."

"I wonder why?"

"No kidding."

"You look a million miles away," she said. "You doing OK? I'm worried about you."

"Right here," Quinn said, reaching for Ophelia's hand and pulling her back into him close. He wrapped his arm around her stomach and started to kiss the back of her neck, feeling her shudder a bit as he placed a hand up under her T-shirt. Her stomach was flat and hard, Ophelia inhaling a deep breath, closing her eyes, tilting her head back into Quinn. Quinn could taste her skin on his lips and moved his hand over the first button of her Levi's, and then the second, and then he slid his hand between her legs. Ophelia became a bit unstable on her feet, reaching back with both hands, arching her back, and feeling for Quinn's hair and face and then turning to him, Quinn kissing her harder now and finding her in his fingertips, the water audibly boiling on the stove, Quinn hoping like hell she didn't hear it. But a buzzer sounded and she pushed him away, catching her breath, buttoning her jeans with one hand and smoothing down her T-shirt with the other. She picked up the paring knife and pointed it straight at Quinn's heart.

"Sit," she said.

"Yes, ma'am."

"Stay."

Hondo peered up from the couch, his rabies tags jingling on his collar. Quinn smiled.

"Drink your beer," she said. "I'll let you know when supper is ready."

Quinn took his beer and found a spot on the couch next to Hondo. He picked up the remote and found *3:10 to Yuma* just at the scene when Van Heflin agrees to take Glenn Ford back to prison. Seemed like as good a place as any to begin.

26

I appreciated you helping," Caddy said early the next morning. "I could've gotten Boom when he gets off at the County Barn, but it'll be nice to get this all distributed before then. It's supposed to get down to five degrees tonight."

"Remind me why we live here again?" Diane Tull said, driving her old Ford, loaded down with boxes of warm clothes from The River and twelve radiators the Jericho General Store had donated. "I could sell seed and feed down in Florida."

"There are times when I think this county is a paradise," Caddy said, leaning against the passenger-door window, farmland and long stretches of pine zipping by. "But then you see the ugliness of what we've done to this place, all the logging, busted-up trailers, and stripping of anything that can make a buck. We didn't need a tornado to rip this town apart. We just needed a few more good years."

"God gives us spring to make amends for it," Diane said. "The wisteria and the daffodils and the trees coming alive again. It makes you remember this is a fertile place. That's the reason our crazy ancestors staked out this land, thinking their families could thrive here. They could grow their own food, hunt what meat they needed."

"Our people came here from North Carolina in 1846," Caddy said. "Before that, they were kicked out of Scotland and Ireland. My momma's family got some Indian in her, too. Choctaw."

"I got some Cherokee," Diane said. "Maybe the reason only this one strand of my hair is white. You think I should dye it?"

"No way," Caddy said. "That's your signature. I think it makes you look hot."

"A hot momma at fifty?" Diane said, driving with two fingers on the wheel, looking for the turnoff on past the Richards place. "Hmm."

"I don't mean to get personal," Caddy said. "But you been dating any?"

"I was seeing this fella from Tupelo last year, nice hair and good teeth, but I found out he was married and had two kids," she said. "I met him online and he said he was divorced. But things started happening that didn't add up. He'd take phone calls outside, come over at weird times, and never stay the night. I finally saw on his cell phone where he'd been texting his wife that he was at a tool convention in Atlanta. When he came back and started to love on me, I told him the convention was closed and he needed to hit the road. And take his goddamn tool with him. He started crying like a little boy, saying he'd been having personal issues, his wife was cold and all that. But, Caddy, I just don't have time for that shit."

Caddy was silent. She stared out the window, passing more clear-cut acres and ugly logging roads twisting into the hills. Seemed like everything of worth in Tibbehah was cut down, loaded on a truck, and taken out of the state. This place must've been a garden back during the Choctaws' time, before a backhoe and bulldozer could rip the guts out of a place.

"I'm through with dating and men and all that mess," Caddy said. "I miss Jamey Dixon every waking second. But to think about ever being with anyone else makes me want to just throw up."

"Hadn't been long, Caddy," Diane said, slowing, taking a left turn down the county road to Fate. They would drop off the heaters at the

Primitive Baptist Church and stop off at ten houses who'd requested cold-weather clothes. Caddy had the names of the families listed in a spiral notebook in her hand.

"Men are good for two things and two things only," Caddy said. "Both starting with the letter *F*. Since I got myself clean, I've learned to fix plenty on my own."

Diane pulled into the dirt lot in front of the little Primitive Baptist Church, a white clapboard building with a small hand-painted sign at the roadside. There were already twenty people outside, waiting in the cold, for them to arrive with the heaters. The preacher, a wiry old man named Shelton Graves, met Caddy and they went through the list together about which families were in luck, which ones would need more sweaters and blankets for the next few days. Mississippi wasn't a place that prepped much for cold weather—the bad nights, the freezing nights, people treated like some kind of strange, cruel event. Back during the ice storm of '94, the worst winter weather most people in the state had ever seen, some houses way out in the county didn't have power for nearly two months.

Pastor Graves and Diane Tull pulled the radiator boxes off the truck and passed them into the hands of a thick-bodied bald man in a flannel shirt and Dale Jr. cap who stacked them neatly. Caddy had jumped up into the back of the truck, sorting through the boxes, looking for the baby clothes to hand over to one of the women who was waiting. Two more boxes, clearly marked in Magic Marker, were dropped off, and then Diane and Caddy were circling out of the lot, with a wave to the pastor and his people.

"What would people do around here without churches?" Caddy said.

"Starve," Diane said.

"I don't know if the South is as religious as it is practical."

"Southerners have never been good at practical," Diane said. "We're stubborn, clannish people who don't like being told what to do. And that makes us easy targets for the greedy."

"I still believe there's a lot of good," Caddy said, smiling. "That took me some while to find out. But if you look for it, believe in it, you'll find it. You look for the darkness and that shit will swallow you whole."

Diane put both hands on the wheel, making a tricky sharp turn, the truck a little hard to handle, as it never had power steering, rolling like a leaden tank down the busted dirt road. "I just like to keep an eye out," she said. "Surprises have never been much fun."

"There's been no official deal offered," Sonny Stevens said. "But that conversation over in Oxford was pure, unadulterated bullshit. I don't care if they got a hundred different rifles of yours, Lillie. You were there to protect Sheriff Colson and you performed your duty."

"Except it wasn't my rifle."

"I know it wasn't," Stevens said. "Y'all have gotten in with some folks who play dirty for a living. I don't care for it, but it's the way they do business."

"They seemed real proud of the timing," Quinn said. "They indict this month, they can take us to trial just weeks before the election."

"They'll lose," Stevens said. "But we can't stop an indictment. Everyone knows you can indict a goddamn ham sandwich."

"So what would a deal mean?" Lillie said.

"Please excuse my legalese here," Stevens said, "but they're just trying to fuck with you. That bullshit they floated past us about that cold case? You think they were just shooting the breeze? You make an arrest and they drop everything. Even if you just work with them, they may back off some."

"Maybe I'll have time to print up some new election banners?" Quinn said. "'Vote for Colson. Indicted on Lesser Charges.'"

"You sure are taking this well," Stevens said.

The law office was hot as hell that afternoon, the old man liking to crank up the heat to nearly ninety degrees, Quinn rolling up his sleeves as they spoke. Lillie fanned her face with a printout of confiscated items from her house. Outside, a brittle wind rattled the windows, rain from earlier freezing along the porch bannister and freezing the drops in the bare trees along the Square.

"I did do a bit of asking around about that case," Stevens said. "Lots of folks remember. But no one—and I mean no one—wants to talk about it."

Quinn nodded.

"I don't see how you can ever make a case on something so damn old," Stevens said. "The DA isn't even offering a realistic time line to make something work. Putting a case together could take y'all years. This rush doesn't make any sense at all."

"Funny thing is," Quinn said, "we were on this already. We didn't need someone trying to bribe us or hold our ass to the fire."

"Welcome to a political shitstorm," Stevens said. "What happened back then was barbaric. There hadn't been a lynching in this town for thirty years before that. People got sick over what happened to those two little girls and didn't want to wait for the process of law. It's an affront to everything I believe in."

"Can you at least give us some names?" Lillie asked. "They don't have to give statements, maybe just lead us in the right direction."

"This happened thirty-seven years ago. It's a history lesson. You're not going to find anyone who wants to discuss it."

"It's not history to Diane Tull," Quinn said.

"Not many folks are going to rally around this fella who got killed," Stevens said.

"Because he was black?" Quinn said.

"Because he killed a young woman and raped another," Stevens said. "There were town people, not county people, who knew what was going to happen to this fella and turned their backs. The man I spoke with was part of a group of men who gave the go-ahead to make this happen."

"Who?" Quinn said.

"I can't say," Stevens said, leaning back into his chair, the day darkening in the windows behind him. "I'm sorry. He's a client. This was said in confidence. He believes his hands are clean."

"You always keep it so goddamn hot in here, Mr. Stevens?" Lillie said.

"It's twenty degrees outside," Stevens said. "We might get an ice storm tonight."

Lillie looked to Quinn. She shook her head. "You want to tell him or should I?"

"Go ahead, Lil," Quinn said.

"That man who was found burned up on Jericho Road never touched those girls."

"How can you possibly know that?" Stevens said.

"Diane Tull saw the man who raped her a few weeks after they killed this man," Lillie said. "It's torn the shit out of her every day with everyone telling her to keep her mouth shut. She blames herself. These good people in town should be ashamed."

Stevens swallowed. He nodded and rubbed his freshly shaved jawline. "I didn't know that," he said. "I never heard they got the wrong man. Is she sure on this? Hell, she was just a little girl."

Quinn nodded.

"Jesus."

"But given our personal shitstorm," Lillie said. "We won't be following up on anything but looking for new employment."

"Y'all lose this election and God knows what kind of people will be running things," Stevens said. "When you came back, Quinn, I had some hope for this place, that Johnny Stagg wouldn't piss his mark on every inch of this county."

"Seems like the new Johnny Stagg has more to lose than ever," Quinn said.

"He's a changed man, Quinn," Stevens said, shaking his head. "Haven't you heard? Everything straight and legal and for the good of this county."

"Might not be out in the open," Quinn said, "but Stagg's got a pretty sweet deal going on the side."

"Beyond the Rebel?" Stevens said.

"Yes, sir," Quinn said. "Nobody can ever say the man suffers for ambition."

27

The first real thing Chains LeDoux ever said to Jason Colson was outside a Tupelo beer joint, both men pissing against a brick wall. Chains was so drunk that he needed one hand to brace himself as he turned to Jason and said, "Who the fuck are you, man?"

Jason finished up, zipped up his fly, and said, "I don't know what to tell you."

LeDoux was a mean drunk, always looking to fight after a few shots of Jack, and tonight he'd had a whole bottle. He stumbled over to Jason, jabbing him with a dirty finger and saying, "Snitches are a dying breed."

"I'm not a snitch."

"You expect me to believe all your bullshit?" Chains said. "You just show up in Jericho and get in with Big Doug, talking about how you make movies out in Hollywood? Bullshit, man. I bet you ain't even been to Hollywood. You're a damn humper for J. Edgar Hoover."

"Hoover's been dead since '72."

"Well," LeDoux said, "whatever Fed got you wanting to break us. That's what all you want, right? You hate us? Hate our kind because we don't work for the man. We don't stand in lines and punch the clock and dance like *puppets. We ride, we screw our old ladies, we get high and loaded. Why you want to shut that down?"*

"I'm not trying to shut anybody down," Jason said. Feeling a little uneasy, as Chains had that .38 tucked in his belt, leather vest wide open, eyes burning hot with Jack and little red pills. "I'm just passing through, visiting some family. Come on, let's drink."

"You're a fucking snitch, Colson," LeDoux said. "Right?"

"Just a stuntman."

"What movies have you done?"

"I've done a lot," Jason said. "I work for an outfit called Stuntmen Unlimited. You don't want me to ride with y'all and that's your thing, man. Either we drink and hang out or I'm gone."

"You're gone when I say, motherfucker," Chains said, "or I'll knock your teeth down your throat."

A few of the boys had wandered outside the beer joint, shouldering past one another, trying to get a good view of what was about to happen, lots of shit-eating grins on their faces. Big Doug wasn't among them. Big Doug was inside chatting up a big-titted cocktail waitress named Connie who told him he reminded her of Grizzly Adams.

"I worked on The Longest Yard, a TV show called Kodiak."

"Never heard of it."

"It's about an Alaska state patrolman."

"I knew you were a fucking pig."

"It's a TV show," Jason said. "I did the stunts."

Chains wavered on his feet, a few of the boys rallied around him, standing behind and around him. Stillwell high as a goddamn kite, wearing big yellow circular glasses and giggling like an idiot, a can of Coors in one hand and cigarette in the other.

"Come on," Stillwell said. "Give him a break, Chains. He don't mean nothing."

"What fucking shows?" Chains said. "I want to know."

"W.W. and the Dixie Dance Kings, a western called Take a Hard Ride with Jim Brown."

"That sounds like bullshit," Chains said, scratching his dirty beard. "How you gonna be a stunt double for some big-ass nigger?"

"You know what? I don't have to tell you who I am. Either you believe me or you don't. I don't give a god damn."

Chains snickered. The door kept on opening and closing to the little beer joint. A couple lazy-eyed women came out and sat on the bikes, passing a joint to each other. His enforcer Gangrene shifting his weight. A lot of smoke. It was July, Mississippi heat coming up through the dirt and gravel.

"If you're as tough as you say, how about I see you take a punch?"

Jason kept that eye contact with Chains. Here we go. Here we fucking go.

"You want to hit me?" Jason said. "OK. Maybe it will make you shut your mouth."

Chains laughed, scratched his bare belly, and spit on the gravel. Music came from inside the joint. Led Zeppelin. "Candy Store Rock." He stepped up two paces, Jason seeing it from five miles away, a big unwieldy roundhouse punch right for his head. Jason did not move, did not duck, did not flinch, took the blow to the jaw and staggered back a bit, rubbing his jaw, feeling the lights go off and on and his teeth rattling a bit. He spit out a little blood and nodded to Chains.

"Now you," Chains said. "See what you got, man. Let's see what you got, fucking stuntman."

"I'm good."

"I said fucking do it."

"I'm good, man," Jason said. "You wanted to take a shot. I let you take a shot. It's what I do. I don't feel things like regular folks."

"I say a Fed would never mix it up with folks like us," Chains said. "Might look bad in court."

Jason felt his jaw swelling and shook his head. He spit some more blood.

"Unless you're scared?" Chains said. "Scared it might hurt feelings and I might shoot your ass."

Jason felt that familiar tension in his neck and shoulders. He nodded and took in a breath, catching the eyes of about everybody in the whole Born Losers standing out in the parking lot, an arrow on a cheap mobile sign offering 2 for 1 tonight. Zeppelin kept on jamming inside the Tupelo beer hall. Jason put his hands on his waist and looked direct to Chains, behind him all those gleaming Harleys, chrome and leather, lined up in just a perfect way.

"Boy is scared?"

Blood rushed into Jason's face, heart pumping like a piston, and he walked up to that nasty, stinky, bearded son of a bitch with wolf eyes and threw a hard right into his soft, sweaty belly and then followed with a left hook that toppled Chains LeDoux over like an lumbering old sack. He was flat to the gravel, eyes closed, sucking in air, as his woman came over and started to comfort him. Big Doug walked up to Chains and spilled some Coors down on his face. Hank Stillwell kicked at him with his toe. And another rider they called Slow Joe helped Chains to his feet, still half conscious, as Big Doug tossed some more Coors in his face, a beer joint baptism.

Chains lolled his head to the side, his whole weight being supported by Big Doug, head and open gray eyes coming around to Jason. He was missing a couple teeth.

He elbowed himself away from Big Doug and staggered toward Jason, pulling out that .38, Zeppelin playing "Tea for One." Jason knew all the songs, as he had the album back at his apartment in Venice that he'd probably never see again. Chains aimed the .38 right between Jason Colson's eyes and said, "Scared now?"

Jason didn't answer.

"God forgives," he said. "Born Losers never fucking forget."

Chains turned his head and spit out a mess of blood, "You know what I do when people look at me like I'm some kind of animal?"

Jason again didn't answer.

"I fucking feed on it, man," LeDoux said. "I love it."

He stretched the gun out farther in his hand, thumbed back the hammer, and squeezed the trigger. Click. He squeezed it again. Click. And four more times, the hammer falling on an empty chamber.

"Fuck," he said. "I guess I forgot to load the motherfucker."

The Born Losers all started laughing, a big fat woman who rode with one of the boys with the shrillest of giggles. Even Gangrene smiled a row of rotten teeth. Chains tossed the pistol over his shoulder and embraced Jason in a big bear hug. "Welcome, brother."

Over his shoulder, Big Doug held up a shiny new leather vest with a back patch reading BORN LOSERS and a front patch reading 1 PERCENTER.

"No need for probation for a crazy son of a bitch like you," Chains said. "Put on your colors and let's ride till dawn."

There were hoots and rebel yells, and the boys showered him with Coors and Budweiser while the vest was slid on him by Chains LeDoux himself, the man's mouth a ragged, bloody mess. Despite every lick of sense he had, Jason smiled.

The engines to the Harleys cranked and gunned louder than ever, Jason feeling the laughter and the brotherhood and thinking to himself, This may be the dumbest goddamn stunt I've ever pulled.

The boys pulled out on the long ribbon of blacktop.

And Jason followed.

28

H ow's your ass feeling?" Boom said. "Heard about the supervisors' meeting and all that shit."

"Just like you said."

"Some men don't have a lick of honor," Boom said. "Some don't have no sense. Seems like those on the board blessed to have neither."

"Bobby Pickens stood tall," Quinn said. "I'll remember that."

"That's because he ain't on the tit," Boom said. "Hadn't been in the crew long enough to make it work for him. Give him time."

"That's hard," Quinn said.

"But the truth."

The paved roads and patches on the bridges had started to ice over across the county by midnight. Quinn and Boom kept to the dirt roads, roving up toward Carthage where the shootings had gone down in April. Quinn had been out officially a few times after the storm, walking the ground with investigators and looking for evidence of the unknown shooter. But since the summer, Johnny Stagg had locked up the front gate, surrounding the acreage with six-foot chain-link and wrapping the entire property with a lot of *No Trespassing* signs.

Quinn parked the Big Green Machine up into a fire road that wound through the woods over the eastern ridge of the valley. The road was grown up in brush and small trees and provided some decent conceal-ment if Stagg had any of his people on patrol. But in all the times Quinn had walked that fire road, watching the airstrip, he'd not crossed paths with a single guard. Stagg too cocky to think anyone would scale the fence and see his operation.

A few months ago, Quinn had cut back a portion of the fencing and closed it back up with metal clamps. He opened it for Boom and himself, and left it open if they needed to haul ass.

The temperature had dropped down to ten degrees, and Quinn wore a black Smith & Wesson shooting jacket, Under Armour thermals, and a black wool sweater with black paratrooper pants and his Merrell boots. He carried his Beretta, a combat knife, a Leatherman tool, and a Reming-ton pump shotgun. Boom wore his old camo Guard jacket and carried a Colt .44 Anaconda, although lately he'd taught himself how to balance and shoot a shotgun using a special harness.

They followed the path nearly two klicks before turning off the road and finding the vantage point Quinn always used to watch the planes land and take off, keeping a log of their tail numbers, with times and dates. He never got any closer than maybe five hundred meters up the hill but had logged in a lot of activity since early November, when the landing strip had been resurfaced and the Quonset huts rebuilt.

Quinn got down on one knee and aimed a pair of Bushnell night vision binoculars. The airstrip was lit up, with tiny blue lights along the runway, and there was a bright white light coming from one of the huts. Three pickup trucks and an SUV were parked along the main road coming from Stagg's front gate. Ice had gathered on the old oaks and scraggly pines. The wind was cold as hell, shooting through that narrow valley and rattling the brittle branches. Quinn passed the binoculars to Boom and took out a small notepad from his jacket, writing down the tag num-bers on the trucks and the SUV.

"Tennessee plates," Boom said. "Johnny been spending a lot of time in Memphis?"

"Johnny goes to the money," Quinn said. "He seems to have lost interest in the Booby Trap and the Rebel. He's there maybe two, three days a week. Most of the time, he's out of Tibbehah County."

"Who's he working with?"

"Don't know."

"You gonna lay all this on the Feds?" Boom said.

"When I can find someone to trust," Quinn said. "The last Feds who came to Tibbehah and I didn't get along. They blamed me for the cartel action around here and bought Stagg's bullshit."

"That was your own damn fault," Boom whispered, handing back the binoculars. "You screwing one of their goddamn agents. Woman was mad as hell when you kept stuff back from her."

"I've made a few mistakes in my life."

"Shit, Quinn," Boom said, "a few? You get a case going against Stagg, how about you keep your dick in your pants?"

"Lesson learned."

"What else you need?" Boom said. "Ain't no reason for that mother-fucker to have this set up without moving drugs or guns or pussy, right?"

"Not sure what he's moving," Quinn said. "Lots of times, I just see a lot of fat cats from Jackson flying in for a quick-and-dirty at the Rebel. They get their pecker pulled and they're on the next flight out. Sometimes Stagg brings some girls out to the huts here."

"Men got to fly to get their peckers pulled?" Boom said. "That's some hard-up shit."

There was some motion by one of the Quonset huts and Quinn peered down along the roadway where the cars had been parked. Three black males in big jackets, two of them with hoods up, walked out to the SUV, a black Escalade, and stood by the hatch, smoking cigarettes. Quinn again shared the binoculars, then handed them back, the men crawling into the

Cadillac. They cranked the ignition, turned on the headlights, but just sat in the road. Exhaust poured from the rear of the vehicle.

"Never knew Johnny Stagg to work with black folks," Boom said, "unless they was mopping the floor at the Rebel or cooking that chicken-fried steak."

"He's got black girls working the pole at the Booby Trap."

"Good man," Boom said. "Progressive as hell."

"Those boys don't look like politicians," Quinn said.

"Nope."

"I'll run their tag," Quinn said. "I bet that SUV is stolen. A throwaway for whatever they're taking over state lines."

"Never knew you racist," Boom said. "Driving while black."

"Guilt by association."

"You want to get down closer?" Boom said. "I don't give a fuck. Let Stagg's boys come on out and say hello."

The SUV finally knocked into gear and made a U-turn away from the huts and back down the road to the exit of Stagg's compound. Quinn nodded to Boom and they followed a little zigzagging trail down the hillside, worn smooth by deer, to the road, where they walked in the shadows to the main hut. The hillside was steep, Quinn and Boom walking sideways to keep their footing.

The hut was windowless, the front door shut against the cold. The big metal building vibrating to the sound of rap music playing inside. Quinn smiled and Boom just shook his head. "Johnny Stagg got him a little juke out in the country," Boom said. "Shaking that ass?"

"His property," Quinn said. "He can do what he likes."

"Got his black friends coming down from Memphis," Boom said. "How you like to see Johnny Stagg shaking that bony white butt?"

Quinn was silent. He held up a hand as the front door to the Quonset hut opened and a girl stepped outside. She was young and black, wearing a rabbit fur jacket and tall white leather boots. She lit up a cigarette and leaned against the metal building. She looked exhausted.

"Ten degrees," Boom said. "Must be hot up in there."

Quinn used the binoculars again where he and Boom crouched in a little ravine and could see the girl's hair, face, and neck were damp with sweat. She finished the cigarette and walked back into the hut, the door slamming behind her, and not twenty seconds later Stagg's boy Ringold walked out and stood in the wide swath of light coming from a security light.

He had on dark utility pants and boots, an Army-green fleece jacket, and a green watch cap over his bald head. He looked to the airfield and checked his watch and moved out of the light and into the darkness by the airfield. He had a weapon in his right hand. As Quinn scanned Ringold with the Bushnells, he recognized a Heckler & Koch MP5 submachine gun. The weapon could shoot eight hundred rounds a minute, often holding a thirty-bullet clip.

Quinn put his hand to Boom's shoulder. Boom and Quinn stayed stock-still.

Ringold walked out onto the airfield, looked to the north, the small blue lights stretching out far into the distance. He was a shadow, machine gun in his right hand, as he moved back to the Quonset hut, still pumping with rap music, and shut the door.

"Feds probably don't give a shit about Stagg running pussy."

"Those boys didn't come all the way from Tennessee for tail," Quinn said. "There's plenty of that in Memphis."

"Wonder who's doing the buying and who's doing the selling?" Boom said.

29

Diane got up early the next morning, earlier than usual, to run by the Sonic and get a Breakfast Burrito for her mother. Her mother lived in an assisted-care facility just down the road from county hospital. Her memory had gotten worse and worse, a radio frequency that would sometimes come in strong and clear and other times faint and distant. That morning, the signal was medium, her mother needing a little prodding when Diane walked in. There was a big warm smile from the wheelchair, her mother sitting crooked in a flowered housecoat, looking out the window, but there was that hesitation of recognition. "Mom, it's me. Diane."

And her mother's smile grew even larger when Diane sat the Sonic sack on the table and opened up the burrito and tater tots. She might have forgotten her own daughter, her own name, and the last twenty years of her life, but she sure knew the burrito and was still exact about the eggs, sausage, and cheese. Tots on the side, and black coffee. And here was her feast.

Her mother, whose name was Alma, shared the room with another woman with Alzheimer's, this woman just recently moving in and not being able to talk, only putter about and hum. She'd sing spirituals and clap and ask you to join in whenever the mood struck her. Luckily, she was off for some therapy and Diane could sit with her mother, wheeling her over to the table and unwrapping the burrito.

"How you been, Mom?"

"Have you seen your father? He's run off again."

Diane's father had been dead now twenty-two years.

"No, ma'am," she said. "Haven't seen him."

"He's like that," she said. "Can't be trusted."

That much being true, the tight-ass Holy Roller preacher eventually running off with the Mary Kay saleswoman in town and starting a new family in Tupelo, working for a right-wing Christian radio station. That was her biological father, not old Mr. Shed Castle, her stepfather, also dead.

"Do you remember when I got hurt?" Diane said. "When I was in the hospital?"

"You had a fine boy," her mother said. "Big, too."

"When that man hurt me, Mom," Diane said. "When I got shot?"

"Who shot you?" her mother said, tilting her head. "You look fine to me."

"A long time back," she said. "I was with Lori Stillwell."

"A sweet girl," her mother said. "A lovely girl. Hair down to her butt. Shiny like a shampoo commercial."

"Yes," Diane said. "Lori was beautiful. Do you remember when that man came for us? That man who hurt us?"

There was a darkness, a passing of light, in the dim blue eyes of her mother. She had a mouthful of the burrito and kept on eating, but there were wheels turning, a shifting and searching somewhere in the mind, trying to place what was being asked. She chewed and chewed. Diane just sat there, a bright sun coming up over the little parking lot facing Cotton Road. "Lori died."

Diane turned to her mother. "Yes, Mom," she said. "Do you recall?"

"Poor girl died," she said. "You almost died. God. Are you all right? Where is your father? Where did he go? I told him he'd get hurt. Those people would hurt him."

"Who, Mom?" Diane said. "Who would hurt him?"

Her mother chewed some more, thinking on things. "These tater tots are crispy. They are just so tasty."

"Where did Dad go?" Diane said. The morning sun seemed to leach all the color from the hoods and roofs of the cars, everything in a dull gray light, cars zipping past on Cotton Road. A sad concrete birdbath outside the window, dirty water frozen in the bowl.

"Lori's father," her mother said. "He wanted your father to come with him. He knew what to do. He was a very bad man. All of those men were bad."

"Who?"

"He had very strange eyes, that one," she said. "He looked like a wolf, with long black hair. Gray eyes. He wanted your father to come. He wanted your father to see what they had done. They were all very proud. I told him no. Where is he? Did he go with them?"

"Where?" Diane said. "Where, Mom? Who are you talking about?"

"Out to that tree," her mother said. "There was a gift hanging from the tree. The man had something for us. He was very happy."

"Who?"

Her mother took another bite, body and head crooked as if the world was spinning a little strange for her, trying to find her balance. Light passed in and out of her eyes. She swallowed. Her hands shook as she lifted the coffee and took a sip, some spilling on the table. Diane wiped it up. Her mother looked up at her, smiling. "Hello," her mother said. "You are somebody? Aren't you?"

"Yes, ma'am," Diane said, patting her mother's hand. "Just a friend."

Lillie Virgil ran roll call at the morning meeting with deputies Dave Cullison, Art Watts, Ike McCaslin, and Kenny. Kenny hadn't missed a patrol since the tornado ripped through his family home, killing both his parents. He'd driven his father, mortally wounded, on an ATV out to the field where his dead mother was found, sucked from their house and tossed a quarter mile away. He buried them, tended to their legal affairs, and set about clearing the destruction on his family land. Lillie had tried to speak to him about it many times, but instead Kenny would rather talk about his dog, a black Lab he'd rescued a year earlier who'd become his best friend.

Kenny arrived first, husky and beaming, looking forward to the day's patrol.

The night had yielded a little action: attempted robbery at the Dixie gas station ("attempt" perhaps too strong a word, as the robber fled immediately when the cashier, Miss Peaches, pulled Luther Varner's .357 from under the counter), a thirteen-year-old girl had run away from home for two hours before being found eating raisin toast at the Rebel, a domestic between a common-law couple, fighting over the purchase of a fifty-inch television, and eight traffic accidents, on account of the iced roads. Most of the ice had started to thaw at first light, but another cold front was expected to pound them tonight and Lillie ran through which wreckers would be on call.

"What'd Miss Peaches say to the robber?" Ike McCaslin asked, rubbing his eyes and giving that slow, easy smile of his. He was a tall, reedy black man who'd been with the SO longer than anyone.

"She knew him," Lillie said. "It was the youngest Richardson boy who lives with his sister up on Perfect Circle Road. He just walked in and said, 'Give it up,' and Miss Peaches aimed the weapon at his crotch and told him to go get his narrow ass back home or she'd shoot his pecker clean off."

"Miss Peaches," Ike said. "She don't take no shit."

"No, sir," Lillie said. "Kenny, you got anything needs a follow today?"

"Need to check up on those mowers getting stolen out on 351," Kenny said. "Mary Alice had a call about another theft last night, but it was on toward the Ditch. Mr. Davis had a zero-turn Toro that he used for work. Someone hooked up the mower to the trailer and just rode off."

"Art? Dave?"

"Same old shit," Dave Cullison said. Dave was still wearing a heavy parka and gloves from running traffic detail at the high school.

"Where's Quinn?" Art said.

"Had a meeting," she said.

"Are those bastards in Oxford going to leave both y'all alone?" Art said. "I'm about getting sick of everyone asking me about it. It's as if people in this county can't recall old cross-eyed Leonard Chappell being an A-1 shitbird since we were kids."

"Don't know," Lillie said, hopping off the desk. "Don't care. Let's hit the road."

Lillie snatched up her cold-weather coat and Tibbehah ball cap as Mary Alice poked her head into the SO meeting room and said that Lillie had some company. "I went ahead and sent him to your office," Mary Alice said. "Hope that's all right. E. J. Royce."

"Yes, ma'am," Lillie said, and then muttered "Shit" to herself, following the hallway to her door. The door was old and heavy, with the top half pebbled glass reading LILLIE VIRGIL CHIEF DEPUTY, along with the official shield of Tibbehah County law enforcement.

She opened the door to find Royce standing by her desk, puttering about, looking through some of her personal effects and smiling up at her as if there was nothing to it. "Morning, Miss Virgil," Royce said. "You asked that I stop by if I wanted to follow up on that old case. So here I am."

It looked and smelled as if Royce hadn't bathed in a few days. He still had that ever-present dirty white stubble on his face. He wore the same threadbare flannel shirt and wash-worn Liberty overalls. He'd removed his trucker hat, the meager white hair that remained on his head stuck up high like a rooster's comb.

"You want some coffee?" Lillie said.

"No, ma'am," he said. "Just figured me and you might have a heart-to-heart, you being the senior of the folks in this office. Quinn kind of came to the scene late. I don't think he understands or respects the work of Sheriff Beckett."

"Sheriff Beckett was on the take."

"That hadn't been proven."

"What you got, Mr. Royce?"

The old man scratched his stubbled cheeks and smiled. His teeth were yellowed and crooked, one eyetooth capped in gold. "Just wanted to see how things was progressing from one lawman to another."

He kind of grinned when he said that last bit, eyes taking in Lillie's posture and hands on her wide hips. Lillie eyed him and nodded a bit. "You just want to know what we're doing since this was your case at one time?"

"Yes, ma'am."

"You didn't seem to be interested the other day."

"Y'all kind of caught me with my pants down," he said. "I was just waking up and not thinking. When y'all left, I started to kind of wonder why you and Hamp's nephew would be kicking all this mess up. Are you some kind of special friends with the Tull girl?"

Lillie was five foot eight in bare feet but five foot ten in her boots that day. She stepped forward two paces and looked down at E. J. Royce's bald head. "Do you have something to say?"

"Relax there, darling," he said. "I don't care which way y'all's pendulum swings. What concerns me is y'all making a mess of what happened. I mean, when it all gets down to it, who gives a shit?"

"Who gives a shit that a young woman was murdered and another raped?"

"That ain't it," Royce said, his eyes glowing with an alcoholic heat. His cheeks so red, it looked as if he'd applied some rouge. "I just can't figure out why y'all have interest in that nigger they strung up."

"Excuse me?"

"We got the right man," he said. "That nigger took them girls. Why on God's Green do y'all want to make something of it? Justice was done."

Lillie crossed her arms over her chest. "Sit down, Mr. Royce."

"I'm just fine."

"Sit the fuck down, Royce."

Royce sat. He seemed amused by the whole thing, grinning and sort of laughing, thinking the world sure had turned into a funny place. He craned his head back and forth, studying Lillie's personal mementos on the way. "Who's that with all them medals on their neck?"

"That was the SEC championship," Lillie said. "I shot a perfect score. I'm prone to steadiness when my mind comes to it."

"Oh, hell," Royce said. "You are a pistol. I can't even imagine what old Sheriff Beckett would think about his wild-ass nephew running the show, ruining his name for some wandering nigger and having some smart-mouth dyke woman as his sidekick. What's the world coming to?"

Lillie did not speak. She breathed slowly. The door cracked open a little and Kenny stuck his portly body inside, obviously listening from the hall. "Everything OK?" he said.

"Mr. Royce was just leaving."

Royce laughed, showing rows of uneven teeth, and stood, putting that old trucker hat on his rooster hair. His entire being smelled of burned-up cigarettes, ashen and dead.

"You know why people like you don't bother me?"

Royce grinned.

"'Cause all of y'all are dying off," Lillie said. "Less and less of you every day. You lost. Thank Jesus."

Royce turned to Lillie, clenched his jaw, and spit on the floor, before following Kenny out of her office. Kenny hung by the door, wide-eyed, before shutting it.

"This man gives you a bit of trouble, you toss his ass in the tank," Lillie said. "And, for God's sake, make sure he takes a shower. He smells like flaming dog shit."

30

G lad you stopped by, Quinn," Johnny Stagg said. "Sure is a fine morning. Cold. But fine just the same. Come on back with me. We can talk a bit."

"I'd rather talk out here, Johnny," Quinn said. "How about right in the restaurant? Just so people won't start talking about me behind my back."

Stagg stopped midstride, having just turned in to the hallway by the public toilets. He nodded, grinned, and said, "Sure, wherever you like, Sheriff. You had breakfast? I can have Willie James fry you up some eggs and bacon. I think we still got some hot biscuits."

"I'm good."

"What brings you here, Quinn?"

"Your man Ringold said you wanted to talk," he said. "So let's talk."

"Come on back to my booth," Stagg said, walking on ahead. "I keep this place special for friends and family."

Quinn ignored the last remark, though he wanted to say that he was neither and didn't want to be. He followed Stagg to the crescent-moon shape of red vinyl and sat down. Stagg had moved some of his famous head shots of celebrities out here. Apparently, one time he'd had the honor of serving Jim Henson a plate of pancakes. And there was Jim in a photo, looking alive and well, with his hand up the butt of Kermit the Frog.

"You want coffee?" Stagg said.

"No, sir," Quinn said. "I need to get back on patrol. We had some accidents last night. Lots of reports to write."

"Probably seems slow after what we all went through after the great shitstorm," Stagg said. "Sure I can't interest you in anything?"

Quinn shook his head. Stagg folded his bony hands in front of him, no one within earshot, the waitresses seating folks near the convenience store and western-wear mart. Nothing more authentic than a straw hat and a pair of boots made in China to ride high in your rig and play cowboy.

"I feel for your troubles, Quinn," Stagg said. "I don't think it's fair."

Quinn just stared at Johnny, breathing in deep through his nose, and kept calm, hands flat on the table.

"I don't like the rumors I'm hearing and what people are saying," Stagg said. "It pained the shit out of me to talk to you like I did last night. You're a good lawman and we're lucky to have you. But it's my constituents who want answers. You can't just blow a fellow lawman's brains out and expect no one to say nothing. Life ain't no John Wayne movie."

"I've always been a Jimmy Stewart man myself."

"Or Gary Cooper?" Stagg said, grinned big. "I see a lot of ole Gary Cooper."

Quinn checked the time, surrounded by big sheets of plate glass looking out on the truck stop business, feeling as if they were floating there in an aquarium. Stagg glancing up and crooking his finger for a waitress and wanting to know if that lemon pie had cooled down yet. If it had, cut him up a nice old slice with a glass of Coca-Cola. "Sure is good," Stagg said. "Mmm-mmm."

"You publicly embarrass me last night and now you want to feed me pie," Quinn said. "I'll ask again, what do you want?"

"I heard you been asking around a bit about a murder back in '77," Stagg said, leaning back in the padded vinyl, licking his lips. "I have to say, I'm a little hurt you didn't come to me, ask me about it. You know, I do have a pretty good memory for all things Tibbehah County."

"OK," Quinn said. "Tell me what I don't know."

"You spoken to Hank Stillwell yet?"

"No, sir," Quinn said. "Not yet. But he's the father of the victim. It's high on the list."

Stagg nodded. The waitress brought him a Coca-Cola but said that Willie James said the pie was still cooling and not to mess with it. Stagg shrugged and drank some Coke. "Y'all sure taking your time."

"Didn't know there was a rush," Quinn said, thinking on the meeting with the ADA in Oxford. The smell of Stagg all over all them.

"It would be to the advantage of everyone in this county if the truth was brought out. All of it. Including what happened after to that black fella."

"Now, that sort of surprises me, Johnny," Quinn said. "You're not exactly one who likes to air the county's bad business. I'd have thought you'd want to keep everyone quiet."

"Come on, Quinn," Stagg said. "I just try and make a dollar like everyone else. I ain't hunting a man like he were some kind of animal. I don't give a shit if he was black or white. You know much about the Staggs?"

"I know your people."

"We been living up around Carthage for nearly a hundred years," Stagg said. "We were all dirt-eating poor. If one family looked to hate another family for being black or white, we didn't survive. That's the way it had always been. All we needed to do was pay that rent to ole man Vardaman and he'd allow us to have a roof over our head. We were all niggers to those people."

"Appreciate the history lesson."

Quinn started to get up. Stagg reached out and clutched Quinn's wrist. "Sit down."

"Take your hand off me, Johnny."

"Those people who done this were animals," Stagg said. "You look down on me, always have. But I swam through a swamp of shit to get where I'm at. Before me, there were the Vardamans and the Stevens and they didn't know how to tend to their own business. Before you were born there was a crew down here who ran things—hookers and dope—and no one had the balls to tell them to leave. You can call me a liar, but I paid your uncle twice a month for him to patrol the Rebel. These people paid him to leave them the hell alone."

Quinn rubbed his eyes. Above Stagg was another picture he hadn't noticed before. Barbara Mandrell and her sisters, with the biggest goddamn hair he'd ever seen in his life. *Johnny Stagg pumps our gas!* written across it.

"Who were they?"

"Miscreants, freaks, didn't have no jobs or no beliefs," Stagg said. "Didn't believe in Jesus. Didn't believe in America. All they believed in was an upside-down, double-fucked world. All for free. Motorcycle gang called themselves the Born Losers. That's about all you need to know."

"I've heard about them," Quinn said. "Everyone in Jericho knows those stories, but they're long gone."

"Is that a fact?" Stagg said. The plate of lemon pie arrived and slid across to Stagg, the meringue nearly four inches thick. He reached for a fork. "Glad to hear it, Sheriff. Because those sons of a bitches just rode through here yesterday, wearing their leather and flying their colors and saying they were back to stay."

"Why?"

"On account of one man," Stagg said. "Chains LeDoux is about to go free. Stick around and I'll tell you about the most evil bastard ever come to Tibbehah County."

They'd called Brushy Mountain the end of the line, but it hadn't worked out that way for Chains LeDoux. They closed down Brushy Mountain three years ago and sent him on to a new prison, Morgan County Correctional, which didn't have the same heroics as Brushy Mountain. You felt like you were a part of history at the old place, fashioned from stone hand-cut by the prisoners a hundred years back, the entrance looking like a castle and the whole prison built in the shape of the cross. Something about bringing hope and promise and that every man could be redeemed. Chains started to feel a part of the place, although redemption was never on his mind, only an escape that would never come. For a few years, he'd taken it on himself to guard James Earl Ray, walking the grounds with the coot, listening to his wild ideas for breaking out, even though the old man had already failed a half-dozen times. One time Ray got as close as the next town and was found by the local police hiding in the bushes, pissing himself.

No, sir. A man didn't escape Brushy Mountain. And now in Morgan City, it wasn't nothing but a waiting game. Two weeks. Twenty years. And then it comes down to two weeks. What a gift.

Was he rehabilitated? Was he a changed man? Had he found Jesus?

Hell no. What Chains liked about the time in that old prison was that try as they might, they couldn't bend him or break him or make him conform to the rules. You didn't get your back broke or whipped or nothing, but they tried to break you with the fucking time. You got one hour in the yard—one fucking hour a day—to look at the layers of rock that had been blasted off the side of the mountain, counting the sediment layers, the amount of time it took, during the dinosaurs and cavemen and shit, when Tennessee was covered by an ocean with fish as big as tractor trailers roaming the waters. Sometimes when he wasn't even drunk on toilet hooch, he'd see the mist rising off the walls of the mountain, covering the rock and the prison, and he felt like maybe he'd walked back in time. Twenty years. A hundred fifty years. Confederates, dinosaurs, and moonshiners running together.

Two fucking weeks. He'd already started growing his hair and beard out, just as it had been. The guards didn't give a shit. He wasn't their problem anymore. He'd gone in a hard ass at forty-five and would stroll out a hard ass at sixty-five, give the finger to the last guard he'd see and jump on his scooter—the boys keeping it clean, oiled, and running all these years. He knew there were Born Losers who were in diapers while he was running meth, 'ludes, and grass up from the Coast. And now they were joining in the brotherhood, wild and free, and taking aim right at the son of a bitch who'd cornholed his ass high and hard.

Johnny Stagg.

There was a mirror made of polished metal over his stainless steel sink. His face had a lot more lines, there was precious little black in the beard and the hair. But the body was strong, a lot stronger than when he came in all fucked-up on pills and booze. He wanted to be like that old Brushy Mountain rock, sit-ups, push-ups, pull-ups, etching his body with road maps of America, places he'd been and places he wanted to see. He'd had a big rebel flag tattooed across his back that said *Southern Bad Ass* and a Harley symbol etched on his flat, hard belly. He couldn't wait to get on that bike, the club meeting him outside the gates of this joke of a prison. To call this place a prison was an insult to old Brushy Mountain. You walked out of that place and you felt like you'd been a part of history.

Here, you did your time. You waited. You made yourself harder and stronger and something more than you were before. He was a rock. He was mist. He was time.

Two goddamn weeks.

31

It was the morning of the Fourth of July and J.T. had bought some barbecue from a carnival vendor and served it up inside scooped-out watermelon halves. The watermelon made the pork sweet-tasting and nice with a breakfast beer. J.T. had the doors to his garage wide open, and even though it wasn't much past ten, the day was growing hot. He had Jason's stunt Harley on his workstation, welding the frame, his assistant Gangrene gone AWOL. The engine, tank, wheels, and the lot sat on a far table, waiting to be reassembled. Jason had left his trailer at the shop, too. Not much room at his daddy's house. Jason knew as soon as the bike was done, he needed to head back west. All of it, the club, Jean Beckett, the whole damn town, pulling on him. Not knowing what else to do, he just sat cross-legged on that grease-stained floor of the garage, drank another cold one, and ate the sweet barbecue.

"It's a brotherhood," Hank Stillwell said, rubbing his thin red beard. "We do for each other. You know? I mean, like if you're short of cash, we pass the hat. Someone has it out for you? They got it out for all of us."

"All for one?"

"Yeah, man," Stillwell said, blowing some joint smoke through his nose. "All that shit. This is our county, we run it. We make our own laws. Our own world. We are the true American badasses who answer to nobody."

"Did you get some barbecue?" J.T. asked, turning off the welding torch, goggles now on top of his sweating head. "That's some good shit. Folks brought that truck all the way down from Memphis."

"You can't turn down a patch, man," Stillwell said. "You'd be the first I ever heard."

Jason looked up from the floor. His chunky brother, Van, was over helping J.T. take the frame off a vise and set it on the ground. Van just shook his head, his gut about to bust his dirty T-shirt. Van being a helluva one to offer personal advice, as he was still living at home after turning twenty, supposedly running things for his dad, but really just not wanting to go out and get a job. He spent most of his day watching game shows and getting high. He wanted to go out west with Jason. But Van Colson in California would be a mistake.

"I would only turn down the offer because I'm leaving," Jason said. "How can I be a part of something, part of y'all, if I'm not here?"

"Chains and Big Doug know that," Stillwell said. "They understand that you're in and out. But he dug the way you acted in Olive Branch. He liked that you're a man with no fear. You get patched and you're patched for life."

Jason nodded. He ate some more barbecue and drank some more Coors. He crushed the can in his hand and tossed it toward the trash. "We must've drank five hundred cases of this when we were making Smokey. The whole movie is pretty much a commercial for Coors. Y'all seen it yet?"

J.T., Van, and Hank Stillwell shook their heads.

"It's a good picture," Jason said. "Can't believe the way it turned out. They didn't even have a script. Hal would just let everyone just let loose with their characters and say whatever came to mind. That Jackie Gleason was incredible. He just showed up, got in uniform, and became that SOB. They call him Buford T. Justice. Just the funniest things came out of him. He tells his son, who's his deputy, that when they get back home from chasing the Bandit all over creation that he was gonna punch his momma right in the mouth. We all were on the set and just broke up on that. That's Gleason. The man's a genius."

"Is making movies like a brotherhood?"

"Jesus H. Christ," Van said, walking to a galvanized bucket full of beer and getting a new one. "Y'all give it a rest."

"Shut up," Hank Stillwell said. "You ain't a part of this."

"He's my brother, Red."

"Nobody calls me Red no more," Stillwell said, glaring at Van. "Call me Hank or Pig Pen."

"You're still Red to me," Van said, belching. Stillwell's dirty looks didn't mean shit to him. "And y'all need to get it in y'all's head that Jason is gone. He's leaving. When? Next week?"

Jason shrugged. "Depends on J.T."

J.T. lit up a joint with the end of his welding torch and then turned it off. He sucked in some smoke and nodded and nodded. "Yeah, man. A week. Two weeks. Got to get some paint. You got a nice job on them Stars and Bars."

"The redneck Evel Knievel," Van said. "That's you, Jason."

"So if you're leaving, really leaving," Stillwell said. "What about you and Jean Beckett? Y'all hadn't been apart. What? She going with you to Hollywood?"

Jason got up off the garage floor, not wearing shoes. His boots sat on the leather seat of his other bike outside. He had on a black T-shirt and faded Levi's, the beard and hair growing truly wild and black. He tossed the shell of the watermelon and came back to where the boys sat around J.T. as he worked, a regular Michelangelo of scooters.

"Shit," Jason said. "She said she'll go if we get married. I said, 'Cool, let's get married.' But she said we got to get married here with her momma and her crazy-ass family. She wants a church and all that and, man, oh man, I'm more scared of that than having a full-time old lady."

J.T. laughed the hardest. Stillwell snorted and Van just shook his head.

"You need to do for yourself," Van said, putting a hand to his mouth as he burped. "You don't need to do for Jean or me and Daddy and, least of all, this here motorcycle crew. What's all that shit mean?"

Stillwell, as narrow and skinny as a board, walked up to Jason's short little brother and poked him in the chest. "You don't get it. You won't get it for a million years. Some men are born different."

"And who's Chains LeDoux?" Van said. "Jesus Christ?"

"You better shut your fucking mouth," Stillwell said, a little loose on his feet. He'd come into the garage twenty minutes earlier with nearly fifty dollars' worth of fireworks that they were going to blow at the clubhouse tonight. He was acting more like a little kid than a man nearly thirty-five years old.

His attitude changed when a young girl walked into the wide-open bay door of the garage. She was real young, probably in her early teens but trying to dress older. She had on an orange-fringed top cut into ribbons, with beads hanging down over her skinny belly, wide-legged blue jeans and tall clogs, her hair pulled back under a kerchief. Stillwell wiped his mouth with the back of his hand and tried to stand tall and sober.

He just nodded at her.

"Can I borrow some money, Daddy?" the young girl asked. Her cheeks were brushed with pink rouge and her mouth was the color of bubble gum.

"If you take that shit off your face."

The girl's face colored beneath the makeup. She looked down to the stained asphalt as Stillwell walked to her, wobbly on those motorcycle boots, and clutched her chin. He turned her face this way and that and reached for an oil-stained rag hanging over J.T.'s Harley.

In front of the three other men, he wiped the makeup off her face with the filthy rag, staining her cheeks and mouth with oil. "Go home and dress proper," he said. "You look like a goddamn streetwalker."

The girl left, crying.

Stillwell walked over to the tub for another beer. None of the men spoke for a long time, Van catching his brother's eye as he left J.T.'s garage, an unspoken warning to back the hell off from all this. Somewhere out on the town square some kids were blowing up a strand of firecrackers.

32

The temperature was dropping fast, and Quinn and Lillie caught Hank Stillwell outside his trailer, chopping wood. He had a neat trailer, a lime green Plymouth and a motorcycle parked nearby under a metal carport, as he collected wood in orderly piles, split and stacked for a billowing furnace attached to the single-wide.

"Mr. Stillwell?" Quinn said. He'd met Lillie up in Yellow Leaf and they both drove their own vehicles to Stillwell's place.

He split the final piece of wood on a big round log with a thwack and looked up to them. He was out of breath, his worn-out jacket hanging loose and open with only an undershirt beneath. He nodded and set another piece of wood on the block but laid down the ax.

"Could use a little of your time, sir," Quinn said.

"Suppose to ice hard tonight," Stillwell said. "Don't like to rely on electric. Co-op takes two days before they get the power back on."

"What're you running?" Quinn asked.

"Y'all want to see it?" Stillwell said, wiping his nose, nodding toward around back. "Paid for itself the first year."

They followed him around the trailer, set high on blocks on a cleared hill. The hill had a nice view of the Yellow Leaf Baptist Cemetery, if you might call a cemetery view a nice thing. The grass was brown and dead across the eroded hills of headstones. The old church, a wooden building, sat next to the new church, a big, wide metal prefab place where they advertised fellowship on Sunday mornings and Wednesday nights. The sign outside was a holdover from the Christmas season. *Santa Claus Never Died for Anyone.*

Stillwell saw Quinn staring. He shook his head. "Baptists don't have much of a sense of humor." He took them in back of the big white trailer and pointed out a decent-sized welded black box with squared pipe running into his home. A wheelbarrow filled with small pieces of split wood stood ready.

"Nice setup," Quinn said. "I have a woodstove furnace. I keep it burning 'most winter long."

"My neighbor up the hill got some of them solar panels," Stillwell said. "His electric bills ain't hardly nothing."

Lillie warmed her hands over the black box as Stillwell opened up its door and stuffed in more pieces of wood. The fire inside glowed a high orange and red with bluish flames. Lillie looked to Quinn, growing bored with the talk of heating and cooling.

"I figure you know we reopened your daughter's case," Quinn said.

"Yes, sir."

"We've gone through the interviews you did with my uncle," Quinn said. "And we've sent out to Jackson for some evidence we hope is still out there. But anything you could tell us would be a big help."

Stillwell nodded, blowing into his chapped hands. "Y'all come on inside," he said. "It's getting colder out here than a Minnesota well-digger's ass."

They followed him around the trailer and up some creaking steps. The trailer was dim, with few pieces of furniture inside and a very small TV on a corner table. He had a few deer heads on the dark-paneled wall and a few big bass. Quinn and Lillie took a seat on a big overstuffed couch covered with a camouflage throw. Stillwell sat down in a big green La-Z-Boy, kicking his feet up, rubbing his reddish beard, the heat blowing hard and hot through the vents cut into the stove's metal walls.

On the kitchen counter, at the back of a tiny kitchen, was a half-eaten grilled cheese sandwich and an open bottle of Mountain Dew. A grouping of pictures of Lori Stillwell faced out from a nearby table. They were school photos, the girl caught in time in fading colors.

Stillwell reached over to the side table and pulled a photo of Lori. He leaned forward in the recliner and handed the gilded frame to Quinn. Her young skin had an oily sheen to it, with a couple blemishes on her cheeks, braces on her teeth, and feathered hair. She wore a long-collared polka-dot top, a chain and cross hung around her neck. She looked eager and happy and very young.

"Y'all been talking to Diane?"

"Yes, sir," Lillie said.

"She can tell you the worst of it," Stillwell said, watching as Quinn passed the frame to Lillie. Lillie studied the photo for a moment, smiled to Stillwell, and then handed the frame back. The home was pleasant and warm. From the spot on the couch, you could see out the window to an open row of pine trees, not the eroded lot of the cemetery. There were hunting magazines on the table and a few more about motorcycles. One called *Easy Riders* with a girl in a green bikini on the back of a black Harley.

"You still ride?" Quinn said.

"Not as much as I'd like," Stillwell said. "Got J.T. working on some repairs right now. I got real stupid a couple years back and got a scooter with a twin-cam engine. Hell, everyone knows them things got problems. It's got messed-up cam chains and shoes. J.T. told me to go ahead and replace that gear system before it throws the whole goddamn engine. It ain't cheap, but better than replacing everything. The Harley people never tell you this shit could cut off the oil to the engine and blow it all. Y'all ride at all?"

"Dirt bikes," Quinn said. "I used to always have Hondas out at my uncle's place. We built a little dirt track just for jumping and messing around. It's been a while."

"Highway riding is something special," Stillwell said. "When I had the money and a good bike, I could clean my head out. If I hadn't had a bike when Lori was killed, I think they'd better gone ahead and took me to Whitfield and tied on the straitjacket. I just rode and rode. Seems like all I did for nearly ten years is stay on that bike."

"And you rode a lot when Lori was alive?" Lillie asked.

Stillwell fingered at his nose, straightened himself against the back of the recliner. He looked to Quinn and Lillie and said, "Don't think it's a secret who I rode with back then."

"Born Losers," Quinn said.

"Among others," Stillwell said. "Joined up with them when I got back from 'Nam."

"Army?"

"101st Airborne, 506th Regiment."

"When?"

"In the shit of it," Stillwell said. "'Sixty-nine through '73. Hamburger Hill. Yes, sir. I was there."

Quinn had a cousin who had died in the same battle back in '69, serving in the 101st but with another regiment. He recalled his great-uncle and great-aunt, sad old farmers who lived not two miles from his farm who had always seemed to be in perpetual mourning until they died fifteen years ago, two months apart.

"You think we'll ever know?" Stillwell said. "Your uncle said I needed to make peace that some things just don't have answers."

"Diane Tull says a lynch mob killed the wrong man," Lillie said.

"Yeah," Stillwell said, hands a bit shaky on the arms of the recliner. "I know about all that."

"You agree?" Lillie asked.

"Yes, ma'am."

"Because of Diane?" Quinn said. "Because of her seeing the man who did this a few weeks later?"

"No, sir," Stillwell said, licking his lips and rubbing his face, eyes void and hovering on a spot between where Quinn and Lillie sat. He was still holding the old gold picture frame tight. "No. I know they had the wrong man from when they set out that night from the clubhouse. They were going to get someone no matter what. I tried to stop it. But it wasn't going to happen. I can make sense of soldiers holding a hill, but this was just blood for blood."

There were a few more pictures on the wall and an old black-and-white of a young man with a crew cut on a motorcycle. A young woman sat behind him, arms wrapped around his waist. The boy, Hank Stillwell, wore aviators and had a cigarette plucked in his mouth.

"What about the man who attacked your daughter?" Lillie said. "After all these years, has anyone told you anything?"

"No, ma'am," he said. "My firm belief is that the boy wasn't from here. He was a hunter, a goddamn animal, coming through looking for young girls. He did what he aimed to do and took off down the road. I believe I have asked every man, woman, and child alive at that time if they ever saw a twisted son of a bitch who had a face like that. I still ask."

Lillie nodded.

"So who was the man who was lynched?" Quinn said.

"Never knew his name," Stillwell said. "Nobody did. He was sick in the head, lived up in the hills. Some said he was a vet, like me. Don't know. Nobody talked much about it later. It was your uncle who set us straight after all this. He knew what we did and told us never to speak about it ever again. He said we'd have to make right with God what we done. He said no court of law could make sense of the savagery. He said that, 'savagery.' Your uncle was a hard man. He didn't want no part of this posse."

"How was it done?"

"I rode off when they caught him," Stillwell said. "I guess that makes me a coward. I said my piece, but no one was listening. It was Chains LeDoux told me to ride off if I didn't have the nuts for it. You know who he was?"

Quinn nodded. "I heard some."

Lillie stood up and looked into the back of the property, to the woods and rows and rows of young pine trees. Quinn turned to see where she was staring and saw two figures walking at the edge of the woods, a glint of light off some field glasses, and then they disappeared.

"You have a lot of hunters around here?" Quinn asked, still watching the woods.

"Some," Stillwell said. "Why?"

"That your property behind you?"

"I got fifteen acres of them pines."

"You may have some poachers," Lillie said. "We'll check it out but you may want to call Wildlife and Game."

Quinn was still seated and leaned forward, elbows on his knees. "So you didn't see it?"

"I saw them catch the man, take him away."

"Are any of the old riders still around?"

Hank Stillwell bowed his head and closed his eyes, nodding over and over to himself. "You are aware that Chains LeDoux goes free from federal charges in a few weeks?"

"Yes, sir," Quinn said. "I just heard the news from Johnny Stagg."

"I ain't forgot," Stillwell said. "I got a lot of guilt and shit. Someone like Chains doesn't have the right to be out and among living, breathing humans. If he comes back to Jericho . . ."

"Bad news?" Lillie said.

"Real bad," Stillwell said.

Quinn stood. The old man remained in the recliner, where he probably spent most of his days and nights. Quinn scanned the woods again but didn't see anyone roaming the edges. Lillie had already walked to the door, fingering at her handheld radio, calling for Kenny to sweep the roads around the Yellow Leaf church for some poachers out and about.

" 'Poachers'?" Stillwell said.

"Who else?" Quinn said.

"It's Chains's people," the old man said, unchanged and not moving from the chair. A quiet heat poured into the room, smelling of sweet red oak. "Y'all realize they're back?"

Quinn nodded, Lillie walking toward the thin metal door and out into the cold. He stood there and looked down at Stillwell, gaunt and graying, shoulder-length hair and beard with still some red in it. He could see the man riding with bikers back in the day.

"When's the last time y'all went out and patrolled around Choctaw?"

Diane Tull performed happy hour at the Southern Star twice a week and an acoustic set at The River at the Sunday service. She liked the performances at the Star a bit better, as she could include her whole band and drink Jack Daniel's on the rocks while she sang. She pulled out a torn piece of notebook paper from her Levi's jacket and read the set list. A little changeup from last time.

1. *"Kiss an Angel Good Morning"*
2. *"I'm the Only Hell My Mama Raised"*
3. *"Come Early Morning"*
4. *"She Called Me Baby"* (*Reworking a bit with* "He Called Me Baby")
5. *"Trailer for Rent"*

The last song of the first set was the newest. Diane didn't care much, if anything, for what was coming out of Nashville these days, but she was really digging what the Pistol Annies were recording. She did like a singer from Alabama named Jamey Johnson. And, of course, good old Alan Jackson. But those guys were hardheaded and not part of that Hollywood sound, where producers never heard of pedal steel, Porter Wagoner, or that a good night of heartbreak and drinking was good for the soul. If she had to hear another song about how much a man loved sitting his porch and sipping sweet tea, she swore to Jesus she was going to blast her radio with her 12-gauge. Country music was about a man and a woman, drinking hard, and getting through life. She was sick to death of folks trying to put a glitter ball over Hank's grave.

"You want another?" the bartender Chip asked.

"I'm good."

"You look like you've had a hell of a day."

"Lots on my mind," Diane said. "Say, go ahead and pop the top on a Coors. I'll bring it up with me."

She took the beer and reached down for the handle on her guitar case and walked up to the narrow little stage, where J.T. had leaned an upright bass, not sure why he changed up from the electric. A mandolin lay at his feet to play for certain songs.

Diane pulled the microphone close to the raised stool and positioned a second mic alongside her Martin guitar. Their drummer was a guy from Holly Springs named Wallace who'd played for a lot of big bands in Memphis and New Orleans. He knew all the songs by heart. They'd only gone through the list a few times, with him nailing every bit.

She passed the list around and then shook her head. "How about we do that new one, 'Hard Edges'? I think I have it down."

J.T. and Wallace shrugged and she dug into the song, the lyrics reminding her a hell of a lot about Caddy Colson, back when she'd been a woman taking off her clothes so the men didn't look her in the eye. Some of the late-night conversations with that girl had left Diane cold. She tried to think about Caddy as she sang and how those hard edges hide that tender heart. Diane enjoying the music so much, thinking how the song would sound better with that lap steel to go with J.T.'s mandolin, that she didn't even mind there were only about seven folks in the bar. She knew from a long time back, you didn't play for the crowd, you played for yourself.

They went from "Hard Edges" and wove back into the set, getting a few songs down the line into that Don Williams classic, "Come Early Morning," one of those songs that brought her back to how much joy the radio and old LPs on her grandmomma's console player used to bring her. J.T. loved it, too, and would work in a harmonica part with the bass. Diane got so into it, she nearly missed the six men in leather and chains walk in the front door of the Star. They wore leather jackets, jeans, and heavy biker boots that thumped on the wooden floor.

Two of them walked up to the bar and the other four took seats close to the stage, kicking back and slumping in their chairs, seeming to already be drunk as hell. They wore beards and tats and motorcycle vests over their jackets. Didn't take long before they were catcalling and calling out requests. Diane had to politely say, in her quiet country voice, "We appreciate you. But we don't do requests."

One of the men hollered out, "So what do you do and when?"

Diane turned to J.T. and J.T. shook his head, leaning in saying for her to forget it and play on. And maybe they had rattled her, god damn them, but she didn't feel like playing "He Called Me Baby" and asked Wallace and J.T. to head into "Tulsa Time." And there were more catcalls and beer bottles slamming on tabletops, shots of liquor, in shadows and neon. One of the men had a bald head and crossed eyes, tattoos across his face and down on his chin, and a weird inked circle across his Adam's apple. He wore a T-shirt without sleeves and kept on staring at her tits as she played, Diane wishing like hell she hadn't worn the glittered tank top reading *Momma Tried* and her tight bell-bottoms.

She kept her eyes down on the Martin, playing on through "Tulsa Time," that long streak of gray hair covering her face and eyes. She finished out the set and then with slow, steady steps walked back to the ladies' room. She splashed cool water in her face and tried to calm herself.

The door opened. In the mirror, she saw the inked man come up behind her. He slid the dead bolt closed.

"You know who I am?" His voice sounded ragged and guttural like his vocal cords had been cut.

She shook her head and held on to the sink bowl.

"You know our colors?"

She nodded.

"I like your singing," he said.

He stood there, arms crossed over his chest, his jeans obscenely tight in the crotch, the scent of him something to behold in the tiny space.

"I like your singing," he said again. "But keep the rest of that old bullshit to yourself."

He unbolted the door and walked from the ladies' room. Diane had watched the whole thing from the mirror over the sink. She breathed and breathed and then dabbed her face again, tucked her silver hair behind her ear, and marched back out for another drink and to start the second set.

When she walked back into the Star, all the bikers had left. She ordered a shot. Until she felt that warm Jack hit the back of her throat, she'd started to wonder if she'd imagined the whole thing.

But they'd been there. She could still smell them.

33

Quinn and Lillie drove the back roads around Yellow Leaf nearly an hour before they spotted the tracks. They were fresh, worn hard and distinct in the mud, and obviously made by some kind of cycle, not a car or truck. Quinn got out of his truck, Lillie riding with him now, leaving her Jeep at Stillwell's place, and they counted three bikes riding along the dirt and into the tree line. They were big wheels, heavy set into the mud, too big and weighty to be dirt bikes.

"You want to see where they go?" Lillie said.

"Why the hell not?" Quinn said.

They followed the tracks only about twenty feet until they saw where the tracks became muddled and had sunk deeper in the mud. The tracks then circled back the way they came and out onto the road. From the turn-around point, they made out distinct boot prints heading into the woods.

"These aren't hunters," Lillie said.

"A kind of hunter," Quinn said. "Trying to spook Stillwell."

"I don't think he spooks much," Lillie said. "He's too worn-out to study on things like that. He seems like he's been waiting on them a long time."

"You heard anything about what he was saying?" Quinn said. "About this gang coming back out to Choctaw Lake?"

"I know that place," Lillie said. "Some shithole shack off a back road. I used to fish by a little river that ran into the lake there. Best place for crappie. But I hadn't seen anyone go in that shack for years."

"When's the last time you been out there?"

"When's the last time I've been fishing?"

"Come on," Quinn said. "Let's check it out."

It was dark when they turned off Cotton Road and headed down south on past Dogtown. There were wooden posted signs from Wildlife and Game about the seasons for hunting and the need to obtain a license. By the edge of the lake, there was a park, with a playground, a couple piers, and a set of public restrooms. Quinn and Lillie drove through the empty parking lot down by the boat ramp and circled off the landing down an overgrown dirt road that seemed to lead nowhere.

"You sure this is it?"

"Look in your headlights, Ranger," Lillie said.

In the narrow beam of headlights were many rutted tracks from motorcycles and cars. The lights shone ten feet ahead into absolute darkness, no moon above, and the road had been so untraveled that limbs and tree branches scraped at the doors and hood of the Big Green Machine.

"Boom won't like this," Lillie said.

"He does love this truck."

"He made that truck," Lillie said. "He got tired of you riding around in that old piece of shit."

There was light ahead.

Multiple headlights and a bonfire lit up a gathering at the edge of Choctaw Lake. Quinn slowed into the elbow of the narrow dirt road, stopped, and cracked the driver's window. In the distance, they could hear what sounded like Mexican corridas, Quinn familiar with the sound of the music through a few run-ins with his old pal Donnie Varner.

"A Tex-Mex biker gang?" Lillie said. "OK. This should be interesting."

"You want to walk it?"

"Hell no," Lillie said. "Let's see what these motherfuckers are up to."

Quinn shrugged. He hit the light bar on top of the F-250 and rode bigger than shit down that gravel road in front of the busted old clubhouse Hank Stillwell had spoken about. There must have been twenty jacked-up trucks parked all around the shack and maybe thirty motorcycles. Out by the lakeside, several oil barrels billowed flame and smoke up into the dark sky. Men and women were walking around, the Mexican music seeming to come from one of the trucks, tall and high, with the back window painted with the face of the Virgin Mary. Quinn slowed the truck at the edge of the party. Everyone with a cup, bottle, or cigarette in hand. The men and women were Anglo and Mexican. They warmed themselves by the fire, tilting up bottles, and then looked at the flashing blues coming from the truck.

"OK," Lillie said. "Now what?"

"We wait."

"Wait for what?" Lillie said. "For them to start shooting?"

"Someone will ask what the fuck we want," Quinn said. "Someone's got to be in charge. They'll want to show us they're in charge."

Quinn kept his window down, the air brittle and sharp rushing into the warm car. Quinn reached into the ashtray and relit the rest of the La Gloria Cubana he'd started that morning. He and Lillie sitting there listening to the sad song sung in Spanish with a steady backbeat and high notes of the accordion.

Not a minute later, a large man in a black leather jacket with a denim vest over it ambled on over to Quinn's truck. He had a shaved head and a lot of ink on his face. At first, Quinn thought he had a small beard, but the closer he got to the truck, Quinn saw it was a Satanic goatee etched permanently onto his chin.

"You dating anyone lately, Lil?" Quinn said.

"Shut the fuck up."

"Here comes Mr. Right."

The man walked up close to Quinn's window and then leaned inside the truck, drunk-smiling to Quinn and Lillie and checking out the squawking police radio and the shotgun Quinn had mounted on the back glass.

"Evening, Officer," the man said.

"Not an officer," Quinn said. "I'm the sheriff."

"Howdy, Sheriff," the man said, laughing. His voice was guttural and rough. His body odor and breath swarmed over even Quinn's cigar. The biker sniffed at the smoke and smiled. "We got some kind of problem?"

"We got a problem, Deputy Virgil?" Quinn said.

"You got a license to operate a beer joint?"

"Ain't no beer joint," the man said. "Just having some fucking fun with my brothers."

"And who are your brothers?" Lillie said.

The man grinned and turned his back to them, thrusting his thumbs at a patch on his back that read BORN LOSERS.

"Y'all have some ethnic diversity here."

"Just some folks down from Memphis," the man said. "They brought the tequila. We breaking some kind of law?"

"You have a permit for that weapon?" Lillie said.

Quinn hadn't noticed the bulge under the coat, but as the man turned to stare, the checkered grip was plain to see. The man grinned some more, reached into his wallet, and presented a folded-up piece of paper that gave him the right to carry a concealed weapon. His name was Chester Anthony DiFranco.

"You want to pat me down?" he said to Lillie.

"You want to shower first?"

The man laughed. "Come on," he said. "Fuck. We done here?"

"Is this your place?" Quinn said.

"Bought and paid for," Chester said. "You need to see that paperwork, too?"

Quinn nodded. "We'll be back," he said. "Just wanted to make sure you know we're around, Chester."

"My name is Animal," he said. "Call me Animal."

"I'll check the property records," Quinn said. "And I'll pay another visit if you're trespassing."

"Man," Animal said. "Trespassing? We're just moving in. This is our welcome-home party. Come on. Get that stick out of your ass and join us for some tequila and Mexican pussy. You look like you might like some of that, too, girl."

Quinn blew a long stream of smoke in Animal's face. He reached for his door handle. Lillie put a hand on his knee.

"Patience," she whispered. She turned to Animal. "Listen, you ugly motherfucker. It may be tough for you to look me in the eye with yours headed in two different directions. But if you want to keep out of jail around here, you will address me as 'Ma'am' or 'Chief Deputy Virgil.' Do you understand me?"

The man pursed his lips and smiled. His eyes did head in different directions. "Yes, ma'am," he said, splitting his index and middle fingers and flicking his tongue between them.

He staggered away. The corridas kept playing from the parked trucks, exhaust fumes from the dually pipes chugging into the brittle night air.

"This won't end well," Quinn said.

"Who are these guys?" Lillie said.

"My uncle used to tell me stories about the Born Losers," Quinn said. "But you know what? He lied to me."

"How?"

"He said he'd run the sonsabitches out of town."

34

There was an ash on Luther Varner's cigarette that must've grown about two inches long before he broke it in the tray, looked to Quinn, and said, "Of course we had problems with those bikers. Everybody knew the trouble they made, things they did out at that clubhouse."

"What about the lynching?" Quinn said. He was seated at a small table at the VFW with Mr. Jim and Varner, getting to speak in private after Friday's pancake breakfast. Quinn had been the keynote speaker that morning, after Mr. Jim had led the vets, young and old, in the Pledge of Allegiance. Luther had cooked most of the pancakes and provided the bacon.

"Sure," Mr. Jim said. "We knew about what happened to that fella. He killed a couple girls and they took him out and hung his ass. One of the girl's fathers was part of the gang. Most people didn't have much trouble with it."

Mr. Jim had the clearest blue eyes he'd ever seen and a giant bulbous nose. After he spoke, he hacked a nasty cough into a handkerchief. The cough had grown worse and worse over some weeks, Mr. Jim saying he just had a cold and to quit bothering him about it.

"One of the girls lived," Quinn said.

"Oh, that's right," Mr. Jim said. "It's been a while. You forget things."

"But nothing ever happened to those bikers," Luther said. "I don't know what your uncle did about it, if anything. I think it was a pretty hot issue. Divided folks."

"Black and white?" Quinn said.

"Nope," Varner said. "Old Testament and New."

"Where did y'all line up?" Quinn asked.

Luther thumped his pack of cigarettes, drew out a long fresh one, and lit it quick with his Zippo. "Whatever we thought at the time was wrong," Luther said. "You're saying the man they got was innocent? I wasn't out there with them, uncoiling the rope. I didn't even know what happened till a few years later. That's why we have society, laws, and courts, so bullshit like this doesn't happen."

"Still can happen," Quinn said.

"Guess it does," Mr. Jim said. "But at least a man has a fighting chance to tell his side of things whether they listen or not."

Luther smoked down half the cigarette, squinting through the smoke, only two other folks left in the old VFW. The hall was a cinder-block building with gray linoleum floors and a lot of plaques, photos, flags, and anything military or about America. Somewhere there was a framed article from the *Tibbehah Monitor* more than ten years ago about Quinn earning his Ranger tab.

"You know much about this gang?" Quinn asked. "The Born Losers?"

"They were some bad motherfuckers," Luther said. "Nobody messed with them. They pretty much kept to themselves. Wasn't like in no movies, where they were chasing the panties off virgins or breaking church windows. All you had to do was look at their head dude and know he meant business. They called him Chains, and the boy had that look in his eye. Haunted? Crazy? Long hair and a beard, animal-wild."

"What about the men who followed him?"

"Some of them were pretty nice fellas."

"Like who?" Quinn asked.

There was a glance, a very brief one, between Luther and Mr. Jim. Mr. Jim opened his mouth and then closed it. He seemed to think for a second and then said, "J.T. either rode with them or fixed their bikes. They spent a lot of time at his garage. But this was a long, long time ago. By the time you were in diapers, most of them had moved on."

"Hank Stillwell," Varner said. "It was Stillwell's daughter they killed. You talk to him?"

Quinn nodded.

"Why are people talking about all this now?" Mr. Jim said.

"They're coming back."

"Who?" Varner said.

"The Born Losers," Quinn said.

"Bullshit," Varner said.

"Nope," Quinn said. "Lillie and I had a meet and greet with them at their old clubhouse out on Choctaw. Met some cross-eyed fella with a throat tattoo. Real personable. We're talking the next generation of shit-birds."

"Seems like all the turds out of Memphis get shook out in Tibbehah," Mr. Jim said. "Can't they go somewheres else?"

The only two other folks in the VFW hall huddled by the front door, deep in conversation. One of the men turned, eyed Quinn, and then leaned back into his buddy. He was a tubby and dumb man named Clay Sneed who'd become a real estate broker—SNEED FOR YOUR HOME NEEDS— after one year at Ole Miss and some time loading trucks in the Guard. He was a couple years older than Quinn. And Quinn recalled something about him being a Peeping Tom at the dress shop who got off with a warning from his uncle.

Quinn sensed something and would have left it alone, except Sneed didn't have the sense to quit turning around. Quinn heard something from the table about the short speech Quinn had just given about ethics, loyalty, and hard work. Sneed said in a whisper that "must take a lot of hard work for kickbacks and a free truck."

Luther Varner and Mr. Jim couldn't hear jack shit. Quinn's hearing was excellent.

He excused himself and walked over to the table where tubby Clay Sneed was snickering. "Glad you enjoyed my talk," Quinn said. "But just how much do you think I make with those kickbacks?"

Sneed's face flamed a bright red. "What the hell you talking about?"

"You just said I take payoffs and got myself a free truck."

"No I didn't," Sneed said. "You're hearing things."

"I was offered a sixty-thousand-dollar Dodge Ram by the county supervisors that I turned down," Quinn said. "That big green Ford parked outside didn't cost a quarter of that. It was customized by Boom Kimbrough."

"This was a private conversation," Sneed said. The other man, a kid in his early twenties, just kept his eyes down on his half-eaten pancakes. "I didn't mean nothing."

"People like you never do," Quinn said. "Can't fault a pig for grunting."

"What the hell's that mean?"

"Think on it," Quinn said. "It'll come to you in a couple hours."

Quinn walked back to the table with the two old men, his two most trusted friends in Tibbehah besides Boom and Lillie. He reached for a coffeepot in the center of the table and refilled a thick ceramic mug with an Operation Desert Shield logo someone had added to the collection. He leaned back into his seat and crossed his boots at the ankle.

"What was that all about?" Mr. Jim said.

"Bullshit."

"That boy need an ass-whippin'?" Luther Varner said.

"For a long time," Quinn said.

Varner stubbed out his cigarette and started to stand. Quinn grinned at the old Marine and told him to have another cup of coffee. "He's not worth it."

"What are you going to do about that lynching?" Mr. Jim said.

"It's been heavily implied that I better find out just what happened," Quinn said. "The DA in Oxford sees himself as the next attorney general. And this case would put his name in a lot of papers and on TV."

"Do people ever do something just for the right of it?" Mr. Jim asked. He started to cough again, the hacking getting worse. Before Mr. Jim tucked his handkerchief back into his pocket, Quinn saw it had been spotted with blood.

Varner did, too, and he and Quinn exchanged glances.

"Did they ever?" Varner said. "I spent my whole life in Jericho and seen and heard about stuff that would've made Norman Rockwell shit his drawers."

"Doing what's right isn't gonna work now," Quinn said, spinning the mug in his hands. "I can only take on one thing at a time, even if it means some people keep clean."

"You're sounding more and more like your Uncle Hamp," Mr. Jim said, smiling big. "He was a realistic man. Before things got real bad, he'd say he had to think tactically on things. Not with anger."

"Yes, sir," Quinn said. "I understand that. But I don't want to be my Uncle Hamp."

Mr. Jim started to cough some more and excused himself from the table. Luther watched him go, finished the cigarette, and stubbed it into the already overloaded tray. "Been smoking and drinking since I was twelve years old and still feel like I could fight and fuck my way around God's Green Earth. My drill sergeant at Parris Island said heaven didn't want a Marine and hell was afraid we'd take over. Maybe that's why we stick around so long."

"How bad?" Quinn said.

"Bad."

"He tell you much?"

"No, sir," Luther said. "Dying is pretty private to a man."

When Quinn returned to the sheriff's office, he found his door ajar and Mary Alice inside, talking to Johnny Stagg and his boy Ringold. She'd served them hot coffee and cold biscuits. Quinn wouldn't have given Stagg the honor of licking his toilet bowl clean. Mary Alice scooted out of the office when she saw Quinn, raising her eyebrows in a look of *What else could I do?* and left the door wide open as she clacked back down the hall.

Quinn took a seat on top of his desk. He didn't say a word.

"I get the feeling she don't like me too much," Stagg said. "Mary Alice told me three times to come back later. I said I'd rather wait."

Quinn nodded.

"You think I could eat one of them biscuits? Or maybe she made 'em with rat poison . . ."

"I guess if you take a bite, we'll find out."

Ringold sat in the chair closest to the window. He'd nodded at Quinn when he'd walked in but remained seated, wearing a black ball cap with narrow sunglasses resting on the visor. He wore a tight-fitting jacket and dark jeans with field boots.

"What do you want, Johnny?" Quinn said. "I gave an inspirational speech this morning and now I'm running late on things. Miss Davis drove her car into a ditch again and some teenagers just stole a box of Slim Jims and prophylactics from the Pig."

"Sorry I missed the speech," Stagg said, "but I'm sure I've heard it in one form or another."

"I heard you made deacon at First Baptist," Quinn said. "Congrats, Johnny."

"I didn't ask for it," Stagg said. "They liked what I was doing for this town. Some people appreciate all I've done after the storm."

"Amen."

"I ain't got time to sit around and square off over smart-ass remarks, son," Stagg said. "We got some real trouble headed this way and I don't think you got a complete grasp of the situation."

"Born Losers are back."

"That's part of it," Stagg said. "Their head man, Chains LeDoux, is also getting out of prison in twelve days. If y'all don't find some reason he needs to be held, he'll be riding back into Jericho bigger than shit. Don't you see they're preparing a hero's welcome out at that sorry ole shack on Choctaw?"

"Lillie and I saw them last night," Quinn said.

"You arrest them?"

"On what charges?"

"Be creative," Stagg said. "Make some up."

Quinn shook his head. The cold biscuits sat on a pink Fiesta plate, half covered with aluminum foil. Two mugs of coffee sat on the other side of Quinn's desk, full, grown cold as they'd waited for Quinn to return.

Quinn scratched at his neck. He wasn't caring for the familiarity of Stagg just stopping into the SO, something that he'd only done a handful of times before. And he sure as shit had never made himself comfortable in Quinn's office. Quinn had made it clear from the first election that he in no way worked for the Board of Supervisors. He sure as hell ran no favors for Stagg.

"How's that old case coming?" Stagg said.

Quinn looked over at Ringold. "You don't say much."

Ringold hadn't moved an inch, shrugging in an offhand manner. The beard on his face was growing out longer than the receding black hairs on his head. He had clear blue eyes and slow, practiced movements. "Sure is a cold day," Ringold said. "Lots of ice on those roads."

Quinn grinned and just shook his head.

"I don't want that man back in Tibbehah," Stagg said. "If you got some kind of personal reasons for not following up on this disgusting act, you need to let me know. Maybe need to get some state people involved."

"Why would this be personal, Johnny?"

Stagg gave that good old preacher grin and leaned forward in his seat. His hair slicked up tall on his head like a rockabilly star from the fifties, down to the ducktail he kept in back. He nodded and rubbed his chin. "What are you hearing about that lynching?"

"I can't discuss a case with you," Quinn said. "You know that."

"I'm coming in here to help your ass out," Stagg said. "I know that DA in Oxford got you and Lillie by the gosh-dang short hairs. What I'm hearing is that you make them look good and they could reevaluate the whole case against y'all."

"Umm-hmm."

"This LeDoux ain't someone you fuck with," Stagg said. "He aims to burn this whole town to the ground."

"Little dramatic, aren't you, Johnny?" Quinn said. "You're making it sound like *High Plains Drifter*."

"Paint the town red?"

Quinn laughed. Ringold hadn't budged. He was still and frozen, flat and hard blue eyes looking to the photos Quinn kept of his time in the deep shit of Benning, the bare mountains of Afghanistan, and the framed flag given to him by a Colonel George Reynolds that had flown at Camp Spann. Ringold had surely been a lot of those places, if not all of them, not commenting or asking about it, maybe knowing his work with Stagg was dirty, soulless, and without a shred of honor. To bring up the connection would be to start on it all. Of course Quinn knew plenty of guys who had come out of the shit in Iraq or Afghanistan feeling like Uncle Sam was just as dirty as Johnny Stagg. Maybe it was better not to talk about it.

"There are living people who saw what that animal and his crew done," Stagg said.

"And I'll talk to them."

"There ain't much time."

"You starting to sweat a little, Johnny?" Quinn said. "Sounds like this man Chains ain't coming back to burn Jericho. He's coming back to burn you."

Stagg nodded. He looked over at Ringold and then back at Quinn. "He'll surely try," Stagg said. "But you really want that trash and filth coming back to our town? We've made a lot of progress since we nearly got swept away by the hand of God. These people are gonna piss on everything we're trying to build here."

"Spoken like a true church deacon."

"I told them."

"Told who?"

"I told people you'd never touch those Born Losers when they came back," he said. "And it won't bother you a lick to see Chains LeDoux flogging his pecker out on the town square. You'll get in with them thicker than thieves."

Quinn stood. He looked down at Stagg.

Ringold stood, too, and Stagg stood between them, his nose and lacquered teeth inches from Quinn's face. "You don't know?"

Quinn stared at the man, thinking about what exactly would happen if he punched Johnny Stagg in the throat and tossed him from his office. Ringold would try to stop it, but most of the job would already be done.

"Your goddamn daddy rode with them sonsabitches," Stagg said. "He was a full-on member of the Born Losers when they hung that man high from that tree out on Jericho Road. That's why you won't touch it. It's too goddamn close."

Quinn didn't say a word. He breathed and studied Stagg's craggy, misshapen face.

Stagg walked out of the office. But Ringold hovered there, hands loose and easy at his side, tilting his head to the side and giving a wry smile, before following behind Johnny Stagg.

35

There was snow two weeks later, not much of it, maybe a dusting of an inch, ice over the bridges and some slick spots on the paved roads. Quinn had gone back to night patrols, Lillie taking on the day. It wasn't even 1800, but the sky had grown black as Quinn met Lillie outside the Dixie gas station, the bright lights and neon shining onto frozen puddles. She parked her Jeep and climbed in the F-250 passenger seat, holding two large accordion folders and an old cardboard box.

"Merry Christmas."

"It's almost February," Quinn said.

"Happy Valentine's Day, then," she said, "if you're into hair samples, dental prints, three shell casings, and an old pair of combat boots . . ."

"Holy shit."

"Yes, sir," Lillie said. "I only had to put in five written requests and call the state office about fifteen times before they replied. But here it is, delivered to the SO today, signature only."

"I wonder why the local DA didn't look for it."

"Because they didn't know," Lillie said. "I got passed around to every son of a bitch in the attorney general's office until I found the archive. And then I had to call the archive with a creative list of search criteria.

This all was filed in 1979 when the evidence was sent for safekeeping. The case was just ID'd as an unidentified body. There was no murder case or corresponding paperwork from your uncle."

"We knew that."

"But here we go . . ."

"Now what?"

"I'm going to drive it over to Batesville in the morning," Lillie said. "With a lot of sweet talk and my charming personality, we should get some DNA results back in a year or two."

"You shitting me?"

"We got one lab for this region," Lillie said. "A year is being generous."

"What kind of shells?"

"Twenty-two long."

"And the boots?"

"Boots," she said. "Black boots."

She handed Quinn the box and he opened the top and reached inside. The boots were very old, cracked black leather with worn rubber soles and smelled of mothballs. They had twelve eyelets but no laces, the topmost eyelets busted from their holes. Quinn studied the tongue of the boot, barely making out the name. CORCORAN. MADE IN THE USA. "These are paratrooper boots from the sixties," Quinn said. "I saw my fair share in surplus stores when I was a kid. I used to love going in those places."

Quinn put the old boots back in the box and handed the box back to Lillie. "More stuff in the files for you to read," Lillie said. "The dental impressions are incomplete. Teeth missing. The lower jaw apparently had been removed."

"If he wanted to keep it quiet," Quinn said, "why in the hell wouldn't my uncle just destroy it? Not send it on as a John Doe?"

"He didn't investigate," Lillie said. "But I guess he figured this fella's life was worth the price of a stamp."

Quinn let out his breath. Light snow swirled in the headlights of his truck. It was very quiet and very cold outside.

"Any word from Miss Jean?" Lillie asked.

The heater ran fast and hard in his truck. "Nope," Quinn said. "She denies my dad was ever part of that crew. She told me she'd rather me quit discussing the matter altogether."

"Sounds like Jean."

"And since that talk, she's gone to half a box of wine a night."

"Hit that nerve."

"Guess so."

"But you believe Stagg?"

"I'd never take Stagg at his word," Quinn said. "But I spoke to J.T. He fixed bikes and rode with the Losers some. He confirmed it. He said my daddy was a full-patched member."

"Between raising hell and making movies, he was riding with a gang?"

"Club," Quinn said. "J.T. said they were just a club and most of them decent folks."

"Chains LeDoux?" Lillie said. "You see his sheet?"

Quinn nodded. "Hard man," Quinn said. "Did three tours with the Marines in Vietnam. Came home to Mississippi to raise hell."

"What'd J.T. say about the lynching?"

"At first, he pretended not to know," Quinn said. "I brought a six-pack with me and after about four beers he said he recalled what happened but believed they got the right man."

"He was with them?"

"He said some of the club didn't go," Quinn said. "He said he didn't see it."

"Would you admit it?"

Quinn shook his head. "Nope."

"And Hank Stillwell?"

"Says he tried to stop it," Quinn said. "He said he called Judge Blanton from a pay phone to talk some sense to the boys because my uncle was away."

"But Blanton didn't want to get involved?"

"That's what he said," Quinn said. "He claims Blanton wanted him to allow God's will after hearing what had happened to Lori."

"Blanton," Lillie said. "Jesus H."

"And Jason Colson, too."

Lillie shook her head, her face half shadowed in the dim light by the pumps. "Did your dad really date Adrienne Barbeau?"

"And Suzanne Somers," Quinn said.

Lillie raised her eyebrows.

"Maybe at the same time."

"Must've been hard for your mom," Lillie said. "Having a wanderer like that around."

"Funny thing is that Jean swears to Christ that he never cheated on her," Quinn said. "I know she loved him. A lot. She'll talk about Elvis Presley all goddamn night, but one word about Jason Colson will send her tearing up, rushing out of the room."

"What happened?"

"He left," Quinn said. "Three or four times. Each time, Caddy and I thought it was for good. But he'd keep showing up like a house cat. Then that all stopped."

"Birthday cards?"

"For a while."

"Calls?"

"Almost never."

"Why?"

Quinn's diesel engine kept on chugging into the cold night, light cutting through the darkness and the long bend of Jericho Road. The little snowflakes hitting the asphalt and burning down to nothing.

"Go relieve that sitter for Rose," Quinn said. "I'll call later."

"Roger that."

Lillie reached for the door handle and started to get out. She pushed a bunch of her long curly hair behind her ear. She was strong and hard-edged, but could be tender and loving, too. She just didn't show that side to people she didn't trust. "You know all the talk about the DA wanting this thing for political points is Grade A bullshit."

Quinn nodded.

"Johnny Stagg is shitting his pants," Lillie said. "Chains LeDoux goes free on Friday."

"We could just stand back and watch," Quinn said. "Might be interesting."

Lillie gathered the box of boots in her arms and shook her head. "Damn, I wish it were that simple."

Quinn watched her walk back to her Jeep and then circled his big truck back to the main road, night dispatch reporting a domestic dispute in Sugar Ditch. A man had threatened to kill his wife. Neighbors had gathered outside the home to watch. OK. Another night.

Quinn hit the light bar and the siren and rode off.

Diane Tull rode out to the Jericho Cemetery with Caddy Colson after closing up the Farm & Ranch that night. Caddy had started off by visiting Jamey Dixon's grave every day, and then, when that became too painful, every week. She sometimes brought flowers, other times just scribbled notes or Bible verses, but always left with two fingers first pressed to her lips and then to the cold headstone. It was snowing just a bit when they got there, a few streetlamps shining on the flat land where Jericho people had been buried since the town's founding.

Caddy used the flat of her hand to brush away snow on top of Dixon's headstone and Diane put a hand on her shoulder and then walked down the rolling hill, the light growing dim, more of the headstones and markers now in shadows. But she could walk there blind, to the big head-stone of Lori's grandfather, who'd fought in World War II, and the other various markers of the Stillwell family. Lori's was curved and simple, a basic inscription:

LORI ANN STILLWELL, MAY 9, 1963 TO JULY 4, 1977.

I will fear no evil as thou art with me.

Diane hadn't been here in a long while, maybe not since she'd come back to Jericho. But seeing the dates, knowing that so much time had passed, that she wasn't that smart-mouth kid anymore but a graying woman with two grown sons, seemed like a dream. It was all there, that funeral, when they'd all stood there on that flat of land. That stuttering, sweating preacher trying to search and grasp and not find one true word to make sense of what happened to her that summer. Diane just remem-bered feeling more sorry for him than anybody, him finally just shutting up, closing his eyes, and praying that Lori would find eternal life and peace and all that sort of thing. This was never an ordained thing or willed by God's master plan. It was just horrible and the preacher knew enough not to say otherwise.

As Caddy had done for Dixon, she wiped away the snow from the top of the granite headstone and just hovered over where they'd buried Lori's body. The ground was hard and cold and she tried to summon up some good thought, maybe a prayer or a song that she knew Lori would have appreciated. She should've brought flowers.

In her mind, she saw Lori smiling and laughing, sitting on that warm stone in the middle of the creek with fireworks cracking overhead, and Diane smiled, too. But the way her mind worked, it all faded to the face of the man who'd forced himself on her and Lori, and then, that not being enough, shot them down on that hill. That disfigured face and the way he spoke with certainty and a goddamn ownership of them both crowded the laughing Lori right out of her head. It always did.

Diane closed her eyes and told Lori she was sorry.

When she opened them again, it had started to snow much harder, falling crooked and cold on the hillside, as she walked back up to where Caddy now stood by the truck.

"Did it help?" Caddy said.

"Nope."

"Me neither."

"They're not there," Diane said. "I don't know where they are, but they're not in this place."

"You know what I want?"

Diane opened the door to her truck and waited.

"I want to go to the bar and line up fifteen tequila shots end to end," Caddy said. "I want to take any pill I can find on the bathroom floor and I want to wake up in about a week, if I wake up at all."

"I don't like that plan."

"Me neither."

The women climbed in the truck cab and Diane cranked the engine, the windshield wipers clearing the view as she turned out of the cemetery.

"I have a fine son," Caddy said. "And good people who need help. That's what I told Jamey. I told him he'd helped me find my strength."

"I don't know if it's strength," Diane said, "but I'm not scared at all. I changed my mind about wanting all this to go away. I want the light to shine on everything that happened. I want people to know about the man that was hung. How could anyone do that and say it was a gift for me? I never asked for anyone to be murdered. Those men left a dark stain on everything since."

"There's something you need to know," Caddy said as they rode back toward The River, where she had left her old truck. "Quinn told me our father used to ride with those men. I'm ashamed of it. But I'm not surprised that's where I came from."

"You're a great woman, Caddy."

"No," she said, "I'm not. But I'm trying like hell to be good."

"I'm not afraid of those bikers," Diane Tull said, taking the curves and turns, shining the headlights up onto that old barn church. "I'm not. Every night, I pray that they'll come back for me."

"Why?"

"I want to look them right in the eyes and tell 'em to eat shit."

36

"You know the worst part about being a goddamn train conductor at a shopping mall?" asked Quinn's Uncle Van.

"Dodging shoppers in the food court?"

"No, sir," Uncle Van said. "Hemorrhoids."

"That kids' train really jostle you that much?"

"It's the sitting," Uncle Van said. "I get paid two bucks a kid to ride them around from Sears, past the Victoria's Secret, and then back down by the playground. You know by that Build-A-Bear workshop?"

"It's been some time since I've been to the Tupelo Mall."

"I'll tell you what," Uncle Van said, frying up a hamburger patty on the stove. "Bring Jason on by and I'll let him ride for free."

"That's nice of you," Quinn said. "Caddy said she had a trip planned."

"That boy's my kin," Van said. "You ever hear me say anything about him being a little dark?"

"No, sir."

"He looks just like your daddy after he'd go down to Panama City Beach and get himself a tan."

Van slipped the burger into a bun and went to his refrigerator to crack open a Bud for him and one for Quinn. They both stood up in his kitchen as Van ate. He lived in a trailer in a little collection of trailers near Fate called Chance's Bend. Van's newest profession at the mall had gone on longer than most of his careers except maybe painting houses. There were a few years that he mainly made a living by trapping coyotes and collecting bounty from a federal grant.

"How's your momma?"

"Fine," Quinn said. "Been a little tight at the farm, with her and Caddy moving in. Momma's house should be finished in a month."

"Damn contractors tell you a month, you better plan on six," Van said, taking a big bite, ketchup spilling on his white T-shirt. "That's the way they work. I know 'cause I used to do that shit."

Van was a fat man with a chubby face and a neatly trimmed mustache and goatee. He'd always reminded Quinn of a Buddha statue. He once saw one in a Chinese restaurant in Memphis as a kid and he remembered thinking at the time that his uncle had suddenly become famous.

Quinn sipped on the beer, not to be rude. He'd be riding on duty till 0600 and the roads were already getting slick.

"Hadn't seen you much since the storm," Van said. "God damn, we got lucky out here. Someone was to fart in a different direction, I wouldn't have nowhere to live."

Quinn nodded. He smiled at Uncle Van, the man still wearing his conductor's hat from his day job. He chewed and chewed and then said, "On the phone, you said you had some questions for me. Go on. Shoot."

"I tried Uncle Jerry," Quinn said. "But he's out on the road, Aunt Dot said somewhere in Texas, and not taking any calls. I needed to learn some things about my dad."

Van stopped chewing. He put down his burger and wiped his mouth. "You hadn't ever asked me word one about your old man. Is he in trouble again? What the hell did he do now?"

"Nothing," Quinn said. "I'm trying to find out what he was doing here back in 'seventy-seven when he started dating my mother."

"He was still working in Hollywood," Van said. "He'd come through maybe once a year to see family, check on your grandfather before he kicked the bucket. 'Seventy-seven was the year our momma died and he came back to help get Daddy settled. He wouldn't have ever come back after that except on account of your mother, trying to make that all work, trying to stay away from those high-flying Hollywood ways and all that shit. Did I tell you he once took me out to the Joshua Tree and we got so screwed-up on mushrooms that I had a four-hour conversation with an iguana?"

"Never heard that one."

"Strange," Van said, taking another bite of burger.

"I know he was in Jericho in '78 and married my mom in '79," Quinn said. "I was born the next year."

"He loved you, Quinn," Van said. "He's a failed man. But he loved you."

Uncle Van removed his conductor's hat as if suddenly realizing he had it on his head. "Damn kids drive me crazy, asking me to toot my horn. But there's some nice ladies out at Barnes Crossing. They got this one gal selling panties at Victoria's Secret. Holy shit."

"What I need to know is if my father used to ride with a motorcycle gang here," Quinn said. "The Born Losers."

Van's face didn't show much. He washed down the burger with some beer. He put down the beer, picked it back up and took another swig. "Hmm," he said. "Define what you mean by 'ride'?"

"Was he a member?"

"No."

"But he hung out with them?"

Van shrugged. His house still showed the admiration he had for his older brother, framed and signed movie posters from *Stroker Ace* and *Cannonball Run II*. Dom DeLuise signing in big scrawl *Don't play with your meatballs.*

"Your old man hung out with lots of folks," Van said. "You got to understand, he was a famous man when he came back to Jericho. Back in the seventies was prime time. He was making all these damn movies with Burt Reynolds and would show up wearing jackets from the latest films. Those real cool silky jackets. He had this one that Burt had given him, one made special by GM for the Trans Am. It had the big flaming bird on it, and I just thought it was the coolest thing ever. You know what your daddy did when I said I admired it?"

"Gave it to you."

"Hanging right there in my closet."

"Around the same time he met my mom, something real bad happened in Jericho," Quinn said. "You recall a man being lynched?"

Uncle Van stuffed his face in what seemed like an act of keeping his mouth shut. He chewed for a while and then shook his head. "I can't recall."

"You can't recall if my dad was around? Or the lynching?"

"Neither."

"Everybody else remembers it."

"Nephew," Van said, patting Quinn on the arm, "I did a lot of drugs back then. My memory is kind of spotty."

"Is it possible that my father was riding a lot with the Born Losers?"

"I guess."

"You need to more than guess."

"What's all this about?" Van said, taking the rest of the burger and shoving it into his mouth, licking his fingers. "You don't want to know this kind of shit about your dad. This was a hell of a long time ago and these were some really bad hombres. These the kind of folks you just didn't mention. You see them riding your way and, man, you better keep your eyes to the ground."

"They killed an innocent man."

"Your daddy wasn't a part of that."

"How do you know if you can't recall?"

"Leave it, Quinn," Van said. "Shit. Sit down with me and we'll watch some fights. They got the MMA on tonight. Those sonsabitches are bad news. You ever think about doing any of that stuff? I know you got all that jujitsu training and Ranger stuff. Lots of them fighters are ex-military."

"I kind of got my hands full."

Outside a small, insignificant window, the snow was coming down in wet clumps. In the center of Van's trailer, a small space heater blew hard in front of a forty-inch television. Quinn nodded to Van, leaving most of his beer on the counter.

"I wish I could be of more help."

Quinn put his hand on his uncle's shoulder and said, "When you decide to do the right thing, give me a call."

"My mind ain't so good these days, Quinn," Van said. "Don't be so hard on me. All I'm equipped to do is ride a fake little train in figure eights."

"You know where he is?"

"Who?"

Quinn didn't answer.

"No," Van said. "I guess I'm like you, I wrote Jason Colson off a while back. He started to turn on himself and there was nothing any of us could do."

"He's alive."

Van nodded. "Leave it," he said. "That man ain't done nothing but break all our hearts for a long, long time."

37

Lillie Virgil had been watching the Rebel Truck Stop since she'd officially gone off work at six. She paid the babysitter to stay late, exchanged her sheriff's office Jeep with her old Toyota Corolla, and found a decent observation point between the diner and the Booby Trap. Quinn would tell her to get home, spend time with Rose, and that he was moving things ahead. But Quinn could be so goddamn straight-ahead that explaining police work to a Ranger was like trying to teach a pit bull to tap dance. She'd been there about two and a half hours, watching the dinnertime crowd thin out and the stripper crowd start filing in. She'd seen Johnny Stagg twice. Once, he'd gone around the restaurant to glad-hand a bit, and, another time, he was crossing the parking lot, whistling, making his way to the Booby Trap.

Lillie had always heard Stagg kept a secret office at the Trap, away from prying eyes, and she didn't doubt it.

She'd about decided this wasn't worth it, at ten dollars an hour for the sitter, when she saw Hank Stillwell get out of that 1970 Plymouth Road Runner, a lovely off-green with a spoiler, and light a cigarette. He leaned against the closed driver's door awhile as if trying to make a decision. He finally shook his head, disgusted with himself, and walked toward the Booby Trap.

This could be interesting or disgusting. Depended on if this was a meet with Stagg or a late-night chicken choke.

Lillie called home. She'd give it another hour.

She'd wait it out.

"I'd prefer you not just showing up like this," Stagg said, eyes widening, looking over his desk at Hank Stillwell, before taking a seat in that big old executive chair. "You should've called."

"I called you eight times this evening, Mr. Stagg," Stillwell said. "Some woman kept on saying you were busy."

"I was."

"Because of the news?"

"I seen it," Stagg said. "I know he's getting out. Ain't no surprise to any of us. Story in the *Daily Journal* about who LeDoux is and what he'd done."

"I did what I could," Stillwell said. "I don't think Diane Tull wants this out in the open. She's a real private person. If she'd told everything and pushed the sheriff's office, maybe then."

Stagg nodded. He opened his hand toward a chair in front of his desk.

Hank Stillwell took a seat, all jittery and nervous, leg pumping up and down like a piston. Stagg just watched the beaten man, a man he'd known when he'd been cocky as hell, with all that leather and denim, long red hair and long red beard. Man used to look like a Viking. Now he looked about as tough as some blue-haired old lady.

"I could do with some more money," Stillwell said.

"That's why you come?" Stagg said. "More? For doing what?"

"I appreciated what you give me," Stillwell said, "but I've run out of food. And the bank says they gonna take my trailer. If I could just get another thousand till the end of the month, I can make it back. I got a job interview coming up at the Home Depot up in Tupelo. Gardening Department. Plants and stuff."

Stagg nodded.

"If I were you," Stagg said, "I'd shag ass out of town."

Stillwell looked like he might be a little drunk, although he wasn't slurring his words a bit. The man's coat reminded Stagg of what quail hunters used to wear when he was growing up. This one looked just about as old, plaid and washed out of any color. Stillwell's leg kept on jumping. Maybe he was on some kind of prescription pills.

"So what if he comes to town?" Stagg said, feeling his face twitch a bit. "What the hell could he do?"

"Blow both our brains out."

Stagg felt his cheek twitch a bit. He swallowed, leaning back into his big chair. "He doesn't want to go back to getting his dance card punched every night," Stagg said. "He's crazy as hell, but I know the truth about LeDoux. LeDoux is a damn businessman. He's already trying to shore up a pipeline between here and El Paso. The other night, he had a fiesta for the cartel boys left in Memphis. They had whores and skag and one hell of a time. A goddamn revival. That's what's on his mind."

"He thinks I'm the man who put him in prison," Stillwell said. "I'm pretty sure he wants that squared."

"Did you?" Stagg said, grinning. This was part of the Stillwell story that he'd never heard. Stagg liked it when the story picked up, adding another layer, getting interesting.

"I took some money from the Feds once," Stillwell said. "Long time ago. They fucked me in the ass and walked away like I was on fire. I ain't proud of it."

Stagg shook his head as if Stillwell was the sorriest piece of shit he'd ever seen. It was one thing to stoke the fire with LeDoux now. But to throw in with the law back when you rode with the man? That was an altogether different matter.

"Always heard they had someone on the inside," Stagg said. "LeDoux pissed off a dear and personal friend of mine up in Memphis. He was the one who sicced the big dogs on them bikers. But I guess they couldn't have done it without you, Mr. Stillwell. Congratulations. No wonder you're leaving skid marks in that chair."

Stagg laughed. Stillwell was shaking all over as if he'd caught a chill. "You got something to drink?"

"We got thirty-one flavors like anyplace else."

"I need some whiskey," Stillwell said. "I need it bad. I had a hard time just keeping my car heading straight."

Stagg craned his head at the bank of television monitors and the black-and-white images of the convenience store, diner, and restaurant. He saw the classic Plymouth parked sideways under a tall lamp. "Fine automobile," Stagg said. "Yes, sir."

Stillwell's teeth chattered and he clutched that old mackinaw coat across his body. His eyes were almost colorless, broken blood vessels across his cheeks. Johnny Stagg didn't think he'd seen a more sorry son of a bitch in his entire life. Almost felt some pity for him. *Almost.*

Stagg let out his breath, picked up the telephone, and told Jelly—a girl who'd gone from top-of-the-pole to fat-in-the-ass and now worked behind the bar—to bring them a bottle of Jack. "What color is that car of yours?"

"Metallic green."

"Original color?"

Stillwell nodded, still shaking. "Bought it brand-new."

"Well, I'll be . . ."

Sometimes Lillie listened to crazy-ass talk radio coming out of Tupelo just for the fun of it. To hear the right-wing nut jobs, a person would think they needed to stock up on water, canned food, weapons, and seal the walls up around them. It seemed to the brain trust operating out of Elvis's hometown that a new Civil War was brewing between those in the White House and regular hardworking families who didn't want to give "urban people"—a new racist code word—free money while American morals were being flushed down the toilets by Hollywood gays. Right after the host advised a caller that the government shouldn't reward people for being unemployed, there was a station break, with a commercial for the network. They desperately needed donations to keep American morals and Christian thoughts alive and well.

Lillie had heard enough. She turned the radio to Classic Country 101 and one of her favorite George Jones songs. *God rest the possum.*

It was about nine o'clock when she saw Hank Stillwell lumbering on out of the Booby Trap, tilting side to side. He looked as drunk as a goat, wandering in the snow. Maybe he'd gotten some companionship inside for forty dollars a song or a hundred to finish things off.

Men . . .

Lillie craned her head from where her Toyota sat in the shadows and watched as Stillwell started to extract the keys from his pocket. She couldn't let him drive, but she wasn't ready to leave.

She had to stop him and reached for her door handle just as Johnny Stagg emerged from the front door, striding across the lot and through the snow, bigger than shit. Lillie stopped. And waited.

Stagg reached Stillwell and grabbed the drunk man by the arm. He'd never in his life seen a man drink down a half bottle of Jack like it were nothing but milk. He held the man upright and told him that he sure had him. OK, he'd hold that note on the Road Runner. He'd even give him until the first of March. Just as a good friend would do.

"But if you can't come up with the thousand," Stagg said, "I can't pull no more favors."

"Yes, sir," Stillwell said.

Stagg handed him an envelope and Stillwell reached into his pocket for his keys. Stagg sought out the one for the car and handed the rest back. Hell, he wasn't about to take the man's trailer, too. Just then, Jelly's fat behind wriggled out into the parking lot with the dumb girl wearing a nothing of a dress and holding a transparent umbrella over her head to stop the snow.

"Jesus, don't you have no coat?" Stagg asked.

The girl shook her head. She looked to Stagg with those same dumb eyes she had when he told her she was gonna bend the goddamn pole. And so he'd put her to work at the bar, selling tank tops and tearing tickets.

Stagg put his hands inside the warm coat he'd bought at Hinton & Hinton in Oxford, treated canvas lined with Indian blanket. "Go ahead, Hank," Stagg said. "The girl is cold."

He stripped off the threadbare mackinaw and handed it to Jelly.

Stagg was getting tired of doing business out in the open, looking around the lot and seeing nothing but the great silent trucks with red parking lights glowing in the dark. He patted Stillwell on the back. "Make sure this man gets home and don't get run over," he said to Jelly.

"Everything's gonna be just fine," Stagg said, turning back to the Trap. "I got Mr. Chains a nice welcome-home gift. Keep him nice and warm."

There was talk, and then the keys in Stagg's pocket, and then the fat girl walking away with Stillwell. That old man might be hard up, but that little pudgy piece of trash wasn't worth the wax on that '70 Plymouth. Lillie watched as the girl helped Stillwell, who was stumbling-wild drunk, into her little Chevy.

Stagg had disappeared quick, back into the Booby Trap.

And Lillie just sat there, thinking on Stillwell and Stagg. Stagg and Stillwell.

She checked the time, knew she needed to get home. But this was a hell of a good time to catch a man. Drunk and pissed-off.

Lillie waited until the girl circled the Chevy around and headed out to Cotton Road. Lillie pulled out behind them, following all the way over the Big Black River, all swirling and indeed black, and through and around the Square.

This was something. Just sit back and let the sonsabitches show you the way.

She reached for her cell to call Quinn. There was a lesson somewhere in this for him.

38

"You don't believe I love you?" Jason Colson said. "How about I climb to the top of the water tower and write it out in spray paint for all of Jericho to see?"

"How old are you?" Jean said.

"I can climb a tree better than a monkey."

"And what if you break your neck, with all those people wandering the Square watching?" she said. "And then people will say, 'There goes Jean Ann Beckett. She killed a man for love.'"

"I could climb that old water tower drunk and blind," Jason said. "You know how I got my start doing stunts?"

"I do."

"Well, it's true," Jason said. "Trimming trees. Taking on jobs that no one wanted to do. I never been afraid of heights, small spaces, or going faster than a speeding bullet. When I was a kid, my brother Jerry and me used to hop freight trains and ride 'em down to Meridian, find another, and ride it back. I liked to ride up on top of the cars. I liked the wind and bugs in my teeth."

"If you're trying to prove you love me, you haven't succeeded," Jean said.

"But if you're trying to tell me to watch out, you're crazy, then you're doing just fine."

"God damn," Jason said. "Look at you."

Jean had on ragged cutoff jeans and a bikini top made from a red bandanna. She'd worn a T-shirt on the ride and tall cowboy boots, to play it safe, Jason taking her to his secret side of Choctaw Lake, in a little place away from the boaters and fishermen. This was a private place he'd been coming since he was a boy, nice and cool, covered in trees. He'd spread out a blanket and they'd eaten some cold fried chicken, beans, and slaw he'd bought in town. Jean lay back, head in his lap, and he stroked his fingers on her belly and rib cage, little goose bumps raising on her pale, freckled skin.

"My brother said if you made any passes at me, to let him know."

"Is that a charge in Jericho?"

"He's a lot older," Jean said. "He's very old-fashioned."

"Just a nice little picnic, darlin'," Jason said. "Nothing wrong with that."

Jason slid Jean's head from his lap and lay by her side, leaning into her and kissing her hard on the mouth. He held the kiss a long time. There was a nice cool breeze coming off the lake. On the portable radio they brought, they could hear music coming over state lines. A little station in Alabama playing an old Bob Dylan song.

Jason leaned onto his elbow and smiled down at this redheaded woman who'd come into his life. He moved his hand down around her belly and tried to move it into her cutoffs, Jean catching his hand by his wrist and bringing it north. Jason smiled.

"If you married me, there wouldn't be any sin."

"You ready for all that?" Jean said. "Mr. Hollywood. Let's not lie to each other. It's the Fourth of July, maybe our last couple days together. This is just a summer fling. Don't lie to either one of us."

"God damn it," Jason said. "I got a can of red spray paint. I will crawl up that old water tower and spell it out."

"And my brother will arrest your drunk ass."

Jason smiled, sliding his bare feet against Jean's, toes touching, leaning in for another kiss, smelling the sweetness of her hair. He came back up for air and touched her belly. "You like this song?"

"Sure," Jean said. "But Bob Dylan is no Elvis."

" 'The Mighty Quinn,' " Jason said. "I heard he wrote this song on account of Anthony Quinn being such a badass. Always liked the way it sounded tough. A man of no fear."

"And what are we doing tonight?"

"You want to ride out to the clubhouse with me?" Jason said. "We don't have to stay or nothing."

Jean looked at him with those green eyes, above that small freckled nose. He saw something there he didn't like, something akin to fear, and that's not the way he wanted these days to end.

"Just us," she said. "That's what you said."

"Just a few beers," Jason said. "OK?"

"No," Jean said, reaching up and gripping the back of his neck, pulling him down close for another kiss. She smelled so sweet, her big chest pushing against his as they breathed together. "This is our private club. And tonight, you stay with me."

"All night?" Jason said, grinning. Not many women could resist his smile.

"If that's what it takes."

39

"A nd how'd that go?" Quinn asked.

"Terrible," Lillie said. "Just god-awful. Am I getting overtime for this shit?"

"What'd he say?"

"Before or after he threw up?"

"Does it matter?" Quinn said.

They'd met up at the Sonic around eleven, the Sonic already closed, Lillie crawling up into the cab of the Big Green Machine. Quinn had the motor going, blowing the heat on high, while they talked. The snow had slowed. Not a single car passed them on the road into town. Everything as quiet as Christmas.

"He said the lynching hadn't been his idea," Lillie said. "He said it had all been Chains LeDoux and some fella named Big Doug. You ever heard that name?"

Quinn shook his head. He reached down into the console between them and grabbed his Thermos. He poured some into his cup and offered it to Lillie.

"Hell, I want to go to bed," she said. "Last thing I need is some caffeine, with this all pinging around in my head. Hank Stillwell may be the saddest man I've ever witnessed. He said he's felt bad the rest of his life for what they did to that poor fella. He admits to being with the gang when they went up into the hills and grabbed him. But when they decided on more than a beating, he took his motorcycle and drove off. He said he went down to Gulf Shores, Alabama, and stayed there for almost two years. Said he worked on fishing boats."

"So who saw the lynching?"

"He named a lot of folks and I wrote them all down," Lillie said. "But there was only one name that jumped out at me."

"Yep."

"Funny, how you can know a person."

"Or not know a person," Quinn said. "There's a lot about my daddy I don't know or care to know. I'm just surprised something like this happened in Tibbehah. I figured any bad shit would've happened on the West Coast. Why would he be so almighty stupid to fall in with some shitbirds like this? He'd already made a name for himself."

Lillie and Quinn sat together in the truck, the scanner breaking up the silence with the voice of a new woman they had on nights. She was talking back and forth with Kenny, who was doing a wellness check on an old couple living in Dogtown.

"I've heard a lot of stories about Jason Colson," Lillie said, "but not a single one about him being mean or having a temper."

"I don't think this was a usual situation," Quinn said. "In times of stress, people come unglued. They don't act themselves. This was right after a fourteen-year-old girl is murdered. Another is raped."

"I asked why they targeted this man," Lillie said. "I kept on wondering was it just because he was there? You know, the first black man they could find? But Stillwell said no. He said someone down in Sugar Ditch had named him. Said the son of a bitch was crazy as hell and had sold off the gold cross that had belonged to Lori. Stillwell said that over and over. 'He had the cross.'"

"That's pretty damning."

"Turns out, this man had found her stuff, her purse, and some other personal items in the trash," Lillie said. "Man was a drifter. He lived out of trash cans and dumpsters."

Quinn drank some coffee, warming his hands on the cup. An 18-wheeler passed the Sonic, driving at a high rate of speed. If he hadn't been busy, he might have chased the guy, told him this was a just a small town, but it was his town and did he mind taking it easy when he came to Jericho.

"So what was he doing at the Rebel?" Quinn asked. "With the stripper and Stagg?"

"I'm getting to that," Lillie said. "Hold on."

Quinn sipped on the black coffee, recalling a tin cup of instant being knocked out of his hand in a dry creek bed in the AFG. A sniper up in the rocky hills taking aim, thinking Quinn's team was coming for him and the twenty insurgents hidden in a cave. No one knowing where to find the sonsabitches until they started shooting. The bullet had gone through the cup and off his breastplate. And then there had been a lot of smoke bombs, flash bangs, and nearly twenty-four hours of zigzagging up that craggy face until they got to the mouth of that cave and brought those boys out, one by one, each replacing the next, until there was nothing left but that cold wind.

"Johnny Stagg took his Road Runner," Lillie said, "he didn't just out-and-out steal it. But took the paper in exchange for a thousand dollars due in a month."

"You got to hand it to Stagg," Quinn said, "he is one prismatic son of a bitch."

"Yes, sir."

"And the stripper was an incentive?"

"Nope," Lillie said. "She was just giving him a ride home."

"God bless her."

"But when I found Stillwell, mind you, he was crashed out on the rug in his living room," Lillie said. "I had to put the toe of my boot up under his chin a few times before he came to. He was a mess. He looked up at me and acted like I had caught him doing something. And so what do you do? I acted like I sure had caught him. He got to his knees—that's when he threw up the first time. Good Lord, if vomiting was an Olympic sport . . ."

"What'd he say?"

Another semi blew past the Sonic, not noticing the light bars on top of Quinn's truck or any of the thirty-five-miles-an-hour signs posted. "Should we chase them down?" Lillie said. "Once you got kids, these fuckers really start to piss you off."

"What'd he say?"

Lillie tilted her head, placed her hands on her thighs, and shook her head. "This wasn't the first or only money he'd been taking from Stagg."

Quinn waited. He reached for a dead cigar in his ashtray. Lillie reached out and touched his hands. "Wait until I leave," she said, "OK?"

Quinn nodded.

"Stagg paid him two thousand dollars to talk to Diane Tull," Lillie said. "Stagg told him to get her good and stoked and to go to the police about Lori. That piece of shit knew it wouldn't take two steps before we'd get on to the lynching. That's a man full of a lot of worry. He must have something real bad going with these Born Loser folks."

"Did you ask Stillwell about it?"

"Yeah," Lillie said. "And he was about to answer when his head dropped in the toilet. I had to drag him to the sofa, and even took off his boots. He could use a new pair of socks, every toe sticking out of a hole."

Most mornings, before driving back to the farm, Quinn would check up on the progress of his mother's house in town. The contractor got paid by the hour and, every time Quinn checked, the man was there right at 0600. He'd had a lot of work to do beyond just putting the roof back together. There was some bad structural damage to the brick walls, and a lot of plumbing, wiring, and flooring had to be restored. Today, the front door was unlocked and open, the contractor not there, as he'd finished two days before.

The house where Quinn had grown up was oddly empty and strange. They'd moved most of his mother's furniture, appliances, and Elvis memorabilia into a storage unit. A good two-thirds of the house was pretty much the same, but the new section didn't have the old blue carpet or the popcorn ceiling. The smell was different, of fresh-cut wood and glue, and the windows were different. Instead of the old wood frames, there was modern, energy-efficient vinyl.

Quinn missed the old windows. He was walking over to inspect the glass and casing when he saw a car pull into the drive. Jean Colson got out of the car, opened the hatch, and lifted out a box. Quinn met her in the driveway and helped her carry a few more boxes into the house.

"Looks like they haven't finished the paint," Quinn said, "just the primer."

"I was coming to town anyway," Jean said. "Figured I'd just bring back some pots, pans, and few cups and plates."

"There's no rush to leave the farm," Quinn said. "That house is yours as much as mine. Hell, you grew up there."

"I appreciate that," Jean said. "But that old house hasn't but one bathroom. I prefer having my own, thank you very much."

Quinn shrugged as Jean walked through the rooms and stared up at the ceiling, the place where that ragged hole had been after the tornado and, for months after, a blue tarp. She walked back to her big empty bedroom and into the kitchen, where some new stainless steel appliances had been installed, the insurance paying out for all the storm damage.

"What do you think?" Quinn said.

"Looks good," she said. "I still wouldn't mind closing off that porch, maybe adding in screen."

"There's always time for additions," Quinn said. "But you got a roof over your head, a new kitchen, and some new windows."

"The windows don't match."

Quinn nodded and rubbed the back of his neck.

"Are you doing all right?" she asked.

"I've been on duty all night, Momma," Quinn said. "I just came by to make sure things were locked up."

"I got a key yesterday," she said, eyeing him. "There's not much to steal."

"Boom and I can help you when you're ready," Quinn said, "but I kind of got used to your cooking."

Jean smiled. "You don't need me," she said. "You got Ophelia to do all that."

"You ever eaten her food?"

"Bad?" Jean said.

"Yes, ma'am," Quinn said. "I wouldn't advise it."

Jean felt along the walls where the Sheetrock had been taped and mudded. Her heels clacked loudly in the open living room as she glanced around at all the space she'd have to fill again. She'd never mentioned it, but Quinn knew she was proud of the home for holding together during the storm. She and his father had bought the one-level ranch in 1982 and it was pretty much all he remembered. From time to time, Jason would still find some of Quinn's buried G.I. Joes in the backyard, his and Caddy's old play fort still up in some pine trees in the backyard.

"I might move to town," Quinn said, "let Caddy and Jason have the farm until they get situated. She talked about using that old trailer at The River. But I don't want Jason out there. She'll get settled, but I don't want her to rush."

"Where will you go?"

"I had an invite to move in with Ophelia," Quinn said.

Jean smiled. "I wondered how long that would take."

"No lectures on me living in sin?"

"Not from me," Jean said. "Sin can sometimes be fun. But some people may not approve. Just don't make a quick decision, with that election coming up."

Quinn laughed and shook his head. "Hell, that doesn't matter," he said. "That thing's lost. People around here think Lillie and I are guilty of murder. The DA in Oxford won't dismiss charges or take things to the grand jury. They're gonna hold things long enough to make sure my name means nothing."

"Lots of folks believe in you," Jean said. "Do you know how many people stop me on the street to thank me for all you've done? Or at church? Or the Rexall?"

"How many folks are going to walk up to my momma and tell her the worst?"

"Think about Ophelia," she said. "That's a nice thing for Caddy. But once I've moved out, she and Jason can take the whole upstairs till they get settled."

Quinn nodded. He put his arm around his mother, light creeping into the front windows and across the new floors. He patted her back and she let out a long breath, smiling and settling into the thought of coming back home after nearly a near.

"Caddy told me you're getting a lot of pressure to solve what happened to Diane Tull," Jean said. "And that mess that came after."

"Yep."

"That's why you wanted to know about your father and that gang."

"I shouldn't have asked," Quinn said. "I know how hard it was to raise me and Caddy. You tried your best to keep him out of our lives and do the best you could for us. To bring him up was wrong."

"No it wasn't."

"He's a dishonorable man," Quinn said. "Let's not talk about him again."

Jean stared up at Quinn. "If you could talk to him, what would you ask?"

"Just one thing," Quinn said. "What did he see the night that man was lynched?"

"It won't bother you to see him, not knowing why he left us?" Jean said. "I'm worried about you more than him if y'all came face-to-face."

"Shit," Quinn said, "I don't give a damn. Lots of men leave their families. I was lucky to have you and Uncle Hamp. Y'all raised me. He doesn't mean a thing to me."

"But it could help you," Jean said, "with the DA's office and the mess they got you in. If he'd tell you the truth."

Quinn didn't say anything. The morning light had crept over the floor and was moving up the walls. Jean stepped away from Quinn for a moment and walked the new hardwood. She put her arms around her waist and stared down as she paced. "I never wanted you to speak to him," Jean said, "but I guess that's my own selfishness."

"What does it matter?" Quinn said. "He could be dead, for all we know."

This time, Jean was silent. She met her son's eye and tilted her head. "He's not dead," she said. "Not yet."

Quinn nodded. "How do you know?"

"Because your Uncle Van goes to see him a few times a year," Jean said. "He comes back and runs his mouth to me as if I give a shit."

"Van lied to me, then."

"He's just protectin' you."

Quinn nodded, not buying it. "How's Van afford to get out west?"

"Your father hasn't been out west for almost ten years," she said. "He's been working at some horse farm in Hinds County, getting himself clean. Some little town called Pocahontas."

Quinn put his right hand into his Levi's front pocket, waiting, thoughts rushing through his head fast. He tried to breathe, slow it all down the best he could, the same way you did when aiming a rifle. Jean walked to her son and put a hand on Quinn's face and said, "Don't let the bastard get to you," she said. "Get your questions answered and then get gone."

Quinn nodded. "Yes, ma'am."

40

Quinn took the Trace down to Highway 82 and then followed the interstate over into Hinds County. He'd been driving straight for about three hours before he found Pocahontas Road, which ran right past an old restaurant shaped like a teepee called, rightly so, Big Teepee Barbecue. He slowed, circled back, and drove into the gravel lot, finding a small building set apart from the teepee, a combo restaurant and convenience store. A sign on the door promised church services in the teepee every Sunday at ten a.m. A bald man with a short white beard came from a back office, wiping his hands on his apron, when he heard the bell. He came on up to the counter with a big smile on his face. "Yes, sir?"

"I'm looking for a man named Jason Colson," Quinn said, wearing official shirt, badge, and gun on his hip. "Lives somewhere around here."

The man's smile dropped. He shook his head. "Never heard of him."

"He's not wanted," Quinn said.

"Why you looking for him, then?"

"It's a personal matter."

The man shook his head some more. "Sorry," he said. "Cain't help you."

Quinn looked around the store, at the little red-and-white oilcloths over the tables and the rows and rows of bubble gum, snack cakes, pork rinds, and cleaning supplies. A big cooler lining a back wall filled with cold drinks, ice cream, and live bait. Behind the register was a fairly decent-sized model of Noah's Ark.

"You put that together?" Quinn asked.

The man craned his neck and scratched his cheek. "Took me three years," he said. "It's completely made of Popsicle sticks. Had me a guy come in last year and offer me five hundred dollars for it. You believe that? I told him I couldn't take it. It brings too many people pleasure to see it and get to thinking about the wicked ways of the world. God could take our asses out again."

"You bet."

"I'm a preacher, too," the man said. "We got services on Sunday. Figured the teepee would make people think on things. I became fully ordained through a course on the Internet. Only cost me fifty dollars."

"Yes, sir." Quinn nodded. "Worth every penny."

The man wore a T-shirt had a big fishing hook printed on it and reading *Hooked on Jesus*. He had a large belly, with the shirt riding up above his blue jeans several inches and stained with barbecue sauce. "You from Jackson?"

"Jericho."

"Where the hell's that?"

Quinn jerked his thumb over his shoulder toward the northeast. The man nodded back at him as if he knew exactly where Quinn was talking about.

"Now, who's this guy again?"

"White man in his sixties, a little shorter than me," Quinn said. "Other than that, I can't tell you much. He might've told you that at one time he worked in Hollywood."

"The stunt fella?" the man asked. "You're looking for that old stunt fella? Hell, yeah. What's his name?"

"Colson," Quinn said. "Jason Colson."

"Yeah, yeah, I know'd him," the man said. "I think he rented a trailer from Mr. Birdsong. He's got him some land down the road divided up in little lots. Ain't much. But he don't charge much, either."

"Where?" Quinn asked.

"You say you're some kind of kin?"

Quinn followed Pocahontas Road to a dirt road with the *No Trespassing* sign the good reverend had told him about. He followed the road for a quarter mile and soon found ten trailers huddled close together on a circular cut-in at the dead end. Quinn got out of his truck, chose the trailer that looked most promising out of ten trailers with little promise, and knocked on the door. The trailer was old and misshapen, with brittle wooden steps leading to it. Inside, a dog started to bark. No one came to the door. He knocked some more.

Nothing. The wind was cold, but the sun had started to cut through the clouds.

He tried two more trailers. At the third one, a skinny old white woman holding a cigarette came to the glass door but didn't open it. She just stared at Quinn. He smiled back at her while she blew some smoke out from her lips and cracked the door. She was wearing a set of pink pajamas and tube socks. "I done paid that ticket."

Quinn shook his head. "I'm looking for Jason Colson."

The woman shrugged. Her eyes were shrunken and sallow, and she wiped her nose while she stood there and waited for Quinn to offer her something. She was skinny, her wrinkled skin just kind of sagged from the bone.

"He lives in one of these trailers," Quinn said. "He's not in any trouble. If that's what you're thinking."

"Good," she said. "Man don't need no more."

"How's that?"

"He's been keeping himself clean," she said. "He paid off those mean men from Jackson. He don't need no more trouble from the law."

Quinn waited a few seconds. "It's a personal matter," he said.

"Why?"

"He's a relative."

"Oh, sure . . ." she said, smiling a row of yellowed and uneven teeth. "Just who are you to him?"

Quinn studied the wrinkled woman, holding herself in the wedge of the door, blowing smoke out into the cold air. The whole thing crazy as hell, that this woman would know more about his own father, feel like she's got to be kind of protective of him. She couldn't stop squinting at Quinn's face. He couldn't answer her.

"Mr. Jason don't live here no more."

Quinn nodded.

"He was living with that woman, Darlene, but they got into it one night and she left," the woman said. "I think she stole his truck. He tossed all her shit out in the yard. She come back and got it, and that's the last I seen of her. She was only with him till his money run out. She said she loved him, but she was just hanging on the man 'cause he used to be a big shot. But I figure you know about who he is, and all the folks he knowed, or you wouldn't be here."

"Yes, ma'am."

"Burt Reynolds," she said. "My Lord. Did you know Mr. Jason once broke a beer bottle off Terry Bradshaw's head? You know, that old quarterback on TV?"

Quinn had heard the story.

"Where'd he go?" Quinn said.

She tiptoed outside the house, delicately, as if leaving her tin shell was going to make her too vulnerable. She smoked more of the cigarette, blowing a long stream into the air. Her voice was as gravelly and worn as a lifetime smoker's should be. She nodded over toward a trailer up the hill on some eroded land. It wasn't the worst on the lot, but it was close. The single-wide set up on concrete blocks, with a rusted roof and tinfoil in the windows. An old red Trans Am, with flat tires and half covered in a tarp, sat in the front yard. The window had been busted out, and the wind ruffled the tarp up over what probably had once been a fine car.

"Y'all are kin."

"Why you say that?"

"You look damn-near just like him."

Quinn nodded, still looking at that relic of a car.

"He works down the road at that big horse barn," the woman said.

"How far?"

"Not far," she said. "You can't miss the place. Biggest goddamn barn I ever seen in my life. He's been working for those rich folks for a while. I hear he's been living up there, too. Real nice, when he's not drinking. Something awful wrong with him. To hear the things come out of that trailer up there . . . That woman Darlene was the devil. She beat him down to nothing."

The barn was fashioned out of river stone and large cypress beams and stood as large as a couple aircraft hangars joined end to end. It had been built high on a hill overlooking hundreds of acres of rolling farmland where horses grazed among Black Angus cattle. Quinn followed a private road that twisted past an endless lake, a big stone mansion, and through the pasture, until he turned uphill and saw the stables and two large open corrals, where some kind of training was happening. The sun was setting over the pasture and turned the air a bright orange through the kicked-up dust.

A group of young kids in thick coats, western wear, and cowboy boots sat on a fence as a man and a young woman stood near a young boy on the back of a small spotted horse. They were talking to the kids, showing them the basic tack, handing over the reins to the kid in the saddle. The man rubbing the horse's forehead between the eyes. The man wore a hat low across his eyes, but as Quinn walked closer, studying him, he could see the guy wasn't much older than himself. He was telling the kids about the right kind of pull on the reins when they were ready to go and when they were ready to stop. He talked about being gentle to the animal and that a kick in the ribs could be firm without hurting the animal.

Quinn recalled a horse that had belonged to his father, a palomino named Bandit. There was a strange feeling as Quinn walked, a little bit of light-headedness with the copper-colored air and the reddening skies. The laughter of the children sitting on the rail. The woman who was helping with the instruction was pretty and blond and smiled right at Quinn as he made his way to the railing and leaned his forearms across the top rung. The girl let go of the horse and came over to where he stood. She had a slow, easy walk, with her boots, tight jeans, fitted Sherpa coat, and feathered hair.

"Looking for Jason Colson," he said.

She smiled some more at Quinn, strangely, as if should she know him, and pointed to the mouth of the barn. Quinn tipped his ball cap and walked toward the door, the feeling of being uneasy and unsettled something very unfamiliar. Before he walked into the big open cavern, he spit into dirt and clenched his teeth.

The floors of the barn were red brick and the ceiling was cathedral-tall, with thick cypress beams crossing overhead. The big sliding doors were open at the opposite side of the barn, hundreds of meters away, and above them was a circular window of stained glass showing two horses grazing in a green meadow. Its colored light shone down onto the bricks.

Quinn followed a lot of empty stalls, nicer than many homes in Tibbehah County, and on through the big central space, its brickwork laid in Byzantine patterns and different colors. Above was one of the tall spires he'd spotted on the drive from the main gates.

Quinn kept walking. Not seeing anyone, not even a horse, only hearing the sound of a radio playing down among the stalls. He followed the music, recognizing the song, "Choctaw Bingo," this one sounding like Ray Wylie Hubbard and not James McMurtry. More reverb and twang through the barn.

His arms and legs felt funny and loose as he spotted a man leaning into a stall over a half door. The man wore Wrangler's and beaten boots, a tight green-checked snap-button shirt and no hat. The man's hair was longish, more gray than blond, his skin the color of stained wood. He had a graying mustache and goatee and he was laughing.

Quinn stopped walking. He just stood there, watching the man, and then a horse leaned its big head out of the stall. The man popped open a beer, the horse taking it from his hand and shaking it all loose from the can, throwing his head back in pleasure. The man laughed and laughed, taking the empty and tossing it. He rubbed the forehead of the horse, walking away from the stall, eyes down, smirk on his face, and then raised them and looked at Quinn.

Quinn just stared.

The man stopped walking, hands on his hips. Something familiar but off about the face. The lines were different. He had a big scar on his cheek, white and zagging, different from the burnt skin. The man took in all of Quinn, eyes and mouth serious as hell, finally just shaking his head and saying, "Well, god damn, ain't you got big."

41

"ow'd you find me?" Jason Colson asked.

"I asked at the Big Teepee."

"How'd you know where to start?"

"Mom told me."

"Didn't know she knew," Jason said, sitting down on a railroad tie outside the barn, staring out at the rolling brown pastures, that big, endless lake where ducks and geese gathered. "We hadn't spoken in a long while."

"Uncle Van," Quinn said. "She knew from him. But he never said a word to me."

"I told him not to," Jason said, stroking his old-dog goatee and mustache. His cheeks and neck were clean-shaven. His clothes were neat and fit well. He'd grown his hair long, not like some kind of hippie but like a man from another time, the frontier days or something. He was darker than Quinn and weighed a bit more, with something off about his mouth when he spoke, like his teeth had been busted out and replaced. Jason seemed nervous as he talked, careful with all his words, as Quinn stood above him.

"I'm glad to see you, Quinn," he said. "You may not believe it, but I am."

Quinn nodded.

"How's Caddy?" Jason said. "Van's told me some things. I've been real concerned."

"How about we just talk about why I'm here?"

Jason looked off and shook his head, not being able to think of another reason his son might come to see him. He seemed like he had started to settle in, would maybe give Quinn the speech about why he left, how it'd been better for everyone but he'd kept real good tabs. He'd be real proud of Quinn's service and all that kind of J.C. bullshit he knew too well from the letters that one day just stopped cold.

"You used to ride with a crew called the Born Losers," Quinn said, not asking but stating it.

Jason nodded, eyes scrunched up, knees bunched up around his chest, looking up at Quinn. "About a hundred years ago."

"Well, some bad shit happened about a hundred years ago," Quinn said, "and you were an eyewitness to it."

"Can you stay a bit?" Jason said. "We can talk about all this stuff. But can I take you out for a meal?"

"Some barbecue at the Teepee?"

"A steak dinner in Jackson," Jason said. "Would mean the world to me, son."

"I don't have time," Quinn said. "I've spoken to a man named Hank Stillwell. He said you were riding with Chains LeDoux the night a black man was abducted in town, taken out to Jericho Road, and hung from a tree. Nobody has forgotten."

"You sure don't waste a lot of time," Jason said. "Can you at least tell me about your mother? How's Jean doing?"

"I don't preach, Jason," Quinn said, "but I don't think my family's welfare is any of your concern. You need to be more worried about your involvement in this lynching."

"I didn't lynch that man," Jason said. "Sure, I remember it. But I didn't kill someone . . . I've fucked up plenty, son."

"Don't call me that," Quinn said. "You don't have the right."

"I said I've fucked up plenty," Jason said. "I go to meetings in the basement of a church every Wednesday. I've gotten up on the horse again and fallen off. Right now, I'm staying on. But any bad things I've done, I've done them to myself."

"That a fact?"

"And my actions have hurt others," Jason said. "I know that. You really come all this way to ask me about the damn Born Losers? I fooled around with that group maybe a month at most. I left town and never hung out with them again. A buddy of mine wanted me to ride and it was just something to do between films."

"Raising hell and becoming a star."

"I wasn't a star," Jason said. "I busted up my whole body and head to make other people stars. Broke my back twice and nearly every bone in the body."

"I figure they don't give Oscars for that."

"I know you're bitter," Jason said. "I don't blame you."

"July fourth, 1977," Quinn said. "Where were you?"

"Hell, I don't know."

"Hell you don't," Quinn said. "You were part of that motorcycle gang. I don't give two shits about the reasoning behind it. I want to know what you saw and where y'all went that night. Uncle Hamp covered the thing because he thought you loved his sister."

"I did love his sister."

"He shouldn't have made this thing OK," Quinn said. "Y'all fucked up."

"Some man killed Hank Stillwell's daughter," Jason said. "Raped and shot another girl. There was this man lived up in the hills . . ."

"How about you follow me to the Hinds County sheriff's office,"

Quinn said. "You can make your statement there. There will be some complications putting this case together, given our situation."

"What situation?"

"Running in my own father for murder."

"I didn't kill anyone," Jason said, standing. The lake behind him had turned a hard copper-gold, ducks skimming the water a bit and then landing with a gentle smoothness in small coves and hidden pockets. Quinn stared at Jason Colson. The old man's forearms stood out, where he'd rolled up the sleeves of his shirt, muscled and corded from plenty of outdoor work.

His face had a plastic quality to it of someone having to fit it back together but not getting the configuration just right. One of the blue eyes was just a little off and Quinn wondered if it might be glass.

"I know I'm not pretty to look at," Jason said. "I wish I'd taken better care of myself. I wish I'd taken better care of you and Caddy. Why don't you go have dinner with me and I'll roll out a list of regrets that will stretch from here to Jericho."

Quinn nodded.

"Did you see Chains LeDoux, Hank Stillwell, or any of the gang abduct that man?" Quinn said. "Did you take a ride with them out to Jericho Road after Diane Tull was found wandering after she'd been raped and shot?"

"I knew you'd find a reason to come after me," Jason said, "but I never figured it would be for something I hadn't done."

The men stood within maybe five feet of each other up on that hill, sunset leaving everything red and black, clouds scrambled above them in weird colors. "You're refusing to make a statement or take part in an interview?"

"What the hell we doing now?" Jason said, rubbing his goatee. "God damn."

"You're coming with me."

"No, sir," he said. "I can't walk off my job."

"You're coming back to Jericho," Quinn said. "You can do it on your own or in cuffs. I got a D ring in the back of the truck where I can chain you."

"Damn, you sure hate me."

Quinn swallowed, hand absently touching the leather pouch on his belt where he kept the cuffs.

Jason bowed and shook his head. "OK."

"You can notify who you like," Quinn said. "Bring any stuff you might need. You might be there for a few days."

"I wasn't part of this."

"You got a lot of explaining to do," Quinn said.

"Nothing to explain."

"We'll get that on record," Quinn said. "And then we'll talk about the charges."

Chains LeDoux walked out of prison as he'd come in, the jeans a little tighter but the old T-shirt, flannel shirt, and leather jacket still fit just fine. A deputy sheriff named E. J. Royce he'd known down in Jericho had picked him up from the correctional center, helped with the out-processing and signed some paperwork, then drove him down the Natchez Trace straight out of the hills of Tennessee and down into Tupelo, where they stopped off at a Walmart and let him get some clean underwear, a toothbrush, and deodorant. He took Chains as far as a Super 8 Motel on Highway 45 where Chains's old lady Debbie was waiting, now a gray-headed grandmother of four but still the kind of woman who opened the door in a nightie and holding a bag of weed and a bottle of Jack Daniel's. They fucked that night like kids.

She helped cut his hair and trim his beard. One of the younger boys had made him a new vest with a new patch and the colors for the Losers. Debbie said they had something real special for him the next morning.

Chains couldn't sleep with excitement.

At dawn he awoke to the sound of what might have been a hundred cycles out in the parking lot, all revving their engines at the same time. He jumped up out of bed, threw on some pants, and walked out, bare-chested, covered in tattoos, and barefoot, and looked down at all those good old boys looking up at the second balcony, revving their Harleys over and over. A few more doors at the Super 8 opened but closed quick.

Chains wasn't able to dress fast enough, Debbie helping him find his boots, combing his long stringy hair and beard, and holding open his leather jacket. He slid into the vest himself.

"How do I look?" he said.

"Like Chains-Goddamn-LeDoux."

He kissed the woman, who he'd laid maybe a million times but who now seemed unfamiliar, hard on the mouth. He walked out on the second-floor balcony and raised his hands, the dozens of Losers revving and hollering until he walked down the steps into the parking lot and a path was cleared through so many faces he didn't know, young men who looked at him with admiration and respect.

He saw a few of the old faces, those who'd come to visit, written him letters, and kept him going on club business. Frank Miller had his arms wide when Chains got close and embraced him in a big hug of brotherhood and friendship, patting his back and saying, "You ready?"

"Hell-fucking-yes."

Behind him stood his old Harley 1200 Super Glide, painted an electric black with an evil jester's face on the tank. The saddle shone and the chrome gleamed in the early-morning light. Chains walked to it, touched the handlebars for the first time in twenty years, and started to weep. A big man with lots of ink on his face and across his throat approached

Chains and offered his hand. He wouldn't see Big Doug here. Big Doug had died in '99 from lung cancer.

Chains threw his leg over the bike, rested his foot on the kick-starter, and fired up the engine. All the Born Loser boys yelled. Up high on the second-floor balcony, Debbie waved. She was crying, too. She said this was it, she couldn't see him again.

She'd gotten married to a good man who she said ran the meat section at a Kroger in Southaven.

The world had changed.

But Chains hadn't.

"Let's go fuck some shit up and raise some hell," he said.

Not one goddamn bit.

42

"Happy Birthday, America, and all you motherfuckers, too," Big Doug said, toasting the Born Losers late that night. They'd been outside the clubhouse for most of the day, shooting guns at bottles and cans, smoking weed, and drinking tequila. Jason was so drunk, it was hard to stand, make his way to the jukebox, and find the Flying Burrito Brothers and punch up "At the Dark End of the Street," one of his favorites. He'd come to the party late, having spent most of the night at the fair, winning Jean an armload of stuffed animals, taking her on swirling neon rides, and driving her home on his bike, a long, intimate kiss before they said good night. She knew Jason was headed back to the clubhouse to see how the boys were doing and she wanted no part of it.

He was having a pretty good time until Hank Stillwell ran through the haze of dope smoke and started yelling through the music that some crazy nigger had killed his baby. The music stopped and the silence of it all was something. Big Doug had to run up to him, pin Stillwell's arms against his side, and tell him to slow down. "What the hell are you talking about?"

Stillwell said some black man had forced his Lori and her friend Diane into his car and rode them out to Jericho Road. where he'd done it. "He raped Diane and shot my baby," he said. "Sweet Jesus! God!"

Big Doug hadn't let go of his arms, not pinning him anymore but hugging him tight. "We got you, bud," he said. "We got you."

"She died," he said. "She died out there in the middle of some field."

Chains hadn't said another word, the whole club getting to their feet, including Jason and the women. Almost everybody was drunk, high, or both.

Everybody had come down from that tall buzz, knowing that one of their brothers had lost a child. A monster was still out there somewhere, rolling through the hills of Tibhehah County, their home turf, looking for more girls, thinking he could do as he pleased without any retribution.

"What'd he look like?" Big Doug said.

"Shit," Stillwell said, "I don't know. He's black. He's stealing white children. He's raping and killing. God!"

Big Doug still held him. Long Tall Sally poured a shot of tequila and brought it to where they stood wrapped together. Stillwell knocked the first one out her hand. But she didn't flinch, Big Doug telling her to do it again, pour out another, and her setting it in Stillwell's hand. He took that one, gulped it down, and then another, and Chains had some reds he placed direct in Stillwell's mouth and within ten minutes he was stoned and glassy-eyed but talking about murder and vengeance and then stories about when Lori was born in Tupelo and how proud he'd been. "God," he said. "She came to see me today. She asked me for money and I turned her away. I told her she was dressed like a whore."

Jason had heard it. He could not look the man in the eye. Someone had found Stillwell a chair as he kept talking. LeDoux marched out of the room, most of the gang following him, to the line of motorcycles. He was giving orders now, telling the boys they were going to ride down into Sugar Ditch and not leave until the blacks gave up their man. "Or we'll burn down every last shack."

Stillwell was alone with Sally. She kneeled and cried with him.

"I tried to talk to Diane Tull's father," he said. "I told him we needed to find this man who did this. But his wife wouldn't let him go. Some people ain't got

297

no nuts. That's why we ride together. A man fucks with one of us and he's fucked with all of us."

He was slurring a lot.

Jason looked to Sally. Sally was crying, rubbing Stillwell's back.

From the open door of the clubhouse, Jason heard, "Burn the fucking place down. We ain't coming back until we found this bastard and hung him high."

The screams and yells brought a coldness to Jason's stomach, sobering him up quick. He felt light-headed and weak, watching Stillwell crumple in on himself, nearly off the chair, the tiny circles on his back from Sally.

Big Doug appeared big and determined in the doorway. He looked right at Jason and lifted his chin. "Come on," he said. "You're a part of us now."

43

Nearly a month passed and Johnny Stagg didn't hear jack shit from Chains LeDoux. He was back in Tibbehah—*Oh yes, sir*—he'd ride the town square bigger than shit with his gang of thieves, tattooed morons, and rejects. Stagg had heard about their bonfire parties, and a few of his boys had a daily stop at the Booby Trap to watch the girls ride the pole and throw some money down for a pecker pull. But the hell that was to follow, the worry that came over Johnny Stagg all those nights, never came back. Stagg figured maybe that time in Brushy Mountain had been good for the man, maybe Chains didn't have hate and vengeance on his mind. Maybe the fella just wanted to drink, get laid, if he was still inclined, and ride those scooters all over the South. Johnny thinking on this and then talking a bit to Mr. Ringold about the strangeness of it, this being the end of February, spring weather coming on now, with the windows open to his first office in the Rebel.

"That's good," Ringold said. "The supreme art is to subdue the enemy without fighting."

"You think that's what we done?"

"I think he may have gotten the message from Mr. Houston," Ringold said. "Burning down their Memphis clubhouse was a bold move."

"Wasn't my idea," Stagg said. "Still don't like it."

"But it showed they weren't welcome," Ringold said. "Them or the Mexicans."

"Fucking Mexes," Stagg said. "We ain't got no border. Down in El Paso or up in Memphis, those cartels have expanded way out from Texas. Atlanta is overrun with them folks. Don't know why anyone thought they weren't coming to Mississippi or Memphis."

"But they were already here?"

"On account of this local boy named Donnie Varner," Stagg said. "His daddy runs that Quick Mart out in the county. You know him? Ole Donnie tried to double fuck the cartel and the ATF. He's in federal prison at the moment. Word has it he done it all for some good-looking piece of Mexican tail."

"What's Houston's story?" Ringold said. "Why won't he do business with them anymore?"

"Sonsabitches tried to kill him," Stagg said. "He was coming out of some disco up on Summer Avenue, drinking champagne and doing what blacks do, and some cartel boys sprayed his Escalade with an AK-47."

"That'll piss you off."

"I think we got things worked out just fine now," Stagg said. "We got LeDoux knowing his place. I got Sheriff Colson knowing which side the bread is buttered on. We get LeDoux back in prison, and that'd be just the damn cherry on things."

"How close are we?"

"'Course you know Colson arrested his own goddamn father," Stagg said. "He cuffed him, charged him as an accessory in that lynching, and kept him in the county jail for three days before he got kicked loose."

"If he didn't have anything on him," Ringold said, "why'd he charge him?"

"I imagine Quinn's got some problems with his old man," Stagg said. "I knowed Jason Colson for a long time and real well. He's a crazy son of a bitch and the biggest cooch hound in north Mississippi. His wife is a fine woman, although she thinks I'm trash come to town, and Colson running out on her was a disgrace."

Ringold nodded. He leaned back in his chair so the front legs came off the ground and his back rested against the wall. "Colson is fucked," he said. "Ain't nobody in this town except for his momma and family will vote for him. He's done."

"Maybe," Stagg said. "Honestly, I don't give a shit. There's a local boy who's thinking of tossing his hat into this thing, was in the Guard and had a couple years with Eupora P.D., and he might be a good fit. You can't trust Colson."

Just then Willie James knocked on Stagg's office door with a shell-shocked face and wide-open mouth. He just kept shaking his head over and over and telling Stagg that he needed to come on with him outside, that there was some trouble that he needed to tend to at that very moment.

Stagg looked to Ringold. Ringold leveled the chair and stood, wearing a Levi's jacket over his automatic pistol. They followed Willie James through a back hall and the bustling kitchen, floor slick with grease, until they turned outside through a pair of doors and watched as Willie James pointed to the a large rusted dumpster and a couple cooks and waitresses who were looking inside a small sliding door cut in the side.

"What is it?" Stagg said. "Shit. Tell me."

Willie James seemed unable to speak. He just pointed.

Stagg walked on over to the dumpster, pissed off as hell that he got bothered for every little thing going on at the truck stop. Last week it was a bird that had flown into the convenience store, and two weeks ago he had to drive a girl from the club to the hospital in Jackson 'cause her fake titty exploded.

"What the hell?" Stagg said, peering through the opening, all that rotten chicken and meat loaf and moldy hamburgers making a hell of a stench. He couldn't see nothing. And then the back of a man emerged, facedown and not moving. Stagg just seeing the shape of him, the old flannel shirt and an arm reaching forward as if the man had tried to crawl himself out of this world of shit. "Well, I'll be. Willie James? You crawl in there and see who it is."

"I'd rather not, sir."

"Get your ass in there," Stagg shouted. "Use a fucking stick or something, but flip his ass over."

Willie James was not pleased, as he used the opening as a toehold and then reached up on the edge of the dumpster and crawled on into the mess. One of the cooks, the fella run the pit, gave him a long busted piece of PVC line, and James stepped over that garbage and rotting shit like the man was gonna turn over and say "Boo."

"God damn it," Stagg said, "do it."

"Hold on," Willie James said. "Shit. Hold on, Mr. Stagg."

Ringold seemed not interested a bit in what was going on, standing back with a couple waitresses and talking about if it might rain later that day. Here they had a goddamn body in the dumpster and he was worried whether he was going to get wet.

Willie James stuck the PVC line under the chest of the poor son of a bitch and used it as a wedge, losing momentum at first, but then sticking it hard and good and getting the body rolled over in the soft bed of garbage. The stench was something god-awful as the fella turned.

Stagg looked through the sliding door. The damn face of Hank Stillwell stared right at him with wide fish eyes and a mouth so big you could put your fist in it.

"Who is it?" Willie James said. "Who is it?"

"I don't know," Stagg said. "Never saw the son of a bitch in my life. Somebody needs to call the law and get this mess out of here. Son of a bitch . . . Hell . . . God damn."

Ringold moved over to the opening, peered inside, and then looked to Stagg. As he brushed by Stagg's shoulder, Ringold said, "Here we go."

"Yes, sir," Stagg said. "Would somebody call the fucking law?"

. . .

"Momma is back in her own home," Caddy said. "I guess Jason and I need to be thinking about getting settled, too."

"I was thinking about moving in with Ophelia," Quinn said. "You can do as you like."

"This is your house."

"This was Uncle Hamp's home and, before that, it was our mother's and, before that, our grandparents', and so on," Quinn said. "It doesn't belong to just one of us."

"Look at you."

"What?"

"You sure want to shack up with Ophelia Bundren," Caddy said. "Good for you. You think y'all will get married soon? Have some kids?"

"Caddy?"

"Uh-huh."

"Can we just sit here without stirring the shit?" he said.

Caddy laughed, Quinn's arm around his sister's shoulder as they swung on the old porch swing and watched the cattle graze out in the pasture. The nights had grown pleasant and the daffodils were big and yellow and in full bloom. Quinn had on a T-shirt and jeans, his boots by the door. Off for the night, Caddy had cooked them all some salmon croquettes, mashed potatoes, and English peas. Quinn drank a cold Coors during and after, enjoying one of the first warm nights they'd had in months, welcoming the end of a long winter.

"I'm not stirring the shit," Caddy said, "but I would like to know just a little bit more about our father. What did he look like? What did he say? Is he as crazy as folks say?"

"I'd back away from this situation like a burning car," Quinn said. "My dealings with Jason were not pleasant."

"You calling him Jason?"

"I'm not calling him Dad."

"He had to have a good reason," Caddy said. "If he didn't have a good one, he would have made one up."

"He tried," Quinn said. "None good."

"And you charged him with murder."

"I charged him as an accessory," Quinn said. "He wouldn't talk. He just sat there not answering any questions. He got some shitbird lawyer out of Jackson to bust him loose. But he's not done with any of this. He has to come back, answer to things. We're putting together a case on the lynching. Lillie and me."

Caddy took in a long breath. Little Jason was inside watching television, a show on PBS about a couple brothers who fight crime against wild animals called *Wild Kratts*. Jason liked animals and thought of himself as an animal protector and rescuer.

"I want to talk to him," Caddy said.

"No you don't."

"Not your decision," Caddy said. "Sorry."

"That's like sticking your head in an oven," Quinn said. "Don't do that to yourself. Keep away from him. Let me put things together, but don't offer yourself up. You were young, but you know he doesn't have feelings. What kind of man walks away from his wife and two kids? Not just walk away but has no contact with us at all? Like we never even happened?"

"I want to know his reasons."

"Who gives a shit?"

"I give a shit, Quinn," Caddy said. "I want to know. When I was young, it about turned me inside out."

"We had bigger issues."

Caddy was silent, not wanting to address that time in the woods, that man following them both, and what had happened in that old and rotten barn. Maybe Jason had loved them once, but he was a man who loved himself so much that he did everything he could to destroy himself.

Quinn had come to the realization that the stunts weren't bravery but cowardice, wanting to break himself into bits so he wouldn't have to feel a thing. Why should he be admired for that kind of bullshit? He and Caddy would have never gone out into the Big Woods if it wasn't for him skipping town . . . again.

"Did he try to talk to you?" Caddy asked.

"Yep."

"Did he try and explain things?" Caddy said. "With him and Momma? And him not coming back ever?"

"Yep."

"Did it make sense?"

"He finally quit talking to me," Quinn said. "Lillie and I tried to break him down, Lillie being really, really good at it. But he just shut up, wouldn't talk about himself and that gang and the hanging of that fella. Disgraceful. People wonder why Mississippi is the armpit of this country."

They rocked some more. A nice warm breeze passed over them, the bright, fun sounds of the television show coming through the open door, Jason giggling inside.

"This is your house."

"You," Caddy said, "get married. Bring her here. Have a family. Don't be frozen. Move on. You're not that type of man. Move on to the next thing, the next story. Grow. Life does not stop."

"Preacher?"

"Is that a bad thing?"

"I have no problem with a woman being a preacher," Quinn said. "Just don't like to hear it from my sister."

Quinn's cell rang. He looked at it, seeing it was dispatch, picked it up and answered. Mary Alice said there was some kind of trouble out at the Rebel Truck Stop, not sure what was going on, but Lillie was headed that way. "Shit."

"What?" Caddy said.

"Somebody must've drove off from the pump without paying," Quinn said. "And Johnny Stagg got his dick in a twist."

"Is he as bad as you think?"

"Worse."

"Stay here," Caddy said. "Don't mess up supper. Let Lillie handle things."

"It's my job," Quinn said. "And I would never make Lillie deal with that son of a bitch alone."

"She's pretty tough," Caddy said. "Toughest woman I ever met."

"I have no doubt," Quinn said, "that Lillie Virgil could handle this whole county without my help."

44

All of the Tibbehah County Sheriff's Department came out to see the homicide. All seven of them.

Lillie borrowed a stepladder from the Rebel Truck Stop to shoot photos of Stillwell's body, not that she had a hard time getting near the corpse. She and Kenny planned to spend the rest of the morning sifting through the garbage for any evidence. She brought a box of trash bags to take anything that wasn't bagged up already back to the county barn. No telling, Lillie said, how long it would take to look through all this crap.

Quinn asked Johnny Stagg for the surveillance tapes.

"Oh, yes, sir," Stagg said. "Only one issue with that."

Quinn waited.

"That's one place we don't keep a camera," Stagg said. "Don't have a lot of folks stealing garbage. Mainly, people just tossing their shit in there without permission. Hardly worth the cost."

Quinn shook his head, asked for everything he had anyway, telling Stagg that a car would've had to pull in view of one of his cameras at some point. Stagg didn't say anything for a long while, hands in his khaki pants pockets, wind fluttering a few hairs of his greased pompadour.

"Or a motorcycle," Stagg said.

"Even if it's who you think it is," Quinn said, "they'd take a truck. Kind of hard to ride around with a body perched in plain sight on the back of your Harley."

"You'd be amazed at the brazenness of some folks," Stagg said, both men standing next to Quinn's truck, watching Lillie take a few more photos. Kenny had backed up his truck to start piling the garbage in. It was cool, but Stagg's face glistened with a fine sheen of sweat. "But you ain't gonna find nothing in that stuff besides steak bones and last week's leftovers. Lord willing, I hope Deputy Virgil has a strong nose and stomach."

"She does."

"You sure admire that woman," Stagg said, wiping his brow with a paper napkin, "don't you? Shame she don't go for your type."

"We been over this ground before," Quinn said, crime scene tape fluttering around the four dumpsters situated at the back of the Rebel. The hiss and pull of 18-wheelers coming from all around them. "Why Stillwell?"

"You don't know?" Stagg said. "Thought y'all had been real chatty."

"That the reason LeDoux would have him killed?"

Stagg opened his mouth, then shut it in a false, toothy grin and didn't say a word.

Quinn shook his head, not wanting Stagg to know about any private conversations he'd had with the man. He never doubted Stagg might've killed the son of a bitch himself and dumped him out back not just to throw folks off but because he was that goddamn arrogant. Stagg's face turned to feign a little sadness as he watched Lillie crawl down the ladder and Ophelia and two men from the funeral home, one being her uncle, lift Stillwell out of the trash and put him in a body bag and on a gurney.

"Two tough gals," Stagg said.

"Pretty clear what killed him."

"Two in the head," Stagg said. "I seen it. LeDoux making a goddamn statement."

"Since you seem to know," Quinn said, "go ahead and tell me."

"On why LeDoux killed him and deposited his dead ass on my property?"

"That'd be the question."

"Shit," Stagg said. "Stillwell told me himself that he was the boy who put LeDoux in prison. He was the goddamn informant for the Feds and somehow LeDoux knew about it."

Quinn nodded.

"He's got a list and he's crossing off names."

"Who else is on that list?" Quinn asked.

Stagg was quiet. His face was as flat as he'd ever seen Johnny Stagg's be. He was the kind of man who'd shake your hand and look you in the eye while selling your ass out far and wide. He reached into a vest pocket and pulled out a rubber comb, running it through the pompadour and ducktail. Before speaking, he popped a mint into his mouth and offered one to Quinn.

Ophelia looked over to Quinn after she shut the doors to the Bundren Funeral Home van. He nodded at her and they drove off.

"Me," Stagg said. "He got no reason to come back to Tibbehah and make trouble unless he thought I was part of the reason he got sent to Brushy Mountain."

"Were you?" Quinn said.

"You see me working with the goddamn government?"

"I think Bobby Campo might disagree with you," Quinn said, "if he wasn't in prison right now."

Stagg sucked on the peppermint and then began to crush it up between his back teeth. Lillie was knee-deep in the dumpster now, passing bags of trash to Kenny and Deputy Dave Cullison. It would be a long night, as Lillie had specific and methodical ways to handle the crime scene.

"I need to help."

"Quinn?" Stagg said.

"I want you to nail that son of a bitch to a tree," Stagg said. "I know'd what you think of me, but he's Satan's pecker personified. You understand? You think them boys at Hell's Creek brought trouble to this county, you wait and see when the clock turns back twenty years."

"It can't."

Stagg snorted and shook his head, Quinn being a young man who didn't know things back then or even now.

"I didn't want to say this, but you need to know something," Stagg said. "You and Lillie had a first-class ticket up Shit Creek. I made some calls, pulled in some favors, maybe knew a few things about that DA in Oxford and his liking of girls who hadn't seen their eighteenth birthday yet. You understand?"

"God bless you, Johnny."

"Grand jury come and gone," Stagg said, "y'all been bothered?"

"They had manufactured evidence and then stepped away."

"Since when have you ever known for people like that to have some kind of conscience?" Stagg said. "I ain't got no political aspirations beyond the borders of this here county."

Quinn nodded, Stagg offered his hand.

Quinn just walked away, put on a pair of rubber gloves, and got in line with the deputies to start sorting through the piles of shit.

"I guess you heard?" E. J. Royce said, just as Diane Tull was about to hang the closed sign in the window of the Farm & Ranch.

"Heard what?"

"Surely you know'd about the commotion out at the Rebel?" Royce said, hands in his back pockets and raising up on his toes. "They just found Hank Stillwell's body in a trash can."

"Oh, God."

"It's true," Royce said. "I heard about it at the Fillin' Station about thirty minutes ago. Figured I needed to let you know."

Tull had the cash drawer out and was counting money out into a zippered bag for the bank. "What happened?"

"I'll tell you what happened," Royce said. "Someone shot him right in the head and tossed him like some garbage."

"I'm sorry to hear that," Diane said, counting out the dollar bills and collecting them in bundles. She could count and talk at the same time, finishing the task and starting to gather the checks into a neat pile. She figured at least a couple them would bounce, and she was pretty sure which ones, but she took them anyway. People had to start prepping now for planting season. She placed them in the bag, thinking about that last time she'd seen Hank Stillwell, never thinking of him getting hurt, only hurting himself.

"Damn shame," Royce said.

"Did you intend on buying something or did you just come in to scare me some more?"

"Lady, I ain't trying to scare you," Royce said, running a dirty finger up under his nose. "I intend to protect you. I don't want something to happen to you when you ain't looking. I know'd your, you know, passion for trying to help folks out. But to an old lawman, this ain't looking good."

"Who sent you?"

"Ain't nobody sent me," Royce said. "Are you implying I know the folks who killed Hank Stillwell?"

"Do you want to buy something? I'm closing in . . ." Diane said, looking at her watch, "in thirty seconds."

Royce shook his head, took off his trucker's cap, and left it hanging by his side. On his right hip, he wore a gun as if the twenty-first century was just some kind of practical joke on the world. He looked shabby and filthy in the same old Liberty overalls and beaten shoes. Diane had on pressed

Levi's and a tight-fitting white button-down shirt, the handmade pair of leather boots shined and gleaming for another show tonight at the Southern Star. She'd changed at the Farm & Ranch, as there wasn't much time between closing and happy hour. She was going to do her makeup in the mirror of her truck. But now this. Goddamn Hank Stillwell was dead.

"Shot twice in the back of the head," Royce said, putting on his trucker hat again. "Lord, I miss them days when we kept the doors unlocked and all know'd each other at church time."

"Good night, Mr. Royce," Diane said, reaching to the table for her set of keys.

Royce didn't move. He walked up close to the counter, placed a liver-spotted hand on Diane's fingers and the keys. "You ain't fucking listening," Royce said. "I don't want you talking to Quinn Colson or his dyke deputy. This ain't a request. It's protection for you. I know'd your daddy. He was a fine, fine man."

Diane snatched her hand away. "I told you to leave."

"I need your word," Royce said. "That's how things used to be done."

"Get out."

"Come on, sugar," Royce said, stepping back from the counter and then walking around it. "You look like you're all dressed up for a long riding tonight. Hard being left by a man late in life. I hate to see it."

The dumb bastard kept walking, a man too sure of himself for too long.

Diane put her hand to the phone but then snatched it away, reaching under the counter for a 12-gauge kept there if they'd ever had a robbery—which they'd never had in the history of the Farm & Ranch. She grabbed the gun, tucked the stock up under her arm, and walked forward quick and hard, pressing the double barrels up under the old man's chin.

Retired sheriff's deputy E. J. Royce stopped cold in his tracks.

"I got a singing gig in twenty minutes," she said, "and I'm tired of you and your shitheel buddies looking in my window. Now, kindly step back, get in your truck or else my delicate finger might slip and I'll blow your goddamn head off."

"Holy shit . . ." Royce said, kind of muttering it as his jaw was closed tight.

"Why are you a part of this?"

Royce clenched his jaw tighter.

"Get the hell out of here," Diane said. "Now."

Royce turned, slowly at first, and then with some old-man speed, gimpy leg and all, looking to anyone outside like a dissatisfied customer, bell ringing upon exit. Diane watched his truck spin out in the gravel and head for the highway. She put down the gun, grabbed her money, and went to turn out the lights and lock the door.

She thought about opening up that first set with Loretta Lynn's "Fist City," feeling about like that.

45

They rode in one big mechanical, growling mass away from the club-house and down south, through the bottomland to Sugar Ditch. It was late, but there were still black men out drinking by the old grocery and kids running wild and holding sparklers by the tight-clustered shacks. Chains got off his bike at the store, the rest of the club behind him, but not dismounting, waiting for what was to come. Jason saw him walk up on the porch and grab the first black man he saw, a young guy in shorts and a blue tank top, and slap him hard on the mouth. An old man who was sitting with him raised up from his chair and Chains pointed a .38 at his head. Jason wished like hell he'd stayed with Jean.

There were words exchanged. Chains pistol-whipped the old man. Finally the young guy pointed down the road, the long, unpaved roads of shacks clustered on that nasty creek, where folks still washed their clothes, bathed, and dumped their sewage.

Chains got onto his bike and just zipped on forward, the kids holding burned-out sparklers standing, openmouthed, as the bikers roared past them in the night, down and around a curve and an old church that sat up on the only high land in the Ditch.

Beyond the shacks, nearly to Highway 45 and the county line, Chains pulled in front of a one-level house, neatly painted white but with a rusted roof. There was a wide-open porch where six or so men sat around two tables drinking and smoking, playing cards. A tall, upright man, young, stood from the group and walked away and into the yard. He wore a white tank top, black dress pants, and no shoes, a cigarette hung loose from his mouth. The other men followed him, standing behind him, backing him.

Some of the bikers did the same with Chains. Not that he needed or wanted the support. Jason followed Stillwell up the crowd facing each other.

"You Dupuy?" Chains said.

"Yeah. What the fuck you want?"

Chains stepped up and pointed to Hank Stillwell and said one of his people had killed his daughter.

"One of my people?" Dupuy said, cigarette bobbing his lips. "Slow down there, Fonzie."

Chains slapped the cigarette right out his mouth. Dupuy didn't move. Chains turned to his boys, who Jason saw now had some pistols out. The Born Losers carried chains, knives, and guns. This whole Fourth of July was turning to shit. Back at the clubhouse, he could have just ridden away, taken off. This wasn't about being tough, brave, a man. This was about being crazy and mean. These people didn't have anything to do with whatever happened to Lori and her friend.

"You tell us where to find this man or we start burning," Chains said. "Shack by shack."

"Go ahead," Dupuy said, thumbing blood off his lip. "Law be all over your ass in ten seconds."

"We are the law tonight."

Big Doug had wrapped some rags around a fattened branch and started to pour a small can of gasoline over it. He flicked open a lighter and got the torch going. He ceremoniously handed it over to Stillwell.

"How about we start with your place?" Chains said.

The black men were outnumbered. The man called Dupuy just shook his head and spit onto the dirt, knowing he was beat. The two small tables on the porch of the old house were cluttered with playing cards and poker chips. And piles of money.

"I heard what happened," Dupuy said. "Them girls yours?"

LeDoux pointed to Stillwell, slick-faced and wide-eyed, holding the torch.

"You ain't got no truck with the Ditch," Dupuy said. "Y'all just got it in for that one."

"You ain't stupid," LeDoux said.

"Appreciate that, Fonz," Dupuy said. "Y'all put out that fire, let me pour some drinks, and y'all cool out. I got some moonshine taste like birthday cake."

"We want that man."

"I'll find him," Dupuy said. "Right now, y'all white men my guests. You dig?"

LeDoux looked to Hank Stillwell and thought on it, slowly nodding. "Don't you fuck me, nigger," LeDoux said, "or we will turn your world to ashes."

Dupuy kept hard eye contact but didn't say a word, just turned to some of his people and then put on a pair of boots. They scattered into the slums as the Born Losers sat on their bikes or sat on the man's porch drinking his moonshine, playing a few hands of cards with the older black men. Someone had some weed. They smoked.

Within thirty minutes, Dupuy was back. He was grinning.

Jason walked up to where LeDoux, Big Doug, Gangrene, and Stillwell spoke to the man. Everyone was smoking, pistol shots and fireworks cracking overhead. A group of ragged kids had come out to look at the motorcycles. One of the Losers let the kids take turns sitting on his Harley, letting them touch the dials and hold the handlebars.

In the small semicircle in the weak light by the porch, Dupuy held up a simple gold cross on a chain. "This look like hers?"

Stillwell snatched it out of Dupuy's hands. "You son of a bitch," he said. "We're gonna murder your ass."

Dupuy didn't react. He popped a cigarette in his mouth and pointed north.

"Boy don't live here," he said, "ain't from here. Came to see a local girl and then she told him to get gone. You see, he ain't right in the head."

Dupuy touched his temple as if it needed more explanation.

"Understand he got a tent up in the National Forest," Dupuy said. "He sold that cross to a man I know for five dollars. Y'all need some directions to get the hell out of my world?"

46

A half dozen of those shitbirds walked into the Rebel at suppertime, taking a seat in the back booth *Reserved for Johnny Stagg, Family, and Friends*. Stagg didn't need anyone to call attention to it, he saw them on his TV monitor, tasseled loafers up on the desk, and motioned over to Mr. Ringold. They couldn't hear what was being said but watched as a waitress came over with a big smile and advised the bikers that they may want to find another place to sit. Whatever they said, it must've been unpleasant and crude, as the woman skittered away right quick, not handing out menus and ice water. A good five seconds later, Stagg's phone rang and he didn't even bother to listen. "Yeah, I seen them."

"Mr. Ringold?" Stagg asked, hanging up the phone

"You could call the police."

"Sure."

"And have Colson take out this garbage, too."

Stagg nodded. "I'd kind of like a little heart-to-heart with Mr. LeDoux," Stagg said. "I don't care to speak to his people. He got something to say about plans, then me and him need to get to talking."

"I'll stand with you."

"Yes, sir," Stagg said. "But I don't care to have another shoot-out at the Rebel, that wouldn't look too good on them AAA maps. This is a goddamn family restaurant."

Ringold kept watching the monitor, sleeves pushed up on his black T-shirt, those tattoos covering his arms from wrist to armpit. Stagg wondered if the man even knew what all had been inked on him. He was as tatted up as any of them Born Losers except his tats were eagles, American flags, and military insignias Stagg didn't understand.

Stagg picked up the telephone, calling Tibbehah dispatch, and told Mary Alice there was some more trouble. "No rush, but why don't y'all send out someone when you can."

Ringold nodded and followed Stagg out of the official Rebel office and down a long hallway, through the kitchen, and into the diner. The waitresses and cooks were nervous as cats, craning their necks to see what was to follow after the run-in with the bikers from the other day and finding that poor son of a bitch Hank Stillwell lying facedown in the trash.

There were six of them in his red vinyl booth, the ugliest, stinkiest bastards the Good Lord had ever put on this earth. They were laughing and carrying on and having a big time as Johnny approached his own fucking table, carrying menus and handing them out personal to each and every one of them. "Mr. LeDoux," Stagg said, "can I get you a complimentary meal? All your boys, too? I'd be honored."

LeDoux, his arms stretched out wide on each side of the booth, smoked a cigarette in a *No Smoking* area. He just stared at Stagg, gray-eyed and wild, with the stringy salt-and-pepper beard and long hair. The baldheaded turd who'd come the other day, the one with the tats on his face, looked up at Stagg as if he had some kind of say, grinning like an idiot who'd just shit the bed. Stagg not taking much notice of the other four, couple old, a couple young, tatted and long-haired, wearing their vests and colors like it was supposed to mean something.

"What we do best is still that chicken-fried steak," Stagg said. "I can guarantee it will make you forget all about anything you got fed in the federal pen."

He could feel rather than see Ringold behind him, and you didn't have to be no military genius to recognize the violence of the man. Ringold kept that gun at the ready and not a man in the booth doubted him for a minute.

"Sure," LeDoux said, lifting his chin. "Bring some for the whole table. And some beer, while you're at it."

"We don't serve alcohol at the Rebel," Stagg said. "This is a Christian restaurant."

"But you can get shots of grain moonshine and pussy pie out back?"

Everyone laughed except Stagg and Ringold. What was so funny?

"We are separate establishments, sir," Stagg said, still grinning. But he was sweating. God damn, Stagg hated when things made him sweat.

And the smell of them fellas—Good Lord, it was offensive in so many ways, testosterone turned to vinegar. Stagg wanted to step back but didn't want to lose the smile or his welcoming stance. He wanted them to come on in, have a meal, and hear how things worked in today's world outside the rock walls of Brushy Mountain.

Stagg turned to Ringold, nodded, and Ringold walked over to a waitress.

"Didn't know if this place was fit to eat at," LeDoux said. "Finding dead bodies near the kitchen? Next thing you know, a man's dick will show up in a hot dog bun."

"Unfortunate, seeing Mr. Stillwell like that," Stagg said, still standing. He would speak to them, be civil, but wouldn't take a sit with any of them. You sit with trash and you stink like trash.

"Motherfucker had a big mouth," LeDoux said. "He liked to talk."

Stagg smiled and smiled.

"He rode with us a long while," LeDoux said. "He was a brother. I was at his third wedding. I comforted him when his daughter died. A shame. We're going to escort the body from the funeral home out to the cemetery."

"Beautiful thing," Stagg said. "Y'all zipping around on them scooters. I know he'd be real honored. Just like some kind of show."

Two waitresses and Willie James appeared with plates of chicken-fried steak, big bowls of mashed potatoes, green beans, and soft white bread. They laid out plates and silverware for the six riders. One of the girls ran off, coming back with a couple pitchers of sweet tea. Another waitress brought some tall plastic cups, her hands shaking. A fine old homecoming for Mr. Chains.

The men, as Stagg expected, all reached across the table like filthy pigs, scooping out and then scraping mashed potatoes and green beans onto their plates, swilling that sweet tea. The bald-headed one lifted a fork to his mouth and Stagg said, "Hold on, sir. You want to join me in a short prayer?"

LeDoux snorted. "Preach, Brother Stagg," he said, clapping. "Preach."

Stagg closed his eyes. "Dear Heavenly Father," he said. "Please bless the soul of Hank Stillwell. He was a good man, if not a smart man, and knew the Devil's ways. May he find comfort in your bosom and be reunited in death with his daughter."

"That's beautiful," that bald shitbird said and then belched loudly. He and the rest of the crew started to eat.

"Fucking nobody eat yet," LeDoux said, smiling. His teeth were yellowed and piss-stained. "I got a prayer, too."

Stagg nodded at him.

"God," LeDoux said, "vengeance is mine and I will repay."

"I knew you got some learning in the pen," Stagg said. "Amen. Amen to us all."

"Sit down," LeDoux said. "Break some bread. I'm too old to fight. Fuck it, man. Just fuck it all to hell and back."

"You sit down with your brother, Mr. Stillwell?" Stagg said. "Before y'all said your good-byes?"

"C'mon, sit down, Stagg," LeDoux said. "I know you tried to keep me inside. But, shit, no harm." LeDoux offered his hand across Stagg's own table. Stagg saw all his own people, all those good and famous folks who'd sat there before Chains: Tim McGraw, Brett Favre (right before he showed his pecker to the world), Mary Ann Mobley, and Jamie Lynn Spears. People who'd made something of themselves.

"No, sir," Stagg said. "Y'all enjoy your meal."

LeDoux shrugged and shoveled some food into his mouth. Outside, Stagg saw a sheriff's office cruiser pull up and roly-poly Kenny Whatshisname get out, talking to the two waitresses who'd brought the dinner. Stagg nodded to the group inside and walked away with Ringold, wanting to make sure that the law knew everything was just fine. Yes, sir. Everything is fine.

"You can't civilize a barbarian," Ringold said. "I tried to do that for six years of my life. A barbarian will look you in the eye, shake your hand, and then shoot you in the back. Or blow himself up."

"Hell," Stagg said. "I don't know."

"That man won't be happy until he's finished you off," Ringold said. "I'll follow you again tonight in my vehicle. You need to talk to Colson about getting some folks to watch your home."

"That woman is unstable, crazy as hell, threatening to shoot my pecker off?" E. J. Royce told Quinn. "Holy shit, you gonna stand for that?"

"And why would she threaten you?"

"Because she's on her damn moon cycle or just hates men," Royce said. "I ain't no psychological doctor. All I know is, I offered her some sensible advice and she done pulled a gun on me. You can't have women pulling guns. What kind of fucked-up world is this?"

They were standing outside Royce's house, his coonhounds milling about, sniffing tires and stretching their long legs. Royce had called Quinn on his personal cell number, Quinn not sure how he got it. He said he had a goddamn emergency that needed to be addressed right now.

"She must've felt threatened," Quinn said.

"Whose side are you on?" Royce said. "God damn. I worked for your Uncle Hamp before you were even born and later while you were shitting your britches."

"True enough," Quinn said. "Do you want to file charges?"

"Yes," Royce said. "Hell, maybe. I don't know. I just want you to talk some sense into the woman. You can't just start whipping out a twelve-gauge on a man."

"What kind of advice were you offering?" Quinn said.

Quinn had his hands deep in his uncle's old ranch coat. The coat, the farm, the job, were the property his uncle willed to Quinn before he took his own life, neck-deep in debt to Johnny Stagg. Sometimes the coat itself felt heavy as hell.

"Shit," Royce said, nearly spewing the words. "She's trying to kick up all this business about that nigger being killed a hundred years ago. That doesn't have nothing to do with her and I was telling her to go ahead and leave it well enough alone."

"I think it had plenty to do with her," Quinn said. "They lynched the wrong man."

"Who the hell said it was the wrong man?" Royce said. "Seems like the right fella to me."

"Diane Tull said it was the wrong man," Quinn said. "She was the victim. She was there. You'd think she'd know better than anyone."

"You being a smartass, son?" Royce asked, cocking his head like a rooster does, standing there in his grassless yard in front of his shack and amid his pack of dogs. "Your father was a smartass, too. You really want to bring all this out? Your daddy was right in the middle of it all."

"Tell me about it, then, Mr. Royce," Quinn said, one hound lifting his head up into Quinn's hand and looking for some kind of appreciation. "I'd like to know."

"You think you know more than me?"

"No, sir."

"You think your uncle was a crook 'cause he fell in with Stagg and I might be a crook, too?"

"Nope."

"You can do what you like," Royce said, "but I'd stand back and let nature take its course. Johnny Stagg is a rotten son of a bitch. You believe that he's the savior of Jericho? Bullshit. He's lining his pockets and looking for ways to cornhole us all."

"Probably."

The wind ruffled the man's thin white hair, shining his red cheeks. He wore a dirty white T-shirt and open canvas jacket.

"You know, I've always enjoyed watching them animal shows on the television," Royce said. "See how one animal group takes over another. You got the fella taking the pictures, standing back, and watching that lion eat that antelope. He could intervene, but why would he? It's just the way of the world."

"And the way of the world is to side with Chains LeDoux?" Quinn said. "Never mind he lynched an innocent man."

"What happened to you in the Army?" Royce said. "You'd sell out your own father for some damn worthless black. A man whose own people served him up."

"How's that?" Quinn asked, the friendly dog trotting away. A bright cold wind swept across the hill where Royce stood, battering his door. The old man, standing sure-footed and mean, wrinkled, brittle-boned, and frail.

"I ain't talking no more," Royce said. "No, sir. Doesn't matter. You won't be sheriff much longer. People say you're finished."

"I've heard that, too."

"You're too quick on the draw." Royce said. "A good lawman needs to think before he acts. You ain't thinking right now worth a shit, Quinn. You really want to look out for the interests of the man who killed your uncle?"

47

They came for Johnny Stagg two nights later, fifteen minutes after he'd left the Rebel and was driving home in his maroon Cadillac El Dorado listening to Conway Twitty on a local station. Ringold was following him in his black Suburban, as he had for the last several weeks, making sure Stagg's house was empty and safe and often sitting on the house through the night so Stagg could get some sleep. But he hadn't gotten but a mile down County Road 382 when four pickup trucks came up on them fast, getting between Ringold's vehicle and the ElDo and boxing him in good. Stagg nearly mashed the brake flat when that jacked-up truck with the Mexican flag and a gold eagle on the tailgate crossed in front. The back glass slid open and a gun slid out, taking aim right for Stagg's windshield.

Stagg decided to just slow it down, drop the accelerator, keep the pace, and see where they were wanting to take him and how the hell Ringold would get him out of this bullshit and earn his pay.

There wasn't much on 382, as most of the land Stagg had logged out. For five hundred acres, the earth shone scarred and barren in the moonlight. Nobody living out on this busted-up land. Stagg had taken out all the trees until he got his ranch house set up on a hill and surrounded by twenty acres of scrub pine, which was plenty for him and the wife he used to have before she left him for a queer hairdresser from Madison.

He dropped down to thirty and then twenty miles per hour, and then the trucks in front, behind, and beside him slowed down. In his rearview, he could see another truck with three fellas in the bed aiming automatic weapons at Ringold's SUV.

Ringold was good. But ain't nobody that good. Goddamn Mexicans.

The El Dorado's engine hummed as Stagg reached under his seat for a shiny .45 with a turquoise grip to aim between the eyes of the first sack of shit who popped up in the window. He'd slipped it to his left side, right beside the driver's door, using his other hand to let down the window and some cold air in.

The entire road and some cedar fence posts and barbed wire glowed white hot and red from the head- and taillights. Maybe forty feet ahead of him, two deer turned to stare, glassy-eyed, from the roadside and then crossed over fast, jumping over the barbed wire fence, tails twitching as they bounced over the barren hills.

Four men approached the open window.

The man in the middle was the tatted-up, bald-headed biker who called himself Animal. Stagg thought about raising that .45 fast and hard in the dark and aiming right for where he'd inked that dreamcatcher on his throat. But that'd leave three, Mr. Ringold being out of the picture, and Stagg could never fire quick enough to stop them from taking his old ass out.

Stagg breathed in a long sigh as they came up on his window, a few more Mexicans on the passenger side, staring at him, reminding him of a safari ride where you could get real close to the beasts.

Animal reached into the Cadillac, across Stagg, and turned off the key. "Get out."

"I'd rather sit right here," Stagg said, holding that gun, "if it's all the same."

"Nope," Animal said, in that broken, messed-up voice. He punched the unlock button on the door, popped the handle, and pulled Stagg out by the front of his Ole Miss sweater-vest, balling it up good and tight in his hand, and throwing him hard down into a dug gulley filled with old leaves, branches, fast-food wrappers, and busted beer cans.

"We got your attention?" Animal said.

Stagg was flat on his back, the wind knocked out good and hard from his lungs, getting his breath back as he lifted up on his elbows, ass still on the ground. He nodded. Wasn't no use fighting.

Animal aimed a pistol at Stagg down in the ditch. All the truck engines still chugging around them on the barren road. Bright lights showing the faces of brown-skinned Mexes and filthy white men in leather jackets and jean vests. Money sure does make for some strange bedfuckers.

"We got a couple options for you," Animal said, "and only one of them keeps your old ass above ground and breathing."

Quinn had gotten the call as he was reaching for his jacket and cap and leaving the sheriff's office for the night. He had an unlit cigar in his teeth and a laptop computer in a green protective shell under his arm. There were some reports he needed to finish, but he was headed over to Ophelia's for supper first. She'd bought some T-bones, sweet potatoes, and cold beer. She would make a salad and Quinn could cook the steaks and bake the potatoes on the grill. It had sounded fine with him and even better with Hondo, who had a sixth sense about such things.

"You wanted to talk?" Chains LeDoux had asked.

Quinn had been looking for the man since they fished Hank Stillwell out of the dumpster. The clubhouse had been empty, as well as the trailer he'd registered as his new address with the Department of Corrections. No one had seen a Born Loser in Tibbehah, and Quinn had heard from an informant that they had planned on a week-long ride along the Gulf Coast.

"Where?" Quinn had said, walking to his truck, Hondo trotting beside him.

They'd agreed to meet right up the road at the Jericho town square. Quinn wouldn't need backup, and if Chains tried to make a move, there'd be dozens of witnesses.

Quinn drove to the Square, parked at the curb, and walked up to the big white gazebo that sat in the center by the veterans' monument. A new brick path had been laid since the storm, names of donors etched on each brick, and small rosebushes had been planted for the spring, deep in rich mulch and covered with pine straw. The night was full-on and teenagers circled the Square, as they had since kids started driving cars, keeping that feeling of the Jericho Square not being a town center but a carousel with lots of honking horns and yelling. Kids jumped from truck to truck, car to car, Quinn knowing he could stop any one of them and probably find a couple beers, maybe a joint.

But he didn't have time or any inclination to roust some high school kids, knowing what he'd been like at the same age.

He turned as he heard the growling of the motorcycle pipes. Chains LeDoux, wearing sunglasses but no helmet, rounded the Square one full time before parking on the opposite side of Quinn's truck. He dismounted the Harley, took off his glasses, and walked with a slight limp up into the gazebo where Quinn had taken a seat. Small Christmas lights winked and sparkled over the latticework.

Chains walked up the few steps and sat down across from Quinn. He wore leather chaps over jeans and had unzipped his leather jacket, showing a printed black T-shirt that read *An American Legend*.

Quinn did not stand or offer his hand. Chains leaned forward, elbows across the leather on his thighs. He seemed more interested in goings-on around him than speaking what was on his mind. After a good thirty seconds, he reached into his jacket and fished out a pack of Marlboro Reds. He popped one in his mouth and with monkey-like quickness turned the box toward Quinn, offering him one.

Quinn shook his head. He fished the old cigar out of his front pocket, lit it with his Zippo, and clicked it closed. They were both seated, both smoking, both watching the parade of cars moving around the Square. Kids liked their country music loud.

"Looks the same," Chains said, "except that corner behind me. That twister fucked things up good."

Quinn nodded.

"Kids are the same."

"Yep."

"I didn't think you'd come by yourself," LeDoux said. "I rode around a bit to make sure. Unless you got some law people in those buildings."

"I told you I'd come alone," Quinn said. "You said you wanted to talk."

LeDoux plucked the cigarette from his mouth, his ratty hair pulled back in a ponytail, gray eyes appraising Quinn, trying to judge whether this guy was bullshitting him but then seeing something in his face that made the man smile.

"You look exactly like your old man," LeDoux said, "except for the haircut. The haircut makes me know you're a square, the law."

Quinn didn't say a word.

"You know your daddy was a full-patched member."

"Hell of an achievement."

"That don't mean something to you?" LeDoux said.

"Not in the least," Quinn said. "He's embarrassed himself in a multitude of ways."

"People like you," Chains said, "don't have it in you like all us. I bet you fucking loved the military telling you when to jump, run, eat, and shit. Some folks need that, can't think on their own."

"I think just fine."

"Reason I called you is for you to know we want a good relationship with the law here," LeDoux said. "We had a good thing going with your uncle. He knew we weren't the boogeymen like you see in those drive-in movies, raping and killing folks. He knew we were a club, not a gang. We respected the law and the law respected us."

"He respected y'all because you handed him off part of the money y'all made dealing dope," Quinn said. "I don't work that way."

LeDoux didn't deny it. He just shrugged and smoked his cigarette. One of the truck drivers honked his horn and flicked his lights at some girls in a little Toyota. The girls slowed and they parked at an angle beside Quinn's truck. The boys got out to talk, leaning in the car, flirting.

"I like this town," LeDoux said.

"Sure."

"It's a good town," LeDoux said. "I thought about Jericho and coming back for twenty years."

"And here you are."

"Goddamn right," LeDoux said. "But I don't want no trouble."

Quinn smoked his cigar and ashed the glowing tip. He leaned forward in the same manner as Chains LeDoux. He stared at the reedy, busted-up convict with the graying hair and the crow's-feet and asked, "Whose idea was it to go out and find the man who killed Lori Stillwell?"

Chains stubbed out his cigarette. He stood. "Don't know nothing about it."

"Of course."

"I'm a free man, sheriff," Chains said. "I just want to ride, drink beer, maybe fish a little. Good fishing here out on Choctaw. Lots of crappie. My boys want the same. You hassle us and I got me a slick Jew lawyer up in Memphis who makes three hundred dollars an hour. You probably seen him on TV talking about personal freedoms."

"I guess we'll be meeting him soon enough."

"I never killed anyone," he said, "'cept in 'Nam."

Quinn didn't say anything, trying to figure out how to nail this guy clean and right.

"How about you?" LeDoux said. "Your hands clean?"

Put your hands on your head, Animal said, "and get your ass out of the ditch."

Stagg tried to use just his legs to climb out but couldn't get a toehold in the dirt and fell back down. He tried at another angle and slipped again and again.

"Shit, crawl on out with your hands," Animal said, now holding Stagg's gun that had dropped in the car. "Go ahead."

Stagg found an old root and used his bad knee to push himself up on the paved road. Another biker reached for the back of his sweater-vest and pulled him on into the road, covered in red mud and bleeding from his knees and hands. His clothes were ruined. He'd lost a fine loafer down in that ditch.

"I want you to understand one thing," Animal said. The boy was jacked so goddamn high, his eyes nearly popped out of his head. Stagg turned down the road and saw the Mexes, three of them, surround Ringold, his man's hands held high over his head as they kept automatic weapons trained on him.

Stagg nodded and licked a busted lip.

"You keep cooking chicken-fried steak and serving up pussy pie," Animal said. "But you're out of everything else. You don't touch Memphis. And we get a cut of all the cooch palaces you're running. That keeps you alive and keeps you well. Nobody gets greedy."

Stagg felt one of his goddamn veneers come loose. He spit blood to the ground, but even in just one shoe tried to muster up some dignity. He wasn't cowering before nobody on his own road. "Y'all can play all you want," he said, "but you've started something y'all can never handle in Memphis. You think them Mexes got your back? No, sir. It's a tough city. Maybe the toughest in America. You can't beat it."

Animal shot a hand at Stagg's shoulder and pushed him back several feet. He nodded to a younger biker, muscled up, with a long, drooping mustache. Animal gripped Stagg's arm, the way a man handles a woman, and pushed him forward to the truck that had cut him off. A Mexican flag painted on the tailgate and a sticker of the Virgin Mary on the bumper.

The bed of it was one of those hatch jobs, sealed on the top, and a flat-faced Mex with black eyes turned the key, lifted the hatch, and opened the tailgate. Animal forced Stagg forward with a rough hand in the shoulder. "Go on," he said. "Go on. Check out your Memphis."

Stagg looked inside to see a human head sitting atop a plastic sheet. It was grayed and bloody, eyes glazed over but seemingly alive.

No swagger, no cockiness left. But there was no doubt he was staring right at Craig Houston.

"When's the last time you saw Hank Stillwell?" Quinn said.

"He's not part of the club."

"He's not part of any club," Quinn said. "Someone shot him twice in the back of the head with a .22."

"Shame."

"He rode with you for a long time," Quinn said. "Figured you'd want to connect to some of your boys when you got out."

LeDoux blew some smoke out of his nose. He looked hard at Quinn. "Go ahead and try and tie me to that killing. Stillwell was nothing. He is nothing."

"You must've hated him pretty bad."

LeDoux rubbed his beard, thinking on it. He shrugged. "You ride with a man, you become a brother. If you don't have that, you ain't nothing but a fucking animal."

"I understand," Quinn said. "I've seen *The Wild Bunch* a hundred times."

LeDoux rubbed his beard. His face twitched into a sort of smile. "What'd your daddy tell you about me?"

"Nothing," Quinn said. "He never said your name."

"Fear will do that to a man."

"What's that mean?"

Chains shook his head, kept on rubbing his beard. A Tibbehah County patrol car circled the Square, Art Watts on duty. Art knew where Quinn had headed and was checking to make sure all was right, an AR-15 on his passenger seat.

"Did your daddy tell you I once tried to kill him?" LeDoux asked.

Quinn shook his head. His tried to puff on his cigar but it had gone out. He flicked open the Zippo and lit it again, a cold wind ruffling the flame.

"Thought he was the fucking snitch," LeDoux said. "I just fucking knew it. The Feds were knowing things coming from inside our own goddamn clubhouse. If it wasn't for Big Doug, your daddy would have had a hole in his chest as big as a dinner plate."

Quinn got the cigar going again. "So what?"

"I was wrong," LeDoux said. "Took me twenty years too long to learn it."

"Good for you."

"I want you to tell Jason that I fucked up," LeDoux said. "I turned on my own brother."

"Tell him yourself."

"Goddamn snitch was right there," LeDoux said. "Standing right by me when I had a gun on your daddy ready to blow his ass off this planet."

Quinn blew smoke into the space that separated them.

"The son of a bitch made your daddy leave Mississippi with his tail between his legs to protect your family. Isn't that funny as hell?"

"When was that?"

"Strange days, back then," LeDoux said. "My head fucked-up on eleven different herbs and spices, knowing the Feds had us close and Johnny Stagg was stoking the flame."

"Then you found out it was Stillwell?"

"I never said that," LeDoux said, grinning. "I don't know nothing about that.'"

"My father's affairs then are none of my concern or yours."

"He'd come back from out west wanted to ride again," LeDoux said. "Hung out at the clubhouse, racing bikes and doing crazy shit."

"I'll nail you for Stillwell," Quinn said. "And that man you lynched."

LeDoux stood, cupped a new cigarette in hand, and fired it up. "Nice to see the law hadn't changed much either," he said. "Your uncle took money from us and now you take it from Stagg."

Quinn walked up fast and hard on LeDoux. He got within an inch of his face, smelling the body odor and smoke. Quinn stared at LeDoux, breathing slow and easy, waiting for the man to react, make just the slightest of moves. LeDoux stared at him with empty gray eyes, turned, and walked down the brick walkway to his bike, kick-starting the engine and zooming out.

The cigar and cigarette smoke intertwined and blew away from the gazebo.

Back in his truck, Quinn recalled an ancient fight between his mom and dad, the crying, yelling, and the pleading at the kitchen table. Jason Colson had left in the middle of the night, Quinn and Caddy's faces pressed against the window as his brown GMC truck bounded out of their driveway, knowing he was gone for good.

He'd wanted them to go somewhere; Quinn couldn't recall where.

And Jean saying she'd never leave Jericho.

48

"W hy didn't you tell me?" Quinn said.

"Tell you what?" Jason Colson said. "That a motorcycle gang wanted to crucify me to a barn door? Pretty heavy stuff for a twelve-year-old."

"Maybe," Quinn said. "But might've made things easier on us if we'd known there was a reason."

"Talk to your mother about that," Jason said, long gray hair combed straight back, neat and pushed behind his ears. "She had a say in all this. She was married to this shit town more than she was married to me."

They'd called Jason back to Jericho for more questioning about the lynching. He'd shown up with his attorney, but Quinn had asked his father for some time first, both of them heading into the interview room by the jail. The attorney hadn't been pleased, but Jason had pulled him aside, whispered in his ear, and sent him off with Lillie. The legal complexities of a son charging his dad with murder weren't lost on the attorney. The man said he hoped all charges would be dropped immediately.

"What I don't understand is why you went back," Quinn said. "You watched those people hang a man and then decimate his body. Then you decide it's OK to go drink beer, shoot pool, and ride the highways with them?"

"I came back to see Doug," Jason said. "He was sick. The cancer had him the first time. I had gotten him some drugs down in Mexico. Same ones Steve McQueen had tried."

"LeDoux said you came back for the Born Losers."

"LeDoux is fucked in the head," Jason said. "He's a diseased individual."

"Yes, sir."

"Whatever you think of me is fine," Jason said. "But I wasn't a part of what happened, or Big Doug, or even Hank Stillwell. There were some of us that stood down when they threw that rope up into that big tree and looped it around that man's neck."

"But y'all rode anyway," Quinn said, "leaving him to die."

"I can't talk about this," Jason said. "I'm just telling you I wasn't a part of it. You can believe me or not, that's your own business."

"Did you see the killing?"

Jason grinned and shook his head. "No, sir," he said. "You're not getting me into this. I've made a new life and I'm living it."

"You should put that bullshit on a bumper sticker," Quinn said. "I bet you could sell the hell out of it."

"Talk to your mother," Jason said. "I've tried to make contact over the years. I tried to find out if she was all right after the storm. You know I rode over to Tibbehah and helped out with the cleanup? Nobody even knew who I was. I saw Caddy handing out ice, almost went to say something. But—"

"Maybe you could have jumped your bike over the wreckage," Quinn said. "It would have been a triumphant return."

"I can't make what I did right."

"But you can do what's right with this," Quinn said. "You don't shut down LeDoux and the killing is just gonna keep going. He took out Hank Stillwell and put Johnny Stagg in the hospital. Stagg's so busted-up, he can't get out of bed. Won't say a word. He told me and the hospital staff he fell off his tractor."

"I don't care about any of it but y'all."

"We can get LeDoux on murder," Quinn said. "Probably some federal charges in there, too. Civil rights violations."

Jason dipped his head into his hands and stared down at the table. He groaned. And ran a hand over his neck to work out the kinks and soreness. "Better bring my lawyer back in here," Jason said. "This wasn't what I thought you wanted to discuss."

"What'd you think? I wanted to know about your time on *Stroker Ace*?"

"That's rough, Quinn."

There was some commotion outside the old wooden door with the frosted window on the top half. Both men talking in the open room, standing, half the room lit by fluorescents and the other half in darkness. Quinn heard Lillie's voice and then a hard knocking on the door. Then Lillie again, then Mary Alice, and the door rattled open and in walked Jean Colson. Her face was without color and she was breathing hard, standing there, looking from Jason to Quinn.

"Hey, Jean," Jason said. "Good to see you."

"I'm sorry," Mary Alice said. "I'm really sorry, Sheriff."

"Quinn?" Jean said. "I need a moment with this man."

Jason's lawyer was standing right there with Mary Alice and Lillie, dressed for some official business in suit and tie, shaking his head over how his morning had been shot to hell. He opened his mouth to make a comment, but Jason held up a hand.

No one said anything for a moment.

"OK," Jason said. "What's on your mind, Jean?"

Jean swallowed, turned her look to Quinn. Quinn picked up his cold coffee mug and walked for the door, brushing through Lillie and Mary

Alice and returning to his own office. Somehow during this day time had flipped on its head and he was ten years old again.

Lillie wasn't slow to follow.

"Wouldn't you love to be a fly on that wall?"

"I was for a long time."

"I bet she's got a lot to say."

"She does."

"First your son charges you with murder," Lillie said, "and then your ex-wife gives you a talking-down-to."

"She's above that," Quinn said. "She's in there doing our jobs for us. She'll get him to confess to whatever it was he did or saw."

"Bullshit."

"You didn't have the misfortune to witness the balance of power in the Colson house." Quinn absently sipped his coffee, ice-cold and bitter. He made a face and put down the mug. "Would you like to make a wager?"

"On sweet Miss Jean bringing him down?"

"Yep."

Lillie shook her head. "No, sir," she said, "I would not."

"Could you bring me a Coca-Cola and one of them bendable straws?" Johnny Stagg said to a nurse as he lay flat on his back. "Sure would appreciate it."

Ringold had just walked into the room. One of his eyes was still swollen nearly shut, and they'd busted a couple fingers, but it hadn't taken long for him to bust free. "How you feeling, Mr. Stagg?"

"Doctor says he might have to wire my jaw shut."

"Can you chew at all?" Ringold said.

"Been drinking my meals out of a straw," Stagg said. "Everything they're feeding me tastes like dog shit warmed over."

"Could've been worse," Ringold said.

"Yes, sir," Stagg said. "I'd rather not study on it too long. Those boys were *artistes* with a tire iron."

"I know I got two, maybe three of them."

"They sure did skedaddle when you got hold of that weapon," Stagg said. "How'd you get it free from that Mex?"

Ringold shrugged. "Didn't have much choice."

"You sprayed the hell out of those bastards," Stagg said. "Wish you'd gotten the big bald fella with the tattooed face. He was the worst with the iron, personally broke my leg and four ribs. Son of a bitch, it hurts to talk. It hurts to breathe. When I go to the commode, it feels like I'm giving birth, pissing blood and all. They would've killed us both, left us in that ditch with what was left of Craig Houston."

"You sure that was Houston you saw?"

"I got a pretty clear memory of it," Stagg said. "Probably will my whole life. They gonna turn Jericho into Juárez while the law's got its thumb up its ass, dealing with family issues and not taking this thing head-on."

"But you won't talk to Colson."

"This thing's gone past him now," Stagg said, using the remote to raise himself up a few inches. Even handling of the remote making it feel like his sides might split. "Son of a bitch, son. Son of a bitch."

"You could ID the ones who did it."

"LeDoux called it," Stagg said. "I want his ass in prison or taken out."

"Might could handle both."

"You ever get a beating like that?" Stagg said. "I was pretty sure I was going to die. Four grown men coming at me with that iron. They were enjoying it. I could smell that tequila on them, them grinning from ear to ear, thinking ole Johnny Stagg is a redneck piñata."

"I have."

"Can I ask you something, Mr. Ringold?"

"Yes, sir."

"That really your name?"

"No."

"Why'd you choose it?"

"Good as anything else."

"And them tattoos," Stagg said. "You got every inch of your arms covered?"

"Yes, sir."

"Why?"

"It tells a story," Ringold said. "People I've known. Men I didn't who I killed."

"I don't like where we're at, right now," Stagg said. "I'm no military man, but our position has been greatly weakened by those pieces of shit out on Choctaw Lake."

"What do we do?"

"LeDoux will undo himself," Stagg said. "He killed old Hank Stillwell. He tried to kill me. And I figure he's got Colson on that list somewhere, too, if he don't want to play ball like Hamp Beckett used to."

"Yes, sir."

"What was that quote you were telling me the other day?" Stagg said. "When we were talking philosophy while they were cleaning the floors at the Booby Trap?"

"Make your enemy mad so they act impetuously."

"And what's that last word mean?" Stagg said as the nurse came in with a can of Coke, top popped, and curved straw held to his mouth. He sucked in a little cold Coke.

"Reckless."

"He's gonna do something dumb and fuck himself?"

The nurse bit her lip, offered the straw again, and Stagg sucked for a good while. She took the can back and set it on the rolling cart.

"Pretty much," Ringold said.

"And we just wait till he does?"

"Yes, sir," Ringold said.

"They think they got us," Stagg said. "But ain't nobody mounting my head on a wall. Or yours. Bring me that phone on the table over there. Yep, that one. I got some calls to make."

49

The pack of bikers rode north, up and around the Jericho Square, and then took the county roads north, past Yellow Leaf and through the hamlet of Carthage and all the way into the National Forest, where Dupuy said they'd find their man. At the edge of the forest, a cop car pulled in behind them from out of the darkness, hitting the red-and-blue lights, Chains slowing and the rest sliding to a stop. The sheriff pulled alongside him and a deputy got out of the cruiser, Jason glad as hell it wasn't Jean's brother but instead a banty rooster of a fella, a deputy he'd seen around named Royce.

Jason closed his eyes and did something he hadn't done in a long while. He thanked God for coming through for all of them. They would disperse, let the law handle this whole thing, and he could get home.

He rubbed a hand over his sweating face, it still hitting the high nineties in the middle of the night. Not even the slightest breeze coming through the big old pines and oaks stretching out into the forest. The trees towering above them, dwarfing the men on the bikes, nervous, agitated, waiting for the law to bring more deputies.

But then the lawman stepped away from Chains, patted him on his back, and got back into his cop car. He turned off the lights on the cruiser but didn't turn around. He shifted forward, the Born Losers following him deep into the forest.

He was giving them a goddamn police escort.

There was a campground set off from the main road with picnic tables and barbecue grills. But few people used this place, especially on the Fourth when it was too hot to camp unless you were near some water.

The cruiser stopped in a gravel lot. He shined his headlights onto a single tent set off from the picnic tables. It was Army, a one-man. A clothesline strung from the opening, where pants, shirts and socks had been strung to dry. There was a small fire, out and smoldering, and then there was a black man crawling out, holding a forearm across his eyes to block the bright light. He moved toward them slowly, shirtless, with a pair of ragged cutoff pants and unlaced Army boots.

He held his big hands wide in an open gesture, confused at all the headlights aimed his way. Hank Stillwell was on him first with a lead pipe and the skinny black man was down on the ground, a crew of the Born Losers taking their turn on him. Jason sat on his bike as the lawman, Royce, wandered over with a plug of tobacco in his mouth.

He eyed Colson with some suspicion.

"Ain't you gonna have some fun?"

"Where's the sheriff?" Jason said.

"Transporting a prisoner to Tupelo."

"Aren't you gonna stop this?" Jason said.

Royce looked at him, spit, and shrugged. "Stop what?"

The man no longer looked like a man but some kind of ragged, bloodied creature. His eyes had swollen shut, teeth knocked from his head, and he was limping, bent at the waist, unable to take in a breath, as they dragged him to the patrol car and tossed him in the trunk.

Chains circled his index finger in the air, got on his bike, and they rode south again. The air felt good and cool on Jason's sweating shirt, him thinking again some sense had come to Royce and that they'd had their fun, taken out their rage, and they'd leave the man at the county jail.

They'd done what they wanted.

But at the town square, the patrol car turned, headed west, away from the sheriff's office and the jail and heading straight down Jericho Road where those girls had been taken earlier that night.

The city turned into the county, crossing a creek, and then there were wide stretches of cleared land and pastures and farms. All along the road, there were a few trailers, some old houses, but a lot of blackness and green rolling hills empty except for the cattle and crops.

The car stopped several miles into the middle of nowhere. The bikers parked on both sides of the highway, everyone dismounting, waiting for Royce to pop the lock so they could hoist the man from the trunk.

Jason would ride away. He'd ride away now and be done with this.

Hank Stillwell walked up to him. He was still not Hank. He was white-faced and speaking so fast it was hard to understand much of what he was saying other than "Gonna hang him."

"They can't."

"They are," Stillwell said. "I wanted that man to bleed. But I don't want this. I can't talk to Chains. You talk to Chains. He's power-crazy. He got the law with him and everything."

They were parked off road, by an endless stretch of barbed wire on cedar posts. There was half a moon, enough light to see the bikers pulling the black man through the cow field toward a big dark farmhouse set off from the road. There was no light in the house and the windows looked to be boarded-up.

But there was a tree. A single thick oak that had probably been there since Reconstruction.

"He won't listen to me," Jason said. "Let's just go."

"Big Doug," he said. "Talk to Big Doug."

"Let's just go," Jason said.

Stillwell was shaking as if it were winter, arms around himself. Big Doug sat on the cop car, smoking a joint. He held a coil of rope in his hands, coolly looking out at the pasture, joint in his big, thick fingers, taking in the whole scene as if it were a beautiful night.

Stillwell and Jason walked to him. They asked him to stop it all.

"Too late, brothers," Big Doug said, thick and strong, shirtless under that leather vest flying the colors. "It's been decided."

"'It's been decided'?" Jason said. "Jesus, this isn't Dodge City. Give him up to Royce."

"Royce wants him hung," Big Doug said. "The deputy said if we don't get it done now, white folks will make a big deal of his innocence. He ain't innocent. He had the cross. That cross was a fucking sign."

Jason left them and hopped the barbed wire and grabbed Chains hard by the arm. The look in the biker's face was beyond wild and mean, it was ecstatic. His gray eyes shined with such excitement and pleasure that he grabbed Jason back by the arm and pulled him in for a hug. "This is it," LeDoux said. "Get the booze."

They brought out the jelly jars of birthday cake moonshine taken from Dupuy in the Ditch, passing around hits of the bright yellow stuff. More cigarettes and joints were lit, men told jokes and laughed.

The condemned sat bloodied and beaten, Indian-style, under the tree. The man could not see, eyes completely closed.

Jason walked over to him and knelt. "Did you do this?" he said. "Did you rape that little girl, kill her friend?"

"Sir," the black man said, "I just found a purse in the trash. That's all I did. I ain't even from around here."

"You a soldier?" Jason said.

"Yes, sir," the busted man said.

"My father was a soldier," Jason said. "I'll get you out of here."

Jason caught the eye of Hank Stillwell and they moved over to where LeDoux stood with Big Doug and Royce. Big Doug had fashioned a noose and had tossed it over his own head, laughing and sticking his tongue out sideways.

"This isn't what Hank wants," Jason said. "That man is a drifter. A soldier like you. He just found that girl's stuff in the trash."

Chains didn't say a word. Royce, plug still in his jaw, just stared at him as if he were speaking in tongues.

Jason touched Royce's shoulder and said, "Do your job."

He hadn't noticed the deputy had his pistol out, cold-clocking Jason on the temple, sending him to the ground. Stillwell bent down to help him. "Y'all stop," Stillwell said. "You got to stop. My baby is dead. My baby is dead."

"Then be a fucking man," LeDoux said.

"Not like this."

"This is the old way," LeDoux said. "The old way."

Big Doug removed the noose from around his neck and walked to the ancient tree, tossing the rope up high over a fat branch. Some of the bikers had ridden their Harleys out in the field and lit up the trunk of the oak. More followed, as Stillwell knelt down to Jason, helping him to his feet. More Harley engines gunned and bumped up and over the rolling hills to that old tree, lighting it up bright in the early hours.

Chains rode up last, taking his chopper across the cow field to the tree, turning around and rolling the bike back by digging his boots into the earth.

Jason and Stillwell walked to the black man. Stillwell asking, "Did you kill my Lori? Did you push her into your car?"

Blind, the man just muttered, "You see me with a car? I don't have nothing."

Big Doug, fat-bellied and serious, walked over to the black man, tossed the noose around his neck and tugged on it to find the proper fit. All the engines gunned and gunned around the big lone oak. Lights now shined high up into the branches, the old house dead and silent on the hill.

The end of the rope was tied to the sissy bar on back of Chain's Harley.

Jason closed his eyes. He touched Hank Stillwell's shoulder, who was shuddering and crying. More fireworks exploded as Chains throttled his big engine.

50

They met before dawn in the parking lot of the sheriff's office with a plan for arresting Chains LeDoux. With Jason Colson's eyewitness account, they had enough to pick him up and charge him with the murder of the nameless wanderer. The tough part, as Quinn explained to his deputies, was the getting.

"And he admitted to it?" Kenny said as they waited. "Said he saw Chains put the noose around him, tie the rope to his bike, and ride off?"

"Yes, sir."

"That's some fine police work," Kenny said.

"All it took was for my momma to shame him."

"Whatever works," Kenny said. "Hell, we got some results. You gonna eat that last sausage biscuit, Sheriff?"

Quinn shook his head, offering him what was left in the sack. He had six deputies riding in three vehicles to raid the Born Losers clubhouse on Choctaw Lake. As soon as he met with the state trooper captain, they could move out, hitting them hard a good hour before the sun came up. They'd get the troopers to stage a roadblock on Jericho Road just in case any broke free or if they needed some help at the clubhouse.

As Quinn told the deputies, "Don't plan for what your enemy might do, plan for what they can do."

"They can fuck us up pretty good," Lillie said.

"Then we plan for that."

Quinn and Lillie had checked out the wooded area around the club-house, the distance to the woods and boat landing and the old trailer where LeDoux had been sleeping since being released. They had a lot of *No Trespassing* signs on their five-acre parcel on the lake. But the way into the compound was a public road, and, walking the ground near the club-house, they spotted only six bikers. Most of his crew worked other jobs, had families and shit to do on weekdays. Being a full-time biker wasn't for most, not unless LeDoux could accomplish what he wanted in Tibbehah and snatch it all away from Stagg.

"You almost feel sorry for Stagg?" Lillie said. "Lying up in that hospital bed, unable to move, looking nearly a hundred years old?"

"Nope," Quinn said.

"Me neither," Lillie said. "Just wanted to know if you'd gone soft."

"I think if we go in hard and quick, LeDoux won't have his pants on yet," Quinn said. "Did you see all those beer cans around that trash barrel? I think they had a throwdown last night and we'd need a goddamn marching band to wake his ass up."

"Or he'd know we're coming and wait in the woods."

"LeDoux's too arrogant," Quinn said. "He doesn't plan. He reacts."

"We knock or we enter."

"We got an arrest warrant," Quinn said. "He doesn't come out, we go in and get him."

"I'm not real fond of busting in a trailer," Lillie said. "Up close isn't my specialty."

"Just like we practice in the shoot house," Quinn said. "No different. I'm in first, then you, Art, and Kenny follow. We arrest LeDoux. And any shitbird that gets in our way."

"Almost sounds simple."

"Yep," Quinn said. "Any riders follow us into town and the troopers pick them up."

Lillie nodded. The radio squawked and Quinn reached inside his truck to catch it. The trooper captain was on his way.

"You want LeDoux to make it to jail?" the Trooper asked Stagg.

They were alone in the hospital room. The only light shining from the bathroom, spread out on the floor, where they spoke in whispers.

"I'd like him to face what he's done," Stagg said, licking his dry lips. "That was always my goal."

"I hate what they did to you, Johnny," the Trooper said. "Jesus Christ, they could've killed you,"

"Got pretty close," Stagg said. "Thank the Lord for Mr. Ringold."

"We got a problem with those same folks in Vardaman shaking down the sweet-potato workers," the Trooper said. "MS-13 with all those crazy jailhouse tattoos and enough guns to take over the state. This ain't the world me and you were born into."

"No, sir," Stagg said.

The hospital was very quiet at this hour, the Trooper sneaking in a few moments before, taking a seat by Stagg's bedside and telling him what he'd heard about LeDoux's arrest. "Colson took his goddamn time," the Trooper said.

"His father is a real piece of work," Stagg said. "I'm surprised he manned up and told what he knew."

"But you don't want us to interfere," the Trooper said, "right?"

"No, sir," Stagg said, mouth feeling dry as hell, that cracked, raspy breathing making it tough to talk. "Just let him get what's coming."

"And if there's trouble at their clubhouse?" the Trooper asked.

In the far corner by the hallway door, Ringold was just a shadow leaning against the wall. Staying, but giving the Trooper and Stagg a little space and privacy to talk about those next moves. Stagg wanted some water, needed some water, but felt weak for asking the men. He wanted a woman nurse to bring it to him, with the straw.

"You mean if LeDoux wants to go out in a blaze of glory?" Stagg asked.

"Could happen," the Trooper said. "Colson wants us to back up their play."

Ringold shifted a bit on the wall, Stagg not able to see his face, only the outline of his body and head, the muscular, compact form of the man.

Stagg opened his mouth, licking his lips. It hurt to swallow and prep his words. "I wouldn't get involved," he said. "I don't need Colson no more. Let him clean up this shit now."

Ringold hadn't moved. The door showed a sliver of light across the floor and up onto the face of the Trooper's square jaw and gray crew cut. He nodded and stood, dressed in full uniform with shield, gun on hip. Protecting and serving the highways of Mississippi.

He walked away, past Ringold, and out into the hall without a word.

Stagg needed water more than ever but couldn't move, calling out to Ringold to get him a cup and straw. But when he'd turned back, the man was gone.

Quinn was driving west to Choctaw Lake in the Big Green Machine, Lillie Virgil riding shotgun with a Remington pump, telling him how much it pained her to be inadvertently helping Johnny Stagg.

"We're doing our job," Quinn said. "What these folks did—"

"They're not people."

"When the law breaks down, you see civilization is a pretty thin veneer," Quinn said. "Law is theoretical, an illusion. Or at least it was to the Afghanis."

"But we're a civilized nation, Quinn," Lillie said. "Don't you know it?"

"Roger that," Quinn said, rubbing his head where Mr. Jim had clipped him close. "We don't knock and hit the door hard."

"I say we wait for the fuck nuts to come out and take a leak," Lillie said. "You know that turd doesn't have a tank set up."

"Snatch him out of bed, cinch his wrists behind his back, and toss him in Art's vehicle," Quinn said. "I want this quick and mean and his ass in the jail quick."

"Yes, sir."

"Can I ask you something, Lil?"

"You bet."

"I want to finish this thing and resign," Quinn said. "Bring in LeDoux and then leave this all for Johnny Stagg to worry about."

"You're kidding, right?" Lillie said. "You want to pull a Gary Cooper?"

"Both of us can find work elsewhere."

"But this is home."

"That was Jean's trouble," Quinn said. "I think she was scared to leave, not knowing what was out there. There's no electrified fence around Tibbehah County. We are free to go as we please."

"I left for a lot of years," Lillie said. "You, too. Don't let the bastards raise their fucking flag."

Quinn was silent, heading down off Jericho Road and on toward Choctaw Lake, the land growing flat, the hills behind them. They soon saw the open expanse of water, a thick mist rising in the false dawn. There were a few ducks, a lot of geese.

"Did he stink?"

"Who?" Quinn said.

"LeDoux," Lillie said. "Who else?"

"I'll let you cuff him and you can decide for yourself."

"You're a true gentleman, Quinn Colson," Lillie said. "Don't let anyone tell you different."

She cut her eyes over at him and they shared a smile, rolling straight ahead, two vehicles following, Quinn turning off his lights and rolling forward slow and easy to the tin-roof clubhouse, leaning hard to the left. Within a hundred feet, a rusted single-wide had been dumped onto some cinder blocks, no lights, but smoke coming from an outdoor furnace feeding heat in through a rigged metal pipe.

Since they'd checked out the clubhouse, two trucks had parked nearby and a couple bikes.

"Fuck," Lillie said.

"Come on," Quinn said. "Grab your weapon."

Quinn reached for his cell and hit the trooper captain's cell number on speed dial. The phone rang and rang. He'd just spoken to the man.

Two men stepped from the clubhouse. Quinn lay down the phone, hit the lights and siren, and the two patrol cars followed suit, the blue-and-whites flashing, slamming on brakes, out in seconds.

Quinn was out with his shotgun, taking aim on the men. Lillie, by his side, doing the same with her gun. His four other deputies backed them up, Quinn not taking an eye off the two bikers as they stood, lit up in his headlights. He yelled for Dave, Art, and Ike to take the trailer.

"Kenny, stay with the vehicles and call dispatch," Quinn said. "Tell those troopers to get their asses down here."

"God damn, they're ugly," Lillie said, shotgun up in her arms as natural as can be.

"Is LeDoux in that trailer?" Quinn said.

The bikers had their hands up but didn't say a word. They were young and scruffy. And silent. They were also drunk and wobbled on their feet.

Quinn heard the door to the trailer bust open and Art and Dave yelling as they entered. More yelling. No shots.

Quinn looked to Lillie, Lillie taking control of the two bikers as he walked toward the trailer with the pump. He had gotten about twenty meters when he saw Art come to the door and say they got him, Quinn running up into the trailer to find Dave Cullison cuffing LeDoux.

LeDoux had his face to the floor of the trailer, the room lit only by the deputies' flashlights. He was laughing like a crazy man. "I wondered when you were coming."

"How the hell would you know?" Quinn said.

LeDoux couldn't stop laughing.

There was a rumbling outside, the sound of guttural engines gunning in unison coming down Jericho Road and straight for the clubhouse. Quinn looked to his deputies as they yanked LeDoux from the floor and pushed him forward out of the trailer and onto the dark gravel lot.

From a quarter mile away he could see the lights of the bikers shining bright.

51

The nurse brought Johnny Stagg a cup of water with a straw and held it up to his mouth. An early gray light filled the hospital windows as she checked the monitors and took his temperature, plumping up his pillows and asking if he needed to take a pee-pee. He said he did but could use some help. The woman, who was black and stout, helped him throw his legs to the side of the bed and held him up while he walked. She was trying to be gentle, but the feeling of those busted ribs and that fractured leg bone brought tears to his eyes. He leaned on her to keep pressure off the left leg.

"You need to sit on the commode and make a deposit?"

"No, ma'am," he said. She held him up as he did his business, the woman saying not to be shy, she'd seen it all. She walked back with him, supporting his weight, as he moved slow, with her helping him settle into the bed.

"You need something, Mr. Stagg, just press that red button," she said. "You see it on the side? Yes, sir. Just press that button you need to go again. They'll be around in a little while with breakfast."

Stagg figured he could send Ringold to the Rebel for some good food, hopefully not having to stay here for long. He'd hire some help at the house. And he'd hire more help for himself. If he could get a man like Ringold, he could get a dozen just like him.

He'd be rid of LeDoux and rid of Colson. He wished things could've been simpler, easier. But with the Mexes coming in, cutting off a man's head and such, he needed violent men to do violent chores.

An orderly lay down a tray on the rolling table. She opened the cover as if revealing the finest meal ever made—some runny eggs and watery grits. The coffee was the color of river water. The orderly began to spoon up some egg and lift it to his mouth.

"Ma'am," Stagg said. "I'm not hungry just now. Do you mind?"

The woman left and Stagg lay there, watching the morning news from Memphis, waiting to hear maybe some news about Craig Houston or the burning of those biker clubhouses. Surely Houston's people were ready for more. But there was nothing, only talk about the rain coming in later that day and Grizzlies returning to top form.

Stagg thought of the humiliation of being beaten down by that biker and those Mexican boys. He recalled his daddy taking him behind the woodshed and taking a fat branch to his exposed backside, whipping him good until the welts began to bleed.

Stagg reached for the fork, hands shaking, having to bend his mouth down to the food because his shoulder and elbow weren't working so good. He scooped up a little bit more the next time, some grits with eggs, and lifted it slightly higher. He chewed and swallowed, a little bit more light shining from outside that hospital window.

He'd just as soon burn down all of Jericho than surrender to them bikers and bean eaters.

Quinn, Lillie, and the deputies tried to make it to their vehicles but had to turn and run into the Born Losers clubhouse, toting the two bikers and Chains LeDoux, when the bullets started to fly. The bikers—Quinn counting fifteen—had rode into that gravel space off Jericho Road and opened fire on the Big Green Machine and the two county patrol cars, automatic rifles busting up glass and sending rearview mirrors flying, tires flattening real quick.

Lillie was talking with dispatch, telling Mary Alice to get those troopers down here fast or she'd be cracking some fucking heads in Jackson when this thing was over.

LeDoux was laughing, where they'd tossed his ass by a ratty old pool table.

This wasn't the scenario Quinn had planned. He'd readied for a tactical operation, quick and clean, getting LeDoux and getting back to Jericho. They were armed with handguns and shotguns, only Lillie bringing a rifle with her. She'd busted out a window facing the road, checking the situation through the scope. "I can get six of them easy," Lillie said. "You think the DA in Oxford would say we were being impulsive?"

"I've gone past giving a shit about that," Quinn said.

"Y'all are on our property," LeDoux said. "Our land. Y'all are the invaders."

His two boys had been hog-tied and left in the middle of the clubhouse. They hadn't said a word or moved from where the deputies had left them.

Lillie steadied the weapon inside the clubhouse, the space smelling of stale cigarette smoke, urine, and vomit. The walls were adorned with pictures of girls in bikinis straddling Harleys and posters advertising beer. Above a makeshift bar was an old velvet painting of a black woman with enormous breasts lying sideways and smiling. It was a well-worn space that smelled and felt abandoned.

Lillie took the shot. And then three more.

"Ha!" she said, reloading.

"Hell is coming," LeDoux said. "Hell is coming."

Quinn twisted his shotgun to full choke. He had his Beretta 9 out on a beaten pool table, away from the windows, laying down an extra magazine from his pant pocket. Dave and Art had set themselves up by the other window, just two industrial-glass panes facing the front. Kenny was now on the cell with Mary Alice while Ike McCaslin checked a back door and barricaded it by pushing over an old cigarette machine on its side. Dawn had come on and hard yellow light filled the road, the bikers finding cover out in the trees, parking their Harleys in the middle of the road to discourage anyone coming in or out.

Lillie took another shot.

Quinn saddled up next to her. From the window, he could see two bodies in the road.

She reloaded the rifle with bullets from her pocket. She handed her weapon to Quinn and he used the scope to see a bald-headed man with tattoos crawling near the cruisers, carrying an AR-15 and aiming it toward the clubhouse.

"They're coming up through the tree line," Lillie said. "I've got six of them behind your truck."

"How bad's my truck?"

"Boom is an artist," Lillie said, "but he's no magician."

Quinn yelled for Art and Dave to get down just as glass shattered and Dave was thrown back, writhing on the floor, smearing the concrete with blood. Quinn ran for the deputy, ripping off his jacket and pressing it to the shoulder wound, as Lillie lifted up her weapon and fired six times.

The automatic weapon was silenced.

Kenny crawled to where Quinn lay with Dave flat on his back, white-faced. Quinn pressed hard on the wound, Kenny now telling Mary Alice they had an officer down and they needed medical help to roll with the cops coming over from Pontotoc and Lee County.

"How many shots you got left?" Quinn asked.

"Don't ask," Lillie said, "unless you want to walk out to the truck for my tac bag."

"They get an inch closer and shoot them," Quinn said. "Art?"

Art had his Glock leveled out the broken window, the cold air battering the ragged blinds against the wall. Nearby, Confederate and Nazi flags fluttered from the ceiling. Dave was clenching his jaw, body convulsing, breathing slowed.

"They're inching around," Art said. "Lillie?"

Lillie fired just once.

"Nope," Art said. "That shit's stopped."

Dave was conscious but in shock, Quinn's jacket was a bright red and he wished like hell he'd brought some QuikClot. The pressure, depending on the wound, would only help for so long.

Someone was pushing against the back door and hitting the cigarette machine. Ike McCaslin fired into the open space. The pushing stopped.

"How'd they know?" Lillie said. "How'd they fucking know?"

LeDoux was still laughing where they'd left him. Lillie told him to shut the fuck up or she'd kick him right in the throat. The other two boys were silent, tossed together in a trash pile by the bar. "Y'all are dead," he said. "Don't you see it?"

"Shut the fuck up," Lillie said, "or I'll shoot your ass right now. You hear me?"

She turned the rifle on LeDoux to make her point. Quinn had made his way to the window, checking out the bikers hiding behind the county vehicles at the tree line. Dave was bleeding out on the floor while help from the other counties was a long time coming.

Quinn peered out again as four more shots cracked off, breaking out more glass.

He walked back to where Dave lay. Lillie exchanging more shots. Even if they could get most of them, it was a long walk back to Jericho. More wind whistled through the busted windows. The old clubhouse felt hollow.

"Sheriff!" a man yelled from out by his truck. "You hear me?"

Quinn looked back over to Lillie.

"They got you," LeDoux said. "They fucking got you."

Lillie walked up to LeDoux and kicked him hard in the side. He yelped but laughed at the same time.

Outside, beyond the vehicles, stood a muscular bald man with a tattooed face. He held an AR-15 aimed at the clubhouse. "Send out Chains," he said, "and we won't finish y'all off. Y'all got about sixty seconds."

Quinn turned to Lillie and handed her the weapon. The pushing was starting again on the back door, the cigarette machine skidding on the dirty floor. The AR-15 scattered bullets across the front of the clubhouse. From the edge of the window, he could see four, five, eight men, at different vantage points.

God damn, everything was so quiet.

So quiet until they heard the revving of a big car engine rolling straight down dirt road. Quinn could just make out the early-morning light glimmering off the windshield as it barreled straight for the gauntlet of Harleys and the clubhouse. The engine gunned harder as it approached the bikes and ran right through them, scattering some and rolling over others. It was a big car, a black SUV. It skidded to a stop sideways and a figure in a black ski mask holding an automatic weapon similar to the bald man's opened fire.

He shot several bikers, taking out the big man with the bald head first, the bald man firing off a couple shots before the bullets hit him in the center mass and left him sprawling. The other bikers behind the cruisers started to run instead of staying with their cover. More shots from the man in the mask and they were down, too.

Quinn ran to the back door to help Ike and Art move the cigarette machine. Lillie was now providing cover for the man in the ski mask, whoever he was, while Kenny kept the compress on Dave's shoulder.

Art shot a skinny bearded man who raised a shotgun to them. As they rounded the corner of the clubhouse, there was a stillness on the lake. The shooter ran back toward the black Suburban and drove off just as fast he'd ridden in. The ducks and geese that had scattered at the gunshots landed back on Choctaw Lake. The birds started chirping again.

The bikers who were left walked from the woods with hands raised. Quinn could hear an ambulance siren.

52

I believe about everyone I know is pissed at me," Quinn said five weeks later, sitting on the farmhouse porch with Ophelia Bundren. It was a warm morning, grass was turning green again, trees beginning to leaf, and out in the pasture three new calves had been born. They nudged up under their mothers, nursing, knee-deep in mud.

"I'm not pissed at you."

"My momma won't speak to me on account of me talking to my dad," Quinn said. "Caddy and I have a strong difference of opinion on a great many things, most of all our dad. You know that's why she moved out?"

"She moved out because she found a house to rent near The River," Ophelia said, sitting on an old metal chair beside Quinn. "Y'all need your own lives. And privacy."

They'd finished an early breakfast, blue and green Fiesta plates, cleaned of biscuits and country ham, sitting on top of an old whiskey barrel.

"I miss Jason."

"I know you do," Ophelia said, reaching out touching Quinn's hand. "But he didn't move to China. Y'all went fishing yesterday."

"I still can't believe Jean won't talk to me," Quinn said. "She knows how important it is to do this the right way."

"It's the honorable thing to do," Ophelia said, "she understands that. She just doesn't know why you're taking your father."

"But you do," Quinn said, reaching for an Arturo Fuente and getting it going with the stainless Zippo, clicking it closed. It would be his last smoke for a bit, a long time on the road ahead, eleven hours' straight drive to the long-dead soldier's hometown in Statesville, North Carolina. There would be a proper burial there. He'd been Army, 196th Infantry, a sergeant like Quinn. Quinn and Ophelia had talked a while about the man, what they knew, and some about how he'd died.

"Why'd he come to Jericho?"

"He'd met a woman," Quinn said. "He'd been part of the last combat brigade to leave Vietnam and came home not the way he left. I'm not really clear on all he did, but I know from his family he saw a lot of action."

"They seem like nice people," Ophelia said. "When we got the dental records match, I was on the phone with his sister for nearly an hour. His parents are dead. The siblings lost touch with him for nearly two years before he wound up here. He just kind of roamed the country, I guess."

"They invited us to the funeral."

"Do they know about your father, his connection to all this?"

Quinn shook his head, ashed his cigar, looked out in the greening pasture, listening to the birds and the cow gently moaning out toward the creek. "But he wants to tell them," Quinn said. "It's important to him. He needs it."

"Your momma said he'll take off before the trial," Ophelia said, squeezing Quinn's hand again. She was wearing one of his old gray Army T-shirts, her bare legs pushed up under the shirt and against her chest.

"Jean and I have some strong opinions on that," Quinn said. "She always gave me the simple explanation of why he left. Turns out that wasn't true. It was a hell of a lot more complicated."

"But he could have come back," Ophelia said. "LeDoux's been in jail for twenty years."

"It's a long way to North Carolina and back. Plenty of time to hear his side."

"So you'll give him a chance?" Ophelia asked. She smiled at him, looking hopeful and young with no makeup, hair in a ponytail. She looked all of eighteen, not a woman who exhumed bodies and X-rayed skulls and dealt with the dead on a daily basis and really enjoyed her work.

"I appreciate you," Quinn said. "You did good."

"You, too."

"Does that mean I have your vote?" Quinn said. "Might be my only one."

"How about we go back into the house and I'll let you know."

Quinn smiled, put down the smoldering cigar, and they walked back inside, leaving the front door wide open.

"I have to admit I'm getting a little tired of looking at pictures of killers and rapists every other day," Diane Tull said, driving her old truck, windows down, engine knocking a little. Caddy Colson sat beside her, after making a run down to The River with five sacks of 13-13-13 fertilizer to jump-start their spring garden.

"Lillie said it might take a while," Caddy said. "She said you've already looked at nearly a thousand."

"Or more," Diane said. "You know what it's like to clutter up your mind with those folks?"

Caddy didn't say anything. And just as soon as it was out of her mouth, Diane wished she hadn't said it.

Caddy's car had broken down, again, and she needed some help running a few errands, now wanting to go with Diane to the sheriff's office. She said she'd like to offer some support, but Diane knew she just wanted to see Quinn, let him know all was well with Jason, their new home, and improvements out at the church.

"What if you never find out?"

"I've lived my life never letting that man take a day from me," Diane said. "That won't change. I think about Lori Stillwell every day. I don't think about that man."

Caddy pulled into the parking lot of the sheriff's office, Lillie waiting inside the conference room. She had several thick books out on the table. They looked old and well-worn. "I have some more photos on my laptop," she said. "But these weren't in the database. I got these from Alabama Department of Corrections."

Diane took a deep breath, removed her purse from her shoulder, and sat at the table. Caddy asked Lillie if Quinn had been in yet.

"Haven't seen him," Lillie said. "We're both working days, but he said he had some business needing tending to."

Diane flipped through the book, page by page, looking at each photo, studying and dismissing them, one by one. She tried not to look at the list of convictions below each picture, as Lillie had sorted them by the most likely possibilites from the mid-seventies to the mid-eighties. Similar crimes, similar assaults on young girls. My Lord, there were a lot.

"Have we exhausted Mississippi?" Diane said, brushing back that gray streak from her eyes.

"Yep," Lillie said. "I think we flushed that toilet. And Louisiana, too. I would have thought for sure that this piece of shit would have floated upriver."

Diane got through a dozen, two dozen, photos of many men, most of whom had been housed at Kilby Prison. Lillie brought her some coffee, Caddy sticking around, waiting for Quinn, talking in whispers about raising children, the new Walmart being built, and some kind of reality show they'd been watching. Diane drank the coffee and checked the time. Carl was running things at the Farm & Ranch, but she needed to get on soon. He wasn't the best on the cash register.

She was halfway through the book, about to quit for the day, jumping two pages ahead, but then something made her flip back. She looked at the mug shot of a man convicted and sentenced in 1980. There was something in the eyes and the self-satisfied grin. And he had those scarred marks on his face. She kept the page open, thinking back to Jericho Road and that slow-moving black Monte Carlo. The way he had snatched her hair, Lori's weeping, being pushed to the ground. Humiliated. "Run," the man had said. "Run."

Lillie was standing over her shoulder. Caddy had walked off to talk to Mary Alice at the front desk.

"Look at that ugly son of a bitch," Lillie said. "Jesus, I hate to put you through all this. That may be the ugliest one I've seen."

She reached over Diane's shoulder, Diane unable to take her eyes away from the photo, Lillie's finger finding details of the man printed out on old-time typewriter. "Got burned up in a prison fire in '83," she said. "I bet it was another prisoner tossing gas on him in the cage. Damn, what a way to go."

Quinn drove north on the Natchez Trace and stopped off at the green rolling mounds built by the Natives about a thousand years after Christ. He parked his truck, a loaner, as the Big Green Machine was still with Boom. It required a lot of body work, repainting, and a brand-new door on the passenger side. He got out and stretched, walking to the sheltered picnic tables looking out on the three mounds. The cigar he'd started that morning with Ophelia was in his pocket and he lit up, sitting there on top of the picnic table, staring out at the biggest of the mounds, knowing it had been some kind of ceremonial center or residence of someone of high rank in the tribe. He'd seen some artists' renderings, way back when he was in school, of some kind of wooden hut perched up high, a holy man speaking to the masses.

Quinn blew out a long stream of smoke, thinking of the warriors back then, all that was left of them buried in those mounds. Long, pointed arrowheads and rocks used for killing. The leader had lived on the bodies of those men and their weapons, standing tall, offering up plans, ideas that would turn to shit in about five hundred years with the white man.

Quinn had smoked down to the cigar band when the big black Suburban drove up and parked beside his truck. The man who walked behind Stagg, Ringold, hopped out from behind the wheel and approached the picnic table. It was a soft, gray day. A light rain had fallen earlier and looked as if it would fall again. Everything was so bright and green, the air charged with gentle warmness that would last a couple months and then turn to an unbearable heat that would bake the streets of Jericho.

"There must've been some incredible battles," Ringold said.

"You know it."

"Never written," he said, "never known. Just those old bones and bits of sharpened rock."

Quinn nodded, tearing the band from the cigar, smoking it down to the nub. Ringold had on a black T-shirt, jeans, and desert boots. The completeness and color of his sleeve tattoos coming right to his wrists, hands clear as per Army regulation.

"You know what I have a hard time with?" Ringold said.

"Being around Stagg?"

"After the service," he said, "I had a hell of a hard time slowing down."

"You call what you do slowing down?" Quinn said. "Being a Fed isn't exactly selling women's shoes."

"It ain't jumping into Kandahar," Ringold said.

"Nope."

"You fucking Rangers," Ringold said, "y'all would rather blow shit up and leave it all in pieces on the ground than try a little finesse."

Quinn tossed down the cigar, stood, and ground it out with the toe of his cowboy boot. "That what you were doing with those bikers out at Choctaw?"

"You complaining?"

"No, sir."

Ringold smiled. "I wanted to let you know, all that shit with the local DA has gone away," he said. "All charges have been dropped. AG has been informed of what you got facing you and some real problems within the highway patrol."

"That son of a bitch."

"Stagg called it," Ringold said. "I heard it straight from the hospital bed."

Quinn nodded. "Appreciate you letting me know," he said. "Can't force this election, but we'll see if I'm still around to do anything about it."

"You'll be around," Ringold said, nodding. "Stagg thinks you're in his pocket. He's adding five grand to your reelection campaign."

"Which I'll send back," Quinn said.

"Keep it," Ringold said, his jaws clenched. Medium height, compact, and muscled. His bald head and black beard made him look like some kind of wild priest. "You want him to think he's protected."

Quinn nodded. They both turned and walked back to their vehicles. A light mist had started to fall. A thin white sun burned hot through some ragged clouds.

"We got a lot of work ahead," Ringold said. "Stagg's got some big plans for this county."

Quinn nodded. He shook Ringold's hand and the men drove off in opposite directions on the Trace.